STRAIGHT ON TILL MORNING

A TWISTED TALE

LIZ BRASWELL

DISNEY · HYPERION

Los Angeles • New York

Printed in the United States of America
First Hardcover Edition, February 2020
7 9 10 8 6
FAC-004510-23059
Library of Congress Control Number: 2019940035
ISBN 978-1-4847-8130-2

Visit disneybooks.com

This book is for my mom and dad, who gave me things I truly love, like ducklings and computers (and not small, obnoxious dogs).

A giant thank you to the best agent in the world: Ginger Clark. You help me see into a bright future—and don't mind tidying up the present.

—L.B.

Prologue

Somewhere in Never Land...

"Wait, did we look over by the Troll Bridge?"

"... We did?"

"What about the Tonal Spring?"

"And the beaches around the Shimmering Sea?"

The asker of these questions was a slender young man of indeterminate age—though perhaps if an observer looked him dead in the face she would notice the last pockets of baby fat plumping his cheeks just above the cheekbones. His eyes and mouth and even nose wiggled and puckered with every word and thought in between, like a toddler telling a very important story to his mother. His hair was mussed up and red, his eyebrows a thicker, darker red.

And were his ears just a touch pointed, at the tips?

The one who answered his questions certainly had pointed ears, though the same observer might be hard-pressed to make out any ears—or actual answers—at all. The boy spoke to what appeared to be little more than a golden light that bobbed and sparkled and tinkled like bells. In fact, the whole scene resembled a mesmerist quizzing a pendulum held from a long golden chain, glittering in the sunlight, whose vague swings returned meanings known only to the occultist himself.

But upon looking more closely, one would see that inside the golden bauble was a tiny woman with *very* pointed ears, a serious face, a green dress, and sparkling wings. Her body was like a series of energetic globes, from her golden hair in its messy bun to her hips to the round silver bells that decorated her shoes. Throughout the conversation every part of her was as animated as her friend's face.

"Really? We looked in all those places? Huh. Well, what about . . . here!"

The boy spun suddenly and grabbed the side of a tree, as if to physically move it out of the way. Really, he was just looking behind it. But there was nothing hiding there aside from some brightly colored lichen, a camouflage moss, and a few grazing unicorn beetles.

From this sudden motion and burst of energy to dead exhaustion; the boy slumped, strangely drained by disappointment and exertion. He slid down to the base of the tree, causing at least two of the shining white beetles to flee into higher branches.

The bauble of light glittered aggressively up and down. It jingled angrily.

"I can't anymore, Tink. I'm beat. I just . . . I just don't feel like it."

The fairy—for that is what she was—zoomed closer, concerned. And it was when her light shone its brightest on his countenance that the most unusual detail of an already fey and wondrous scene became apparent. For no matter how intensely she glowed, no matter how perfectly yellow and dazzling the sun in the sky shone, neither source of light managed to produce a shadow off the boy.

The bauble jingled in tones of hope.

"I don't know. We've looked *everywhere*. Twice. Tink, I just don't know where it could be!"

The bauble swayed quietly, pensively. Almost as if the fairy within was in that rarest state of all for fairies: deep thought.

Possibly *bothered* by something.

But the boy, even in his diminished state, still kept his attention permanently fixed on himself. He did not notice.

She jingled once, tentatively.

"Naw, I don't feel like flying. Not right now. I think I'll

just rest here for a while. You go on without me. I could use a nap. Then I'll feel better. I just know it."

The fairy jingled worriedly around his face.

"Just . . . go look without me." He swatted her away like a gnat, sleep already overtaking his body once the decision had been made. "Don't feel like flying . . . anymore. . . ."

He yawned a giant, repulsive yawn, and was soon snoring.

The fairy regarded him silently. She hung in a cool shadow of the generous tree, spun gently by a summery breeze.

They were at the edge of the Quiescent Jungle, which was the friendliest forest in Never Land. The leaves of the trees spanned every shade of golden green, and the creatures who lived there were all harmless and mostly furry. The air smelled like ripening blackberries—although it was not quite the right season—and a whisper of cool moistness hinted at a delightfully icy stream somewhere nearby.

Only a fool would want to leave. Only a genius would choose to nap there.

But Tinker Bell was twitchy. She had a rather dark inkling of where the shadow *could* be, since they had effectively proven where it could *not* be.

And if her friend ever found out that she'd had this inkling all along, he would be very cross with her indeed.

She floated silently over to his face, her golden sparkles illuminating every lash, every freckle, every pore. He blew out through his careless lips, and his breath lifted up the ends of his long, shaggy bangs. She hovered above his pug nose. After debating and biting her own lip, she gave him the tiniest quick fairy kiss on it.

Then she steeled herself and zoomed into the sky like a bee bent on finding its way home after a day of foraging nectar.

But she was not going home.

She was going to look for Peter's shadow in the scariest place of all.

She was going to London.

London

Yes, it's a scene re-created so often it has become almost a caricature of a trope, but let's go through the process once again anyway because it's necessary, even to this story.

Low clouds do not *blanket* the sky, for that implies coziness and comfort. No, these clouds mask the sky, weigh on the sky, choke the sky. They are strengthened by smoke from below, the trickling-upward effluence of a hundred thousand chimneys that decorate the landscape like unhealthily angular flowers. The slate-and-clay-shingled, higgledy-piggledy rooftops seem to extend forever in an industrial upside-down version of the fairy-tale hills and dales in a children's book with bright pictures and bad perspective. Everything—*everything*—is in shades of gray and black. A great gray river slinks through the city like a tired but friendly snake, hobbled by bridges far less impressive than their names imply.

(Don't believe me? Look up *London Bridge* and gaze at its pictures. An utter disappointment.)

Of course there's Big Ben, the giant clock with equally giant gunmetal and copper hands that an astounding number of fictional characters have wound up standing on at one time or another. Its bells, along with *all* the church bells of the city, toll the hour menacingly with the obvious mournful implication of time passing, death coming, soup's getting cold.

On the cobbled streets below the towers and rooftops, weather has some impact and energy; the almost-rain and morning mist combine to make a wet, stinging atmosphere that has men swirling into greatcoats, nannies bundling up their charges, and mums shouting, "Come out of the garden, you'll catch your death in the fog!" Also many, many umbrellas. So many black umbrellas with the usual spindly frames—like insects or skeletons or whatever—that watching them pass is almost torturously jejune.

There.

London.

End of one century, beginning of another.

Got it?

Good.

Halfway between where the umbrellas ended and where the sky should have started, maybe twenty and a half feet below the tallest chimney, was one particular casement window. Gazing out of it was a young woman in an unfashionable pale blue dress. Her hair was a popular shade of brown and her eyes an exquisitely normal blue for that time and place.

At first she looked up at the sky, but it was impossible to make out any shapes in the clouds because of their utter completion, filling the heavens from one end to the other in the same unbroken shade. So she looked down. But the dismal garden below soaked up the wet like a moldy sponge; there were no puddles, no reflections. The tree was sodden.

Nothing in this stolidly real vista was alterable by even the strongest imagination: there was no foothold for pirates, fairies, golden carriages, knights, or even a hint of swashbuckling. Someone from the street had thrown a brown banana skin over the fence, and there it lay, out of place in the English yard, attesting to the banality of global commerce and how it didn't bring with it sultans or magic horses—only bananas.

Wendy sighed and turned from the window. Afternoons were the hardest.

In the mornings she still saw her tutor, and there were chores and writing exercises. After elevenses was a *good improving book* recommended by the bookseller, the one with the handsome nephew.

By then Mrs. Darling had usually either gone to pay visits or was busily engaged in correspondence with her delicate blue pen at her elegant secretary. The gloom never seemed to affect her even if she did stay home all day; she was always gracefully and slowly attending to some task or other: her face; her toilette; her sewing; the little expense book she kept for the house; the pantry; their unpredictable cook, Mary. Wendy used to watch her mother engage in these endless circuits with delight, but that feeling was now tempered with confusion: how could someone remain so serene and glowing while working through the same indoor errands, rainy day in and day out?

Wendy still enjoyed it when Mrs. Darling included her in some of her "feminine rituals," which usually involved the proper application of powders and creams, tips on how to polish her nails, or ideas for sprucing up an old bow. She loved it when they had enough extra house money to go for a fancy tea out at Saxelbrees, just the two of them. Wendy would admire her mother smiling and laughing beneath her many-times-renewed hat, and would think once again that she was the most beautiful mother in the world.

She wondered when she herself would attain that delicate beauty, confidence, and perfection of manner.

But these outings were rare. And anyway, even the most appealing things lost their glamour when held up to the imaginary delights of Never Land.

Wendy turned to her bureau. Normally she tried resisting until the end of the day, as a sort of reward. Like the opera creams her mother secretly indulged in. Mrs. Darling smiled so blissfully while she chewed—she sometimes even popped one before dinner if it was an especially trying day!

Often, when tempted to peek into the drawer too early, Wendy could assuage her longing by pulling out the tiny notebook she always kept with her. It had a very slim blue pencil that perfectly fit down the spine, and was nearly full of her neat, enthusiastic words. Well-thumbed pages were titled with things like "Peter Pan and the Pirates and the Unexpected Zeppelin" or "Peter Pan and Tiger Lily versus the Cyclops of the Cerulean Sea." And she had illustrated "Captain Hook Is Taught a *Timely* Lesson by Peter Pan" with a little picture of a clock she had carefully copied from the mantel, as well as the eyes and nostrils of a fierce crocodile—the rest of whose body she had no hope of depicting accurately, and thus chose to submerge.

But today the words looked bleak and worn, and the empty lines beyond them bleaker still.

Wendy couldn't resist anymore. Not today. Not when everything was so *particularly* gray and dreadful and hopeless.

She slid open the creaky wooden drawer and picked up an inky-soft bundle that lay neatly folded within. It shook out like a spider's web, softer than silk and without the little catchy bits that clung to rough fingers. Its outline deformed easily. Only when she laid it out on the floor completely flat could she coax the shadow into its proper shape: Peter Pan.

Four years ago Nana had torn it from the boy. For four years Wendy had kept it carefully safe in her top drawer, waiting for Peter to come back and claim it.

Michael and John gave up first.

In the beginning they had been even more exultant than she at the discovery; in Michael's case, jumping and crying and generally bouncing off the walls. John had pushed his ridiculous glasses up on his nose and tried to speak in grown-up terms of *actual evidence* and *irrefutable facts* and the like.

But . . .

Weeks turned into months. Into a year. Into four years.

There was no *more* proof, no more evidence, no more sign of a visitor from Never Land. And though the boys kept stealing quick looks at the shadow, Michael soon began to remark that it was "kind of crummy" and "a bit faded" and John muttered darkly about *manifestations of another realm* and *meteorological phenomena.* Somehow, astonishingly, it became just another piece of bric-a-brac, a souvenir from an earlier time or an only slightly more exotic place, like the tiny mosaic mirror Mr. Darling had bought from a man who was traveling back to his home in Kashmir.

But every night since then, Wendy had gone to sleep burning for Never Land. She hoped, the way some questionable but trendy pamphlets suggested, that if she thought about what she desired most of all before she fell asleep, she would dream of it. She drifted off whispering, *Peter, I have your shadow. . . . Peter . . .*

She often woke with a strange golden feeling, like she had just touched the boundaries of Never Land—something about wolves and strange fruit and freedom—but then quickly forgot it; the feeling never stayed.

Wendy rubbed a thumb along the edge of the shadow and shuddered. If she wasn't careful she would begin weeping.

What had she done wrong?

What was so repulsive about her that Peter Pan wouldn't return—even for his own shadow?

What about her was so lacking that *no one* from Never Land ever sought her out again?

She dropped the thing back into the drawer and slammed it closed, crushing a knuckle into her mouth to keep from sobbing.

Soon it would be time to prepare tea, and she didn't want her mother commenting about unattractive red splotches on her cheeks or rings under her eyes.

In the afternoon her brothers came home, and things should have been better.

"John, Michael," Wendy said with relief as their boyish humors and exuberance filled the otherwise silent house.

"Greetings, Sister," John said, handing her his hat while pecking her on the cheek with a vaguely sarcastic air. He was bound for a real university someday, perhaps even Oxford, and had already begun effecting the irony and insouciance necessary for a sojourn there. Michael just kicked his boots off willy-nilly and threw his coat on a chair. Of course, other families had maids to deal with such situations, but aside from the Darlings' general lack of excessive funds, Wendy enjoyed the routine.

At least, she used to.

*Tsk*ing mindlessly, she picked up Michael's jacket and smoothed it out, hanging it up properly.

"Wendy, you're a damn fool for not continuing your studies within the sphere of public education," John announced, sounding like someone else.

"It's *heaps* of fun, too," Michael growled, a stormy look on his face. He was a less subtle wielder of sarcasm than his older brother.

"Well, Father said none of the daughters of his clients go—and they are all very respectable girls. And anyway, I have all the time and books I need," she added, a little hollowly. It had seemed like the right choice to decline when her parents had—somewhat reluctantly—presented her with the option of attending one of the newfangled public schools. Why should she spend time cooped up in a crowded institution and be treated like a child when she could have a tutor and then putter about the house, dreaming and keeping things in order like an adult?

"It's dumb. I *hate it*. School and its stupid rules," Michael shouted. " 'If you don't eat yer peas, you can't have yer pudding!' Stupid lunch matron."

"Now, Michael, I'm sure they just want you to have a nutritious, healthy supper," Wendy said, feeling the comfortable role of *mother* easily slide over her with its dulcet tones and indulgent smiles, banishing any uncertain feelings from the moment before.

"Are there any of those French biscuits left?" Michael asked hopefully. "The ones you made?"

"The ones I and *Mother* made? Perhaps. I'll set out some and serve you a nice cup of proper tea while you go upstairs and bathe. And then, if there's time, I'll tell you a story before bed."

"Oh, Wendy and her stories," John said with a smile

and not *quite* a roll of his eyes. "I have too much reading to do. Like *actual* reading. Of *actual* history. Plus, Wendy Darling, I find your tales have a bit of a Freudian bent to them these days. Haven't you noticed? It's all *fathers* and *sons* and *missing mothers.* . . ."

"I'm sure I have no idea what you're talking about," she said frostily. And indeed she didn't. But his tone was nasty enough.

"I want three lumps in my tea! And milk!" Michael called over his shoulder as he stomped out of the room.

"Oh," Wendy said, suddenly remembering. "Mother is supposed to come home from her dinner with Mrs. Cradgeapple early tonight—if you hurry, you may get to say good night to her before you turn in!"

"Oh. Yes. *Mother*," John said thoughtfully. "Haven't seen her in *ages*. Tall lady? About so high? Would absolutely *love* to catch up with the old hen."

"John!" Wendy put her hands on her hips.

"Tootles, Sister. Off to read some more Swiss psychology. You know those Swiss. All chocolate and timepieces and subtext." John made an elaborate bow and pretended to tip the hat that was no longer there.

Once he was gone, Nana, curled up comfortably in her early retirement by the fire, gave Wendy the sort of questioning look that only a really intelligent dog could.

"Yes, I see the muddy tracks they left on the floor," Wendy sighed. "And no, I don't know what to do about them. Boys! They grow up so fast."

Now *that* was an interesting idea.

Never Land was full of children who never grew up— but what about a boy who grew up too fast? Literally. Like . . . hatching out of an egg as a baby and then attaining the height of a man by the end of the day.

"They watched the egg with expectant faces," she murmured, trying it out. " 'What's it gonna be?' asked Cubby. 'How should I know?' Peter laughed. 'It'll be something great, though—you can count on that!' "

Yes. That was lovely. She pulled out her little notebook. Now that her brothers no longer cared to hear Wendy's stories, she had to put them *somewhere*.

And maybe, someday, someone would like to hear them again.

Michael came back down dripping wet and yet somehow barely clean—there was still chalk on his neck. He guzzled his tea and madeleines and stomped back upstairs to play with his lead soldiers. John hadn't bothered descending yet, probably caught up in his books about real soldiers being played in the wars of kings.

Wendy sat by herself in the kitchen, regarding the

notebook and the abandoned and untouched tea plates. Madeleines were all the rage right now and it had been wonderful spending the afternoon trying to make them with Mother, but after the first day they had sort of dried out and become a little tasteless. She picked one up and tentatively dipped it in her cooling tea, then nibbled its now soft edge. *Much* better. They almost tasted a little bit like sunshine— like warm, exotic days. . . .

Her mind whirled. Suddenly, she saw a ship bobbing in tropical waters, and herself on a beach. It was another Never Land dream she was remembering—but this one had felt so real! The sailors—pirates—were singing, and Hook was bowing from the waist, as perfect and gallant as John had been awkward and foolish. In the sunlight and open air the captain seemed far less terrifying.

But maybe it was because of the wolf at her side, the one she had befriended so long ago, growling and ready to kill for her. Maybe that was why she was brave.

A pity you can't stay here . . . the captain was saying. *That rapscallion utterly abandoned you to such a dismal, gray life in London Town. . . .*

She had frowned. "Do *not* talk about Peter Pan that way. You are a *pirate*. You make people walk the plank and burn their ships."

And yet never in my most evil and wretched moments

would I abandon a lady like yourself to such a fate. He really has no heart, not even a black one like mine.

"I am *not* abandoned. He left me his shadow," she said, perhaps a little too boastfully.

Hook's eyes widened at that.

You . . . have . . . his shadow, you say?

Wendy felt her lip quiver a little but stilled it. A mistake?

"It is nothing to you. And I am fine, thank you very much."

After all those stories you told about him . . . all that time you devoted to enriching his legend . . . and this is how he treats you? By leaving you . . . and making you be caretaker of his shadow, no less. . . .

Wendy in the dream didn't cry. She wouldn't, not in front of a villain like Hook.

Wendy with the madeleine did.

She put her head on her arms and wept herself to sleep.

Hours later she was gently woken by the soft touches and sweet perfume of her mother, who somehow, without actually picking up the nearly grown Wendy, managed to gather her daughter in her arms and gently lead her upstairs.

"What in the blazes is wrong with her?" Mr. Darling growled. "Asleep at the table like a serving wench?"

"Shhh," Mrs. Darling cooed. She gestured with her

hand, making him scoop up the notebook Wendy took with her everywhere.

"Mother," Wendy murmured, waking a little. "Oh, Mother, you look so beautiful."

"Thank you, dear. You're so sweet. . . ."

Mrs. Darling helped her out of her dress and fixed her hair, more shadowy apparition of eyelashes and perfect coif than parent of stuff and substance. Wendy enjoyed being treated like a little girl again. She snuggled into her bed drowsily and heard her parents talk.

"Something's got to be done about her," Mr. Darling swore, shaking the notebook for emphasis. "There's something not quite right about that girl."

"She's just a little . . . blue. She needs a project," Mrs. Darling said. "A boy. Or maybe a charity."

"Charity? How about a Darling charity?" Mr. Darling huffed. "Courtships are all very well and good but require dresses and hats and all sorts of expensive shenanigans. That was always the advantage of Wendy . . . she never wanted the things other girls had."

"No," Mrs. Darling said with a touch of sadness. "She always wanted something . . . else."

And Wendy dreamed quickly forgotten dreams of foreign seas and wolves.

In Bocca al Lupo

Wendy opened her eyes, dreams of hidden cabins and friendly wolves and menacing pirates disappearing into the dim morning grayness. She had absolutely no desire to get up and perform the start-of-day rituals she used to relish: washing her face with fresh, cold water, giving her hair a hundred solid strokes before pinning it back, going through her dresses and deciding which one to wear, which one to mend, which one perhaps to embellish a little.

But despite her whole-body unwillingness to begin this process, routine took over. Habits, especially healthy ones, become easily ingrained in people like Wendy. Without even meaning to she rose and turned and neatened her bed, smoothing the pillow out so it would look pretty and inviting when she went to lie down again that night. She drifted over to the basin of water and splashed her face (without looking in the mirror), ran the brush through her hair (only fifty-seven times), and examined her nails (dispassionately; she decided they didn't need to be buffed).

Moving made her feel better; accomplishing little things gave her dim sparks of satisfaction. Before long she had the boys up and out of bed, a whirlwind of toast and tea and brushing down jackets. Some of the brothers' energy managed to rub off on their sister. And Nana, bless her, tried to help like she used to, holding a spare white cuff in her mouth, waiting patiently and dolorously until one of the passing boys—Michael—grabbed it and patted her in thanks. It all ended when John blew an airy kiss and pulled his reluctant brother after him out the door.

"Goodness," Mrs. Darling said, appearing for a moment in the foyer like a tentative daytime ghost. She was resplendent in her white froth of a nightgown, and prettily covered her mouth for a delicate yawn. "Whatever would I do without you, dear."

She kissed her daughter on the head and Wendy fell to warm pieces under her praise. But then the figment retreated back upstairs to perform her own ablutions and the lower house was released to the normal workaday world. Wendy had toast and tea and settled down for her French lessons with Mademoiselle Gabineau. Not satisfied with her main subject of expertise, Mademoiselle also had strong opinions on history and maths, lecturing angrily—and often incomprehensibly—in her native tongue about the first topic while not letting Wendy give up on the second. "You must keep a house someday, wiz all of ze accounts," she admonished. "And make ze right decreases when knitting a jumper."

Wendy didn't deign to reply, uninterested in either application of maths. She surreptitiously stroked the pages of the tiny notebook in her apron pocket and dreamed of a well-spoken, logical, and utterly evil witch.

The day *seemed* like it was going to progress along the same lines as the one before it, and the one before that, and the one before that—but sometime before tea there were strange noises downstairs, outer doors opening and closing and a deep-throated male voice sounding out.

It was far too early for Mr. Darling to be done with business already. Concerned, Wendy tripped down the stairs as fast as she thought it decorous to do so. Nana waited at the bottom, doing something she rarely engaged in. She was *growling.* Very softly.

"Dear Nana, what is it?" Wendy asked, growing even more nervous. The dog was large but not much of a wolf, and probably too old to do any real damage to an intruder.

"Oh, what a funny thought. 'Not much of a wolf.' Wherever did that come from, I wonder? *Wolves* indeed."

It was just prattle, but talking aloud to herself always made Wendy feel brave. And anyway, if the house was being invaded, it was up to her to defend its inhabitants and silverware.

She stuck out her chin and pushed open the front hall door with a carefully composed look of indignation on her face.

"Now see here, villain—!"

She stopped immediately, presented with a very odd scene.

Mr. Darling *was* home early. It was rare to see him by day in a full suit, coat, and hat; usually when he came home it was dark and he went straight upstairs to change into his slippers and smoking jacket. He held his arms strangely, as if one were broken and he were cradling it with the other. Also unusual was that Mrs. Darling was with him, a gloved hand resting lightly on his shoulder.

Mr. Darling looked utterly confused by his daughter's words, his large, bushy black eyebrows rising nearly to the top of his head.

"Wendy? What in blazes is the reason for that tone? I? A *villain*?"

"Dear, whatever is the matter?" Mrs. Darling asked with an indulgent smile.

"I heard noises—I just thought . . . I'm so glad you're home early today, though, Father! Wait, did you hurt yourself? Did you break your arm? Is that why you're—no, if you had, Dr. Sorello would be here with his treatments and nasty draughts. Is it some sort of holiday? I don't think I had it in my datebook. Is it a birthday? Are the banks closed? Or—no! Oh no, Father. You didn't lose your job, did you? You and Mother look so radiant, that can't be it. Is there other news?"

Mr. Darling looked more and more blown back by the torrent of Wendy's words, as if a wind were physically assaulting him.

"All right, all right," he said, unable to think of anything better to quiet her.

"Wendy, dear, we've brought you something," Mrs. Darling said through soft laughter. "Show her."

Mr. Darling moved his arms and revealed the reason he had been cradling them so carefully.

At first Wendy thought it was a rat, which would explain its size (small), its color (white), and Nana's discomfort (extreme).

But then a fat little pink tongue lolled out of its mouth and large black eyes blinked in excitement. It panted and pawed at Mr. Darling's arms, excited but obviously unsure what it wanted to do. Its little ears, no larger than the corners of a lady's pocket handkerchief, were actually quite huge compared to the thing's head and didn't seem to be able to move very much, as they would have on a German shepherd or Nana.

"Oh," Wendy said, blinking. Her carefully read and reread books of *Manners for English Girls and Boys* had nothing she could draw from for this sort of situation. "Oh. A small dog."

"It's a teacup terrier. Isn't it the most darling thing?" Mrs. Darling said, rubbing her face against its and kissing.

Mr. Darling looked unsettled by this physical display of affection, the dry nose touching the wet one.

"Yes, well, all the girls seem to be into them right now. Carrying them in baskets . . . bows in their fur . . . taking them to the park . . . I don't know. You don't hunt with them, I'm fairly certain. We just thought you could use . . . ah . . . a little friend."

"We were afraid you were getting lonely in this big old drafty house," Mrs. Darling said, taking her daughter's hands and squeezing them.

Wendy, so talkative before, now had nothing to say. Mr. Darling always complained about how *tiny* their house was, endlessly comparing it to those of his business associates and of the managers whose ranks he wanted to someday be among. Mrs. Darling never said anything obviously unkind about their home, but did often refer to it in painfully obvious terms: *adorable, cozy, manageable, charming, doll-sized.*

"Oh . . . yes . . . lonely . . ." Wendy said, seizing on that one point, the one that was most reasonable.

(Nana whuffed indignantly. What was she, a piece of furniture?)

Her parents waited expectantly.

The polite thing to do, Wendy realized, was to walk forward and put a hand out to the tiny dog and let it smell her. She made herself do so.

The teeny puppy snuffled its wet nose all over her hand and seemed to lick—or slurp—her, like a jungle creature from one of her adventure books. Something horrid that ate ants or honey or anything else that required sucking up. It barked several times in a manner that was both strangely too quiet and somehow extremely irritating.

"Thank you, Father," Wendy said, carefully removing her hand as if for the purpose of hugging him. It wasn't entirely a lie; she did indeed want to envelop Mr. Darling's large form and rest her head on his side, smelling his aftershave and his general father-ness. Her mother hugged her on the other side and kissed her on the forehead.

They loved her, that was more than obvious.

They just didn't understand her.

———

Wendy did make an effort to try to see what the puppy could do.

(With Nana watching in stern disapproval.)

It would run into the middle of the room and then wag its tail like it had accomplished something truly incredible.

It would run up into her arms and lick her chin.

It would scamper along next to a ball that Wendy rolled.

It would *not* make any actual attempt to stop the ball, grab the ball, fetch the ball, or do anything with the ball aside from barking at it in that tiny yip that made Wendy want to lean over and say *"Pardon me?"*

Eventually, with two hours until the boys came home, Mother and Father now nowhere to be seen, and nothing else to do, Wendy found an appropriately sized basket, tied a ribbon around it, tucked in Snowball (really, what else could she name it?), put on her coat, and attempted an outing. She left her notebook behind, encumbered with her new pet and umbrella.

Nana also remained inside, aloof and disapproving.

While she felt a little ridiculous, Wendy had to admit that the cold, slightly damp air felt good on her face. *Moisturizing,* her mother would say. *Invigorating,* her father would say. The little dog peeped out of the basket and looked around blankly with no actual interest in hopping out and getting a firsthand sniff of the many wonders they passed. Wendy nodded to other walkers, most of whom regarded Snowball with amusement or delight.

And then, down the path, came the demonic Shesbow twins.

They were clad as was their wont: in similar dresses of different hue, similar hats with different flowers, similar parasols with different tassels. Outfits just alike enough to give a nod to the sisters' ostensible sameness, just a bit off to remind the viewer that they weren't the same person at all.

Wendy froze and considered heading back the other way, as if she had forgotten something. She could see the steely blue of four Shesbow eyes and didn't feel strong under their lantern gazes, especially after the caroling party last Christmas.

But they had spotted her, and she had something interesting to distract them with, so maybe it would be all right. Wendy stuck out her chin and walked forward bravely to meet her fate.

"Miss Darling," Clara said with the beginnings of a coldly amused smile. "It's so lovely to see you out and about in public, especially after—"

"Oh! What is that you have there?" Phoebe cried, spotting the basket.

"Him?" Wendy almost blew it immediately. Was the dog even a him? She hadn't bothered to check. "He's new."

"Oh—oh, how *perfect*," Phoebe simpered, holding out

a delicately curled gloved finger. The puppy obligingly sniffed and she practically screamed with delight.

"He's adorable," Clara said flatly, to the point as always. "When did you get him?"

"Well," Wendy said, stalling. She hated the way that, despite the girls' continually bad treatment of her, she was flushing and eager for any kind word of acceptance. Telling the specifics of the puppy's origin might spoil the chances of that happening. "The house was feeling a bit lonely, don't you know? And I thought, well, what I need is a nice little companion to keep me company and to absolutely indulge."

"Isn't he the *sweetest*," Phoebe cooed.

"I'm gratified to hear you've taken on a project like this," Clara said, tapping her parasol and trying to sound like her grandmother. "Everyone was worried, you know."

"Worried? About me? *Every*one?"

"Oh, please, Wendy. After Christmas it became fairly obvious what your future is. Your brothers will go to university, and you will be stuck helping your parents, and then probably care for your nieces or nephews as their spinster aunt."

"With cats," Phoebe added, not looking away from petting the dog. "You would have cats, of course."

"Quite right, lots of cats."

"People . . . are talking . . . about me? As a spinster?

With—cats?" Wendy's mind was too overcome with this new information to even take offense at it. She was sixteen, for heaven's sake! She had time. She had just moved out of the nursery not that long ago. . . .

And to think of a husband? *Now?* There were so many other things to think about. Balloons and submarines. Airships and pirates. Deepest Africa and farthest Australia. Peter Pan and fairies and mermaids and centaurs . . .

"But now this," Phoebe sighed, throwing her hands up at the dog as if there were no words. "You know, Alice has a little dog, too! Oh, we should all go walking together! Wouldn't that be fun? We could bring a ball, or something like that."

"He could accompany you to one of our teas sometime," Clara said thoughtfully. "We have literary ones, you know. Almost like our own salon."

"I would like that very much," Wendy responded before she could decide whether or not that was true. Or if *she* had even been properly invited at all; it almost sounded like Snowball was really the intended recipient of the offer. Then again—*literary* salon. That was a place for stories!

"You could absolutely meet someone there, perhaps, someday," Phoebe added. "Someone dreamy, who likes dogs, like you."

"It's a project," Clara said, eyes glittering. "Making you

acceptable and finding you a match. But you must promise not to do that thing—not to run off at the mouth the way you do. No one finds that attractive or ladylike."

"No one at all," Phoebe agreed. "You really will end up all alone."

"I don't want to be alone. I have Snowball now," Wendy said, trying to make her thoughts come out the way they were flowing in her head. It didn't seem to be working. "But I couldn't possibly think of a match. Now. And I can't help talking—I like stories, and telling them. And really, isn't there another choice? Besides a match, and spinsters, and cats? Something—else?"

"You're doing it again," Phoebe said kindly. She put a finger to Wendy's mouth. "Shhh."

And then the sisters nodded to each other, in full agreement, full of themselves and very happy.

"I'll send round my card," Clara called as they walked off, arm in arm.

Wendy stood there watching them go and then looked at Snowball, who gazed dimly back.

This could be the beginning of something really big, and quite different. If she could do things properly, her lonely days batting around the house by herself would be over—there would be teas and salons and parties and group dog walks.

And boys.

And dances and happily-ever-afters, where she would attend balls and cotillions, and have a husband and children like Michael and John, and a different, perhaps less lonely old house.

Was that what she wanted?

Was it better or worse than what she had now?

Wendy managed one giant breath.

It was enough to get her home, running and heaving in a most unladylike fashion.

Ireland

When she burst through the front door, Wendy was for the second time that day surprised by the presence of her parents.

She was a little frazzled, the dog basket dangling on her left elbow while she shook out her umbrella with her right hand, and deep, deep in her own thoughts. She needed time to reflect, to figure out the possibilities resulting from her interaction with the Shesbow twins. This meant journaling. *And* fiction. With her father home from work early and the new dog and everything, it felt like a day out of time, a holiday—so why *not* spend the afternoon writing up her latest ideas for Never Land? She would indulge herself, the same way other girls did with naps, baths, and dresses.

She had been playing with the idea of linking all her stories together somehow, maybe into a novel. . . .

"Oh," she said, blinking at the unexpected sight of her mother sitting at the kitchen table, her father standing over it, both with very, very serious expressions on their faces. Like someone had died.

And there, under her father's hand, was the very notebook she had just been thinking about.

"Mother, Father," she added, feeling something flutter and flop somewhere between her stomach and heart. *A new organ,* she told herself crazily. *One whose sole purpose is to react to the uncomfortable tension in the air.*

"Wendy," Mr. Darling said in his lowest, most managerial voice.

"Darling," Mrs. Darling said. "I think . . . I think we had better talk."

Mr. Darling coughed suddenly, like he was trying not to look nervous.

Wendy had the strange notion of asking if *she* had been let go from the firm.

"You read my notebook," she said instead.

"Yes, and really, darling, your writing is *quite* exquisite," her mother said quickly. "Really. I had no idea you were so talented with words. Your descriptions . . . Your characterizations . . . Mademoiselle Gabineau has never mentioned your facility. At all."

"She is unaware. May I have it, please?" Wendy said, unable to keep her eyes or attention off her book. The little dog waggled frantically in the basket, causing it to swing. She barely felt it.

"The thing is, darling," her mother went on, "the stories themselves are . . . well . . ."

"Oh, enough of this blustering around," Mr. Darling exploded. "They are the product of an infantile mind. The febrile imaginings of a child. I thought you had *done* with all this Peter Pan nonsense years ago! You're *sixteen* now, for heaven's sake, Wendy!"

"It's my fault," Mrs. Darling said apologetically. "I have always indulged my baby girl."

"You haven't changed at all since you were little, Wendy. These silly stories—"

"They aren't silly," Wendy said, offended by the word.

"Well, yes—yes they are, because they aren't real! None of it is *real,* Wendy! Not a deuced thing! And you write them with *yourself* in the stories, like you're some kind of hero, like you're still pretending with your baby brothers! Like you *think* it's all real!"

"I never believed it was—"

But her voice caught in her throat.

She couldn't do it.

She could never knowingly lie about Never Land—she would never betray it that way.

Her parents saw her swallow. They saw her hesitation, her refusal to finish the sentence.

Her mother's head sank toward her chest, and this hurt Wendy most of all.

Mr. Darling cleared his throat again.

"I think you have some growing up to do, Wendy. I think you need to see the world as it is, and what must be done in it to live a full adult life. I think you need a break from these environs and thoughts."

"Father, what are you—"

"The Rennets have a cousin with a country house in Conaught. Their governess had to take a leave of absence on account of her mother passing away," Mrs. Darling said quietly, almost musically. Like delivering the news in operetta format somehow made it less unappealing. "You will join them for several months and care for their five boys."

"*Ireland?*" Wendy cried. "It's . . . a long way off."

It was the first, the only thing she could think to say: she had been looking at a map of the British Isles just the other day to help fill in some descriptive passages of Never Land, and had been drawn to the county's green meadows and hills.

"I know, darling, and I will miss you terribly—" her mother started.

"Now stop there." Mr. Darling held up his hand to silence her. "Brave heart. We're doing this for her own good."

"You're sending me to *Ireland*. You are *exiling* me. To care for a bunch of . . . of . . . nasty little boys I don't even know!"

"Think of it as an adventure! Like in your stories!" Mrs. Darling said brightly. "They could be your Misplaced Boys!"

"*Lost* Boys, Mother. And no, they can't."

"Well, think of it as a nice little excursion from London, then. A vacation, really . . ."

"You're hiring me out to complete strangers hundreds of miles away just because I write stories about Peter Pan?"

It wasn't really a question. It was a reaffirming of the facts as presented to her.

"It's not just about the stories," Mr. Darling said, looking desperately at his wife.

Mrs. Darling raised an eyebrow. She may have been soft in many ways, but Wendy's mother never, ever lied.

"All right, it *is* just about the stories," Mr. Darling sighed. "And I think you could do with a break from each other for a while."

"We will keep the notebook safe here with us while you go," Mrs. Darling said soothingly.

"But they're *my* stories. They're *mine*. They belong to *me!*"

Mr. Darling threw up his hands. "Wendy, they are not the product of a happy, normal girl!"

"No, I suppose *not*," Wendy cried, and she fled upstairs, the basket with the dog still swinging from her arm.

Wendy Makes a Decision

This at least could be said about Snowball: the little thing curled up on Wendy's neck and breathed his soft wet breath on her cheek while she lay on her bed, dry-eyed and insensate. Nana sat loyally on the floor nearby, perhaps withholding her disdain for the new interloper in view of her mistress's distress.

"Ireland . . ." Wendy finally whispered. "I don't want to go to Ireland.

"Unless . . . *maybe* I would if I got to go in an airship.

"Or if I went by regular ship, while chasing pirates.

"Or if I wasn't alone. If I was brought there by . . .

"*Peter Pan.*"

This time hearing her voice aloud didn't make her braver at all.

"Peter Pan," she repeated bitterly.

"*Peter Pan*, who only visited when I couldn't see him. Peter Pan, who left his shadow and never came back for it. Who never came back for *me*."

She turned her head to look out the window, but all she saw was gray. The same gray that was inside her head; the two reached out to each other, like sensing like. Wendy closed her eyes, severing the connection. But it was still gray behind her closed lids.

What had happened?

Somehow her life had gone from heady days of playing games with Michael and John and telling stories about pirates to . . . passing time until they came home. And then there were no more pirates anyway. Something had slipped out of her hands. There would be no pirates of any sort in her future. No fairies, no Peter Pan, no Never Land. Just banishment to another family in another drearily real country. And there? And then back home? The same: social mistakes, misery in a crowd, boys who probably didn't like her anyway.

She sighed and looked at Snowball. "Pretty doggy," she said, giving him a pet. "When they gave you to me they were only trying to make me happy. They really do think this nannying abroad, this . . . . *gothic situation*, would be good for me. But I don't like gothic novels, Snowball. They're dreary.

"I suppose it could have been worse, like an arranged marriage. All right, perhaps that's going a bit far. It's really a bit more Charlotte than Emily. 'A serious introduction to a proper boy,' then."

She carefully moved Snowball so she could give Nana a good petting too.

"I thought *Peter Pan* was the proper boy for me. But all I have is a shadow of him."

She paused for a moment, wondering if that sounded too dramatic.

"But I really did think he was going to come back, Nana. At least to fetch his property. It's his *shadow,* for heaven's sake. What is he doing without it?"

She went to the bureau and opened the drawer and regarded the black non-object that lay there unmoving, darkening the shapes under it.

"He mustn't need it anymore," she said thoughtfully.

"He mustn't *want* it. Anymore," she added after another moment.

Nana let out a sound somewhere between a growl and a chuff. Almost like she knew what Wendy was thinking.

Wendy herself wasn't sure what she was thinking. An idea was just beginning to form in her head—an extremely alien idea, but one that opened a space in the clouds even before it was fully formed, like a sigh that precedes great things.

Things that did *not* include Ireland.

Acquiring these things would be tricky, however.

Apart from maths, nothing in Wendy's life was strictly transactional—though certainly there were times when the boys were younger that she'd had to divide time into five-minute slots so each could have a turn playing with a favorite toy. And, of course, she often overheard Mr. Darling going on about how if Mrs. Darling bought a new hat they wouldn't be able to afford a new tea service—and her mother calmly agreeing, to her father's never-ending surprise (for she was practical underneath her lashes and perfume, and quite good at maths).

But the idea of *worth* . . . of *trade* . . . of something having value to someone else in a way that was useful to *her*, to Wendy . . . this was new, and a little frightening.

Here were the facts: Peter Pan didn't value his shadow anymore, apparently.

But someone else might.

No, scratch that; someone else *did*.

She wouldn't let herself think beyond this. She wouldn't let her mind chatter the way her mouth did, ruining everything. This time she would *do*.

She looked around until she found the perfect thing: a delicate linen and lace envelope for keeping her nightgown in that she had done a pretty job of embroidering. She carefully scooped up the shadow, folded it, and slipped it in.

What else might she need?

A sewing kit, a tiny lady's knife, a muffler, a half dozen extra hairpins, some string and ribbons. She put all this along with the envelope into a worn leather satchel and slipped it under her bed.

Then she took out a pair of stockings and began to darn them, an innocent and useful task should anyone come upon her unexpectedly.

Hours later, Michael and John returned home full of their usual youthful energy and droll remarks. Wendy neither remonstrated them nor laughed softly; her brothers remarked on her distracted nature.

When Mrs. Darling came into the kitchen it was with a tentative step and furtive looks.

"How is your little pet?" she eventually asked.

"What? Oh, he's absolutely adorable," Wendy said, remembering to toss Snowball a tidbit of mutton. For Nana she reserved the bone.

"You can . . . take him with you, you know. To Ireland. He would be a delightful little travel companion."

For a moment, just a moment, Wendy looked at her mother—*really* looked at her, steadily and clearly.

"You would never send the boys away."

The statement fell hard and final and full of more meaning than anything that had ever been said in the kitchen before.

"But they didn't write the . . . fantasies. . . ." her mother said quietly.

Then Mr. Darling came in, loud and blustery, talking up Irish butter and clean country air.

Mother and daughter both ignored him.

Wendy went to bed early that night, claiming fatigue. Since the sun had almost won its daily Sisyphean battle with the weather, the sky was light a long time before the air became heavy enough to subtly infiltrate thoughts with sleep.

"Hook . . ." she whispered, finally drowsing.

"I have his shadow. . . ."

Ramifications

Wendy woke as the clock tolled midnight. If she had any doubts about the reality of her situation or the rashness of her escape plan, this clarified it all immediately. Of course, midnight: the witching hour.

A foggy memory of instructions whispered to her in dreams guided Wendy's hands through the act of slipping on her boots and lacing them up, of wrapping herself up in a coat and grabbing her satchel.

She tiptoed down the hall, pausing to look into Michael and John's room. They were both peacefully asleep. John's glasses hung precariously from the headboard above him and a book was slipping out of his arms. Michael had fallen unconscious with the force of a tot: immediately and completely, no book, and he hadn't moved from that position at all.

"Goodbye—for a little while, at least," she whispered. "You have your own adventures now. It's my turn this time."

Despite attempting to be a ladylike sister, Wendy knew just as well as the boys where the squeaky stairs were and how to hold on to the banister and silently swing to a more polite step. Mr. Darling was snoring; the house was otherwise silent, and she had a clear path to the back door. . . .

Except for Nana, who sat resolutely in front of it.

"Now, Nana," Wendy whispered. "If you really loved me, you would let me go."

Nana made a sound of doubt in the back of her throat.

"Nana. I am *not* going to Ireland. Michael and John don't need either one of us anymore. You need a safe, warm, loving home and a good fire. I need . . . something else."

Nana's doggy eyebrows raised plaintively. She whimpered a question.

"Well, all right. I'll tell you, so that if anything happens to me you may tell the authorities. I'm making my way to Never Land."

Nana sighed, as if to say *I wish I had never grabbed that shadow.*

Then she slowly stepped aside and gestured at the door with her head: *Well, there it is. Go on.*

"Thank you for understanding," Wendy said, kissing her on the head. "I'm grateful."

She opened the door the smallest crack. *"Able to slip through sideways . . . Wasted away with love and longing,"* she whispered spitefully. "Stupid John and his stupid Ovid."

She drifted down the walk carelessly for a moment, stunned by the night. The moon had come out, and though not dramatically full or a perfect crescent, its three quarters were bright enough to turn the fog and dew and all that had the power to shimmer a bright silver, and everything else—the metal of the streetlamps, the gates, the cracks in the cobbles—a velvety black.

After a moment Wendy recovered from the strange beauty and remembered why she was there. She padded into the street before she could rethink anything and pulled up her hood. "Why didn't I do this earlier?" she marveled. Sneaking out when she wasn't supposed to was its own kind of adventure, its own kind of magic. London was beautiful. It felt like she had the whole city to herself except for a stray cat or two.

Despite never venturing beyond the neighborhood much by herself, she had spent plenty of time with maps, studying them for someday adventures. And as all roads lead to Rome, so too do all the major thoroughfares wind up at the Thames. Names like Vauxhall and Victoria (and Horseferry) sprang from her brain as clearly as if there had been signs in the sky pointing the way.

Besides Lost Boys and pirates, Wendy had occasion-ally terrified her brothers with stories about Springheel Jack and the half-animal orphan children with catlike eyes who roamed the streets at night. As the minutes wore on she felt her initial bravery dissipate and terror slowly creep down her neck—along with the fog, which was also somehow find-ing its way under her coat, chilling her to her core.

"If I'm not careful I'm liable to catch a terrible head cold! Perhaps that's *really* why people don't adventure out in London at night," she told herself sternly, chasing away thoughts of crazed, dagger-wielding murderers with a vision of ugly red runny noses and cod-liver oil.

But was it safer to walk down the middle of the street, far from shadowed corners where villains might lurk? Being exposed out in the open meant she would be more easily seen by police or other do-gooders who would try to escort her home.

"My mother is sick and requires this one particular tonic that can only be obtained from the chemist across town," she practiced. "A nasty decoction of elderberries and slippery elm, but it does such wonders for your throat. *No* one else has it. And do you know how hard it is to call for a cab this time of night? In this part of town? *That's* the crime, really."

In less time than she imagined it would take, Wendy

arrived at a promenade that overlooked the mighty Thames. She had never seen it from that particular angle before or at that time of night. On either bank, windows of all the more important buildings glowed with candles or gas lamps or even electric lights behind their icy panes, little tiny yellow auras that lifted her heart.

"I *do* wish I had done this before," she breathed.

Maybe if she had, then things wouldn't have come to *this.* . . .

She bit her lip. A decision had been made; it was time to follow through on it. There was no room for weakness or second thoughts in a hero, and if nothing else, Wendy had to be the hero of her own soul. She found the closest set of stairs down to the river and descended lightly, keeping an eye out for thugs and cutthroats. There was no one around at all—no one visible, anyway—except for a suspicious old man in a broken top hat sucking on a pipe on the opposite bank.

She stood at the edge of the turgid black waters and waited.

A breeze rose, curling the little hairs that strayed from Wendy's chignon. She realized with a start that the air now had the sharp tang of salt. Of the *sea.* The wispy fog that had seemed to follow her from home was now joined by its big brother, which swept down the river like a swift, dark carriage. Thick tendrils preceded it, scraping this way and that just above the water, as if feeling a clear path for the billows that followed. In a very short time Wendy was once again surrounded by gray. She couldn't even see the stairs up to the road.

Everything was still.

And then, emerging out of the darkness like a wraith, a single yellow light bobbed in the inky distance.

Slowly and steadily it grew closer.

Wendy sucked in her breath.

The light resolved into a lantern hung on a yoke. . . .

No, not a yoke—a *prow*!

Incredibly, unbelievably, a silent galleon glided down the Thames toward her. Its sails were furled and its masts as thin and bare as the bones of a broken ribcage rotting on some ancient, forgotten battlefield.

The ship paused improbably in the currents.

Nothing moved in the foggy night but a single black flag rippling in the salty breeze, its skull and crossbones faded and yellow.

Wendy forced herself to stand still, waiting, as motionlessly as she could, her heart pounding loudly in her ears. She had made her decision. She had taken an action. These were the results, and she would deal with them.

"Well, well, well," came a voice from the deck.

Then came the measured *clops* of surprisingly hard and

high-heeled boots on the planks, approaching the railing. Wendy gritted her teeth.

Captain Hook leaned over and grinned at her.

He was exactly and precisely the way she had imagined—*remembered*—him. Long, black, ridiculous curling locks. Probably a wig. Long face, clear of the dissolution of rum but ruined by the joint devils of villainy and insanity. He obviously thought himself a duke in a red-and-gold coat, prim breeches, and mostly spotless stockings. A feather stuck out of his oversized hat; a Jacobean collar throttled his neck. Above his smile was a mustache waxed and styled to within an inch of its—probably dyed—life.

Yet Wendy gulped.

Seeing him was different from imagining—remembering—him. He looked utterly absurd, and that was exactly what made him terrifying.

"Ah, Miss Darling. How are you on this fine night?" he called, saluting her with his hook, sharp and golden, the only thing that glittered in the dim light of the solitary lantern.

"Very well, thank you!" Wendy shouted back. Manners stepped in, bless them, when the mind scrambled away to hide. "And you?"

"Oh, I couldn't be better, thank you for asking," he answered with an oily smile. "That is, assuming you have brought what you said you would."

"I have it. I have Peter Pan's shadow here." She took out the satchel and showed it to him.

"Oh, excellent, excellent girl."

Any pretense at politeness, any mockery he exhibited, disappeared entirely as visceral excitement took over. The greed on his face was both reassuring and nauseating. He rubbed his hand and hook together with tangible glee.

"Do we have a deal?" Wendy asked, clearly and loudly.

"Yes, yes, of course. Passage to Never Land. In return for one shadow."

"And *home* again," Wendy pressed. "When I wish to return."

"And passage home again," Hook said impatiently. "Yes, yes. As for when you wish to return, that can be a tricky business. Getting *here* . . . without pixie magic or flight . . . is an uncertain thing. My crew wasn't too keen on the idea to begin with."

"That was the deal. Never Land and home again," Wendy said, pulling the satchel away from his view and making as if to put it back in her coat.

"*Of course, of course,*" Hook said desperately, eyes never leaving the satchel. "Never Land and home again. Without question. Just be aware that we are not some sort of ferry service, Miss Darling. We are *pirates*. With limited magical means. You cannot on a whim decide you've missed

Mummy and Daddy long enough and expect to be transported instantly. These things take time."

"All right, I will take that into due consideration," Wendy said. "Otherwise, promise?"

"Oh, I promise."

"Swear . . . swear by the pirates' code!"

Hook looked exasperated.

Wendy put her hands on her hips.

She knew about boys trying to sneak out of promises. She had two younger brothers. You had to be *very specific* with your orders and wishes, or they were as wily and untrustworthy as evil genies. And what was a pirate, really, but a boy grown, with a real sword and a mustache?

"Swear it," she repeated.

She could have sworn she heard muffled laughter from behind him on the deck.

Hook sighed.

"All right, all right. I *swear* on the pirates' code: I, Captain Hook, promise that in return for Peter Pan's shadow I shall grant Wendy Darling passage to Never Land *and home*—when circumstances allow it."

"All right then," Wendy said, trying to sound surer than she felt. She had just won a battle of wits with a pirate, just like in a story. Why didn't she feel triumphant?

"Come on, men, let's welcome our passenger aboard!"

Hook grinned again at her, a smile that narrowed to points at the corners of his mouth that were as sharp as those at the ends of his mustache, as the end of his hook.

There was a thumping and pounding on the deck. A rope ladder unrolled over the side, bumping and bouncing on its way down, the last step landing neatly at Wendy's feet.

She took a deep breath, set her jaw, and climbed up.

Wendy Among the Pirates

As might have been guessed from the preceding pages, Wendy hadn't much experience interacting with the world at large; that is, people who weren't her family, shopkeepers, neighbors, or other audience members at the theater. Yet despite this innocence she had an immediate sense that perhaps these pirates were not the nicest people to be left alone with. It was one thing to tell tales of swashbuckling battles and the backstory behind the bosun with the eye patch—and quite another to actually be in their midst.

Captain Hook presented his men with a flourish. They stood neither in neat rows nor at attention—with very little respect at all, actually—and beheld Wendy far too boldly for her liking. One skinny chap with large gold earrings who slouched provocatively to one side actually gave her an appalling wink.

Their clothes were not the bright primary colors of nursery room imagination; they were salt-faded and dull. Their faces weren't merely unshorn and artfully streaked with a daub of tar; they were *grubby*. All shades of skin were dulled with not enough washing. Wendy found her hands twitching, the urge to grab a cloth and scrub them almost overwhelming all other thoughts.

"Men, this is Wendy Darling. Wendy, this is me crew. Crew, she is a *guest* aboard the *Jolly Roger* and I expect you swabs to treat her as such."

"It's bad luck to have a woman aboard," one large old pirate with a red bandanna growled. "Worse than a cat. Brings storms and swells."

"Oh . . . I think it's the *best* sort of luck to have a lass on deck." A man with one eye and a loathsome leer grinned at her disgustingly.

"If any one of you touches her," Captain Hook said with a very false smile, "you'll be feeding the sharks before you can draw your next breath." He leaned on his heels and put his hands on his hips, a movement that threw his splendid jacket back and revealed the twin pistols that were holstered elegantly on his hips.

This made Wendy feel a lot calmer but a little vexed.

What if the pirate was saving her life, or wanted to arm wrestle? What then?

"This whole thing is a bloody waste of time," a third pirate scoffed. "We should be out attacking ships, looting gold, and plundering treasure!"

"And so we shall. But in the meantime, she has given me something more valuable than all the gold in Never Land," Hook said airily. "Peter Pan's *shadow!*"

He unfurled the poor limpid thing and flapped it out to show them. The shadow hung limply from its neck where the pirate held it, struggling only a little.

The pirates looked mostly unhappy at the sight, a smidgen angry, and not just a little uncomfortable. Seeing a shadow hanging there apart from its owner was unnatural and might make the heartiest and blackest soul shiver, but even Wendy could see there was more to it than that.

"And what will that get us?" demanded an orange-haired lout with a northern European accent.

"Why, it will get us P—" Hook paused with a not-very-subtle side-eye at Wendy. "It will get us something we've always wanted. Well, something *I* have always wanted. And I am your captain. So it's what you want, too—or at least it's in your best interests to want it. And when I have it, we will be done with Never Land and all its silliness forever, and there will be only plundering and loot from here on out. All right?"

There were muttered grumbles of grudging assent.

"For now, I'm putting the shadow in safekeeping, in the trusted hands of Mr. Smee."

At this the pirates looked even *more* uncomfortable—and disgusted. Possibly resigned. They threw up their hands and slowly dispersed, growling and unsatisfied and muttering curses.

"So there you are, my dear," Captain Hook said, bowing to her. "A loathsome lot, to be sure, but you're safe among them while we're on our way to Never Land."

"What time shall we get there, if you please?" Wendy asked politely.

"We don't deal with time or clocks or watches on the *Jolly Roger*, Miss Darling. Except for figuring latitude and longitude. Pirates are free from such civilizing constraints and demonic inventions of man. We have none of those infernal contraptions on *this* ship, I can tell you."

Wendy narrowed her eyes. What a strange thing to say—and there was a strange look behind his bluster. Fear? Could it possibly have been *fear*? He was afraid of something. Something he wasn't telling her.

"All right, well . . . Approximately how *long* will it take to get there? Surely pirates aren't entirely free from the passage of time, what with meals and sleep and the like."

"Oh, you're a very clever girl, aren't you, Miss Darling?

Well, these things aren't precise, but it shouldn't be more than a day or so."

"And how are we to get there?"

Captain Hook gave her a knowing smile. "I suppose if you were with Peter Pan he would say something like *oh, second star on the left,* et cetera, et cetera. And you would fly through the sky, straight to the island of your dreams.

"Alas, my lady, pixie dust and good magic are rather out of a pirate's reach. We had to go a different route, and it nearly cost poor Major Thomas his life. Possibly his soul. It was a bit unclear. Anyway, he's a useless lubber and prone to grog. Not much of a loss there."

Wendy's eyes widened and her hand went to her mouth in dismay, but Hook was already touching his hat to her and spinning away, chuckling over the shadow he held.

Now alone, she looked around the deck nervously. There were no benches or chaise lounges as on a proper transport vessel. Because of the lateness—or the earliness—of the hour, the pirates mostly went belowdecks to their bunks. None of those remaining seemed particularly happy about the strange motion of the ship, gliding along with-out oars or sails or any human help at all. They occupied themselves with other pirate-y pursuits: five-finger fillet on an upturned barrel, surreptitious sips from leather flasks, shouting over a game that involved rolling with what looked very much like knucklebones instead of dice.

(*And how were those come by?* Wendy wondered.)

She fidgeted with her fingers a bit the way she did at parties, and then decided that the dice throwers seemed the least dangerous.

"My, those are certainly unique implements you're playing with," she ventured.

The pirates just grunted.

"Of course, I don't approve of gambling at all, but Father has a lovely pair of dice that he keeps with his jewelry. They're not . . . bones. At least, I don't think so. I believe they're ivory. Although I suppose that's basically a sort of bone, isn't it?"

The pirates frowned and tried to ignore her.

"They have real pips on them, carved and painted. They really are quite lovely. Of course, I *am* against gambling, and so is Mother. It's not a proper occupation for anyone, even men. But his dice are quite pretty and nice to hold, and they warm up in your hand so. And how do you know which side yours land on? Without pips?"

The pirates stopped their game entirely and stared up at her in exasperation.

"Well, I've never played before," she said, a little defensively. "I'm not asking you to teach me. I'm just wondering. I should have to say no if you asked me, wouldn't I? Seeing as gambling and games of chance are immoral. So please, I'd rather you didn't ask."

"Weren't going to," one of the pirates grumbled. And with that, he swept the dice up into his bag and left her alone with the other players, who gave her nasty looks before they, too, retreated.

Wendy wilted. Life aboard the pirate ship was actually surprisingly similar to a fancy party, the type she hated. With dressed-up girls and boys and men and women and tea and tiny sandwiches and aspic and someone showing off on the piano. No one wanted to talk to her at *those* gatherings, either. It was like Christmas all over again.

She wandered forlornly across the deck and looked out over the railing.

The sky was blank. Fog surrounded the ship and there was no more breeze. It was as if they had reached the middle of the night, the middle of nowhere. Everything stood still except for a few tendrils of Wendy's hair and the black flag. She shivered, pulling her coat more closely around her. She didn't want to be alone. But the five-finger fillet players looked . . . dangerous.

And then Wendy saw salvation.

A lone pirate was sitting cross-legged on the deck, looking squint-eyed and studious, pulling at a string on his pants.

He was sewing!

Wendy brightened like the sun. Now *there* was a subject she could feel confident about.

She walked up to the fellow and watched for a moment as he ineffectually stabbed a giant needle into a piece of cloth that he held awkwardly in place on his pants, trying to cover a hole.

"Excuse me, if you don't mind me saying, but I'm afraid you're doing that entirely wrong," Wendy said politely.

The pirate looked up at her, one eye still squinted. She wondered if it was a permanent affliction.

"Well, I ain't got me a seamstress to fix up my fancy pants now, do I?" He cackled. "'What Mother can't do, sons must *makes* do,' as they say."

"Ah—I don't know about that," Wendy said, trying to work the words out in her head and failing. "But if you'll hand it to me, I'll have a go."

The pirate's eyes widened. Without a second thought, he shoved the whole mess over to her, including his pants— which, as his brightly striped knickers attested, he had apparently not been wearing.

"Oh!" Wendy blushed and turned around.

The pirate cackled again. "What, you think I'd stick it with a needle while it's on me own skin? I'm unskilled, not *daft*, ye silly co'. Now settle down. Ye can't see me privates or me bum, and there's them that wear less on washing day round here, so ye'd best get used to it."

"Well!"

Wendy tried to rearrange her shocked expression while busying herself sorting through the mess of cloth. He was right, of course. She was in alien country now: a ship full of uncivilized men. All she could do was act properly, like a decent civilized person, as there was no guarantee that others would.

She settled herself down on a tipped-over quarter cask and smoothed out the pieces. Actually, the pirate had made a very nice, neat little knot to begin with. But that made sense, she supposed. Sailors had to be very good at knots, hadn't they? She bet they would be excellent at macramé, or even crochet, if patiently taught. . . .

Wendy whistled and hummed to herself and felt much better with something familiar in her hands. In a short while the patch was finished and held tightly on by tiny and neat little stitches.

"There, all done. You can see how I—oh!"

There was a crowd around her now. Pirates, speechless and wide-eyed to a man.

"*BLIMEY!* Do mine next!" one said, whipping off his shirt.

"No, me! I got no seat on me trousers!" another begged.

"No! Me next!" whined a third.

"All right, all right now . . ."

She put her hands on her hips, feeling crowded and overwhelmed. It was on the tip of her tongue to say that as long as she was on board, she would do any minor repairs and mending that were needed. Might as well make herself useful, right? That's what she always did: made herself useful, and as a result she was always needed. And liked.

Then again . . .

She had paid her passage on this vessel. A very dear one. She wasn't a scullery maid; she was a customer.

"My jacket's fearful cold when the wind blows—I'll give ye a halfpenny if ye do it first," a fourth pirate said slyly, seeing her hesitate.

The others caught on fast.

"I'll give ye me grog ration! For me pants!"

"I'll give ye a whale-bone needle and carve ye a thimble, if ye like. Can ye *make* things, too? Like a muffler for cold days?"

Well, that's better, Wendy decided. *I think.*

Pirates were *very* transactional—and seemed to respect you more if you were as well. In some ways it was rather a windfall: who knew what other supplies she would require for her foray into Never Land? In her dreams and stories there was always just the right-shaped stick or rock or key discovered at the last possible moment. But was the real Never Land like that?

And, of course, the pirates would have to talk to her now.

Take that, Shesbows! thought Wendy, very pleased with herself.

There was no sun to mark the passage of time. After her third mending project, Wendy began to grow restless. She asked the hovering pirates the precise o'clock but they all shook their heads.

"Without a sun ye can't use no sundial," one said, pointing to the dark gray wall of fog around the ship. "And Hook don't allow no modrun clocks nor watches nowhere on account of that crocodile what took his hand. It tocks like the clock it swallowed."

Aha . . . Now it made sense! She had called the creature Tick-Tock in her own telling of the story. Hook's hand had given the beast a craving for more of the pirate captain, and it followed the *Jolly Roger* everywhere. The noise of the clock it had swallowed always presaged its appearance.

(The boys would shriek with glee when Wendy said things like: "But wait! What was that? Off in the distance? *Tick . . . tock . . . . tick . . . tock.*" "IT'S A CROCODILE!" Young Michael would cry.)

"That thing hasn't been around for years," another pirate said. "Probably dead from indigestion. But Hook, he still thinks it's out there somewhere."

"He can't bear being reminded of it. Thinks the beast is still after 'im," said a third. "Every time he hears a clock it drives him batty."

She wondered what had happened to the crocodile in the real Never Land. She hadn't killed it off in her own stories—yet.

But despite the lack of clocks, lunch came anyway, and blessedly just in time. Wendy's stomach was growling in a most unladylike way. She followed the crew to the mess hall. Each pirate presented his own bowl to the, er, sous chef. It was then filled with glop that might have been a chowder or a mulligatawny. One polite fellow (whose waistcoat Wendy had fixed) offered to give her his own bowl once he was done. She discreetly tried to wipe it out. The tall, slouchy pirate with the two big gold earrings saw this and cackled.

"Have you anything of your own you would like fixed?" Wendy asked him, trying to change the subject and distract attention from her covert actions.

"Oh, I'm plenty handy with a needle and thread," the pirate said, posing for her. And in fact, he was more solidly dressed than the rest. Everything was mostly clean, if not perfect, and unpatched. "I just don't let it get out too much, know what I mean?"

"I suppose I do," Wendy said uncertainly as the pirate winked at her.

"The name's Zane," he said with a bow. "Alodon Zane, at your service."

"Wendy Darling at yours," she said with a curtsy.

"MISS DARLING, WHAT ARE YOU DOING IN HERE WITH THESE LOUTS?"

Captain Hook was suddenly filling the door like a bad omen and roaring like an enraged lion. At her dismay and the other pirates' shock, he immediately softened his voice. "My dear, you're a *guest*, not a midshipman. Come dine in my quarters. Mr. Smee will serve us."

Wendy shivered. She *might* have read a few books that were not strictly approved by Father or prescreened by the bookseller. In those typeset pages, she'd had glimpses of the greater world—even if she didn't fully understand it. She knew it was not proper to be alone in the company of a strange man.

"Dinna worry," Zane whispered into her left ear. "He's not . . . I mean, Hook's a lunatic, but he loves decorum. Your maidenhood is safe with him. Not yer throat, maybe. But the rest of you is."

"Thank you?" Wendy whispered back. Then she returned the bowl to the pirate who had provided it. "Thank you, sir, but I suppose I will be dining on the lido deck instead. Your generosity is very much appreciated."

"Oh, yes, me too. Absolutely, ma'am," the pirate blustered, bowing.

Lunch with a pirate captain could have been many things: terrifying, spooky, embattled—even romantic, given the right circumstances.

But in reality, lunch was . . . awkward.

Wendy sat up properly and used her best manners.

Captain Hook bowed and flourished and removed his hat and pulled out a chair for her. The table was a tiny fold-out thing spread with a fancy cloth, silver utensils, and a clever golden candelabrum that was held upright on chains so it didn't tip with the waves. It was all very lovely, and for the first moment Wendy was overcome with the precise perfection of the scene. There was even a spinet piano in the corner of the room.

"I do play, if you're wondering," Hook said, following her eyes. "A bit harder since the . . . well . . . *hook*, but I make do."

They settled down to empty plates.

"Mr. Smee," Hook called politely.

No one came.

"Mr. *Smee*," he said again with a growl—while still smiling at Wendy.

Silence.

"MR. SMEE!" the captain finally cried, slamming his hook down on the table. "Blast that man. He'll be at the grog again, no doubt."

He leapt up and crashed through the door, muttering under his breath.

"Confounded . . . lazy . . . overpaid . . ."

Wendy sat stiffly and continued to look around at everything she had already looked at.

Eventually Hook came back, awkwardly carrying a plate of carved beef, a bowl of neeps and tatties, and a beautiful if stale-looking baguette, all cradled in his hand and hook.

Wendy leapt up to help, but he *tsked* her back down and actually quite neatly and deftly laid out the feast.

"Good help is so hard to get," he said apologetically. "I should have had him walk the plank years ago, but we go way back. . . . He's even saved my life a few times. It's like keeping an old dry cow around because you can't bear the look in her eyes."

"Oh," Wendy said uncertainly.

They concentrated on serving themselves in silence. Wendy wondered if this was what having a distant uncle was like—an odd grown-up who didn't know how to interact properly with young people and who often said inappropriate things.

"So I'm curious, Miss Darling," Hook finally began,

with a casual tone so false Wendy's ears practically curled at his words. "Whatever made you come to the rather rash decision to trade Peter Pan's shadow to his greatest enemy in exchange for passage to Never Land?"

Wendy was *about* to interrupt and point out that Hook wasn't Peter Pan's *greatest* enemy. Depending on how you looked at it, Peter Pan's greatest enemy could have been growing up, his own sense of self-importance, or his more immediately dangerous foes: the warlike, winged L'cki, the Fangriders of Upper Hillsdale, or the Cyclops of the Cerulean Sea. Hook was a *recurring* enemy. Not his *greatest* enemy.

Then she thought better of mentioning it.

"Well, you know, he never came back for it. He just left it there," she said airily. Trying to ignore the agency she had in the decision, that what she had done wasn't *right*. That these words were *false*. "What was I supposed to do, keep it around for the rest of my life among my trinkets and bric-a-brac? Hanging after me? You seemed to want it more than he, and I wanted a little holiday. Everyone is happy. Shall I pour you some water, Captain?"

"Thank you, my dear, but I'll stick to this lovely Barolo. A very interesting . . . argument—*justification*, maybe? Now don't look at me like that; it's just us, Miss Darling. But surely you of all people know that Never Land is a bit trickier than that. There is no *holidaying* there, like Blackpool or the South of France. You have made quite the commitment. I can't help but wonder what drove such a pretty, innocent little thing like you to such desperation—abandoning her life and family to leap into the unknown, and trading in her hero's shadow in the process."

Wendy had mixed feelings at these words. On the one hand, they made her sound a little epic.

On the other hand, was her life really that dire? Her family loved her. Nana loved her. Ireland was terrible, but it was for only a short period of time, right? And *safe* . . .

She looked up at the pirate, suspicious. In her stories Captain Hook was always planning, always conniving. He had an angle on everything, even if that angle was stupid and resulted in ridiculous defeats. So what was he driving at now?

"Yes, it shall make a fascinating chapter in my memoirs, won't it?" she said as haughtily as she could, pouring herself another glass of tar-scented water.

"Won't your family miss you—the Mister and Missus Darling?"

"I don't really know how time operates between Never Land and the real world. Perhaps I'll just have been gone a day," she answered carelessly. "Perhaps it will be a blink of an eye. Perhaps this is all now a dream and I will wake when it's over, back in my bed. Either way, Mother and Father have their hands quite full with Michael and John. I daresay they shan't miss me beyond needing to write an embarrassing explanation to a certain family in Ireland. I just hope Nana remembers to feed Snowball.

"But what about you, Captain Hook? What exactly are your plans for Peter's shadow? Are you going to keep it and hold it over his head forever? In return for your . . . hook?"

"*Forever?*" Hook sat back in his chair, looking astonished. "Oh no, no, my girl. I have no desire to continue this endless charade with Peter Pan any longer at all. I have wasted far too much of my life on it. My crew hasn't looted a merchant vessel or stormed a port in years. No, I am done with Never Land. Rather permanently. I think it's high time I put it and Peter behind me. *Rather permanently.*"

"That sounds a bit ominous," Wendy observed.

"It was supposed to. I'm actually quite thrilled by the fact that you will be here as an audience to his and its fate."

"What precisely are you going to do, if I may ask?"

"Well, my dear, unlike the villains in *your* quaint little tales, I am not daft enough to reveal my cunning plans to anyone—a hero or even a bystander like yourself—before carrying them out."

Wendy took some umbrage at the term *bystander*—wasn't she on a pirate ship headed to Never Land of her own volition? Didn't she *invent* much of the world he inhabited?

But there were more pressing issues than her own ego.

"Of course not," she agreed, around a sip of water so she wouldn't choke on her subterfuge. "But surely you couldn't keep such ideas entirely to yourself. Even a great captain like yourself needs help with the dirty work. And perhaps a sympathetic ear."

"Well, you are right there, of course," Hook said, swirling his deep red wine in its glass. "But I have Mr. Smee, who holds all my secrets dearly. He alone is aware of the not so happily-ever-after that awaits all of Never Land.

"And I'll have you know, Miss Darling, I was rather despairing of ever being able to carry out all the details needed for my plans. Your offer of Peter's shadow came like a miracle out of the blue—finally Mr. Smee and I can get to work on it!"

Wendy . . . was, however inadvertently, responsible for setting in motion one of Hook's most murderous schemes? That involved all of Never Land? *Rather permanently?* She swallowed and tried to stay calm.

"Lucky break for you, I suppose," she said casually. "But how *does* it involve Peter's shadow? You couldn't have made all of these plans without knowing for certain you could get it, and—"

"Tut tut," the captain said, shaking a finger at her like a

schoolmarm. "It's highly impolite to question a pirate captain so closely when he has invited you to lunch, don't you know? Terribly bad form."

And Wendy ground her teeth, defeated.

The moment lunch—or whatever it was; the world was still gray and formless—ended, she escaped back to the deck. Her eyes had that dry, crusty feeling of having been open too long from being up too late. How long had it been since she had left the house? It was mad not having clocks or watches around. Despite just eating a rather substantial meal she felt a little light-headed. But not queasy. Even with the rhythmic rocking of the ship, she walked steadily and her stomach remained firmly digesting the surprisingly good repast.

"Lady! Missy! Miss Darling!" A pirate ran up to her, a loop of string in his hands. Two other pirates came reluctantly behind, looking chagrined. One of them cradled a badly bleeding hand.

"My goodness, whatever happened here?"

"Me and these louts was just arguing about the proper play of cat's cradle," the pirate with the string said. "The White Duke here kept flubbing it up."

"I had to cut him," the second pirate admitted, pointing at the wound on the third's hand.

"Can you show us how to do it, proper-like?" the Duke asked, heedless of his injury.

Wendy gave them all a severe look.

"Let me take care of this poor fellow first and *then* see what we can do."

She took the pirate's bloody hand and gently peeled open his fingers for a better look. It wasn't so bad, really—just deep and narrow. All it needed was to be thoroughly cleaned before infection set in. For this they used some pure rum and one of Wendy's precious handkerchiefs. The pirate tried not to swear during her judicious application of the stinging cleanser.

Only then did she take the loop of string and demonstrate the proper sequence of cat's cradle. She even included some of the more difficult variations like the clock tower and the bishop's cap.

Delighted, the pirates clapped her on the back rather harder than she would have liked and strode off, guffawing and chatting like there had never been a row to begin with.

Wendy sighed and shook her head. If all of Never Land's adventures were as easily won as that, she was in for a nice time indeed.

She leaned on the gunwale and looked out. Was it getting lighter? Really this time?

Yes! The rosy fingers of dawn had finally slipped through the fog and gently pulled it apart, separating the tendrils, weakening it.

Wendy watched in fascination. She almost never saw the sunrise except in winter and that was through her window, under the gray sprawl of London Town. Nothing like this. As the sea lightened and the sky began to clear, the two elements resolved themselves into colors unlike anything she was used to: brilliant emerald and deep aquamarine, pellucid azure and shining lapis. It was so storybook perfect she wouldn't have been surprised at all if the sun came out with a great smiley face drawn on it.

"Miss Darling," came a whisper behind her.

Wendy spun around. A cadaverously skinny pirate stood there, the one who had leered at her so loathsomely before. His one eye was narrow and lecherous, his smile thin and frightening.

"I don't believe we've properly met yet. How do you do?" Wendy said, putting out her hand.

"Oh, I do just fine," the pirate growled—and pushed her back up against the railing.

Wendy was caught before she could even figure out what was happening. It took her a moment to find her voice and one more to realize that, despite struggling, she had no ability to fend off this attacker.

"Unhand me!" she cried.

The pirate laughed, his foul-smelling breath nearly asphyxiating her. Wendy screamed.

The pirate leaned over her—

A shot rang out.

So loudly, so close, she felt its hot wind singe her face.

Her attacker looked surprised and then slumped to the deck.

A pool of blood formed under his head. As his body crumpled into a more permanent position, she saw the perfect hole behind his ear where the bullet had gone in.

Wendy knew from stories that this was the time when women screamed and screamed and screamed—and sometimes men, too. But she was just happy to be able to breathe freely again and to have the monster off of her. She felt little of anything except relief.

Hook stood on the deck posed either heroically or demonically, depending on how you read the scene. He had his pistol out and aimed in case the foul miscreant rose again and a curious golden two-cigar holder balanced in his hook. Smoke rose from both cigars as well as the muzzle of his gun.

The rest of the crew appeared as silently as rats (and just as curious) from all parts of the ship, including the crow's nest.

"Miss Darling, are you hurt?" Captain Hook asked, his tone soft and flat.

"No, I don't . . . I'm a little . . ." She touched her mouth and throat, wiping away the grease from the dead man's fingers. *Then* she began to shake. "I'm . . . physically, I'm all fine."

"Mr. Smee, have the crew remove this . . . filth at once," Hook said with a curl of his lip, the gun and cigars still held steady. "And someone bring Miss Darling a draught of something to restore her spirits."

"Oh, I don't . . ." Wendy began. But then again, maybe a drop of something might not be such a bad idea. The shaking had spread to her feet and parts of her body untouched by the villain, and she was having a hard time reining in all the ants she felt crawling on her skin.

Three pirates came forward—none of them named Mr. Smee, Wendy was fairly certain—and unceremoniously dumped the body overboard. A fourth brought a mop and duly began scrubbing the blood and brains away. Two more rushed to her side, one holding a silver-and-crystal decanter and the other a matching cup, both of which looked like they were from Captain Hook's personal stash. Someone held her upright and someone else poured a few drops of a liquid, thick and amber, into the glass. She downed it in one gulp, feeling all eyes on her.

It burned just as she'd imagined it would. Her eyes felt like they were spinning in their sockets.

"Begging your pardon, Cap'n," she heard someone say as she staggered a bit, still trying to collect herself. "But we're back in our proper seas now, Cap'n. And on course for Never Land."

"Thank you, but right now we have more serious things to clear up here," Hook growled. He looked over the crew, into each and every man's eyes. The muzzle of his gun followed closely.

"*This* is how you treat her?" he demanded, his voice carrying across the deck although he didn't shout. "I bring you someone to be your *mother*, and this is how you treat her?"

"Oh," Wendy said, apologies coming to her lips far too easily, the deadly niceties of social convention, the stupidity of being raised by the Darlings. Or maybe it was just the drink. "Most of them were gentlemen. They didn't all treat me badly. It was just that one fellow and—I'm sorry, what?"

She blinked as his words caught up with her brain.

Captain Hook put his arm protectively around her shoulders, careful not to burn her with the cigars. He addressed the men with a tone of great disappointment.

"I bring you a *lady* and a *gentlewoman* to take care of all of you, and this is what you *do*?"

"We would never!" one pirate called out piteously.

"Valentine is a villain, everyone knowed it, he's the worst!" another called out.

"We wuz nice to her! I gave her me own bowl for lunch!"

"She fixed my pants up real good—I'd never harm a hair on her head!"

"WELL, YOU ALMOST LET *THIS* HAPPEN!" Hook roared, firing his pistol in the air.

Wendy winced at the repetition of the loud sound, the ringing in her ears. But it didn't stop her from speaking.

"Excuse me? I'm sorry, I don't believe I quite understand what you're saying," she pressed. "I'm glad to have helped out here and there while aboard, but as someone just said—we're not far from Never Land now. My journey aboard your lovely ship is nearly over. It will soon be time to disembark. I'm not here to be a mother to anyone. I'm here to have adventures."

"And adventures you shall have," Hook promised. "After we leave these cursed waters of Never Land, we shall travel the high seas, plundering and looting along the way, and you shall fix our pants, do our laundry, mend our wounds, and generally take care of us. And probably do a *much* better job than Mr. Smee."

"I shall do nothing of the sort!" Wendy protested, almost stamping her foot. "We had a deal. I bought passage to Never Land for Peter's shadow."

"Yes. And here we are, *almost* arrived." Captain Hook said this politely, but a nasty grin stretched across his face. He indicated the horizon with his gun: far off in the distance was indeed a pale bright line, a glowing golden beach. "That was what you bargained for—and that was *all* you bargained for.

"I never promised to put you ashore."

Tink Among the Salarymen

The way to London was not unknown to fairies; it was just rarely used anymore. Smog was bad for wings and the new machines made for strange dreams in children; fewer and fewer were of the sunny meadows and hidden vales that once captured their imagination.

When Tink appeared in the sky above, it was as if a shy star had worked up the courage to appear among its brighter cousins. She glimmered golden and faint at first . . . and then brighter and nearer . . . but never any larger.

The sound she made as she descended, however, was not the music of the spheres or anything so celestial. It fell somewhere between *angry hornet* and *angry percussionist shaking a rack of bells for the worst ever Christmas concert*.

Below her all of London was gray and rolling and endless

and eternally the same. If she squinted, the little fairy could almost pretend that, instead of houses, the streets were lined with the hives of meerrabbits. Maybe from the wrong side of the savanna, but friendly nonetheless.

The thing was . . . Tinker Bell never actually paid attention when Peter took her on these jaunts. She loved hearing about Peter's babyhood; she loved revisiting his lost home. But she *hated* going to Ugly Wendy's house. She had no idea how Peter had even found the girl and her stupid, snotty little brothers. Somehow the stories that Wendy told of his exploits ad nauseam had reached his pixie ears in a way that was just quintessentially Pan-ish.

It was near Kensington Gardens, wasn't it?

She flew the way she vaguely remembered they used to go, following the Thames and keeping an eye out for pockets of green among the gray, brown, and black.

Aha—at last, something familiar! She recognized the updraft that suddenly lifted her high into the sky and made it difficult for someone as light as she to land anywhere. Peter never had any trouble. Once in a great while she clung to his collar while he dove through gusts, and these were the best moments of all.

The sky was just beginning to lighten as Tinker Bell touched down delicately inside a park. She felt some fairy familiarity; magic had not entirely deserted this ancient place. But these fey folk were of earthly origin and she had no time for such riffraff. She was Never Land empyreal—and she had work to do.

As she peeped around the garden gate and up the street, she realized that things looked very different when you were down among the ugly buildings and not high above them. At least it was early and she had the city mostly to herself while she explored. There were only a few humans around this time of the morning.

A solitary girl hurried along, looking over her shoulder every few steps. She was large and ugly—was it Wendy?

Tinker Bell approached her eagerly.

But no, up close it was obvious the girl's dress was shabby and poor and her eyes darted about in fear; they didn't hold steady in dreams.

Toward this not-Wendy girl a pair of men strode broadly. Their voices were loud and their dress obviously fine even to a forest pixie's eyes: great silk and wool capes, shiny top hats slightly askew, walking canes with glittering knobs. Much like foxes and wolves they had obviously been out all night hunting for whatever rarefied things these humans craved—eyeglasses, taxes, creampuffs.

"*EGADS*, is that the dancer from the Moulin Rouge? The one you liked so much?" one of the men said, guffawing, pointing at the human girl.

"Good evening, sirs," she said, pulling her collar close and trying to hurry past them.

The other man put out his hand and stopped her, then looked her up and down.

"No, she's a bad copy. Still . . ."

"Please, sirs, let me go. I'm just on my way home."

"From what nefarious activities, I should like to know," the first man said with a snort. "Would anyone even miss you? At 'home'? All the decent girls have been in bed and asleep for hours now. They're not out wandering the streets at night, looking for trouble."

"I ain't looking for trouble. Just let me go," she pleaded.

Tinker Bell's eyes widened as she watched the man reach out to touch the girl's cheek.

Before she knew what she was doing, the little fairy was suddenly zooming in between the two, pelting pixie dust into the man's eyes.

The reaction was immediate: he howled and clawed at his face like a madman.

His friend drew back in surprise.

The girl saw her chance and ran off, mouthing silent thanks to her mysterious savior. The ball of light now zooming away brightened visibly—thanks to a new believer in fairy magic.

"I can see!" the man moaned, falling to his knees. "I

see too much! The world . . . as it really is . . . the great god Pan . . ."

But Tink was already whisking down the street, that adventure over and forgotten.

There were plenty of helpful street signs in this London—if only she could read. She remembered a big tree at the house; that's how Peter always found it. A big tree in a tiny yard with an unused doghouse below. The windows to the nursery were on level with the highest branches of that tree, so they could perch there and listen. If Peter was especially enamored of the story they would glide silently over to the roof and lie on the slate shingles, half listening, half dreaming.

Some of the street trees were indeed large, grand, and imposing—and sadly penned in, surrounded by cobbles and flagstones. None were in a yard.

Human movement increased as the sun rose. Lamps were doused and people came out; they were sweeping the streets, hurrying into shops, unlocking doors with big keys. Tinker Bell buzzed unseen over everyone's heads, looking out for young women of a certain height.

Aha! There!

A young woman in a *very familiar* blue dress entered a bookstore and coughed to get the bookseller's attention. How perfectly Wendy!

Tinker Bell zoomed down to see if she was indeed her; this girl definitely seemed more likely than the first one. All right, her skin looked darker, and her hair, too, but who could tell? Humans were strange. Maybe they changed now and then.

"I have a question about a book. Please," the girl spoke softly.

No, that was definitely not Ugly Wendy. Ugly Wendy wasn't shy when she spoke. She was loud. And to the fairy's ears, strident and pushy.

"My wares are far more refined and intellectual than what will satisfy the likes of you," the shop owner snapped without looking up from his own book. "I doubt you can even read. Where are you from?"

"My parents are from Barbados, sir. I was born in England and am a citizen."

"Hardly. Please leave my premises at once."

"But—"

"Get out. Now. Or I shall summon the constable. Your kind is *not* welcome here."

The girl sighed, shook her head, and left.

Tinker Bell also buzzed off, confused and full of unquiet thoughts. She paused to catch her breath and sort things out— and also to suggest to a couple of nearby mice that they would probably very much enjoy comfy nests made exclusively out of a shop's worth of shredded books. They agreed and scampered off, summoning dozens of their friends.

Wendy *was* a big ugly girl. That was just the truth of the matter. And she took Peter's attention away from Tink, despite being big and ugly.

But . . .

Was this the world she lived in?

Where random men might try to hurt her?

Where even if a girl was polite, people . . . ignored her? Yelled at her? Made fun of her?

Was this why Ugly Wendy stayed inside all the time telling stories to her brothers?

Because it was safe?

Because she could be whatever she wanted?

Maybe her brothers were also ugly, but at least they treated her with respect. . . .

Tinker Bell shook her head, trying to physically beat the thoughts out. They were complicated and negative and felt strangely similar to the ones she had about Peter and convincing him that his shadow wasn't in London. There was something . . . *icky* about them. Like the bad-smelling graklemud you could never completely get off. You always thought you had, but there would be just a tiny bit somewhere and you wouldn't be able to find it and you would stink embarrassingly for days.

She rose into the air to fly her mind clean. She skimmed along the roofs and chimneys and spires of London, spiraling out wider and wider, expanding her search.

Sometime mid-morning, when the tired sun crawled into its work clothes of smoke and mist, Tinker Bell finally found the attic gable she remembered from years before.

But unlike every other time when she and Peter had come to hear stories, the windows were shut and fastened tight.

Tinker Bell frowned and whizzed back and forth. She rapped on the glass angrily with her tiny knuckles.

No one was there.

She zoomed into the garden and up to the kitchen door and knocked, trying to stick her head into the too-small keyhole. She jingled furiously when she got stuck there for a moment.

Then she heard a scratching on the other side, almost like a response to her knocks. She redoubled her efforts, slamming against the wood feetfirst.

The door pulled slowly and laboriously inward and she tumbled into the Darling household.

There were no humans about; only the dog was there. She regarded the fairy with large, woeful eyes. But the little fairy didn't stop to say hello or thank you. She zoomed like an angry hornet from room to room until she found the stairs and zipped up them—and then a second set of stairs when she realized her destination lay on the next floor.

The low thudding steps of Nana came up slowly behind her, as well as a doggy sigh or two.

Here was the terrible room. Where Ugly Wendy told her stories to her brothers while Tink and Peter stayed outside looking, listening in. With all of its stupid, ugly, large human tools and bits and pieces littering the room . . . though it seemed there was far less clutter than the last time. She flew chaotically back and forth, over lamps and trunks, into the wardrobe and amongst the clothes, causing dust of both the general and pixie varieties to spray about indiscriminately.

"Woof."

Nana had finally made it to the top of the stairs and sat down on her haunches with resignation, knowing it would do little good to try to physically stop the fairy.

Tinker Bell stopped her buzzing around and hovered in front of the dog, angrily jingling questions.

"Woof . . ." Nana said, rolling her eyes toward the bureau.

Tinker Bell flew into the half-open top drawer so hard she bonked against the back. She might have gotten trapped inside had Nana not put up a massive paw to stop the drawer from closing.

The fairy looked around frantically, lighting up every

corner with her glow. But all of the shadows behaved normally, twisting and shrugging and shrinking and growing with her movements. None were Peter's.

She flew out and glared at the dog.

Nana didn't respond, hearing something with her giant dog ears that even the pixie couldn't at first.

Something horrible was waking. Bones clicked into place as it stretched its feeble limbs . . .

And realized it was all alone.

"Yip! Yipyip yipyip yip!"

Tinker Bell froze. *Another* dog? Where were the humans? Where were Wendy and her two brothers? What was going on here?

She hadn't realized how much she had expected things to be exactly the same as before: three children in the nursery, Nana puttering about, furniture and toys askew. Everything had changed subtly and strangely like a spring after a bad winter, when plants came up where they hadn't before.

Fear began to sneak through her anger.

She jingled tentatively.

In answer, Nana just jerked her head toward the window. Peter's shadow—and Wendy—were somewhere behind the clouds. Beyond London.

Tinker Bell jingled a hesitant question.

"Woof."

Tink's facility with dog speak wasn't perfect.

So there was no way to be certain that Nana had said anything at all about *pirates*.

Right?

Without a second thought Tinker Bell took off as fast as she could, out of the house and into the clouds.

Interlude:
A Dog's View

Some readers might well be curious: was Nana upset at being left home from all these adventures—school, Never Land, doings with pirates and pixies?

No, she was a dog, with dog dreams. Few things made her happier than the stories in her own head when she was hunkered down in front of a warm fire with a full belly.

She *would* have appreciated some gratitude, however, for time well served. Perhaps a nice juicy steak on her birthday and Christmas—and maybe the occasional Tuesday as a welcome surprise.

Unexpected Help

"I WILL NOT!"

Wendy sat with her arms crossed and legs primly together. Before her was a washtub full of hot salt water, suds, pirate clothes, and stink.

A half dozen half-naked pirates glowered around her, arms also crossed—though some were holding knives in their fists.

"But you're the mother of the ship now," one said—Screaming Byron, whose jacket she had patched. It was only the second or third day and she had already learned most of their names. "The washing's your responsibility."

"Absolutely *not!*" Wendy snapped, glaring at him so violently he almost fell backward. "I already take issue with the whole *idea* of being your mother, but being your *scullery maid* is entirely out of the question! Go find someone else to do your dirty work. My mother's beautiful hands never scrubbed a nasty pair of pirate unmentionables, and neither shall mine!"

The men looked at each other in surprise; apparently this was an idea new to them. Mothers always did the wash, didn't they? But perhaps they hadn't much experience with the type.

One leaned forward with his long knife and actually growled.

"Oh, cut me if you will, Ziggy," Wendy said, rolling her eyes. "*That's* proper behavior toward a mother. Let's ignore the fact that not a single one of you has presented me with a posy, or a badly done but affectionate drawing, or a pretty shell you found, or even a—" She had been about to say *kiss*, but thought better of it at the last moment. "Even the tiniest token of your appreciation. And after I sang you all that lullaby last night!"

The pirates looked, if not exactly chagrined, then at least a little thoughtful.

"We're new at this," the one with green teeth said: T. Jerome Newton. "Ain't never had a mother before. Don't know the rules."

Another—Djareth—cleared his throat. "Well, if you're

not ginna do the wash . . . then just . . . set a nice table tonight then. With folded napkins? Maybe?"

"We'll see," Wendy said levelly.

The pirates shuffled off, muttering, chastised.

Wendy collapsed. It had taken all of her will to remain indignant and cold. Their knives were actually absolutely terrifying, and the pirates' behavior was violent and insane.

"And here I am, *negotiating* with them," she said with a disgusted sigh, kicking the washtub. "They've made me their slave, and I'm telling them I won't do the very worst of the work."

She sighed and picked up the finished clean clothes, folding them. These she dropped into a basket, trying to remember which thing belonged to which pirate so she could place each on the proper hammock and they wouldn't just tear into the pile, throwing things all over the place as was their usual custom.

What a mess.

She had escaped her boring, dismal life in London only to enter an even more dismal one in Never Land! Where were the wishes? Where were the palm trees? Where were the adventures on savage shores?

What to do?

She could see one terrible possible future: one in which she remained with the pirates and became a little hard like them, praising some and castigating others, wrapping them all around her finger until they did her bidding like good little boys. Maybe even to the point of rebelling against their father.

Er, Hook.

There was of course a far more immediate and pressing concern than her eventual career aboard the *Jolly Roger*: the fate of Never Land itself. Hook had definitely implied its—and Peter's—destruction at his hand. Somehow she didn't believe that "rather permanent" meant the decision of never docking on its shores again.

Despite some sly questioning of the newly friendly crew, Wendy received no answers about Hook's plans: the pirates didn't know, nor did they care. They were sick of Never Land and eager to get on with their privateering on other seas. That was all they cared about.

(Which of course begged the question: *What* other seas? She'd never really thought about the rest of this world, beyond the island where Peter and the Lost Boys lived.)

And somehow her handing Peter's shadow to Hook helped him with his plot.

She had to escape, to find help—to find Peter Pan. There was nothing else for it.

But how?

As she carried the basket of clothes toward the hatch

that led belowdecks to the crew's quarters, Hook swooshed by her, all ruffles and coat and double cigars in their fancy golden holder.

"How goes it this morning with you, Mother?" he asked, a sly smile on his face.

Wendy felt a twist of violence in her stomach. It had been bad enough when John and Michael joked about how rarely they saw their own mother and how Wendy had taken her place. It was of course worse when these murderous hooligans called her Mother. But there was something specifically, especially nasty about Hook's use of the word. The way a quarrelsome old husband might say it to his old wife. Not that there was anything *untoward* about it; the captain wasn't at all suggesting anything inappropriate in their relationship.

It was just . . . wrong.

"This morning is going most terribly, Captain Hook. I will organize, fold, and mend the crew's clean clothes. But I will *not* do the washing. I have my limits," she said firmly.

"Ohh, whatever. We can have that done ashore if we must," he said, rolling his eyes as if she were silly for even mentioning it.

"And how are *you* doing this morning?" Wendy asked coldly. "Or, shall I ask, *what* are you doing?"

"Just the usual captainy, piratey things," he said,

whirling his hand in the air. "Trying to figure out the proper route to take . . . with a little spectral help. . . . And then we shall set sail."

Wendy didn't like the sound of that at all. "A little *spectral* help? Do you mean Peter Pan's shadow? What are you doing with it?"

"Miss Darling." He leaned forward and grinned eerily into her face. "If you were so worried about its fate, perhaps you shouldn't have traded it away in a deal with the devil?"

And with that, he spun and strode off, obviously pleased with his answer.

Wendy felt what remaining energy she had drain out through her feet, slide along the planks, and spill overboard.

She sank to the deck, resting her head on the pile of clean clothes, and began to weep.

What had she *done*?

She *knew* it was wrong. She knew it. No good would ever come of trading Pan's shadow. Any arrangement made with Hook and his pirates could never end happily. She had known that in her heart, and still she had done it, desperate to escape to Never Land.

And now it seemed like all of Never Land was going to pay for her rash decision.

"Pirate's life got ye down, love?"

Wendy looked up, wiping her tears. Standing there in a

swaybacked, repugnantly self-assured slouch was Zane.

"I thought I was coming here to have adventures," she said disgustedly, wiping her tears. "Not to be a *slave* to *pirates* for the rest of my life while Never Land is utterly destroyed. I have to get out of here."

"Ah, so many of us look for adventure and wind up as slaves, one way or another," the pirate said philosophically. "When you're young, you think the world will make room for who you are and what you want. . . . And then you find the world of adults is even more limiting than the world of children. With no room for adventure, much less yer own thoughts."

Wendy regarded the pirate curiously. This was the most thoughtful, intelligent thing she had heard on the ship so far.

He laughed quietly at the look on her face. "I'll get ye out," he promised.

"Really?" Wendy asked, surprised out of her usual politeness. "But . . . why?"

"Because some of us always have to escape, to hide in plain sight, to fight with the world to get the adventure we deserve. Ye'd think a pirate would be the freest person in the world, wouldn't you? But even here there are other people's rules to follow. And men don't like what's different—at least not at first, now do they?"

"No, I suppose not," Wendy said thoughtfully. She

wasn't entirely sure what he was driving at. Maybe he didn't want to be a pirate? Maybe he wanted to be something else altogether. What if she and the boys, just by imagining it, had cast him in the roll of buccaneer forever? What if he wanted to be a shepherd, or even a banker? The poignancy of his words struck her heart.

"I might be trapped in the part I play . . . and maybe it's *because* o' that, but I can't stand to see others what are constrained against their will, too. And maybe it'll be a good deed what goes against my own litany of skullduggery.

"But enough o' ruminatin'. The captain's involved in that shadow nonsense and the crew is getting restless. He's promised we're soon back to our villainous ways, so when the tide turns on the morrow we'll be off—or there'll be mutiny, mark my words. You'll have to get out tonight, just before dawn."

"I can't swim," Wendy said, looking doubtfully at the water below. "At least, not very well."

"There's a one-man dinghy for repairs and whatnot I'll toss over the side. But you'll have to slide down the rope to it, and I don't think I could spare more'n one paddle without raising suspicion. If you care enough about your freedom, you'll figure out how to use it right."

"I feel like that is some sort of metaphor you could apply to your own life, sir."

The pirate laughed again, and not at all like a villain.

"Just make sure you're up before the Southern Cross fades from view, and meet me stern side."

"Not that I am not greatly appreciative of all of this," Wendy said politely, "but what is to keep Hook from turning around to look for me? Even if I manage to figure out how to row with one paddle, I daresay it's unlikely I could be on the beach outrunning a crew of angry pirates bereft of their . . . mother."

Zane gave a thin smile. "Oh, don't you worry about that, love. I'll just say, 'What's that? Anyone hear the tickings of a clock?' And Hook will have us speeding out of here like that old dead croc is on his pants. Or he'll *say* it's the croc—but between you and me, I think it's just the sound of time passing that puts the fear of the devil into him. I think he knows somewhere in that musty head of his that his old companion is long gone.

"Anyway, our beloved captain is mostly engaged in other pursuits. You're a pretty thing, and useful, but a thin detail in the calamitous fable of our captain's life. He's after bigger prey."

"Bigger prey?"

"Ain't it obvious? His using the shadow to somehow find and get Peter Pan. Thought we were *done* with that nonsense years ago," Zane said, sighing.

"But what about his first mate, Mr. Smee? It sounds like he's very loyal to Captain Hook. Won't he see through your ruse and try to persuade Hook to chase me?"

At this the pirate just laughed and kept laughing, wandering away and slapping his knee. It wasn't pleasant laughter, and despite the rescue she was being offered, it left Wendy uneasy.

To stay up, she tried a trick she'd read about in a book: she drank several pints of (tar-scented) water just before bedtime.

(This was hard to keep from the pirates, who drank nothing before bed besides their grog ration and whatever flasks they had hidden.)

The crew had made her a private "bedroom" belowdecks among the ship's stores, and to their credit, they hung there a very nice hammock and covered it with whatever they had that passed for cushions. Hook even contributed a tiny fringed velvet pillow that looked more like a jellyfish than something fit for a bed. Wendy contemplated it now, wondering what hapless ship or manor it had been looted from.

She drifted off, almost pleasantly, in the gently rocking hammock.

It didn't seem like any time had passed at all when her eyes snapped open to utter darkness. The terrible, disturbing noises of a ship full of sleeping pirates came from the berths above her: snoring, tossing, turning, talking or whining in their sleep . . . as well as other far more unmentionable noises.

Wendy tipped out of her hammock as quietly as she could, wincing at the creaks from the newly knotted ropes. Then she strapped on her leather satchel (now full of strange bits and bobs and pirate treasures) and climbed the ladder.

The pirate noises reached a crescendo as she pulled herself up onto the gun deck right behind their quarters. Her mind whirled through all the possible scenarios of being caught. She expected a hand to clamp down on her shoulder at any moment, her flight discovered. Although she tiptoed, it was probably unnecessary: the ship rattled and groaned like a haunted mansion as it rode the little nighttime waves. The planks she walked didn't squeak at all.

Shaking and trembling she finally made it out to the main deck, where a great gulp of fresh air and an upside-down bowl of stars were a welcome relief. She studied the sky and finally managed to locate the Southern Cross, which was already fading in the false dawn. *Funny that Never Land skies should be so similar to the real world's,* Wendy thought. Not *London's* skies, of course, for rare was the night that one could see stars through the fog. And that particular constellation was of course absent from northern heavens.

The mizzenmast rose like a great sentinel. She cast a wary eye up to the crow's nest, but it was empty; perhaps the most dreadful pirates on the seas of Never Land didn't need to post a lookout for Royal Navy ships or potential foes. Still, the cockiness (or laziness) of it irked her sense of propriety.

She edged up to the rail and looked down. Directly below her was the balcony that hung off the captain's quarters. While it wouldn't have surprised her at all to see the nearly inhuman Captain Hook awake and smoking his infernal cigars, pondering whatever insanity it was that kept him going, the balcony was blessedly empty.

Far, far below that was the black sea, little white tips of its baby waves playing in the starlight.

"Quietly done, young miss," came a voice from behind her.

She spun around. It was just Zane, but now he was shaking his head.

"That is, I *was* impressed with your sneaking, until it were obvious you had no idea I was here. You'll never survive Never Land if you're not on your guard."

"Survive *Never Land*?" Wendy whispered indignantly. "It's a place of fantasy and imagination. I *lived* Never Land growing up. It is mine as much as yours."

"And how well do you know yourself then, I wonder,"

the pirate said softly. "Anyhow, look." He pulled back a tarp that was lying on the deck, unnoticed amongst the dregs and bits aboard a pirate vessel. A *very tiny* dinghy was revealed. It was more like the coracles children played with at the seaside than a proper boat.

Wendy sucked in her breath but didn't say anything.

The pirate picked up the boat and gave it a surprising throw: it arced out almost like a fishing line before dropping to the water with a very minute splash. It could have been a large fish leaping from the water. Angelic blue phosphorescence dazzled for a moment in a ring around the boat before fading.

"Down you go, lassie," Zane said, pointing to another rope tied to the railing.

Wendy looked at the old frayed-looking rope and the sea far below.

But she was an English girl. She squared her shoulders, took a deep breath, and saluted the pirate.

"Thank you, sir. I shall endeavor to repay your kindness someday."

"Nobody salutes on a pirate ship," he said with disgust. "We're all equals here, except for the captain. More than anywhere else in the world, I might add. You should think about that some, missy. Off you go, then."

He hoisted her up over the railing, making sure her hands were tight around the rope.

Then he let go.

Aside from antics in the nursery and some games when she had gone to school, Wendy's physical activity had been limited to bracing constitutionals around the park. *Fast walks*, in other words. Barring a few morning stretches, her arm strength was delimited by chores.

She was terrified.

But she closed her eyes, wrapped her feet around the rope, and . . . slid.

What it must have looked like from a distance! A tiny, pale girl slipping down a thin rope from a galleon that floated silently on the midnight sea. Her light blue dress ballooned around her like a paper lantern lit from underneath, yet it was not without a certain amount of grace that she made her way to the icy waters below.

Zane had fished the dinghy as close to the ship as possible, so only half of Wendy's skirts got wet as she awkwardly transferred to the tiny boat. The equally tiny paddle was hooked in just under the hull as neat as a child's play set.

She waved once to the figure on the ship high above her; whether he waved back or was even still there at all was impossible to tell against the blackness of the sky.

Wendy gritted her teeth, settled herself on her knees, and began to row.

This was the point where, if she were telling the story to Michael and John, she would say something like this:

"And so the hero struggled, arms growing weak, a glittering sheen of cold perspiration covering her brow. She felt faint. In the east, rosy-fingered dawn was just brushing the sky, but all else was black: the black vault of heavens above her, the black sea around her, the black distant shore, the thousand slimy things that lived in the murky waters below and occasionally brushed the boat with their black fins.

"Countless hours passed.

"It was all she could do to keep her eyes fixed on the shore and her strength at the paddle. The terror of being captured and the need to escape drove her through the harrowing gauntlet of exhaustion and fear. Wearily—but triumphantly—she passed through to the other side. Though the task seemed endless, nevertheless she persisted."

But the real Wendy was growing weak and utterly fatigued. The whole thing seemed less heroic and more like a scene from some farce: she was paddling a prop boat, comedically dipping her oar on one side and then the other, frantic and ceaseless, making no headway along the silken scrim.

Above where the sun would eventually rise, a few decorative clouds swept tentatively past: sleek, long, thin, and dark purple, unlike London clouds. The air itself was somehow lightening, glowing a sort of pale green.

Was time finally passing? Was she actually making headway?

At first Wendy thought she was hallucinating, delirious with exhaustion. But the shoreline *did* seem a little closer. When she let herself turn around once or twice in fear, straining her neck, the pirate ship, too, seemed a little farther away.

After a time, Wendy looked down and saw that the sea was only a couple of feet deep and as clear as drinking water. Despite a thousand different ingrained rules telling her *no* (don't get your feet wet, you will catch cold; don't ruin your skirts in the salt water; don't get your clothes wet *also* because they will become see-through), our hero was fed up with the boat. She slipped her boots off and tied their laces around her neck. She carefully undid her stockings and did the same with these. Then, holding up her skirts, she stepped out into the water.

It wasn't cold at all.

She felt like an idiot standing there in such a lovely current, skirts raised like some sort of fainting milksop from a terrible operetta. So she let them drop and strode to shore, pushing against the water. Little fish she couldn't quite see scooted out of her path.

The sun pushed its way through the purple clouds and its light grew on the beach strangely and organically, starting out weak and white and then ripening strong and yellow. Wendy cast a final glance back. The ship and she—the only two tall things in an endless flat plain of water and shore—seemed to regard each other in wonder. Then she turned from it and stepped onto land. The dry rattle of coconut palms swaying in the distance filled the air when the sound of the ocean began to recede.

Wendy had arrived in Never Land.

Never Land

The beach sand was crunchy and perfectly golden, like—well, like in a winter Londoner's wildest imagination. Wendy walked inland watching her feet, her toes curling and spreading into the sensual granules. Halfway to where the shore met the jungle was a perfectly picturesque shipwreck. She clambered up it, holding on to the helpfully curvy trunk of a palm tree for balance. With a hand to her forehead, Wendy surveyed her new kingdom.

She was perched at what was obviously the edge of a cove, Pegleg Point just to the south and west of her. Despite its scurrilous reputation the place looked downright pleasant. Tiny waves of sparkling aquamarine lapped at the edges and were probably delightful to splash in. Out of sight to the northeast lay Mermaid Lagoon. Off the shore beyond that would be the nefarious Skull Rock, riddled with caves where pirates hid their loot.

Emptying into the cove was Crocodile Creek, a wide, sparkling rivulet whose source was somewhere in the Black Dragon Mountains (Michael had named them). These were a wild range in the center of the island that grew bleaker and spikier to the northern, or Hyperborean, shore (John had named that). While the closer peaks were green and clear, the farther ones were gray and shrouded in mist and mystery.

And if one followed Crocodile Creek toward these mountains, through the Pernicious Forest and Quiescent Jungle (both John's touch), one eventually came to the Hangman's Tree, hideout for the Lost Boys. But in the very northwesternmost part of the island, there was . . .

There was . . .

Wendy frowned.

She couldn't remember—or she had never described it, or had never dreamed it. Or maybe she had, and then she had forgotten it? There was *something* there, but it was like it was wiped from her memory completely.

Or maybe the reverse—maybe it was unimagined yet. And therefore unexplored.

The sun was a brilliant lemon yellow, the sky a bracing

blue. The sea wind whipped Wendy's hair into an obliging jig.

Her adventure was beginning! Her quest to find Peter Pan and save Never Land!

But, truth be told, *while* she was living the adventure, it didn't feel like one. It felt horrible. Not at all like the stories she made up. Never Land wasn't supposed to be actually dangerous. Never Land wasn't supposed to have murderous grown-ups in it. Pirates shooting each other seemed awfully funny in the context of a bedtime tale, but the blood on the deck had been thick and ugly and she could still hear the way his head had hit the planks. Pirates attacking ladies had never been part of *her* story.

And neither was laundry.

"And that poor pirate," she whispered. "Zane. What was his story? I didn't make it up. . . . What did he mean he was trapped?"

Never Land was not as simple—or as innocent—as it had seemed. Wendy would have to stay on her toes whilst there. But everything *looked* just as bright and sunny and perfect as ever. Her shadow was as black and strong against the sand as a child's drawing, and . . .

Wait, was the shadow crossing her arms?

Wendy looked at her own arms, which were first at her sides, and then snapped to her chest in surprise.

Her shadow still kept her arms crossed. And was now shaking her head as if to chastise.

Then she flexed her hand and curled it into a menacing hook. Shadow puppets without the puppets.

There was no doubt at all what she was trying to say: she was upset with what Wendy had done, selling Peter's shadow. Of course shadow-Wendy was worried about shadow-Peter Pan. Here she was simply free to express it.

"He didn't *want* his shadow," Wendy muttered to herself—and her shadow—for the thousandth time.

She still didn't believe it.

Wendy took a deep breath and straightened her shoulders. Whatever, it was done. She had already dealt with some of the results of her actions and would now see to righting the additional wrongs she had created as a result. She would go find Peter.

She would save Never Land.

And if he was angry with her for what she had done—well, she would deal with it and accept it as fair punishment for her actions.

She hopped off the shipwreck and wandered toward the greenery at the edge of the cove. Trying not to notice or hope that her shadow was coming along and behaving, trying to keep her eyes on the jungle ahead.

A strange structure untangled itself out of the background like a hallucination, not part of the natural landscape.

It was a funny-shaped, almost spherical, green podlike thing woven from living branches of trees and vines. A trellis of flowers hung down over the opening that served as a door.

Wendy was so delighted tears sprang to her eyes.

It was her Imaginary House!

They all had them. Michael wanted his to be like a ship with views of the sea. John had wanted to live like a nomad on the steppes. And Wendy . . . Wendy had wanted something that was part of the natural world itself.

She tentatively stepped forward, almost swooning at the heavy scent of the door flowers. Languorously lighting on them were a few scissorflies, silver and almost perfectly translucent in the glittery sunlight. Their sharp wings made little snickety noises as they fluttered off.

Her shadow made a few half-hearted attempts to drag back, pointing to the jungle. But Wendy ignored her, stepping into the hut.

She was immediately knocked over by a mad, barking thing that leapt at her from the darkness of the shelter.

"Luna!" Wendy cried in joy.

The wolf pup, which she had rescued in one of her earliest stories, stood triumphantly on her chest, drooling very visceral, very stinky dog spit onto her face.

"Oh, Luna! You're *real*!" Wendy hugged the gray-and-white pup as tightly as she could, and it didn't let out a single protest yelp.

Although . . .

"You're a bit bigger than I imagined," Wendy said thoughtfully, sitting up. "I thought you were a puppy."

Indeed, the wolf was approaching *formidable* size, although she was obviously not yet quite full-grown and still had large puppy paws. She was at least four stone and her coat was thick and fluffy. Yet she pranced back and forth like a child, not circling with the sly lope Wendy imagined adult wolves used.

"*You're* not a stupid little lapdog, are you?" Wendy whispered, nuzzling her face into the wolf's fur. Luna chuffed happily and gave her a big wet sloppy lick across the cheek. "Let's see what's inside the house!"

As the cool interior embraced her, she felt a strange shudder of relief and . . . *welcome* was the only way she could describe it. She was home.

The interior was small and cozy; plaited sweet-smelling rush mats softened the floor. The rounded walls made shelves difficult, so macramé ropes hung from the ceiling, cradling halved logs or flat stones that displayed pretty pebbles, several beautiful eggs, and what looked like a teacup made from a coconut. A lantern assembled from translucent pearly shells sat atop a real cherry writing desk, intricately carved and entirely out of place with the rest of the interior.

Wendy picked up one of the pretty pebbles in wonder,

turning it this way and that before putting it into her pocket.

"This is . . . me . . ." she breathed. She had never been there before, but it felt so secure and so right that it couldn't have been anything *but* her home. Her real home. Here there was no slight tension of her back as she waited for footsteps to intrude, for reality to wake her from her dreams; there was nothing here to remind her of previous days, sad *or* happy ones. There were no windows looking out at the gray world of London. There was just peace, and the scent of the mats, and the quiet droning of insects and waves outside.

"Never Land is a . . . mishmash of us. Of me," she said slowly. "It's what we imagine and dream of—including the dreams we can't quite remember."

What an odd thought. "Zane was right. It *is* an island that knows me better than I know myself."

She could easily envision herself falling asleep on the scented mats—adventuring was exhausting work—but she went back outside instead. Luna leapt beside her.

In the bright sunlight her shadow reappeared, jumping and waving her arms and trying to pull herself away from Wendy again.

"We *are* going after Peter Pan. I promise. We'll certainly need him against Hook and whatever he has planned. But I really don't know where to even begin looking for him! I suppose we'll just start. In *that* direction." And with that, she strode resolutely ahead, Luna leaping beside her.

(If she had snuck a look, she might have seen her shadow wag her head back and forth as if making fun of her, then snap back to aping her mistress's movements—if a little slower and more reluctantly than they were actually performed.)

Large-leafed plants at the edge of the jungle reflected the sun rather than soaking it up, their dark green surfaces sparkling white in the sunlight. Some of the smaller ones had *literally* low-hanging fruit, like jewels from a fairy tale. Behind them was an extremely inviting path into the jungle with giant white shells for stepping-stones. And rather than the muggy, disease-filled forests of books that seemed to kill so many explorers, here the air was cool and pleasant and not too moist—although Wendy could hear the distant tinkle of water splashing from a height.

"Oh! Is that the Tonal Springs? Or Diamond Falls?" Wendy wondered breathlessly. "Luna, let's go see!"

She made herself *not* race ahead down the path, but moved at a leisurely, measured pace. Like an adventuress sure of herself but wary of her surroundings.

(And yet, as she wouldn't realize until later, she hadn't thought to grab her stockings or shoes. Those got left in her hut without even a simple goodbye.)

Everywhere she looked, Wendy found another wonder

of Never Land, from the slow camosnails to the gently nodding heads of the fritillary lilies. She smiled, imagining
John as he peered over his glasses and the snail faded away
into the background in fear—or Michael getting his nose
covered in honey-scented lily pollen as he enthusiastically
sniffed the pretty flowers.

The path continued, winding around a boulder into a
delightful little clearing, sandy but padded here and there
with tuffets of emerald green grass and clumps of purple
orchids. It was like a desert island version of a perfect
English meadow.

"Oh, Luna, isn't it beautiful? Let's go see!"

With the loud *snap* of a horse rider's crop a white vine
whipped out across the path at her ankles.

"Oh!" she cried, stumbling forward.

But she didn't fall; another vine shot out across her
chest. She bounced jarringly into and then off it. This one,
too, was ugly and poisonous white—but also slightly sticky.
Her dress got caught and so did her throat, already bruised
from the impact.

Another vine whipped behind her so she couldn't fall
backward. Couldn't escape.

"What the deuce!" she cried, pulling at the vines. They
were tough but stretchy and gave rather than broke under
her hands.

More of them—slowly now, like they had all the time in the world—coiled around her wrists and ankles. Their viscous sap itched and burned where she struggled, and it was an unhealthy scarlet color.

"No grown-ups allowed."

Out of the clearing stepped the speaker of these words, a strange little fellow indeed. He was short and fat and as clear and crystalline as a blob of molten glass. His head was a misshapen oval on top of his body. A peaked crystal hat sat on his head, and he held a sharp shard of a spear. The only color on him at all was his eyes, strange and tan, like two butterscotch candies pressed into the face of a snowman.

"What?" Wendy asked indignantly, trying to understand the harsh words from the otherwise almost adorable figurine.

"No grown-ups allowed."

He turned to face her, but not like a normal person; more like a cross between an owl and some sort of hideous, broken toy. His body didn't move. Instead, his *head* spun smoothly and slowly and farther than it should have until his pupilless eyes locked on hers.

Probably. It was hard to tell what he was looking at.

"I am not a grown-up!" Wendy sputtered. "Let me through!"

"*You are sixteen,*" the guard said tonelessly. "*The time of parties and balls and weddings and husbands has commenced.*"

"It has *not* commenced," Wendy said with great dignity. "I'm here in Never Land, aren't I?"

The creature's button eyes didn't move at all but somehow darkened.

"*You should not be here in Never Land.* No grown-ups in Never Land. *No fun killers! No bringers of pain and boredom! GET OUT!*"

Wendy blinked at the ferocity of the ridiculous, strangely terrifying little thing. It leaned forward, bringing the tip of its spear perilously close to her stomach.

Where on earth had it come from? She had never invented any such monster. True, adults *didn't* figure in her stories of Never Land except as incidental characters—pirates and their ilk, villains and foils. Never Land was supposed to be an island of endless fun for children like her and Michael and John, but she had never said anything specifically about prohibiting grown-ups or threatening them with spears.

"*You make the days long. You make the food terrible. You make us go to* school!*"

Wendy caught her breath in shock, recognizing the tirade. *Michael.* Michael had horrifyingly once told his own father that he hated him—actually hated him—for making him go to school, where the seats were hard and the lessons worse. And for forcing him to eat their mashed peas.

Also, now that she thought about it, the shape of the little creature wasn't unlike something Michael had made out of mud once. *Puppin*, he'd called it.

Yes, this whole scenario felt a bit like Michael, now that she thought about it. A crazed, all-powerful Michael.

"Now, you listen to me—" Wendy began in her best adult voice, as if she were speaking to Michael.

Bad choice.

"NO MORE LISTENING!" the thing screeched madly, pushing itself as high and far into Wendy's face as it could. *"YOU GO AWAY NOW. FOREVER. TO FOREVER PLACE!"*

It reached back its arm to hurl the little spear—

But Luna had had enough.

She threw herself at the horrid thing. Her claws made little *tinging* noises as they scraped harmlessly against the crystalline surface. Her teeth slipped from the creature's neck, unable to get a good hold or sink into real flesh.

While the creature was distracted by this Wendy took the opportunity to try to free herself. She rocked back and forth as hard as she could against the vines, pushing her arms and legs out as far as they would go. The tendrils gave just enough for her to be able to slip her right hand out. She immediately reached into her pocket and grabbed the stone she had taken from her hut. Summoning as much *boy-chucking-rocks-in-a-fountain* as she could, Wendy hurled it full-force at the creature's bulbous crystalline stomach.

There was a very satisfying *crack*.

As soon as the tip of the rock hit its "skin," giant ragged cracks appeared from the impact point. These rapidly winnowed out through the rest of its body, growing like Jack Frost on a windowpane—but much, much faster.

The thing's mouth hung open and it dropped its spear. As the fractures spread it waved its arms back and forth helplessly, like a puppet or a windup toy.

When the cracks reached its head and became so numerous that its body was almost opaque, the thing exploded.

Its glittering bits hurled themselves every which way through the dappled sunlight in a beautiful wave of *tinkles* and *pings* one might expect to hear from baby angels playing harps.

Wendy flinched and covered her face. Where a shard hit her skin it immediately melted, running down to the ground with little droplets of her own blood.

"Well," she said uncertainly.

Luna jumped back and forth over the thing's rapidly disappearing body, barking last warnings and triumph.

"Goodness," Wendy added.

She let herself experience one more moment of shock,

then forced herself to focus and work at pulling away the vines. They were unpleasant to touch (and sticky and itchy) but actually not that hard to wrestle out of now that she had one hand free and no distractions. In fact they were strangely like a pair of her mother's hose the three children had once gotten into *massive* amounts of trouble for using to tie up Michael when he was "kidnapped by pirates." Same color, even.

"Hmm . . ." Wendy said thoughtfully.

Then, a little nervously: "I suppose that's the last of them?"

Luna barked, and it *sounded* like an affirmative response, but Wendy couldn't be certain.

"I think it was really going to kill me," Wendy murmured, putting her hand out. The wolf immediately came over and leaned against her friend, sensing her need. "Isn't it funny . . ."

There were a lot of thoughts in Wendy's head, and none of them were actually funny at all. They weren't even clear or formed thoughts; just a mishmash of feelings, misgivings, and the unnamed, fetal beginnings of ideas. Not a situation she was used to: possessing a quiet mess of genesis with no articulation. No pronouncements, aphorisms, or decisions came readily to her tongue.

"Isn't it funny," she tried again. "I thought Captain

Hook would be the only real villain here. I mean, the only one I would bump into, because of the shadow. And here I have run into a villain I didn't even know existed . . . one my brother invented as some sort of protector or savior. It's not really clear what that thing was, is it? But all of *my* stories were perfectly clear and straightforward."

She looked around at the trees and the foliage, the sky and the ground. Things she had brushed by in quick descriptive phrases to the boys—*desert island, tropical plants, venomous but beautiful insects*—were solid in more detail than she could ever imagine, down to the tiny veins on the leaves. Apparently Never Land got "worked on" when she wasn't even talking to the boys . . . they imagined things on their own. Or at least Michael did. To a little child, the idea of *No Grown-Ups Allowed,* to the point of the death, might seem reasonable. Funny, even.

Time passed for the three siblings in London . . . but it didn't in Never Land. Michael's whims and fancies remained the same here while he grew up in London. And these whims seen through older eyes were not harmless. They were diabolical.

"Never Land isn't just a simple place of childhood dreams—because childhood dreams are actually never simple. Oh, I do wish I could write that down in my little notebook."

Her face suddenly constricted into a cartoonish expression of terror as she recalled a younger John, furious at the Shesbow twin who had tweaked his cheek and giggled at his hat and glasses. "Girls shouldn't be allowed to talk at *all*," he had growled at her. "To boys, anyhow."

How had the rest of the conversation gone? Had he made an exception for his sister? Had Wendy laughed and remonstrated him?

More to the point, was there some sort of horrible punishment zone for girls in Never Land devised by the fiendishly clever—but undeveloped—mind of a preadolescent John?

Luna was watching with giant unblinking yellow eyes as Wendy worked out all these things, far more patient than anyone Wendy had ever known.

"We must be on our guard," she said, kissing the wolf on her nose. "This place is tricky. Far trickier than I ever dreamed. The dangers I *expect* are not the only dangers. Who knows what other horrors my little brothers dreamed up? Then again, if Never Land were as simple as my own childish fantasies, it would be no fun at all. Toffee trees and mazes easily solvable by a simple application of *left left right left*. Where's the challenge in that? I *am* sixteen now, whether or not I am an adult. I should expect more!"

Wendy dusted off her dress. The sun had moved slightly

in the sky; ideas and creatures might be eternal in Never Land, but still night came. *Time* still existed. Decisions had to be made. Luna pranced back and forth in front of her, yellow eyes gleaming with excitement. Ready to go.

But where to?

The Mermaid Lagoon. Obviously.

Peter Pan often visited the mermaids in her stories. Maybe she would find him there, or get help from the friendly locals. But also . . .

Mermaids!

And they would be *very* helpful in a maritime war waged against apocalyptic pirates.

And maybe along the way Wendy could look for fairies. They were powerful little denizens of Never Land, weren't they? Surely they could use some magic or something against Hook.

(Plus: *fairies!*)

And . . . what about the Lost Boys, by Hangman's Tree? Maybe she should find them first. They would know where Peter was. And they would be terribly useful—how many stories she had written about their battles with the pirates! And how lovely it would be to have a visit, too. All of those clever things Wendy had invented for them, like the slides down to the hideout from hollow trees . . . How marvelous to see it in person, to understand how Never Land had worked out the details. Maybe Peter would even be there already!

She gulped a little at the thought.

Or . . . maybe the Lost Boys later.

Really, the best thing was to round up an army to defend Never Land, wasn't it? She could find Peter and apologize to him—and bring him up to speed on Hook's nefarious plot—later.

"Yes, mermaids first. And then maybe fairies. I wonder where we should go to find them?"

And her question was answered, in true Never Land fashion, as a fairy dove headfirst into Wendy's chest.

Meanwhile, on the High Seas...

Captain Hook paced back and forth in his cabin predatorily—but not at all like a wolf. More like a military commander with a motive and possibly a bad back. The angry movements and swishing clothes made the captain's quarters seem even tighter than they already were; he filled the space with his plumes, red jacket, and frustration. There was room for nothing else besides his rage. When he was interrupted—rarely—the interrupting pirate stayed outside, unable or unwilling to come in.

"*Talk*, bloody *talk*, and this will all be over!" Hook swore at his prisoner. "Just tell me where Peter Pan is. Once I have him you can go!"

Pan's shadow writhed and shrank before the captain, but didn't answer.

Its lower body was cinched tight with a silken cord, only a little string of shadow sticking out the bottom of the knots—possibly its toe. The rest puffed up and out like a dark genie out of a bottle, though its arms were also stretched and tied. It squirmed and distended itself pitifully in an attempt to get free.

All of the usual sorts of torture had little effect on the thing: discarded implements were strewn around the floor as testament to their uselessness. Knives, pincers, hot brands, tacks through the nails, fingernails drawn across slate boards. He even had a drunk Smee play the concertina, but the terrible music had no effect on the shadow at all.

(It did, however, make the captain want to put his own ears out with his hook.)

The shadow had *some* presence in the real world; otherwise the cord wouldn't have held at all. But the rules that governed it were tricky and, well, Hook wasn't the most logical and thorough practitioner of the scientific method. He grew frustrated often and tantrums came quick.

The captain stewed, rage boiling up quietly behind his eyes and face again.

And then, in the silence of this latest lull, a quiet ticking began. Distant and weak.

Hook's prodigious brows shot up to the top of his forehead.

He dashed out of the cabin, throwing papers and chairs aside, and ran to the railing—nearly knocking a pirate overboard along the way.

Tick.

Tick.

Tick.

He started to let out a sigh of relief. Just some of the rigging snapping against a mast, or . . .

Tock.

What passed for Hook's heart almost stopped, clenched in an invisible icy fist.

He staggered away from the railing, hands over his ears so he couldn't hear it anymore.

Tick.

Tock.

Tick.

Tock.

"No, no no no no no! Not *now*! It was all coming together!" he cried, rushing up and down the deck in a panic. "I was practically *handed* Peter's shadow. And once I used it to get Peter, I could blow everything the boy loves to smithereens—while he watched! It's the greatest revenge ever planned by any villain *ever*! And I was almost *there*!"

He ran back to the comforting darkness of his cabin and threw the door violently shut behind him.

"WE ARE RUNNING OUT OF TIME HERE!" he screeched at the shadow. *"I* am running out of time! Can you hear that? It's the vile croc, come for me! So talk, blast you!"

"Maybe it *can't* talk," Smee suggested from the corner of the room, where he had waited quietly until the captain's fit had passed.

"Of course it can't talk," Hook swore, raising his eyebrows at his first mate's predictable stupidity. "It's a *shadow*. But it could make a sign, or write something. . . . I *gave* it the bloody slate, before I made those dismal noises! It didn't even bother to try."

"Maybe it can't write. Maybe Peter Pan can't write. Can he read?" Smee asked curiously. "Never seen the lad with a book or nothin' . . ."

"Why, that's . . ." Hook paused, thinking. "Actually, that's a very good point, Mr. Smee. The *sadly ignorant* Peter Pan probably can't even write his own name—uneducated lout."

"So maybe he's not worth your time," Mr. Smee hazarded. "Such a useless, adventurous, young, enthusiastic . . . er, I mean *utterly uneducated* boy. A right simpleton. Not much of a nemesis, right? Maybe you should just forget about him, like the crew's been suggesting. Forget about all of Never Land. Just put it behind you. Let's go out and find us a merchant vessel or pillage a seaside town. Right now. Like in the good old days."

"*I won't let Peter get away! I won't let him escape me this time!*"

"But Cap'n. It's a never-ending chase," Mr. Smee pointed out as gently as a mother consoling a child chasing his own shadow. "Oh, sometimes it seems like you get the best of him, but he always gets the best of you in the end, and then he slips away. Maybe it's time to . . . let it go, like? Move on? Wrap up that part of your life and enjoy what's enjoyable now? The sea, the sun, the blood of your enemies . . ."

"But . . . but I *want* him," Hook whispered, lips trembling. "He always gets away from me and it's *not fair*. He took my *hand*. He took the best of me."

"Nawww," Mr. Smee said, patting him on the back. "Not the best of you. Your hook is so useful, ain't it? And shiny. He didn't take nothing away. He gave you a deadly weapon, and a boatload of memories, and a souvenir. Let the lad go. You're the bigger man. You're the only actual *man*, as it were. So maybe it's time you—"

"*WHERE IS PETER?*" Hook roared suddenly, whirling on the shadow, leveling an accusing hook at it.

The thing flung itself backward in fear but did nothing else.

It didn't even shrug, which one would assume even an ignorant, badly behaved, etiquetteless shadow of an uncivilized simpleton could resort to.

Hook's eyes narrowed.

"Maybe you don't know *exactly* where he is. But you have some idea. You're part of him. You even act like him. There is some sort of ley line or force that connects the two of you. If I set you free, you might even fly off yourself, in search of him, lonely in your bodiless state."

The thing bobbed quickly and wretchedly up and down. It tipped its head toward the small porthole window. *Let me go,* it was obviously pleading.

"*AHA!*" Hook said triumphantly. "You *do* have some idea. The direction at least. Now that the two of you are both back in Never Land, you can somehow sense where he is. You couldn't when you were trapped in London."

"Almost like a compass," Mr. Smee said whimsically, chuckling from deep within his large belly. "Always pointing north, in a manner o' speakin'."

"Always pointing—what?" Hook blinked. "Almost like a compass, you say?"

He rubbed his chin thoughtfully.

"Now *that*, Mr. Smee, is an interesting idea. . . ."

Pernicious Pixies

Wendy stumbled backward. She wasn't hit hard enough to fall down, but the tiny points of the fairy's—feet? Fingers? Head? *Stinger?*—jabbed her right in the middle of her rib cage, knocking the wind out of her. It would probably leave a nasty bruise.

She warily regarded her attacker. The fairy—again, Wendy assumed—was an angry tinkling ball of light with the prettiest girl imaginable inside. Diminutive but . . . *solid,* with a scandalous lack of decorous dress. All she wore was a ragged green shift which barely covered her hips and thighs and breasts and was gathered dangerously over only one shoulder. This was both shocking and delightful; it made the tiny creature resemble statues of ancient nymphs and nereids Wendy had seen. Her hair was even done up in classical style, a goddess-like bun of hair so golden it glowed. Tiny pointed ears curved their way through the few dangling tresses. Her eyes were enormous and not even remotely human: they were far apart and glaring.

The crowning glory was, of course, a pair of delicate iridescent wings sprouting from her back. Their shape was somewhere between butterfly and dragonfly. They were clear as glass and thin as onion skin.

The fairy chimed and jingled angrily, shedding little sparkles of golden light that danced for a bit in the air before drifting down to the ground and fading. Wendy couldn't tell where the girl's lovely tinkling sound was coming from, exactly. At first she thought it was bells on the tiny shoes but close inspection revealed nothing. The chimes, like the dust, seemed to come from her very essence.

"Oh my, I'm so sorry," Wendy breathed, apologizing for her . . . standing? Being? In the way of the beautiful little thing? "Are you all right?"

The tinkling grew more insistent. The fairy bobbed up and down in the air and balled her tiny hands into fists.

She aimed herself at Wendy's chest again and struck her.

Prepared as she was for it this time, the pain was no worse than a bumblebee accidentally knocking into her and then buzzing drowsily off into the sunlight.

"Whatever is the matter?" Wendy asked patiently. "Have I done something wrong? Will you tell me?"

Luna barked once, forefeet planted firmly and defensively.

The fairy suddenly dipped down to the ground. The light emanating from her dimmed.

"What is it?"

The fairy stamped on the dirt and pointed at it.

"Am I trampling your flower?" Wendy asked, stepping back carefully and examining the prints where she had just stood. There were no crushed petals there, just some grass and sand. No dead insects, either.

The fairy gritted her teeth in frustration and flew back up to Wendy. She grabbed a lock of her hair and yanked, hoisting it over her shoulder like the heaviest rope on a ship.

"Ow! Hey! What is it? You merely have to tell me!" Wendy cried, stumbling farther into the clearing, trying to free her hair from the pixie's grasp.

Apparently satisfied, the creature released her grip and dove back down to the ground . . . and walked. Slowly and carefully out over the ground, along . . .

"My shadow," Wendy said slowly.

A sinking feeling came over her.

Her shadow crossed her arms knowingly.

"Not *my* shadow, of course," Wendy said, biting her lip. "Peter Pan's shadow."

The fairy nodded twice, slowly and solidly—no misinterpretation possible.

Wendy sighed. The time of reckoning had come far sooner than she expected. She had hoped for a *little* more time in Never Land before her choices caught up with her. How did this fairy even know about it, really? Wendy thought she would only have to apologize to Peter. Not anyone else.

(Of course she also rather hoped that the imminent doom of Never Land would overshadow any mistakes or transgressions on her part.)

"I don't have it. Anymore."

The fairy's eyes widened. She started to move, uncertainly—perhaps to pull Wendy's hair again, perhaps to shrug: *Why?* Perhaps to make motions to get a fuller explanation . . . but Wendy's guilty conscience was way ahead of her.

"I traded it to Captain Hook in return for my passage here," she said calmly.

Her shadow did a sarcastic little curtsy, as if to say, *Thank you. Now we're getting somewhere.*

The seconds stretched out to infinity as Wendy watched the fairy register what she had said. She could feel the tropical sun on her back, feel the breeze from the sea lift the little hairs off her forehead, smell Luna's clean but doggy fur scent as she waited for a reaction.

When the fairy's eyes had widened further than it seemed possible, she dove at Wendy again.

Here and there and everywhere at once—pinching, pulling, yanking hair, biting.

Wendy covered her face and flung herself around the clearing, trying to get away from the creature without hurting her. It was like being attacked by an angry swarm of bees or a dozen fairies at once.

"Oh! Stop! Please!"

Luna leapt up and bit at the air, snapping and growling and trying to grab the annoying flying thing that was hurting her friend.

As she slapped madly at the air around her, Wendy prayed that neither one of them actually injured the fairy.

Finally Luna's muzzle smacked the creature hard on her tiny behind, and she went tumbling head over feet, straight into a tree. She slid down it, landing in a heap among the roots.

"Oh no, are you all right?" Wendy cried, immediately running over despite the myriad pinches and tiny cuts she had suffered from the attack. She knelt down and cradled the stunned fairy carefully in her hands. The fairy sat up, swaying woozily. Then she leaned over and sank her teeth into Wendy's thumb.

"Now stop that this instant," Wendy said sternly, gripping her a little more tightly around the middle. "Let us try discussing this like adul—ah, like civilized people. I take it you are a friend of Peter's?"

For yet again, this creature—this particular fairy—wasn't one she had invented in her Never Land tales. And she didn't imagine her brothers could have come up with anything like her.

The tiny girl pouted and frowned and crossed her arms sullenly. It was so adorable Wendy had to work very hard not to giggle.

"Well, I'm very sorry about what I did. I'm not proud of it. I messed up," she admitted. "But look here. Your friend Peter *left* his shadow in my bedroom. Ages ago. Four years, in fact."

The fairy blinked at this. Wendy couldn't be sure how intelligent the fairy was; she took quite a bit of time to process this new information, and with surprise.

"Yes! Four years I've kept it safe, free from dust, awaiting Peter's return. Of course, I had every intention of giving it back! I'm not a thief. But he . . . never returned."

The fairy looked uncomfortable. Her eyes darted to the side and she squirmed a little in Wendy's palm.

"For years I waited for him," Wendy continued, trying not to sound *too* sorrowful. She was in the wrong, after all. "Every night I told stories about him, watched the night sky for him. . . . Then they moved me out of the nursery.

Michael and John went to school. I was left all by myself, alone and waiting. And still he never came.

"I grew a bit despondent, I suppose. The boys didn't want to hear my stories anymore. If it wasn't for the shadow I would have begun to think I had imagined every last moment of Never Land. Life was just so dreary and dreich. . . . And then my parents bought me this stupid dog. . . . Not you, Luna," she added before the wolf could even react. Luna wagged her tail happily. "And *then* they decided to send me away to Ireland. *Ireland!* They only want to see me settled down with some nice boy with a nice job at a nice office somewhere, or as a spinster governess in some remote location, and I don't want either of those things. Not yet, anyway."

Despite her anger, the fairy made a questioning tinkle that wasn't too hard to interpret.

"Well, I don't know *what* I really want. I want to see Never Land, obviously," Wendy answered, indicating the world around them. She opened her fingers, loosening her grip on the fairy. "I want adventures. I want . . . I don't know, other things. Certainly not to do laundry aboard a pirate ship for the rest of my life.

"Yes, I'm ashamed of what I did. It was a bad deed. But Peter can't have missed his shadow much, since he never came to get it."

The fairy tinkled angrily at her, rising up off her palm and clenching her tiny hands once again into tiny adorable fists.

"All right, look, before you start again, two things. One, I'm perfectly willing to make amends for what I did," Wendy said, squaring her shoulders. "Whatever it takes. Right now."

Her shadow stood up straight upon hearing this, intrigued.

The fairy frowned at her suspiciously.

"I'm absolutely serious. Also, number two, and potentially far more importantly: either as a result of my actions or alongside of them, Never Land is in trouble. Captain Hook seems like he means to destroy the whole island. We need to stop him—*and* find Peter. He and his shadow are involved somehow. And I will do whatever it takes to accomplish both things."

She meant it. She conjured up images in her head of all sorts of brave Englishmen and realized she couldn't think of a single face. But the idea of dying at sword point or being forced to walk the plank in a dramatic rescue attempt was somehow still easier to swallow than an eternity of serving aboard a pirate ship as a nanny and scullery maid.

The fairy narrowed her eyes, obviously reevaluating the human.

Then she nodded. Once.

Not enthusiastically.

"Shall we go then?" Wendy asked primly. "Last I saw, the pirates were headed north, or what would have been north in England. Up the coast. We need to get some help to stop them, I should think. More of you fairies, perhaps? And mermaids might be helpful. Or we could arrange some sort of boat, one with cannons, I expect, and a willing crew—"

The fairy stamped her foot angrily—then lowered herself back down onto Wendy's hand so the big human girl could actually feel it. She shook her head. She pointed into the jungle.

"I'm sorry, I don't . . ."

The fairy snarled in frustration. Then she made a big show of miming the act of looking for something or someone, hand shielding her eyes from the sun, peering into the distance. She pretended to find the thing and marched very dramatically toward it. She had a whole conversation with this thing, which was now obviously a person, took him by the hand, and pretended to fly off.

Then she and he either battled a small army together or succumbed to St. Vitus's dance; it was hard to tell which.

"Oh—you want to find Peter Pan *first*?" Wendy said, suddenly realizing what it all meant. "Find him and bring him along to get his shadow back from the pirates?"

The fairy nodded excitedly, and for a heartbreaking second looked absolutely delighted that Wendy understood.

"But I don't know how much time Never Land has! And do you even know where he is?"

The fairy shrugged and looked exasperated, throwing her arms out to indicate all of Never Land. Wendy wondered, from the way the fairy was acting, if the two friends had ever been separated before this happened.

In spite of her determination to save their world, Wendy was ashamed to admit her first reaction was *No, let's not go find Peter first*—only because then she would have to tell her hero straight off that she had sold his shadow to his enemy. It was one thing to admit wrongdoing to a random fairy, but to the person you've slighted himself—well, that took a different kind of courage. "Perhaps he isn't so useful right now, without his shadow?" she ventured.

The fairy frowned and pointed again.

"But perhaps we should drum up some other help against the pirates first?"

The fairy crossed her arms and closed her eyes haughtily, shaking her head.

"Oh, please," Wendy said. "Even *with* Peter Pan, the two of us can't take on an entire pirate crew. In all my stories about Peter Pan he fights Captain Hook man to man, not against *all* of them."

The fairy turned her head away and sniffed.

Wendy rubbed her head. She hadn't had a lot of experience cajoling people—beyond her father, at least—much less an irrational little creature like this. The thing wouldn't listen to logic or reason.

But of course, she was a fairy. Why *would* she put up with terribly human ideas like logic and reason?

Wendy thought about her mother's gentle arguments with shopkeepers when the Darling account came up a bit short.

"Well, how about this," she said, using her best *reasonable* voice. "Let's do go fetch Peter. But perhaps we should *start* with the Lost Boys? He's always with his crew. So he might be there, or they might know where he is. And if he's *not* there, we can see if they're interested in joining us for our big run-in with the pirates. All right?"

The fairy pouted and looked suspicious, as if she thought Wendy were trying to trick her somehow. But she couldn't find anything obviously wrong with what had been suggested, so she nodded. Reluctantly.

"All right then, let's—"

And the fairy took off like a shot, a golden bauble that zipped high into the air and disappeared.

"All right," Wendy repeated, uncertainly, watching it go.

"I can't fly," she added after another moment.

The clearing was silent except for the chirping of a single insect. It regarded Wendy through what looked like a very tiny pair of spectacles.

"I'll just walk then, I guess." She adjusted her dress and looked at Luna. "Shall we? I think . . . I think the Hangman's Tree is due north of us, and a bit east. We may need to bushwhack. A pity I don't have a machete or some such . . ."

Just as Wendy set foot into the shady, vaguely threatening undergrowth, there came a distant tinkling sound. The bauble of golden light tore back through the sky and stopped suddenly in front of her like a confused meteor. It hovered up and down angrily. Within the glow, the fairy tapped her foot and pointed to the sky.

"I can't fly," Wendy said politely. "I will have to meet you there. It will take me rather longer than you, I should expect."

The fairy looked like she was going to explode in frustration. Her face turned red and her tiny hands became grasping, strained claws. Her shoulders rose up around her neck.

"Ah . . . sorry?"

With a strangled cry, the fairy flew at her. Wendy threw her hands up over her face for protection.

Nothing happened.

When no pinches or bites occurred, she hesitantly lowered her arms.

The fairy was flying in loops and swirls around her, shedding fairy dust as she went. Throwing it at Wendy.

Delighted, the human girl raised her arms up to fully experience what was happening. Delicate golden sparkles floated down and kissed her skin. Where they touched, Wendy felt *lighter*. Tiny pains she hadn't even realized she felt entirely disappeared, and any weariness vanished. She felt rested, energetic, eager, and—*airy*.

"Oh! Fairy dust! Will this help me fly?"

The little fairy crossed her arms and nodded. She looked over Wendy with an appraising eye, perhaps seeing if she had done a good enough job. Then she nodded again, satisfied, and buzzed off into the sky.

Wendy raised her arms. She felt like the wind itself!

Nothing happened.

"All right," she said. "Here I go!"

Did the ends of her hair lift a little, or was that just the breeze?

Sparkles continued to twinkle on her arms for a bit before settling into her skin. She worried: Was there a time limit? Did the magic fade if not used properly?

And with that worry, she felt the earth solidly under her heels again, her full weight bearing down on the soil.

"Oh, oh oh oh," she cried, panicking. "Don't do that, don't think bad thoughts. I don't think the fairy dust likes that. It won't work if I think bad thoughts."

She then had to stop herself from worrying about not flying *because* of worrying and bad thoughts. It made her head a little crazy.

The fairy hovered a good twenty feet up with her arms crossed and an impatient, bored look on her face.

"Sorry," Wendy called as brightly as she could. "Never done this before! Doing my best here!"

The fairy rolled her eyes. Wendy winced. Nothing she did or said seemed to endear her to the pretty little thing at all. She wished she could do something *right*, immediately, the first time.

The fairy dove down and grabbed Wendy's left thumb with both her hands and pulled. Wendy caught her breath, delighted by the tiny, warm touch.

Luna barked. She didn't at all like the unfriendly creature coming too close to her mistress.

Wendy was torn, not wanting to upset the fairy—but not wanting to upset her wolf, either.

"Oh, it's all right, girl," Wendy said, putting her other hand out for Luna. "She's just trying to help."

The wolf pushed her nose into Wendy's palm, licking it and forcing the hand up over her head to encourage scratching behind her ears. Wendy felt a rush of warmth and affection for this friend she only knew from dreams, who loved her so fiercely and unconditionally.

She felt herself lighten.

The fairy also must have felt it somehow, because at that exact same moment she tugged, beating her little wings, trying to fly backward and drag the girl *up*.

Wendy rose onto her toes.

Luna barked again, less worried and more perplexed.

"*Oh!* It's working!" Wendy cried.

In that moment, all of Never Land became everything she had always imagined it would be. She could do anything. The sky was blue, the future full of infinite good.

The fairy still held her hand, obviously trying to keep a skeptical, annoyed look on her face. But her lips moved in a strange duck-billed twist, as if she was working very hard to keep them frowning. Her whole face had lightened, the scowling darkness removed like a storm whisked away by a whimsical and beneficent god. When she impatiently rolled her eyes and twirled her fingers, it wasn't with anger this time; it was encouraging: *Come on, come on! More of that!*

"But . . . more of *what*?" Wendy asked, distracted by the feeling of weightlessness, Luna, and her own thoughts.

The fairy tapped her head then pointed at the human girl and shrugged dramatically.

"What? What was I thinking? Is that what you—yes, it was. Well, I was thinking about flying—no, I was thinking about Luna, actually. What a good girl she is and how wonderful it is that she loves me. . . ."

Wendy's toes left the ground entirely.

"Oh! Oh! It's happy thoughts! I see it now! They make you fly!" she cried, clapping her hands.

And with that, she slipped the surly bonds of the earth and rose slowly, twirling into the sky. The fairy kept one tiny hand on hers, steadying her ascent.

Trees and bushes below her waved in the mild tropical breeze like undersea plants. Wendy wasn't as terrified of the height as she had thought she might be. The change in perspective was a little thrilling, a little startling, but that was all. It was like she merely had nothing to do with the ground anymore.

Luna barked.

"Oh, Luna, I'm all right, I—"

The fairy let go.

Wendy suddenly listed to the left. It was as if the fairy were the only thing anchoring her to the sky. She thrashed wildly, making flailing swimming motions that did little to help. The earth rolled sickeningly below, looming close.

The fairy immediately grabbed her again.

Wendy felt everything . . . *stabilize*. The lightness on

both sides of her evened out and she bobbed steadily again, feeling somehow supported by the air around her.

The fairy waited a moment and gave her a look—*All right? Are you ready?*

Wendy swallowed and nodded.

The fairy—slowly—withdrew her tiny hand, drawing it across Wendy's skin until just a finger touched, and then nothing at all.

Wendy remained steady this time.

She laughed. Out loud, like she hadn't laughed in years—honest, billowing peals of pure joy. Her skirts swished and spread out. Gravity had no effect on her anymore—nothing tugged at her shoulders, feet, neck, mind, ears—she was weightless, untouchable.

Luna barked. But it was a bark of excitement this time, a *wow look at us and you and me and that's all great yes!* bark.

Seeing this, the fairy dipped down and started to sprinkle some dust on her—but the wolf ducked neatly out of the way. She pranced back and forth, her back bending and shimmering in the sunlight. She barked again politely. *No, thank you,* she was obviously saying. *I'll go my own way.*

The fairy shook her head—*Who wouldn't want to fly? Silly thing!*—then buzzed up to Wendy's nose and snapped her fingers imperiously.

"All right, yes, yes," Wendy said, too happy to take

offense. "I'm coming. Forgive me—I've only flown in my dreams before!"

The fairy rolled her eyes and took off toward the gray mountains. More slowly this time.

And Wendy, spreading her arms out to catch the wind, happily followed.

The Lost Boys

Wendy followed the fairy as best she could without becoming distracted by the details of the landscape below. Some things looked *exactly* as she had imagined them (the savannas of Upper Hillsdale, for instance, and the multi-level pools of the Tonal Springs). But some things were subtly different and others entirely unrecognizable. Far to the northwest was the area she couldn't remember very well: in reality it turned out to be a peninsula shrouded in a heavy gray and viscous fog.

Maybe it really is masked by the elements because it hasn't been described yet, or used in a story, Wendy thought.

To the south of that was a strange, balding mound of a hill that was just crying out for an obvious name. Was it

John's invention? Or Michael's? Or . . . someone else's?

And, wait a moment, what about those someone elses? *Other children? Besides me and Michael and John?* Wendy suddenly wondered. Did they make up whole areas of the island in their own games? And was there any part of Never Land that was just—itself, not prone to the stories and imaginations of children? Was this fairy with her a *native*, as it were, or the result of some little girl's dream?

Maybe Wendy could get some answers once everything with Hook and the shadow was sorted.

Luna ran far below them, disappearing into the jungles here, reappearing on a trail there, keeping an eye on the two fliers and barking at their shadows.

(Wendy's shadow waved insouciantly at her as she rippled over the treetops and clearings.)

The fairy was already descending toward the center of the island, which wasn't really that big.

Despite the very obviously *non*-temperate flora near the beach, here the Pernicious Forest became solidly northern (if not quite Hyperborean). There were pines and oaks with their surprisingly familiar leaf shapes that spoke of cool, moist shadows below. But these grew alongside palms and vines and exotic flowers and the like, a mishmash of ideas. Spot in the middle of this mess was a scrubby clearing that was just short of terrifying and very long on *creepy*. A giant dead tree stood in the center. Its gnarled, broken-off branches and twigs were like bones grasping at the sky, as if the tree were still fighting its fate a hundred years after its death. What looked too regular to be vines turned out, of course, to be the frayed ends of ropes and nooses, all sizes and shapes. "For all sorts of necks, I suppose," Wendy said thoughtfully.

The grass and weeds around the tree had been trampled into dry brown dust by unknown activity. Standing like sentinels on the cardinal points just outside this circle were other gigantic trees, but these were very much alive. Almost too alive.

Wendy carefully and slowly lowered herself to the ground, wobbling a bit as she went. She was hoping for a perfect, graceful landing like a Russian ballerina *en* one *pointe* but had to settle for a mostly-on-two-flat-feet stumble. She bowed forward with momentum, managing to catch herself before completely tumbling over her own head.

The fairy had disappeared, presumably into the hidden hideout of the Lost Boys.

"Luna?" Wendy called. *"Luna!"*

An answering howl came from somewhere downhill and to the south: the wolf was on her way, but still far.

"All right, I'll see you in a bit!"

She made a barefoot circle of the clearing, the weight of

her dress now feeling strange as it swished against her legs, catching against the little hairs on her skin. She studied the living trees on the perimeter carefully and was quickly rewarded for her efforts: giant knots in their trunks had suspicious black cracks around them. Body-sized holes rose up from their roots with edges that seemed strangely smooth, as if they had been polished by constant use.

"They're not actually hidden that well, are they?" she mused. Anyone, not just clever Wendy, with an eye and a moment's thought could tell there was something off and a little too *frequented* about the area. Did the pirates really never find Peter Pan's hideout? Had they ever actually looked? It brought to mind the idea of when a child plays hide-and-go-seek with his mummy and tries not to giggle while posing behind something too small to adequately camouflage him. The family dog, for instance. Or a small ottoman.

Wendy shrugged and primly stepped through a door, feeling just a *tad* superior.

So she was more than a bit taken aback when the floor fell away mechanically below her and she tumbled, heels over head, down a hard and lumpy ramp.

She landed on an equally hard floor, a mess of dress, hair, and sash, legs splayed and vision spinning. But she could see enough to notice a *very* smug-looking fairy hovering in the air before her, arms crossed.

"Oh! I'm really here! This is Peter Pan's hideout! . . . And yours, too," Wendy added quickly just as the fairy began to frown.

The place was as delightful as she had imagined. The cave under the Hangman's Tree was perfectly dry and smelled mostly fresh—with only the very slight tang of dirty little boys. The ground was even, and, if not neatly swept, then at least covered with an assortment of skins and rugs. One particularly large sheepskin near the firepit had its soft and thick fleece turned upward, showing indentations where it was obviously slept on. Other beds were stashed willy-nilly around the cave: some nestled in hollows made in the walls themselves, some in the cradling arms of gigantic roots that stuck through the ceiling. Some were hammocks hanging from those same roots.

There were a few civilized details, like chairs that looked as though they had been purloined from more modern and elegant domiciles—a red velvet recliner, for instance, which would have been far more at home at Mr. Darling's club than in a cave. *Wherever did that come from?* Wendy wondered. But the rest of the furniture consisted primarily of things like barrels cut in half with moss for cushions, and the stumps of trees with hastily hammered-on backs. Enormous mushrooms made for tables. Some of the lanterns were fungus as well—softly glowing bluish-green "flowers" that spread in delicate clumps just below the ceiling.

"John would just have a field day with those, I'm certain," Wendy said with a smile.

One large barrel was placed under the end of a hollowed-out root to collect rainwater. There were shelves and nooks for the few possessions considered precious by the Lost Boys: piles of gold coins, interesting animal skeletons, shiny crystals, captivating burrs and seedpods. Also more strange detritus of the civilized world: a hinge, a pipe, a knob from a drawer, a spanner, and even a pocket watch.

"Oh, this is all . . . amazing! Not that it couldn't do with a bit of a woman's touch." A proper cauldron could be hung from a chain above the fire for soups and stews, for instance. The rugs could be beaten out a bit. Where was the washtub? And the out-of-place, ornate gold frame that cleverly delineated a window could have used a nice little chintz curtain to keep bright light and prying eyes out.

Oh, she could do so *much* with it! Imagine if it were hers, and all the Lost Boys, too; she would take care of them . . .

. . . like young pirates. . . .

Wendy struggled with that thought. In many of her stories about Never Land, she kept house for Peter and them much like Snow White for the dwarfs. And they revered her and promised to never leave her and always brought back the best little trinkets from their adventures. . . .

An inquisitive tinkling brought her out of her reverie.

"I don't know where they are," Wendy answered, thinking she had guessed the question. "But I'm sure they'll be back soon. . . ."

With an irritated swoop, the fairy grabbed one of her locks and pulled, flying to the far corner of the cave and forcing Wendy to stumble quickly after to avoid any pain.

"You don't have to—oh!"

The fairy let her go and pulled aside a piece of bright gold-and-pink silk hanging on the wall. Behind it was the fairy's own private room.

She had a soft bed of bright green moss with several iridescent feathers for a counterpane. A shelf mushroom served as an actual shelf displaying an assortment of dried flowers and pretty gewgaws the fairy had collected. There was a charming little dining table, somewhat bold in irony: It was the cheery but deadly red-and-white amanita. The wide top was set with an acorn cap bowl and jingle shell charger. In the corner, a beautifully curved, bright green leaf collected drops from somewhere in the celling much like the water barrel did, but this was obviously for discreet fairy bathing. An assortment of tiny buds, rough seeds, and spongy moss were arranged neatly on a piece of gray driftwood nearby to aid in cleansing.

"Oh my," Wendy sighed. "This is the most beautiful flat I have ever seen."

The fairy tried very hard not to look pleased.

"The accessories . . . the flowers . . . the *furniture*. It's all *perfect*."

Maybe the fairy didn't precisely blush, but she did allow a single grudging smile.

Wendy felt her heart leap. They were, despite the fairy's initial hatred, growing closer.

Maybe.

Suddenly the cave resounded with bumps and knocks and disturbing echoes from above. The furniture—fairy *and* full-sized—shook.

"What's that?" Wendy cried. "Are we being attacked?"

The fairy rolled her eyes, once again dismissive of her human companion.

As the first boy's body tumbled into view, Wendy understood: the Lost Boys were home.

They came flying down the tunnels' slides, landed neatly, and unfurled like ferns or strange creatures. These were the lads Peter had rescued from orphanages and the terrible fate of *growing up*. In her stories, Wendy always had them wearing the skins of animals.

And so they did, sort of. The first boy definitely had on a real bearskin, as real as the rug on the floor, and the animal's claws were worn over his hands like gloves. The next one, the tallest, had on the tail of a fox, but he also sported the bright red coat of a traveling salesperson and a red felt hat beaten into two peaks to resemble fox ears.

There was a set of twins with black gloves and black masks plastered directly onto their faces somehow. They also had fluffy striped tails affixed to their gray baggy overalls— which they wore *with no shirts on underneath.* Scandalous, like poor street ruffians. Wendy searched her mind for what animal they could possibly be and finally came up with *raccoon,* a creature from the Americas that was supposed to be terribly smart and devious but quite prim, habituated to washing its hands and food before dining.

The smallest Lost Boy was no more than a toddler. He also wore real fur, a beautiful black-and-white hide with a strangely pungent but not entirely unpleasant smell. Another New World creature: a skunk. They could spray their stink in acidic streams to deter predators. *Very useful defense for one so small and helpless,* Wendy found herself thinking.

Right in the middle of the group, neither the tallest nor the shortest, not the fattest or the skinniest, was an approximation of something that was not quite a rabbit. A long, *very* used dove-gray tailcoat had an equally long black tail with a white tip on the end. A leather headband that held back short brown hair sported two long, floppy gray ears.

"Oh! Hello!" Wendy said, clapping her hands together in delight at all of them.

They looked up at her with a little surprise, but not much more. A shadow hung over them and in their eyes.

"Who's this, Tinker Bell?" the tall fox asked.

The fairy flew down in between them and tinkled and jangled.

"A *Wendy*? What's a Wendy? Oh, *she* is. The Wendy. I get it."

While Wendy was pleased with this introduction, she felt a little slighted. She had loved fairies, always loved fairies. How come the Lost Boys could understand what the fairy said, and she couldn't? And they even knew her *name*!

"Pleased to meet you," Wendy said, very properly holding out her hand.

The fox looked at it.

"I'm Slightly," he said. He couldn't have been more than fifteen, but there was something in his eyes that seemed both older and younger. "I'm the leader when Peter's not around. This is Skipper." He gestured at the rabbit thing, who looked away. "And these are the twins."

The two raccoons bobbed their heads and grinned.

"How d'ya . . ."

". . . do?"

Wendy grinned, charmed by the way they acted in perfect unison.

"Cubby." The bear bowed and growled. He pointed at

the littlest one, standing next to him. "This is Tootles. He don't talk much. He's a baby—but, I mean, a *fierce* baby. Don't scrap with 'im."

The skunk had started to look annoyed and sulky, but then smiled broadly, easily lulled by quick-thought words of praise.

"How do you do," Wendy said, leaning forward to the little skunk. His smell was actually less offensive than what was coming off some of the other ones. She had to resist the urge to crinkle her nose or hide behind a scented glove (which she didn't have, anyway). Slightly seemed to be the only one who bathed at all. His dark skin was free from the permanent layer of grubbiness that covered the rest of them. As with the pirates, Wendy desperately wanted to scrub them with a nice boar-bristle brush, starting with the fierce baby.

Tootles melted under her attention, practically swooning.

"Whatcha doing here, The Wendy?" Cubby asked, displaying a set of teeth pocked by the occasional absent baby tooth.

"I'm here because . . . well . . ."

Any internal struggle she had about confessing her use of Peter's shadow and handing it over to the pirates was immediately cut short as Tinker Bell dove in, literally and figuratively, bouncing up and down and angrily shedding sparkles as she obviously told what she thought was a tale of betrayal and near-murder.

Slightly nodded and said, "Uh-huh," madly understanding everything the fairy jingled.

"Oh . . . so *that's* what happened to his shadow," was all he said when she finished. Then he collapsed contemplatively onto a giant mushroom chair that bowed a little under his weight.

Wendy tried to stave off her anxiety while waiting for his reaction, conclusion, or decision, by running her hands through Tootles's wispy hair.

Meanwhile, Skipper kept staring at *her*, unblinkingly, either in awe or disgust.

"But . . . wait . . ." Slightly finally said, frowning. "There's one part of your story I dinna get, Tink. His shadow was in London the *whole time* and he never thought to look there?"

The fairy began to sway back and forth in the air, her face twisting like a child's between contrived innocence and a brow furrowed in deep thought as she desperately tried to come up with a better answer.

"Oh, Tink," Slightly said, shaking his head. "Did you *keep* him from going back? Were you *jealous* of The Wendy?"

"It's just Wendy," Wendy corrected, unable to stop

herself even as she processed this new information. She looked at the fairy in shock. That pretty thing had been *jealous*? Of *Wendy*? A plain, boring London girl living with her brothers in a nursery, inventing tales of a world more wonderful than their own? Tinker Bell had Peter Pan himself! All Wendy had were stories and his shadow. And the *fairy* was jealous?

"But . . . why?" Slightly pressed, echoing Wendy's thoughts precisely.

The fairy looked taken aback by this honest question.

Then she stuck her tongue out at Wendy, put her hands on her hips, and turned away, fluttering her wings provokingly and buzzing. Skipper shook his head in acute disgust.

"She says it was stupid the way he always made her go to London and sit outside your window," Slightly translated. "And then forced her to listen to *you*, The Ugly Wendy, tell long and boring stories about *her* friend."

"Oh dear," Wendy said, unable to think of anything else.

"That's Tink," the fox boy said with a sigh. "No one gets between her and Peter."

"But I wasn't, I didn't, I couldn't even . . ."

"Aw, don't worry about it. She'll come around," Cubby said, rolling his eyes. *"Girls."*

"Oh, there is so much I must make up for in Never Land, and I haven't been here a day!" Wendy cried. "Starting with you Lost Boys. Slightly, I am deeply sorry for what I have done. Trading in Peter Pan's shadow for passage to Never Land was a base, cowardly thing to do."

"What?" Slightly—and all the other Lost Boys—looked at her in surprise. "Why are you sorry? Wasn't no other way you could get here. Grown-ups ain't allowed. Pretty clever, really. Besides . . . *pirates*, you know? Hook was the one that tricked you. They're the bad guys. They're always scheming to get Peter."

"So you forgive me?" Wendy asked timidly.

"I guess it's Peter's got to do that. You should, um, probably talk to him," Slightly said, but he seemed uncomfortable saying it. He looked over at Skipper, who looked away.

"What? What's going on?" Wendy demanded. "Something is going on. You're not telling me."

"It ain't nothing," Skipper murmured.

"It's just that no one's really talked to Peter . . ."

". . . since he lost his shadow," the twins said.

"He's been real ornery. Gotten way worse lately," Cubby said, rolling his eyes. "No fun at all. Him and Slightly been going at it."

"Going at it?" Wendy asked in shock. "You've been fighting with Peter Pan? Your leader?"

"Peter said it was time for Slightly to get out of Never Land . . ."

". . . because he was growing up," the twins said quietly.

The rest of the Lost Boys looked embarrassed. Like it was something they would rather die than reveal to an outsider.

Slightly frowned and worked his jaw, rapping his fingers on the table in nervous anger.

"Aye. He did. He said I was growing up and there weren't no place for me here anymore."

"But—that's unheard of! No one gets kicked out of the Lost Boys! *Why?* Why did he say that? Was it anything you did at all?"

The fox boy shifted in his chair and then suddenly leapt up, going to look out the window. "I was just getting sick of it . . . you know? I been here the longest. Done it all. 'Go hunting.' 'Talk to the mermaids.' 'Battle the pirates.' 'Raid the L'cki.' 'Get raided by the L'cki.' 'Tease the Cyclops.' It's always the same things."

"He begun to *miss* things," Cubby whispered, like it was too awful to mention aloud. "He thinks he can remember his mother."

"He misses *beds* . . ."

". . . and hard things . . ."

". . . and nurses . . ."

". . . and being indoors all the time!" the twins said in disgust.

"I don't ever," Slightly swore, spinning around. "I don't want any of *those* things. I just . . . I want different things. New things. Aright, and maybe a bed. So what's wrong with that? I just had some ideas about things we could do and Peter just . . . Peter just . . . *laughed* at them."

"*You* look like a mother," Tootles ventured, tugging on Wendy's skirt. The Lost Boys looked at him in surprise.

"Oh, why, thank you, darling," Wendy said, scooping him up—reminding herself to wash her hands thoroughly as soon as she had a chance. The skunk boy snuggled into her soft chest. "So . . . because of this, he threatened to throw you out?"

"Peter don't like change," Slightly said, scowling. "Anything different—unless it's a newer, better game that *he* thought up—is growing up. And bad. So *I'm* bad. And I'm growing up. So I have to go."

"And do all of you agree?" Wendy asked, shifting Tootles onto her hip so she could turn and look each one of the Lost Boys in the eye.

None of them met that look.

"No," Skipper finally said, eyes to the ground.

"We love Slightly," Tootles murmured.

"He's all we got when Peter's not around," Cubby said.

"He's a good . . ."

". . . leader," the twins said.

"Well, I don't suppose it's entirely up to Peter, then, is it?" Wendy said. "Is he the *king* of Never Land?"

"No! No one is!" Slightly swore. "That's the whole point, right? No growing up and no rules and whatever you want and fun all the time. If you *want* fun," he added thoughtfully. "I don't always want fun. And don't freedom mean you get to do what you want, at least sometimes?"

"Absolutely correct. Well, all right then. You will stay if you so desire," Wendy said, carefully putting Tootles back down. "That's sorted. No one is the boss of you here."

"That's it?" Cubby asked, surprised.

Wendy nodded. "Why not? It's Never Land. Do as thou wilt—isn't that the whole of the law here?"

"Huh," Skipper said thoughtfully.

"I don't think it's quite that simple," Slightly said. "At least not between Peter and me."

"Well, I don't think there's much I can do there. The two of you will need to work things out on your own. Just as I need to apologize to him myself. Tinker Bell and I are actually here trying to find Peter and help him get his shadow back. Which may ameliorate his mood a bit, and tone down the tension in your little tête-à-tête."

"Ameliorate . . . ? Tet-a-*what*? You memorize a dictionary or somethin'?" Slightly scoffed, waving his hand at her. "Aw, who would *want* to go back to London?"

"Who indeed," Wendy said dryly. "But listen: besides having Peter's shadow, Hook also has something terrible up his sleeve for all of Never Land. Deadly, and *rather permanent*, as he said."

"What? Like destroying all of Never Land?" Skipper asked.

Tinker Bell nodded.

"But why?" Slightly demanded.

"I have some theories," Wendy said, "but I think it's mostly because he's mad. Anyway, we need to stop him, and I don't think we could defeat the pirates on our own, just the three of us, me and Tinker Bell and Peter. Even with Peter reunited with his shadow. Can we count on you?"

The fairy rolled her eyes and turned her head away with a sniff.

"Aye, of course," Slightly said, sticking out his chin. "Whatever my beef with Peter is, a man needs his shadow. O' *course* we'll go with him to get the pirates and save Never Land!"

"That's the spirit, Slightly!" Cubby cried.

"We'll show those stupid pirates . . ."

". . . and that *stupid*, stupid Captain Hook!" the twins crowed.

"Wonderful," Wendy said warmly. Everything was coming together! She had met the Lost Boys, rallied them to her cause, and now they would come with her, and of course the fairy—*Tinker Bell*—couldn't object. It would be like trying to resist a cheery force of nature, a good-willed waterfall, once they decided to come along. "So where do you think Peter is?"

"Sometimes when he's down he goes to Mermaid Lagoon," Cubby said, rolling his eyes. "Talks with the fishgirls."

"Aye, I'd try there first," Slightly said, nodding.

Wendy tried to quell the quick thumping of her heart. *Mermaids!* First she got to see her fairy—who admittedly was much more hostile than she had imagined, but Wendy was working on that—and now *mermaids*! With glittering scales and flowing hair! Everything was turning out so wonderfully.

"All right then, lead the way!" she cried.

"Ah . . . well . . . you go on ahead," Slightly suggested. "We'll just wait until you bring him up to speed. Once you tell him about what you did, and where his shadow is, and give him some time to . . . you know . . . *react* to that."

"He might be very angry," Cubby said, nodding.

"Or very happy," one of the twins said.

"*Too* very happy," the other one added.

"He might fly off and go by hisself," Skipper mumbled.

"Or fly off the handle—right at you, or Tink. Or Slightly, even."

The fox boy nodded. "I don't know *how* he'll take all this news. You tell him, let him work it out for a bit. I don't want him taking nothing out on me because he ain't got his head on straight. He's sore enough as it is."

"But together we can convince him, or argue with him. And be ready to immediately go get the pirates!" Wendy said desperately. "Power in numbers!"

"'Do as thou wilt,'" Slightly quoted back at her. "We wiln't. Not until Peter's all right with all of this and all of us."

"'All of this' sounds like a terrible idea," Wendy said forlornly.

But the little fairy smiled, looking more than a touch smug.

The Lost Girls

Luna chose that moment to burst onto the scene.

She had found one of the "secret" doors to the hide-out almost immediately and scrambled down—much more elegantly than Wendy. She barked happily, pleased with her entrance and audience.

"Wow! A wolf!" Cubby said in awe.

"He's so fierce!" Skipper sighed.

"*She's* mine," Wendy said proudly, going over to pet her. "And I'm hers."

"That's incredible. She's beautiful," Slightly said, a little jealous but more impressed.

As she ran her hands over the wolf's coat, Wendy saw with dismay it was covered in burrs and mud. Luna panted—a little laboriously—and leaned extra hard against her human friend. It was obvious she was exhausted. Still part puppy, she was too young to realize when she had worn herself out.

Honestly, Wendy was feeling a little done in as well. Flying was hard work. And so was being kidnapped by pirates.

"Poor girl! Well, if we *must* go on alone," she said (a little peevishly; she couldn't help it), "I think we will require a bit of rest and refreshment here first."

The fairy looked outraged and put her hands on her hips. She made a very obvious walking motion with two of her fingers, then pointed to the door. *No. We have to keep going.*

"I'm sorry, *you* might be used to spending most of your day on wing," Wendy said politely, "but while it's glorious sport, like something out of a dream, well, *unlike* a dream, it's a bit exhausting. Like all sports, really. And Luna had to run here on foot. She's had it."

The fairy frowned at Luna and then tossed her head. Like she was saying, *Fine, all right, but only for your wolf. Not for you.*

"You heard her, boys! It's teatime!" Slightly cried.

In a sort of reverse of Snow White's story, the boys ran around gathering what provisions they could like dwarfs desperately making everything nice for their lady guest. The twins quickly filled a basket with berries and fruit. Cubby found a big bowl of nuts. Slightly blew embers into a lovely little fire and put the kettle on (where they had gotten the kettle, a highly decorated affair of blue and gold enamel, was a mystery). Tootles somehow managed to carry and set out a stack of mismatched cups: wood, bone china, and coconut shell. Skipper brought out a pot of golden comb honey.

While this happy chaos was happening, Wendy took the opportunity to approach the fairy alone, in a—very slightly—quieter part of the hideout.

"Tinker Bell?" she ventured. "So that is your name?"

The fairy looked at her in surprise—then grudgingly nodded her head.

"Did you . . . Did you really keep Peter from going to London . . . on purpose?"

Tinker Bell looked away, but she didn't disagree.

Wendy was torn. More than anything she wanted this beautiful little fairy to be her friend, to like her back, to initiate her into the secret world of flowers and fey folk. But she had to know the truth.

"Did you really do it because you were . . . jealous of me?"

Tinker Bell crossed her arms and scowled at her. She jingled something disdainful.

"Of . . . *me*?" Wendy repeated, indicating her torn

dress, her size, her brown hair, her overall very un-fairylike plainness.

Tinker Bell nodded, a little less certainly.

"Well, I think that's very flattering. Perhaps even the highest compliment I've ever been paid—no matter how backhanded. I thank you."

The fairy rolled her eyes. Wendy sighed. She sat down heavily on a barrel.

"If we are being completely honest here, and I feel we should be since we are companions in this strange adventure, then I should tell you straight: I *do* like Peter Pan. I used to worship him, in fact. I used to dream about him, too. I suppose if he had actually come to me, I might have . . . well, who knows. He's all I ever cared about, really, besides Mother and Father and Michael and John and Nana, of course."

Tinker Bell had an *aha!* look on her face, and waggled an accusing finger at the human girl.

"But I never even saw him while I was awake, Tinker Bell," Wendy pointed out. "These thoughts of him were just that—all in my imagination. I am very sorry it upset you to come and listen to my stories. But I was never even aware that you and Peter were there. You have had such amazing, *real* adventures with him here in Never Land. All I ever had was his shadow."

Tinker Bell blinked. It was obviously an entirely new idea for her.

"It was a very naughty thing you did to Peter out of jealousy, Tinker Bell. Preventing him from getting his own shadow . . . And what *I* did was naughty, too, trading that shadow to his enemy to come here. Far more naughty, really. Especially since it seems to have resulted in putting all of Never Land in danger. We *both* have a lot to answer for. Apologies and reparations to make. Together."

The fairy looked outraged at this suggestion of any similarity between them. But then she recovered herself, crossing her arms again. *Go on,* she seemed to say.

"And look, here we are, talking about Peter while he isn't even here at all! In person, or in shadow form!" Wendy said with a laugh. "Is he really the king of Never Land, after all? Invading our conversations and making everything about himself even when he's not present? Hook can't stop talking about him, the Lost Boys are depressed about him, you are constantly jealous around him, and I—well, I sold him out when I couldn't have him. It's ridiculous, really, the effect he has on all our lives.

"Tinker Bell!"

The fairy jumped at the sudden, direct address: Wendy was looking at her sternly, full of purpose, shoulders back and jaw firm.

"You and I must resolve not to discuss him any longer, at least until everything else is settled and we have properly saved Never Land. Surely the two of us have other things we could talk about that don't involve a boy. Other things that warrant our attention. Pirates, flying, the job of getting this shadow back, beating Captain Hook. The adventures *we* have. Our lives. The life of a fairy. The life of a plain human girl. That should be more than enough for many hours of solid conversation. So enough talk about him for now. Are we agreed?"

The fairy looked at her as if it were a weird thing to ask.

And Wendy supposed it was a *bit* odd. Wasn't Peter the very reason they were thrown together in the first place?

But then, as the thought *really* wound its way through her mind, the fairy relaxed. She shook her head from side to side, as if sloshing the idea around and physically measuring it.

Finally, she nodded. She put out her tiny hand.

Wendy grinned, thrilled to have made some headway with the fairy at last.

She very carefully took the tiny hand between her own index finger and thumb and gave it a gentle but solid shake.

"Excellent. This should make our task that much easier, as well as our working together."

Tinker Bell narrowed her eyes at that—maybe the

idea of actively *working together* with the human girl, or at least expressing it out loud, was still a bit much. But she didn't jingle or otherwise comment. Whatever their feelings toward each other or Peter were, they had a job to do.

The tea was filling but strange. Wendy could have done with some proper sandwiches, pastries, or crackers. And she had to sneak the questionable day-old rabbit meat to Luna, who snapped it up discreetly and happily. But she appreciatively drank the strange reddish-brown decoction of leaves and twigs the Lost Boys swore was just like proper tea if you didn't think about it too much. And in truth, it wasn't bad; it just wasn't East India Company Darjeeling. It had a warm, almost cinnamony taste.

Luna had a big bowl of fresh, cold water, and Tootles insisted on having his tea the same way, on the floor. After that and several stale biscuits, plus a little rest (and more tummy rubs than any puppy could really ask for from a hideout full of instantly devoted fans), it was finally time to leave.

Outside the air was as fresh and bracing as Never Land air ever was. A *great* day for flying.

But while the two girls were getting ready to say their goodbyes, Wendy noticed that Skipper kept looking at her strangely—almost in fascination.

"Is there something wrong?" Wendy asked, of course immediately needing to fix whatever problem there was.

"Nuthin'," Skipper said, turning away so she couldn't see his face.

Wendy wasn't the girl at parties who caused boys to blush. But she had seen it happen with others, like at the spring dance when John was caught off guard by a hello from Alice Cotswaldington. He had turned red, turned away, and choked into his punch.

This wasn't that. Skipper didn't seem to be *blushing*, exactly, and there was little wonder or fear in his eyes. He grew nervous under her scrutiny.

"Come on, you can tell me," Wendy prodded. "Is it that you actually want to join me and Tinker Bell? Looking for Peter Pan, I mean?" She tried to keep the hope out of her voice.

"No!" he cried. He immediately looked down and lowered his voice to its usual mumble. "I don't want to see Peter right now. Maybe not even after he's finished being angry or whatever. Maybe not ever."

His voice . . .

It hit Wendy all at once. Skipper's constant staring at her and his reluctance to speak. The especially baggy clothing he wore and soft, almost babyish face he had despite his height. The obvious desire not to be noticed by the new girl while being unable to take his eyes off her.

"Skipper, you're a *girl!*" Wendy exclaimed.

The Lost Boys all turned around at her cry.

Skipper swallowed and hardened her look, but that was all.

"Sort of," Slightly said with a shrug.

"What do you mean, *sort* of?" Wendy demanded.

"She ain't like *you,*" Cubby said.

"Not like me? She's *exactly* like me!"

"She doesn't wear . . ." one twin began.

". . . dresses and ribbons," the other one finished.

"She don't talk like you."

"Her hair's short."

"She don't feel like a mother."

"Yes, yes, but those are all just externalities!" Wendy protested. "She and I both have . . ."

Well, nothing that could be said aloud in mixed company.

How old was Skipper? Old enough to be reminded of these things once a month?

Skipper's eyes were tortoiseshell, her eyelashes short and black. Wendy found herself imagining the Lost Boy with long hair in a proper girlish curl down her back, a ribbon round her neck, and a simple but fetching strolling frock . . .

And realized it would have been ridiculous.

This girl was perfectly at ease and comfortable in her

jacket and animal getup. Anything less freeing would have forced her to stand weirdly or made her look like a clown.

"But . . . how are you a Lost Boy?" Wendy finally asked, baffled.

"Always wanted to be one," Skipper answered, voice strong now that she had decided to speak. "I saw Peter come and take boys away from the orphanage. *Only* boys. Everyone knew that. Only *boys* could become Lost Boys. So I became a boy. The nurses forgot. They hated me—they hated who I was when I was a girl. They could barely read, so I changed my name in the books. I was a boy. And then, when Peter came, he took . . . me."

Everyone was quiet during her little speech. As if it were as natural and acceptable an escape plan as selling Peter's shadow.

"But why did you want to leave the home? Did they . . ." Wendy leaned in close and lowered her voice. "Did they hurt you . . . as a girl? Is that why you wanted to leave?"

Skipper gave her a look of shock and revulsion. "*No!* I just wanted to be free. Like all of us. To not have rules and not brush my teeth and hunt and fish and have fun all day. To never grow up. Ever."

"Right on, Skipper!" Cubby cheered. "That's my Lost Boy!"

"But she's not . . ." Wendy started to correct.

Slightly smiled at her confusion.

"She *is* a Lost Boy," he said gently. "One hundred percent. Like all of us."

"But that's the problem," Skipper said sorrowfully. "I'm not *exactly* a boy."

"All right," Wendy said uncertainly. "But . . . if it's always been like this, why are you worried about it *now*?"

Skipper shrugged but looked a little desperate. "Peter don't know. Not really. And Peter wants to kick Slightly out 'cause he wants new things. Peter's *always* talking about silly girls. Stupid girls. There are so many . . . all over Never Land . . . and you in London. . . . And I guess Tink *says* he likes you, but you're not like him, you know?"

Wendy considered this. True: Peter would never ask someone like Wendy to be a Lost Boy. He never did, in fact.

What would happen if she suddenly popped up in his crew?

"I see your point," she said slowly. "I think, however, we can get this all straightened out. No need to worry about it right now. We'll find Peter, retrieve his shadow, beat the pirates, have him make up with Slightly, and . . . then deal with you, however you wish. All right? But we'll wait until things are a bit calmer and he can see things with a clearer head."

Skipper nodded a little unhappily, but she had the

look of a child who has just cried and is in the feeling calm and being mollified stage, tears having been sniffed away. Wendy wondered if the girl ever cried—*had* ever cried in her strange, short life—at least in front of other people.

"But, ahh. . . ." She couldn't stop herself from asking, from leaning in and whispering: "Don't you find it a little . . . bothersome to be with these wild boys all the time?"

For an answer, Skipper opened her mouth and let out a terrifically loud burp.

"*Nice* one, Skip," Slightly said, touching his hat and bowing to her. The rest of the Lost Boys cackled and laughed and cheered and tried to follow suit, with considerably less success.

"Well," Wendy said, trying not to appear flustered or embarrassed, "I suppose that answers that."

"Mermaid Lagoon is that way, when the two of you are ready," Slightly said, pointing to the southeast. "How will you go? There's the path east and south beyond the Tonal Springs, or will you be trying to sail across the Bay of Skull Island?"

"Neither," Wendy said politely—and perhaps just a little smugly. "We'll be taking the *ether*."

And with that, she neatly rose up off her toes and a few feet into the air.

The Lost Boys cheered, crowed, and guffawed at that.

"Tink! You gave an outsider *fairy dust*?" Slightly called in mock outrage. "My my, how far down in the world we have come."

Tinker Bell stuck her tongue out at him. Slightly made a very inappropriate, rude gesture back at her that Wendy had only seen thugs and urchins use. But he was laughing. The fairy tossed her head derisively.

Wendy wondered about their interactions. Tinker Bell had her own room in the Lost Boys' hangout. Yet she seemed to treat them as meanly—or, at least, indifferently—as she did everyone else. For their part, the Lost Boys seemed to not to care what she thought, or they simply accepted that it was just part of her touchy personality. *Maybe it's not just me,* Wendy thought. Maybe the fairy was naturally prickly and bad-tempered to everyone.

But she doubted if Tinker Bell had ever physically attacked a Lost Boy the way she had assaulted *her* back at the clearing with the crystal creature. And she couldn't imagine Skipper acting the way Wendy had, stepping away and apologizing. The Lost Boy probably would have cracked Tinker Bell across the pate for such behavior.

Luna yawned, turning herself around several times before sitting down heavily next to Tootles. The little boy laughed and rubbed his face into her fur. The wolf looked wearily up at Wendy: *Are we really taking off again so soon?*

Just look what a lovely group of playmates we have here. I could use a nap, too. . . .

"Can we . . ."

". . . keep her?" the twins begged immediately.

"Just for now?"

"She's so tired!"

"Nobody can *keep* her," Wendy said. "She's her own person."

And yet . . . insomuch as Luna was anyone's, she *was* Wendy's. She was Wendy's dream dog, the perfect companion for adventures in Never Land.

But was she a pet?

Perhaps something created in Never Land was never really a Londoner's to begin with.

And the wolf really was just a puppy—a very large, very tired-looking one at that.

"Tinker Bell," Wendy said as casually as she could, relishing the use of the fairy's name and the intimacy it brought, "what do you think about Luna? Perhaps she *is* looking a little exhausted."

Tinker Bell considered the wolf, then nodded slowly. She pointed at the Lost Boys and shrugged: *What better place for a puppy to stay?*

"All right then, goodbye for now," Wendy said, dipping down to give Luna a big hug around her neck and shoulders. The wolf licked her all over.

Then the girl sighed and rose into the air. Tinker Bell followed—a few feet away, of course.

At least, Wendy thought, *we two have just had our first completely neutral conversation: no anger, no recriminations, no insult jingles. It is certainly a step.*

She waved at the Lost Boys. "It was lovely meeting all of you."

"See you! Send us a signal as soon as you've sorted stuff out with Peter!" Slightly called.

The Lost Boys leapt and capered and yelled after them. Tootles and the twins broke into a wild twirling circle dance. Skipper gave a shy wave with a half-smile. Cubby howled like a wolf rather than the bear he thought he was. Luna joined in, a great doggy smile on her muzzle.

It was a charming scene—and Wendy dearly hoped that would not be the last she would see of her beloved wolf.

The Water Girls

Once they were out of the jungle, Tinker Bell chose to hug the curving coast rather than cross the water, which would have been faster. And when Wendy took a detour over the waves to get a closer look at a whale spouting she realized why. The mild breezes that kept her cool on the beach were whipped into much stronger versions of themselves over the ocean. She found herself suddenly pitched out of control by a rogue gust and in danger of being batted out to sea—or of a good dunking.

"A bit too Icarus there," she chastised herself, using her arms to somewhat un-prettily flap her way back to land.

Tinker Bell wisely only skimmed over the shallowest wavelets that encroached on the beach. She dipped a finger into the surface as she went, throwing up a pretty little spray that made rainbows in the golden sunlight. Fish leapt over her wake, flashing silver. Wendy caught her breath at the thoughtless beauty of it all. The fairy didn't care how others perceived what she did—she just *did*. Whatever she wanted. The results were often grace and spectacle.

When Wendy did whatever she wanted, people hated it. Like at parties. Like at Christmas, when she had been so full of the beauty of the season and the festive caroling music that she had made the mistake of enthusiastically telling everyone how a Never Land holiday might be run. Utterly unaware (at first) that not only did the people there not care about the holidays of an imaginary world or its cleverly invented trappings, but also that they were more than a little horrified that these stories came out of the mouth of a sixteen-year-old, and not a child.

(She had also been unaware at the time that her behavior would become the prime topic of jokes and gossip for the next season.)

Back in the reality of Never Land, the dark peaks of the Black Dragon Mountains glowered in the far distance, ominous smoke circling them like a scarf. Gray and brown twists of vapor rolled around each other like serpents, the air so thick it had texture and mass. Everything together fooled the eye into thinking there was an actual dragon—the size of a city—slithering through the landscape.

Maybe after they found Peter Pan and saved Never Land Wendy could explore those mountains and look for real dragons. She wondered how long the fairy dust would last.

It would, of course, be far more fun with someone else along. Even a foul-tempered fairy.

The northern side of the Mermaid Lagoon was a rocky, leisurely half-moon with a strip of jungle clinging to its stony spine. Flickering through green shadows were bright birds in orange, green, and yellow flocks. Here the clean, salty slap of the sea air was replaced by a heavy atmosphere of exotic blooms and ancient, earthy decay.

Tinker Bell headed for a gray ledge studded with palm trees, a hidden platform from which they could survey the water below. She landed silently and then crawled to the edge to peep over the side, keeping her body flat and out of sight from the ground.

Wendy did her best to emulate the fairy but her long skirt kept tangling in her legs. Frustrated and in a huff, she decided it was safe with no one but a girl fairy around to see her and hiked the dress up between her knees. Ignoring Tink's eye roll at her awkward maneuvers, she leaned over the lip of the rock for a look.

A paradisiacal lagoon lay below them. The water was

an unbelievable, unreal turquoise, its surface so still that every feature of the bottom could be admired in magnified detail: colorful pebbles, bright red kelp, fish as pretty and colorful as the jungle birds. A waterfall on the far side fell softly from a height of at least twenty feet. A triple rainbow graced its frothy bottom. Large boulders stuck out of the water at seemingly random intervals, black and sunwarmed and extremely inviting, like they had been placed there on purpose by some ancient giant. And on these were the mermaids.

Wendy gasped at their beauty.

Their tails were all colors of the rainbow, somehow managing not to look tawdry or clownish. Deep royal blue, glittery emerald green, coral red, anemone purple. Slick and wet and as beautifully real as the salmon Wendy's father had once caught on holiday in Scotland. Shining and voluptuously alive.

The mermaids were rather scandalously naked except for a few who wore carefully placed shells and starfish, although their hair did afford some measure of decorum as it trailed down their torsos. Their locks were long and thick and sinuous and mostly the same shades as their tails. Some had very tightly coiled curls, some had braids. Some had decorated their tresses with limpets and bright hibiscus flowers.

Their "human" skins were familiar tones: dark brown to pale white, pink and beige and golden and everything in between. Their eyes were also familiar eye colors but strangely clear and flat. Either depthless or extremely shallow depending on how one stared.

They sang, they brushed their hair, they played in the water. In short, they did everything mythical and magical mermaids were supposed to do, laughing and splashing as they did.

"Oh!" Wendy whispered. "They're—" And then she stopped.

Tinker Bell was giving her a funny look. An unhappy funny look.

The mermaids were beautiful. Indescribably, perfectly beautiful. They glowed and were radiant and seemed to suck up every ray of sun and sparkle of water; Wendy found she had no interest looking anywhere else.

Sometimes when he's down he goes to Mermaid Lagoon. Wasn't that what Cubby had said?

Of course, it made sense: just a few moments of *watching* these mysterious beings made Wendy feel light and happy all over. But . . . imagine having to compete with them.

Even if the fairy and Peter Pan weren't—*involved*, romantically, this would have been a hard act to follow.

What kind of girl, even just a friend, wouldn't grow jealous of a crowd of the most extraordinary, delightful creatures on the planet? Ones to whom your best friend turned whenever he was down?

Stupid girls. There are so many . . . all over Never Land . . . and you in London. . . . Skipper had said that. Who knew what other sirens populated this island? Selkies? Fairy princesses? Normal princesses? Pirate queens? Dryads? Naiads?

Wendy decided to say nothing about the exquisite beauty of the mermaids.

"Ah, there they are. But I don't see Peter Pan," she said instead, narrowing her eyes and casting her gaze to every obvious shadow and cranny.

Tinker Bell shook her head slowly, thoughtfully.

"Perhaps we should . . ." Wendy's voice trailed off.

The old Wendy would have stood up and marched on down to find out where he had gone, questioning the pretty mermaids closely.

The new Wendy, Never Land Wendy, paused.

She had been held hostage by blackhearted pirates when she had thought she had made a simple deal.

She had nearly been killed when crossing a harmless-looking clearing.

And these beautiful, innocent-looking mermaids, in their

beautiful lagoon—were they actually what they seemed?

Were their teeth just a little sharper than those of their human counterparts?

"Perhaps we should continue to surveil the situation from up here," Wendy said finally, sitting up straight-backed, her legs crossed. She cupped her hands around her mouth.

"Hallo down there! Good afternoon!"

Immediately the mermaids froze. Some dove down into the water. They made esses of their bodies like snakes, keeping their heads above the surface. All fixed her with their large, unblinking wet eyes.

The one on the largest rock alone stayed where she was. She had tightly braided purple locks and gripped the sides of her gray stone with fingers that now seemed a little more clawlike than human.

She relaxed when her eyes found Wendy.

So did all of the other mermaids, as if they all saw her at the same time. As one.

"Don't be afraid!" Wendy called. "I'm not going to hurt you."

"Oh, that's nice," the—leader?—said. Her tail began to swish behind her on the rock, the tip of her fin just touching the water, flipping it so little droplets spit into the air. The other mermaids began slowly moving again as well, treading water or beating their tails. They kept their faces halfway below the surface, however, noses firmly beneath. It was more than a little disturbing. While Wendy knew logically that mermaids could breathe underwater, it seemed very unnatural to hold themselves that way. No bubbles burbled up.

"Humans are *always* trying to catch us," the purple one said, pouting. "Nasty piratesss . . ."

"I'm not a pirate!" Wendy said quickly. "I've just escaped from being their prisoner, in fact."

"Nasty piratesss," another one said, pink-haired, kicking herself above the water for a moment so she could speak, her tail working and sliding.

A little surprising, because serpents can't speak, of course, Wendy thought.

Then she wondered what had suddenly made her think of serpents.

"Humans want to steal from us. A lock of our beautiful hair . . ." a red-haired one growled. Her locks weren't merely ginger; they were a flaming, tomato, poppy red. Red as a ladybug or the lips of some inappropriately dressed woman.

"Oh, I wouldn't do that," Wendy promised. "Though your hair *is* beautiful. It's the most beautiful hair I've ever seen."

Tinker Bell rolled her eyes. But the mermaids rolled in the water, smiling and—hissing? They seemed to like what she had said quite a bit.

"We can't see you very well," the purple one called out. "We can't see *your* hair. Our eyes don't work very well above water. Come down so we can see you."

"Yess," a green-haired beauty begged. "So we can see your hair."

"So we can comb it," another said.

"So we can brush it," a third said.

The mermaids swam back and forth in the lagoon, pleading and making dizzying patterns. They were beautiful and plaintive and hypnotizing to watch.

Wendy's heart tugged with a terrible pain. Such a scene had only existed in her wildest, most secret fantasies, ones she hadn't even told her brothers about: How she would make friends with a beautiful mermaid and the two would comb each other's hair, and laugh and sing. And *maybe* the mermaid would make fun of her voice, for Wendy could manage simple hymns and popular songs all right, but she was no siren. And then they would trade combs; Wendy would give the mermaid the silver-handled brush the Darlings had given her for Christmas one year, and the mermaid would give her an ivory comb, or maybe one made from a fish skeleton with tiny white translucent teeth. And they would forever remain friends, and even if they were far apart, they would think of each other every time they brushed their hair.

Wendy wanted nothing more than to lean over and plunge into the water below, to sit on a rock and have them do her hair in proper mermaid style. Long and down and flowing, with a flower or sea star for decoration.

But their enticements were a little overmuch, their teeth a little sharp.

"Oh, I would dearly love to, after I've asked a few questions," Wendy said apologetically.

"What?" the leader called out, putting a hand to her ear. "I'm afraid I can't hear you."

"I said I have a few questions!"

The mermaid was silent—all of them were silent. They stared at her without blinking. It was like she had reached a dead end in a game.

Wendy groaned inwardly.

"I will come down to talk to you," she said, regretting every word. "But not to the water's edge. I'm afraid of falling in, you see. I'm not a terribly good swimmer."

She thought it was a good story. But Tinker Bell shook her head and slapped a hand over her face.

There was another ledge just a little bit below the one they sat on that still seemed a safe distance from the water.

Wendy clambered down to it as neatly as she could, trying not to further tear her already ruined dress. Never Land was not easy on one's clothes. Perhaps that's why the little fairy's skirt was all ragged at the hem. If Wendy wasn't careful, she'd wind up in animal skins and purloined gear like the Lost Boys . . . or, heavens forfend, as naked as the mermaids!

Tinker Bell was wary, taking a long, lingering moment before drifting in a lazy spiral down to where Wendy now stood four or five feet above the water. She crossed her arms, upset that they had given in even this much.

But the mermaids leapt and played in joy at this development, swimming up close to and almost under Wendy—and then away again on their backs, like otters.

"What are you *wearing*?"

"Take it *off* this moment!"

"You can't swim in *that*!"

"I do not plan on swimming anytime soon. As I mentioned before, I cannot swim very well," Wendy said primly. "And anyway I . . . *we* . . . came here with rather urgent business. . . ."

"Bah!" The blue-haired mermaid stuck out her lip and splashed water with the tip of her tail so expertly that it hit Wendy squarely in the face.

The mermaids laughed and tittered and dove and flipped.

"Here's to *business*," another one said, hitting her tail even harder on the water. This time Wendy managed to cover her face, but it was a much larger volume of water, drenching her head and her hair. It was a hot day and the water was cool, so it wasn't the most unpleasant thing at first. But the jungle air at the edge of the lagoon was close and her dress stuck to her in clumps now, not likely to dry anytime in the near future.

Her shadow seemed outraged; she shook herself from top to bottom and wrung herself out like a towel, throwing little shadow droplets everywhere.

Tinker Bell peeped out from a large monstera leaf she had managed to duck behind. Her eyes widened in wonder at the giant, salty droplets that ran down her green shield, but then she noticed the sopping wet human girl. She giggled, pointing.

"All right, all right," Wendy said gamely, trying to keep her smile. Her shadow straightened herself out and set herself back in place behind Wendy—but *very* behind Wendy, keeping her as a sort of bulwark against more splashes of shadow water. "Very funny. But really, I'm here for a rather serious quest. You see, Peter Pan has . . ."

"Peter Pan!" the red-haired one sighed, flipping herself onto her back and swimming dreamily across the lagoon.

"That Peter Pan . . ." A green-haired one whistled.

"What do *you* know of Peter Pan?" the purple-haired one still on the rock asked, eyes narrowing.

The pink-haired one swam up close to Wendy, near the bottom of her ledge, listening intently.

"Well, he and I have some things to . . . sort out," Wendy stammered. She didn't want to admit that she was responsible for his shadow now being in the hands of pirates—whom the mermaids obviously feared and hated. And they didn't seem to have a great attention span. It would be difficult to make it all the way to the end, when she explained how she was trying to make reparations for what she had done.

The pink-haired one grinned strangely up at her.

"Yes?" Wendy asked politely.

But the mermaid just fixed her with giant caramel eyes and held up a vine draped over her hands.

"I don't understand," Wendy said. "What—"

Suddenly, the mermaid yanked. The vine snapped taut; the other end clung to a tree that was *behind* Wendy. She was thrown headfirst into the water.

Not the best swimmer even in calm situations, Wendy panicked, throwing her arms over her face as if expecting another splash. She hit the lagoon in the worst sort of tangled position, mouth open as she tried to cry out.

Salt water immediately ran down her throat and up her nose. She coughed and choked and sneezed, flailing her arms around and trying desperately to right herself. Her dress swirled and caught around her legs and waist, tangling her limbs utterly and weighing her down.

Her toes touched the bottom.

This shocked her into thinking again, and she kicked off it toward the surface.

"HELP!" Wendy called out as soon as her mouth was out of the water—instead of breathing, which might have been a better call.

A mermaid took this opportunity to grab her hair and yank her head back.

Wendy's lower half flipped up as her torso bent backward underwater, forcing a river's worth of water up her nose.

She coughed and floundered. Opening her eyes underwater didn't cause any extreme discomfort, although what she *saw* did: the sinuous forms of mermaids cutting back and forth through the current, quick as knives.

She tried to paddle to the surface, old lessons finally kicking in. She pushed her legs hard, hoping to connect with one of the glittering, slick bodies.

Her left foot did, and it was just enough to propel her to the surface.

She didn't waste her chance this time; she sucked in a deep breath of air.

The mermaids leapt and porpoised around her, their

grins hard and white. Their mouths seemed a little wider than they should have been, their teeth even sharper.

One of John's random facts popped into her consciousness: how some sharks had *four rows* of teeth, one inside the other, to more quickly disembowel their prey.

"Tinker Bell!" she cried. "Help!"

The fairy hovered in the air, watching the commotion thoughtfully.

Or . . . could it have been . . . *disinterestedly?*

Slimy, strong hands grabbed Wendy's waist and tugged. Down.

But the mermaid didn't manage to pull her entirely underwater. She had expected the human girl to be as light and lithe as one of them.

So the next mermaid leapt *out* of the water and landed with her hands on Wendy's shoulders, trying to push her down from above.

Once again, this mermaid wasn't strong or heavy enough to do much besides dunk Wendy for a moment. But they were learning. Hands and mouths grabbed at her body and dress, pulling and pushing and trying to drown her with their combined efforts.

"Tinker Bell!" Wendy spluttered.

The fairy, hanging above the lagoon, shook her head slowly.

That was the second to last thing Wendy saw.

The last thing was the fairy flying off, away into the jungle.

Tinker Bell had given up on the human girl and her hopeless situation.

Wendy went under.

The Drying-Off Girls

Wendy's thoughts as the water closed above her head were a strange mix of things.

Primarily it was panic and survival, her body thrashing and arms circling, mouth shut tight, trying to keep from breathing in the water that was now all around her.

And obviously her mind touched a bit on her rapidly approaching and inevitable death.

But there was also a surprising amount of disappointment. She and Tinker Bell had finally been starting to make a connection, even if it was just over a common goal. The fairy had even given her pixie dust to fly! And then the little thing had revealed herself to be no better than any of the other heartless members of Never Land—pirates, crystal monsters, murderous mermaids. She was utterly selfish, only concerned with her own problems and adventures.

Wendy couldn't hold her breath any longer. She opened her mouth and . . .

The water was suddenly clear of mermaids and the weight holding her down was gone.

She popped to the surface like a child's toy in the bath, free of all hands, tails, mouths, and other impedimenta.

Coughing and spluttering—as quietly as she could—she sucked down great, painful gulps of air.

No one attacked her.

She kicked to the side of the lagoon, muscles screaming. Whatever had happened, she had to get out of the water before the mermaids returned.

She was almost too weak to pull herself up onto the ledge and scraped the sides of her legs raw while scrambling for a good foothold. Once finally up, her muscles and lungs desperately wanted her to lie there and recover. But Wendy forced herself to roll until she was a good arm's length away from the water and clear of any sneaky vines.

She took many amazing breaths while looking up at the sky. It was an intense deep blue and the palm fronds were black against the sun. It was bliss just to be alive. Even the little clouds of gnats hovering around her face didn't bother her. Anyway, they were sort of cute, with what looked like giant red and yellow feathers trailing from their heads and behinds.

Eventually she recovered enough to sit up. Salt water poured indelicately out of her nose and down the back of her throat, burning it even more. Water sloshed in her ears dizzyingly. If she hadn't known better, with the way her head was aching, she would have thought there was salt water up in her brains, too.

The mermaids were all still there, roiling in the water, lashing their tails and whipping up foam, fighting.

Each other.

"It's mine!" the purple one cried. She was no longer so queenly or stately upon her boulder throne. She was in the water with the rest of them, wide mouth even wider with toothy glee, holding up what looked like a piece of fruit. Something orangish but elongated like a banana.

"No, it's mine!"

The red-haired one leapt out of the water like a dolphin and snatched it out of her hands.

Two more mermaids dove after her, and so the roiling rebegan.

Tinker Bell hovered out of harm's way above the water, shaking her head disgustedly. She had another piece of fruit in her hands, a small reddish thing rather like an oversized cherry.

Now Wendy understood.

Legends told of how mermaids craved fruit because there was nothing like it in the sea. They would trade pearls and gems and long-lost treasures for a single apple, according to old sea chanteys the boys used to sing.

Tinker Bell had managed to distract the mermaids and make them turn on each other just by pelting them with bananas—like a mean child at the zoo.

"Oh, well done," Wendy tried to say aloud. It came out a rasping whisper. She coughed and more water came out—along with a thin trickle of blood. Nothing serious, she decided, being a practical girl not prone to flights of panic or hypochondria. It wasn't tuberculosis or cancer; it was just the result of her throat being scraped raw. But the taste and feel of it combined with the salt water threatened her already turbulent stomach.

Despite the whisper, Tinker Bell, with her fairy ears, had heard what she had said, or at least caught the tone of it. Her eyes widened in surprise.

"That was very clever. Very, very clever," Wendy said, her voice slowly gaining volume. "Good show."

Tinker Bell—*blushed?*—and gave a timid smile.

The purple-haired mermaid below took the distraction as an opportunity: she leapt high in the air to snatch at the cherry thing the fairy held.

Tinker Bell buzzed straight up out of reach, dropping the fruit as ballast as she went.

The mermaid caught it and laughed with glee.

Wendy glared daggers at the sea creatures as she wrung out her dripping, tangled, sodden hair.

These were the majestic beings she had imagined brushing it?

"You're quite *literally* the worst," she growled. "The. Worst."

The purple mermaid took a salacious bite out of the cherry and grinned at her wickedly.

The rest of the mermaids calmed down, the last of the fruit having been torn into several pieces and devoured by the lucky—or most vicious—ones.

"We were just having a little fun," the pink-haired mermaid said with a pout.

"Fun. That's *all*," the green-haired one said, floating on her back.

"We were only trying to drown you," the red-haired one added innocently.

"As I said," Wendy said flatly. *"The worst."*

Tinker Bell flew over to her, careful to avoid the reaching hands of the mermaids. She blanched when she saw the raw skin and sheets of blood on the human girl's legs. Wendy grimaced and ripped off a wide strip of hem from her already bedraggled skirt and carefully dabbed at the wounds. The salt water was, if not sterile, then at least safer than anything coming out of the jungle. Once her legs were clean, she tore the makeshift bandage in two, wrapped one around each leg, and tied them neatly.

"We came here to get your help in finding *your friend*, you know," she said when she was done. "And saving *your land*. We know where Peter Pan's shadow is and came here looking for him so we could get it back. And also—"

But it didn't matter that their entire world was being threatened by psychotic pirates; the mermaids only heard or cared about one thing.

"Peter Pan?"

They paused whatever they were doing at his name, bobbing in the water like floats on a fishing line.

"Why didn't you say you were here for Peter Pan?" one of them asked.

"I DID!" Wendy barked angrily, so unlike herself that Tinker Bell blew a couple feet away in surprise. "You were too busy trying to lure me into the water to listen. You horrible, murdering fishwives!"

"We didn't know it was about Peter *Pan*. . . ."

They began to dreamily glide and drift through the water.

"We know he lost his shadow. . . ."

"He hasn't been the same without it. . . ."

"So sad, our Peter!"

"We'll help him get it back. . . ."

"And then he'll be happy again!"

Wendy gritted her teeth, trying to control her temper.

"All right. You can start by telling us where Peter is. We were told he came here."

"He *did*!" the red-haired mermaid said, as serious as any toddler telling an actual truth. "He always comes here when he's sad."

"We cheer him up."

"We . . . make him happy again."

Tinker Bell grew red in the face, literally red, literally glowing, and her wispy brows became thunderheads.

"All right, yes, good, whatever," Wendy said quickly. She didn't want to hear any more, either, honestly. What a little harem he had here in Never Land! "When was that?"

"He came when the first moon was a tiny sickle," the green-haired one said thoughtfully, putting a fetching finger to her lip, deep in thought.

"An ickle-sickle," the red-haired one giggled.

"And he left just two mornings later!"

"No time at all with us, this time," one pouted.

"So *boring* . . ."

"So *sad* . . ."

"All right. Please stop. Tinker Bell, how long ago was that? I'm afraid I'm quite unfamiliar with the phases of the moon here. Moons, I suppose." For all she knew, time ran backward, or made no sense at all.

Tinker Bell cocked her head, thinking, then jingled four times.

"Four days ago? That's bad news," Wendy said grimly. "He could be anywhere by now. Did he mention at all where he was going?"

"Yes," the purple-haired one said grandly, trying to regain her original poise. "He said he was going to petition . . . the First."

At this, everything became silent. The mermaids stopped chattering and bobbing. The jungle noises faded into the background. Tinker Bell shuddered. Even the waterfall seemed subdued.

"All right, then, that's something," Wendy said, trying to sound bright despite the apparent dire connotations of the mermaid's words. "And where do we find 'the First'?"

"Hopefully," one mermaid said as she turned a lazy barrel roll, "you don't. And they never find you."

"Helpful. As always." Wendy stood up to wring out the rest of her skirts. "Thank you for the information. And who knows? If it turns out to be useful, I may *not* direct the pirates to your lagoon after we've dealt with them."

"Oh! You're so mean!" the pink-haired mermaid cried in dismay.

"*Really?* Are you *kidding* me?" Wendy demanded.

She felt a tiny tap on her hand.

Tinker Bell squeezed her finger and shook her head. *It's not worth it.*

Wendy realized the little fairy was right. If Tinker Bell, who had just as much—if not more—reason to hate these mermaids than Wendy, could walk away, well, so could she.

"Good day," she growled with as much dignity as she could muster. Feeling her dress drip-drop in tatters and streams behind her, her legs scandalously bare but for the bandages that now wrapped them, Wendy marched into the jungle unsure of the direction she was going except that it was *away from the mermaids*. Beside her was someone who might not be her friend yet, but who at least didn't seem to want to kill her.

Which was beginning to seem like a very rare thing indeed in Never Land.

Meanwhile, on the High Seas...

"I thought you said my idea was a good one," Mr. Smee said doubtfully from behind Hook. "I thought you was going to use the shadow like a sextant or compass or whatnot to find Peter."

The captain stood ramrod straight at the wheel, his lower jaw jutted out. That was one thing you could certainly say about Captain Hook—when he was moved by a plan (his own) or an emotion (his own) or a crazy idea suggested by another member of the crew (somehow reinterpreted as his own), his bravery and clarity of purpose surpassed those of the finest storybook hero. His antics might not have made a lot of sense to an outside observer, but he carried them through with the enthusiasm and fearlessness of a toddler who didn't know any better.

Right now the outside observers were his own crew, who pretended to do their tasks while visibly unnerved by the sea changes going on around them. Most gave up and just twiddled their thumbs or daggers, trying to listen in on the captain's plans.

"Yes, but the bloody thing's a *shadow*," Hook said with great disdain. "I can't put a gold needle in its mouth and align it with north, now can I? I need someone else's expertise on the matter. Outside direction on how to filter its essence into compass *form*."

"Yes, Cap'n, I see that, but . . ." Smee swallowed. "Madam *Moreia*?"

"I don't see anyone here with a better idea," Hook said with a sniff. "I don't like the idea too much meself . . . but there's times a villain has got to rely on a little help from his people. His *community*, as it were. Exchange some trade secrets. My expertise is piracy, not black magic. Moreia is conjured out of the darkest fears stupid little children have of old women and their unknown habits. She'll help. Out of professional courtesy, if nothing else."

"Unknown habits?" Zane protested, overhearing. "Everyone normal's got a granny. Smacks of ageism, don't it?"

"Not if it's *specifically* the unknown habits," Major Thomas suggested. "For years I didn't know that the foul-smelling cack me nanna smeared on her rump every morning was anti-wrinkle cream. Thought it was oils decocted from the placentae of unborn babes. So she could fly or sommat."

"What was the recipe?" the Duke asked, trying to sound casual.

"Oh, shut up, you lot. I said *stupid* children, didn't I?" Hook roared. "Who knows why they fear their old neighbors and not rabid dogs or Staphylococcus aureus or stepping out in front of oncoming carriages? Now SHUT UP and let me remember the passage over Soulsucker Reef!"

The heavens turned murky and thin. In patches between strangely resinous clouds, the sky was black with cold, un-glittering stars—despite its being late afternoon. A wind picked up, so hideous and unclean that even the most wretched pirates shuddered and held their noses against the foul stench. Polluted thoughts came with it, and not the usual familiar nightmares of witchery like ravens and cats and curses; these were presages of end-times: battle-fields crawling with things no longer quite human, the dead and decaying in piles on the ground to every horizon, the wrenching howl of the last person alive.

Far too quickly for some on board, a rocky island emerged out of the mist. Hook muttered *port port, starboard a bit, keep it steady* to himself, his eyes as cold and unblink-ing as the alien stars above.

There was a dock on the otherwise empty island. Despite the crew's desperate pleas to weigh anchor farther out, their captain refused.

"You, none of you, would still be here when I was done," was all he would say, without his usual bluster and speech-ifying. The truth was enough to silence the men.

Ever so carefully, Hook piloted the ship in. Strange apparitions appeared on the dock. Their mouths dripped to the planks and they flickered in and out of view at irregu-lar intervals . . . but they caught the ropes thrown down and tied them neatly to solid-seeming cleats. Soon, for bet-ter or worse, the boat was fastened tightly and in no danger of drifting off.

Captain Hook seemed almost jolly as he put on his hat and adjusted his mustache. "You're with me, Smee."

"I was really hoping you wouldn't say that," the other pirate murmured sadly, pulling his own cap down over his ears.

The captain grabbed a jaunty walking stick and saun-tered down the gangplank. "I don't think I need to tell you fellows no shore leave here, today," he called over his shoulder.

The island wasn't much more than a single rocky promontory rising up out of the sea like the longest claw of a dying antediluvian beast. On the tip of that claw was Madam Moreia's hut.

"What kind of witch lives on an island?" Smee muttered as they left the dock and clambered up the narrow path that spiraled around the island (allowing the witch several perfect views of approaching visitors). "Shouldn't she be in a nice snug little house in the woods somewhere, luring children in with candy and then eating them?"

"This is the oldest kind of witch, Mr. Smee. If you had any education at all, you would know all about the Greeks and their very, *very* scary witches."

"Guess I'm glad I never got a proper education, then," the other pirate said, looking around woefully.

At the top of the promontory they walked across a precarious bridge to the hut: a gnarled mess of driftwood, strange black vines, and what looked like seaweed or possibly human flesh stretched taut for a roof.

Hook took off his hat and rapped.

"Madam Moreia? It's Hook! Come to visit!"

The door opened of its own accord after a suitably spooky pause.

The inside of the hut was of course much larger than the outside, but so dark and cramped and filled with indistinguishable things that the effect was much less grand than it could have been. A primitive fire burned coals on the floor without a ring or anything around to contain it.

Tending the cauldron suspended above the flames was a bent-over old woman. Her skin was thick with grease and soot. Great ropy locks of hair were mounded on her head until they practically doubled her height. When she turned to fix a pair of milky eyes on her guests, Smee's heart almost stopped.

"Ah, Hook! Such a long time!" she cried, surprisingly merry. "How's my favorite handsome pirate captain?"

"Very well, Moreia, very well," Hook said politely, leaning over and submitting himself to a kiss on the cheek that left a gray lip print.

"You want something, don't you," she said with a sigh. "You never just come to visit. Ah, well, what's to be expected among the evil? Polite behavior? *Niceties?*" She cackled and slurped from the ladle she held. "I'm just cooking up a nice bowl of baby bits. Care for a bowl?"

"None for me, thank you," Hook said, trying to sound regretful. "Maybe Mr. Smee would."

"Who? *Oh.*" The witch looked up and made a big deal of winking at the first mate, although not quite in the right direction. Perhaps because of her cataracts. "What do you want, then? May as well get right down to business, eh?"

"Well, I'm having some *shadow* issues," Hook admitted with a sigh, sitting down in a comfy red-velvet chair whose hard parts were carved from human femurs and tibias.

"Shadows, mm? Tricky business. For mortals."

"Yes, well, it's *Peter Pan's* shadow. So trickier than most, I would say."

"*Peter Pan?* You're still chasing after that wretch? Well, well. Some things never change in Never Land."

"It is what it is." Hook crossed one leg over the other and sniffed with great dignity. "But I had this rather brilliant idea that I could use his shadow—currently in my possession—to lead me *to* him. Like a compass."

Mr. Smee nodded eagerly—then frowned, perhaps remembering where the idea had come from originally. Hook was careful not to look at him.

The witch sucked her tooth, stirring the soup thoughtfully. "Not a compass . . . There's problems with enchanting the shadow down so small. For long periods of time. Especially if you don't plan on staying near the equator. No, a compass won't work. You need something more human-sized. Like . . . a Painopticon."

"What's that?" Hook asked eagerly.

"I think it's the thing you're looking for. The engineering of it escapes me. Was mentioned in one of me books over there."

The witch gestured to a shelf, which had on it things that made even Hook squirm: moldering jars of foul-smelling ointments, shiny black plants that looked more liquid than fiber, cloches protecting half-fleshed skeletons that could have been human or reptile—and which moved a little when not looked at directly. *Also* a set of musty black-bound books, some of which had blinking eyeballs set in their covers.

"Splendid, splendid!" Hook said enthusiastically—concealing his disgust. "How much for the lot?"

"If you were a good fellow, I'd say free—the chaos and pain released by your attempting to use them would certainly make it worthwhile," the witch said with a smile that wasn't entirely unkind. "But since you're one of us, I have to charge. Let me see. . . ."

She waddled back and forth in front of her fire, a giddy, almost childlike look on her face as she tapped her tooth in thought.

Hook fidgeted.

Smee whispered, *"You don't think she'll make us get her more babies, do you, Cap'n?"*

"Even I have my limits," Hook whispered back.

The witch whirled around, and both men jumped like boys caught by a teacher.

"All the rum on your ship!" she declared happily. "Not the grog. The real, pure stuff. Also any cones of sugar. And a silk dressing gown."

"Absolutely," Hook said in relief. "Whatever you like. It is yours."

Moreia rubbed her hands together in excitement. Strange oils came off them but disappeared into dust and smoke before hitting the floor. Smee began to inch toward the exit.

"Oooh, I haven't had a real drink in years. And there's spirits like it, too."

"And you look like a woman who deserves a nice gown to eat your, er, breakfast in," Hook said politely.

The witch cackled. "Oh, the dressing gown is for a bit of a disguise. . . . There's a handsome young merman I rather fancy. And who, I might add, could stand to be taught a lesson or two."

"Well, I'll leave you to your projects," Hook said hastily, standing up.

The witch rolled her eyes and spat. "Least I'm honest about *my* issues. Chasing Pan, indeed. Put your anger at lost youth into violence, I say. Go burn some villages or raid one of the other islands. Become a despot. Keep yourself busy."

"I'll just have what you ordered sent up here by a couple of my men. With some extra goodies for you, of course," Hook said, pushing the door open with his rump and bowing out.

"Oh, you're too kind. I'll have one of my own 'men' bring you the books once I get what I want. I don't suppose I need to tell you there is no way your ship is leaving these waters until you hold up your end of the bargain?"

"And I don't need to tell you that my cannons are aimed at your lovely house on the off chance you don't hold up yours, of course."

"Always a pleasure, Hook." The witch grinned and blew him a kiss.

"For me as well." The captain tipped his hat before setting it on his head and closing the door behind him.

He and Smee stood for a moment in the dismal half-light of the weird island and its foul vapors, breathing deeply in relief.

"That weren't pleasant, if you don't mind me saying so, Cap'n," Smee eventually said.

"No . . . but I wonder," Hook said, thoughtful. "Maybe what we feel now . . . that's how people feel when *they* deal with pirates. I mean, we're frightening, too, aren't we? Killing and looting and looking generally fearsome . . . Isn't that why the heroes always come after us?"

"Never thought about it that way before, Cap'n," Smee admitted, scratching under his hat. "I guess that's why you're the cap'n, Cap'n! Always thinking the deep thoughts and whatnot."

"True," Hook said, nodding. "Too true, Mr. Smee. 'Tis a burden of leadership. You know, I will almost miss her when she's gone, with the rest of Never Land. Poor old witch. Now let's back to the ship. I want to get her the rum and be out of here as soon as we can. And I think it's high time for a bath and a shave. . . . I always feel unclean after dealing with her."

"That's the thing! One bath and shave coming right up, Cap'n, sir!" Mr. Smee said happily.

And the two brightly colored pirates descended the steep spiral path, the only red and blue and gold things for miles around. Hook's feather bobbed jauntily in the air. He even smiled despite the foul breeze.

Soon he would have the shadow showing the way. . . . Peter Pan was as good as gone, along with the rest of Never Land.

Steps

Tinker Bell's glow lit the dark understory of the jungle with a sprightly—if feeble—twinkling. Whatever triumph Wendy had felt upon surviving the mermaids soon dissipated into the dark, moist, enveloping atmosphere.

She was walking away from creatures she had dreamed of meeting since she was a very little girl.

"Thank you," she said aloud, eventually.

Tinker Bell looked at her.

"For saving me," Wendy elaborated.

Tinker Bell blinked, as if she hadn't thought about it. Wendy watched expressions flit over her face as quick and transparent as the wings of a dragonfly (or a fairy); there was no need for language. The fairy frowned, obviously recalling details of the previous hour. Then an expression of wonder and an unguarded smile appeared: she *did* save Wendy, didn't she? The smile grew into a rosy grin as she remembered her own heroics, a pleased, proud smugness settling over her features.

Finally she looked up at Wendy—as if just remembering that the person she had saved was still there. And perhaps that person was someone she didn't want to like.

She rolled her eyes and shrugged. *No big deal.*

"Well, it meant a lot. To me," Wendy said, refusing to let her companion retreat so easily from the conversation. "I didn't think . . . Well, I didn't think you were going to come back for me. I had thought you left. For good."

The fairy flew up toward Wendy's face, settling inches from her nose. She put her tiny hands on her hips in exasperation.

"Well, really, how was I supposed to know? You've made it quite clear that you don't have the fondest feelings for me. From the moment we first met. You were boxing me about a bit, remember?" She didn't mean to overemphasize her statement, but she couldn't help rubbing her arm where the fairy had pinched her extra viciously.

The fairy looked thoughtful.

"Well, you *did.*"

Tinker Bell really was like a child, Wendy decided.

Her intelligence and wisdom *in the moment* were certainly advanced and adultlike. But anything that required reflecting on previous moments or her own past behavior, any consideration of intangible elements like consequences or empathy, was as impossible as the close observation of a distant world. Tinker Bell of earlier in the day was an entirely different creature from afternoon Tinker Bell, alien and divorced from her.

The fairy looked left and right, as if trying to figure a way out of Wendy's rather obvious and telling statement. Then she cocked her head, as if remembering something, and opened her mouth, waggling a finger at the human girl.

"I know, I know! I sold Peter's shadow. I put all of Never Land in danger. I deserve your ire. Which makes it only *more* likely that you would abandon me to be drowned by the mermaids—especially if it looked hopeless." Wendy sighed, feeling the heaviness of the last few days fall solidly on her shoulders. "All I ever wanted was to be friends with a fairy, or a mermaid, and go on an adventure. I didn't mean for all of this to happen. I don't know how many times I can apologize, Tinker Bell.

"Look, I know I said we shouldn't discuss him anymore. . . . But really. Ask yourself. Why do you like Peter Pan?"

The fairy looked up, surprised at the apparent change in conversation.

"Is it because he's different from everyone you would normally spend time with? Is it because he leads you on great adventures? Is it because he draws you out of your pretty, delicate little bedroom and you get to battle pirates with him and do great things?"

Tinker Bell gave a tiny nod.

"*I* liked Peter—the idea of Peter—*for the exact same reasons.* I always dreamed of going on great adventures, of battling pirates, of exploring caves and finding treasures. Because there *are* no adventures or pirates in London. Not for girls, anyway. All of the stories I read are about boys and men. Oh, there are a few, rare female explorers . . . but I am not one of them. I need a little help to get going, do you know what I mean? I don't seem to be able to escape my own bedroom in London without someone giving me a bit of a push. Peter Pan would come and save me from all that dreariness.

"Had I known about you, and how you already had a . . . relationship with Peter, a strong and—perhaps rightfully—jealous one, I would have been much more careful. But I would still want *a* Peter Pan. I would still want adventure. But I would in no way have put myself between you and *the* Peter. Your Peter."

Tinker Bell frowned as she slowly processed these words.

"Really. You needn't have hated me," Wendy said with

a wan smile. "You could have just said something like . . . 'Back off, woman! The fair lad is *mine*!' And then we would have shaken on it. Or whatever it is dumb men do when they come to some dumb manly agreement."

The fairy's mouth tugged to the side in a snarky smile. She knew exactly what Wendy was talking about, the ridiculous gestures of a gender prone to extroversion.

"And then maybe you could have eventually introduced me to some fairy prince. . . ." Wendy said lightly, with a smile. "Just like my mother is always trying to get girls to introduce me to their brothers or cousins or whatever."

At this Tinker Bell frowned and made a little gagging motion, sticking her finger on her tongue.

"No, I suppose there's a reason you spend time with Peter and the Lost Boys, and not males of the fey kind," Wendy said, laughing. "Perhaps they are as boring to you as London boys are to me. Anyway, without Peter—or you—I had to find my way here myself. I didn't understand the cost or consequences. I'm getting my adventure finally, even if it's not exactly the one I wanted. I just wish—I really, really wish—we could travel together more as friends. I'm not your enemy, Tinker Bell. If I had known about you, I would have been your greatest fan."

Tinker Bell was silent. For once her face and body were unreadable, an enigma.

"Anyway, we should probably get going," Wendy finished, a little lamely. She already felt like she had pulled a real Wendy, talking too much, revealing too much, feeling too much. All in the open.

But Tinker Bell still seemed frozen in thought. Almost as if once Wendy had got her thinking about things she had never considered before she couldn't easily give them up, like a cat worrying a toy.

"You should probably lead," Wendy added politely, "Since I have no idea where we are going."

The fairy tipped her head back and took the human in, as if really looking at her for the first time. She paused for a moment in what appeared to be a *new* thought, judging by the spark in her eyes.

"What is it?" Wendy asked.

Tinker Bell opened her mouth. Widely. *Very* widely. Wider than it seemed should have been possible for such a tiny creature. Wendy couldn't help noticing familiar, almost mermaid-ish rows of sharp, perfectly white teeth. Was every resident of Never Land equipped with such weapons? Such mouths? How dangerous *was* this place?

"I don't know what you . . ."

Tinker Bell closed her mouth, then opened it again widely and pointed at Wendy.

"You want me to . . . ?" Wendy asked, opening her own

mouth—but not *quite* as wide as Tinker Bell had. She was a little self-conscious. Mother and Father had always told her to chew with her mouth closed, of course, and ladies didn't yawn or speak while eating, at least not without hiding behind a properly gloved set of fingers.

But she opened up a *little* wider, seeing the fairy's growing impatience and fearing her retribution.

"Ike ish?" she asked.

In answer, the fairy shook her wings and spun—hurling a stream of fairy dust directly onto Wendy's tongue.

Wendy and the Fairies (Finally!)

What Wendy felt was a spray of something that could only be described as *golden*. Light, effervescent, slightly dry. Fizzy, like the horrible mineral waters Mother sometimes made Father take to aid his digestion. But not with the terrible metallic taste. For the brief moment she could taste anything at all, it was sweet—or no, maybe sour like lemons. No, not that, either—more like sparks from a fire.

All too soon it was gone, down her throat or up her nose or dissipated into her flesh and brain.

A wave crashed through her body starting in her sinuses. She was frozen all over, and then sweating and shuddering, but in the next moment felt like herself again.

"What was—thank you—why did you—"

Tinker Bell jingled.

Can you understand me?

"Yes, of course, but what did you just . . . Wait, what?"

Just like that, like nothing at all, everything the fairy said made sense. Like it had always made sense when taken all together: her jingles, her wing flutters, her eye movements . . . The human girl just hadn't been able to understand it before.

"Your . . . dust," Wendy said slowly. "Somehow it allows me to understand you. The way everyone else can."

Tinker Bell shrugged and did a slow spiral in the air, apparently now bored with the conversation. She zoomed up to a palm leaf to examine a bug there: something like the unicorn beetles but with an iridescent rainbow mane that fluttered in the breeze. She jingled quietly and nuzzled it.

"Well, this will make things a lot easier," Wendy said happily. Did the dust allow her to understand just Tinker Bell, or all fairies? What about all the creatures of Never Land? How long would it last? Did it change other parts of her? Was it poisonous? If she had been doused with fairy dust to fly, and imbibed fairy dust to hear fairy language, how much more of her was there to infuse with the substance? Would she become—she secretly hoped—fairy herself?

Magical translating dust aside, she also understood

without anyone saying it that despite this apparent change in their relationship status, the fairy would still not stand for the usual Wendy-barrage of questions. They might be on better terms now, but they weren't bosom companions.

Not yet, at least.

"All right then," Wendy said, patting her dress down and dusting herself off—as best she could—while ordering in her head a careful list of questions she would dole out, slowly, over the course of her time with the fairy. "Where do we find these First?"

Tinker Bell shrugged.

"Oh," Wendy said, perplexed. "But—when they said that thing, about him going to see the First, you looked like you knew of them. You looked, if you don't mind me saying so, worried."

I am worried.

"About what? Are they dangerous?"

Tinker Bell swayed this way and that on a whisper-soft breeze so faint she might have summoned it with her own wings.

The First are . . . the first. The first inhabitants of Never Land. The first spirits of the place. Ancient. They were here before mermaids and pirates and fairies and the dreams of men. They are Never Land. Whatever Never Land was when it was born. We are all . . . a result of them, and you.

Wendy frowned, considering this. The history of Never Land had never occurred to her as a discrete idea before. Never Land was Never Land, a place of infinite happiness and adventure, where anything you could imagine was possible. Did theories like geology, the true age of the Earth, and Mr. Darwin's evolution hold for imaginary lands?

"Where do fairies come from?" she asked, thinking it was the simplest entry into a complicated subject.

The first laugh of a baby. A special baby. So they say. Tinker Bell smiled wryly. *We are here, we appear, sometimes there are more of us. I awoke under a leaf, curled up like a drop of dew, complete. Tinker Bell!*

But . . . also *we come the usual way.*

She made a face.

"But there *is* a connection between you and the imagination, the *minds* of human beings," Wendy hazarded.

I guess so.

"When I tell a story about Never Land to my brothers, am I making it up? Or am I just repeating something, which my inner mind already knows—a story that has already actually happened, in Never Land?"

Who knows? I don't.

Who cares? I don't.

"But we're talking about the nature of your existence! Your *world's* existence. Doesn't that make you wonder at all?"

I am. *You* are. *Everything else is talk.* Tinker Bell jingled, a little impatiently. *What's important is getting Peter's shadow back and figuring out how Captain Hook plans to destroy Never Land.*

"No, no, of course, you're right," Wendy said—but a little distractedly. She did *not* really agree. Details mattered to her. Which hand of Hook's Peter actually cut off, for instance. How many masts the *Jolly Roger* had. The precise workings of an entire world, the rules by which it existed . . . Well, besides soothing her constantly tumbling mind, knowledge was power. The more she knew about Never Land, the safer she was—and the more successful their quest would be. "But—just—what do they look like? The First, I mean?"

They do not look like men or fairies or mermaids or pirates or animals or insects or fish or plants. They look like nothing—and everything at once.

Wendy sighed. "All right. I see. But if they're so dangerous and unknowable, why do you think Peter went to see them?"

The fairy looked disgusted at yet another question. But then she thought about it.

Maybe he thought they could get him a new one.

"A new . . . shadow? Can the First do that?"

They are Never Land. Why did I give you the dust to hear if you won't listen?

"All right, all right. But—*would* they do it?"

At this the fairy looked troubled.

They don't talk or listen to reason . . . or they do things for their own unknowable reasons. Big things. Scary things.

"So they are opaque and random? Powerful and whimsical? Unknowable, inscrutable, and unpredictable, like an Old Testament sort of god?"

Tinker Bell looked at her for a long moment.

Sure.

"Lovely. I suppose we must go then and chase Peter Pan together to the demesne of these terrifying gods of Never Land. How do we go about finding them?"

Their place of being is never constant for very long. We will need to ask where they were seen last.

"Oh, dangerous whimsical gods—on something like the *Flying Dutchman*. This gets better and better. So how do we find out where they are?"

I have been asking the Small Friends, the many-legged companions of the woods. But I think we shall need to seek fairy help.

The *OOOOOOH!* that Wendy couldn't quite suppress in her throat had to be caught and killed physically with her hands: she clapped them over her mouth and held tight while the sound tried to come out.

Tinker Bell did something that was a like an eye roll

stopped midway, with a *tiny* smile thrown in for good measure.

Unfortunately, this is not the best place to do it. We're at the edge of the Qqrimal Range in the Pernicious Forest, and things live here that feast upon fairy kind. We tend to avoid this area. And we certainly don't draw attention to ourselves while here by gathering in groups. But hopefully there will be one or two of my kind about, traveling through.

Besides predators, my brethren avoid human contact. Hide somewhere and peep out.

"Absolutely!" Wendy breathed, only a little disappointed not to be involved in actually meeting them. *Watching* fairies up close was still more fairy contact than she'd ever had before . . . even if it didn't seem fair somehow, now that she could understand what they said.

She found a clump of shiny, large-leafed plants and arranged their long canes until her body was hidden from view. There was a nice hole in one of the leaves through which she could spy. The hole was still being worked on by a "Small Friend," a caterpillar with purple scales instead of fur. It looked at Wendy in dubious surprise. Or so Wendy assumed. It was hard to tell with its faceted but depthless golden eyes.

"Excuse me," she whispered. "I'll just be here for a moment."

She was unsure if the fairy dust gave her the ability to communicate with otherwise unspeaking Never Land creatures, but the thing *did* give her a long, hard look before going back to the business of chewing and ignoring.

Tinker Bell, meanwhile, was drifting with purpose up to the highest leafy branches of the jungle. Her light glowed warmly off the leaves below, the droplets seeping off their thick veins, the sweet sap running down the trunks of the trees. It made the whole clearing look . . .

Well, like it was touched by fairies, Wendy thought with a smile.

All her life she had looked for fairies in more mundane places, experiencing a rush of hope and warmth whenever a scene even palely imitated the one before her now. Candles at Christmas, fireflies in the park, flickering lamps in teahouses. The sparkling leaded glass windows of a sweets shop on winter afternoons when dusk came at four. A febrile, glowing crisscross of threads on a rotten log her cousin had once shown her out in the country: fox fire, magical mushrooms.

And here it was, for real! Tinker Bell was performing what appeared be a slow and majestic dance. First, she moved to specific points in the air around her, perhaps north, south, east, and west, twirling a little at each stop. Then she flew back to the center and made a strange bowing motion, keeping her tiny feet daintily together and putting her arms out gracefully like a swan. As she completed each movement, fairy dust fell from her wings in glittering, languorous trails, hanging in the air just long enough to form shapes. She started the dance over again, faster this time.

And again even faster. Her trail of sparkles almost resolved into a picture, crisscrossed lines constantly flowing slowly down like drips of luminous paint.

Wendy felt a bit like John, overwhelmed with a desire to try to reduce and explain and thereby translate the magic. But she also felt a lot like Michael, with an *almost* overwhelming urge to break free from her hiding place and see it up close, to feel the sparkles on her nose, to run a hand through the sigils not for the purpose of destruction but from a hapless, joyful desire to be part of it all.

Tinker Bell finally stopped, breathing heavily.

Wendy held her own breath.

And then . . .

Out of the darkness . . .

An answering glow.

The Never Land Empyreal

Like a firefly in the mists or fish from the darkest deep, the light came bobbling through the jungle gloom. This one was tinged orange like the last ember of a really good fire. Wendy felt warm all over just looking at it.

The tiny ball of light soon resolved into another fairy. She had darker skin than Tinker Bell's that was orangey red at the tips of her ears—which were a little longer than the other fairy's, and more pointed. Her hair was hard to focus on, more foam or spirit than actual strands: a cloud of dark reddish brown that had ribbons dividing it into two big puffs, each the size of her head. She wore a simple poncho belted around the middle—but it was hemmed nicely and not ragged like Tinker Bell's. The belt was prettily tooled and had an intricate metal-and-gem buckle that

Wendy desperately wanted a closer look at (with a magnifying glass).

Well, I didn't even know you knew the Call.

If Wendy had expected some sort of intricate fairy greeting ritual, she was more than taken aback by the new fairy's *very* casual tone.

Tinker Bell opened her mouth, and Wendy waited, wincing, for her usual intemperate response.

Instead, the fairy took a deep breath.

I know the Call, sister. I am fairy.

Really? I haven't seen you at any of the midseason fetes, or the blossom gatherings, or the acorn hunts, or . . .

I don't like crowds.

You don't seem to like much of what it means to be fairy.

More and more was revealed about Wendy's temperamental little friend! Fairies were apparently gregarious—social creatures, like people. Or horses. Not the lonely solitary haunters of hills and isolated groves Wendy had imagined, who came together for the rare dance around a ring of mushrooms.

But Tinker Bell obviously shunned the company of others like herself, preferring the company of a few giant humans like Peter Pan.

I need help. Tinker Bell put out her arms in supplication, trying to change the subject.

I'll *say,* the other fairy retorted with a raised eyebrow.

Then: *I was hoping this was a Friends Invite; I don't usually travel so far into the Pernicious Forest. It's dangerous—there are qqrimals around here, you know. I'll bet you don't even have any nectar or cake to offer a weary fellow traveler, do you?*

Tinker Bell shook her head morosely, looking at the ground.

Wendy started to fumble around in her bag. Along with her hastily thrown-together belongings, she was sure there was a packet of throat lozenges, maybe a mint pillow or two. Then she remembered her main directive: to stay hidden. She couldn't help out her little companion even if she wanted to. Reluctantly, she settled back down.

A third glow appeared during this awkward silence; it zipped along more definitively through the gloom and then stopped in the space next to the two fairies, revealing itself to be a fairy prince.

All right, perhaps it was just a male fairy.

But either way Wendy was thrown. He was *devastatingly* handsome.

He had bark-brown skin and high cheekbones and a broad chest—and he sported a neatly folded kilt and sash that did little to cover said chest. His head was shorn and his ears were extremely long, tapering to filaments that waved gently as he spoke. A weapon like a sword hung from his waist, hilt-less and slender and golden.

Even at his diminutive size, he radiated confidence, martial skills, and a general calmness that spoke to all the best characteristics of a leader of men *or* fairies.

Oh, it's Tinker Bell! What a surprise. And hello, Berryloon.

He was polite enough to Tinker Bell, but he bowed to the other girl.

It's more than a little dangerous for the three of us to be gathered together here like this—every qqrimal in the area will sense our presence. What's the emergency?

I don't know, ask her, Berryloon snorted, tilting her head at Tinker Bell.

I have to find the First. Have either of you seen them, or heard about them lately?

Both the fairies looked shocked at her question.

What is this about? the boy fairy asked seriously. *Are you in trouble?*

Tinker Bell looked a little cagey. *No—not me.*

Who then?

Peter Pan has lost his shadow, and seeks them out for help.

Berryloon burst out laughing. The male fairy just looked greatly disappointed. Wendy cringed, feeling like the look was directed at her as well.

Bell, let the boy to his own fate, he suggested, putting a hand on her shoulder in a brotherly fashion. *For how long are you going to keep rescuing and following after that big ugly human?*

He's not human! Tinker Bell responded angrily, so angrily that she put her hands on her hips and her backside lifted up as her wings buzzed.

All right, calm down, he's not . . . exactly . . . human, the boy said soothingly—while giving Berryloon an eye roll. *But his friends are. Tinker Bell, if he's such a great not-human adventurer, he can take care of himself. And* you *can come with us to the Pinkpetal Harvest!*

Oooh! Berryloon—well, *squeaked* would be the closest approximation to the way she jingled. She spun and grabbed the boy fairy's hands. *Me too! Let's be partners! We could even trio, if little miss boring wings here will come. . . .*

As nasty as it sounded, Wendy could tell that Berryloon was making a real effort to reach out to Tinker Bell. The offer was genuine despite her tone, whatever it all meant.

Tinker Bell shook her head. *I have to find Peter. I know where his shadow is—it's with the pirates. And they're planning to destroy all of Never Land! Peter needs to hear about this before he reaches the First and makes some sort of terrible bargain. Or mistake. And then we'll go after Captain Hook and stop him.*

Planning to destroy all of Never Land, Berryloon sneered. *Uh-huh.*

The boy fairy sighed, shaking his head. *It sounds like just another round of games between Peter and the pirates. But all right, Bell. A comrade of mine saw the demesne of the First appear on the northwestern corner of the island, at the base of the Chanting Peninsula, east of the Shimmering Sea.*

Thank you, Tinker Bell said with relief, and gave him a little bow.

Good luck, weirdo, Berryloon said with a toss of her head. *Guess we'll see you next time you need something, or you finally tire of the company you keep. Shall we?*

Hand in hand, she and the boy fairy rose perfectly in tandem, more gracefully than the most skilled ballerinas Wendy had ever seen, more smoothly than any ice-skaters.

And then—just before they disappeared into the depths of the jungle darkness as little bobbing glows, the boy fairy turned and winked.

Directly at Wendy.

She fell back, overcome by the direct, smiling gaze of the tiny man-at-arms.

Strange thoughts popped into her head: shrinking, or growing, clinging to a boy as he rode up into the air on the winds, his dragonfly wings beating strongly behind them.

Breathless, she staggered out of her hiding place, feeling a trifle disconnected from things.

Seeing Tinker Bell knocked sense back into her. The little fairy was hanging in the air like an old toy tied to a string to amuse a baby or a cat but then forgotten: she twisted a little right and then left as the breeze nudged her. Her gaze was fixed on the disappearing lights of her "friends."

Poor Tinker Bell!

How entirely wrong Wendy had gotten her! What she had *thought* was fairy affectation—artfully ragged dress, tousled hair in a messy bun, snobby and antisocial behavior—was not *de rigueur* for fairies at all. The other two seemed to spend all of their time at parties and gatherings. They both had neatly tailored apparel complete with perfect, high-fashion little accessories. Tink cared less about her appearance than whatever quest she was currently on, whatever fun she was having, whatever the Lost Boys and Peter were up to, whatever her own mischief involved.

Oh yes, Tinker Bell did appreciate the finer things, like her delicate little bedroom. But on her own terms and, most importantly, on her own. She didn't fit in with other fairies. And *they* obviously had issues with her chosen way of life.

No wonder she was so enamored of Peter Pan. She finally had a companion like herself. And of course she would be jealous and unwilling to share—without him, she might be alone.

"Tinker Bell?" Wendy said softly.

The fairy spun around in the air, obviously not having heard her approach. Her eyes were filled with brightness and wet. She shook her head to physically remove any traces of emotion and crossed her arms resolutely.

"Tinker Bell, I . . ."

Wendy bit her lip. The sort of person who abandoned her extremely cozy people to live a wild life with an unapproved-of boy, a girl who wore tatters and didn't care . . . well, she wouldn't be the sort of girl eager to discuss her feelings. She was obviously already embarrassed by what the human girl had witnessed.

"I feel like we should get started on our way to this Enchanted Peninsula, shouldn't we?"

Tinker Bell let out an audible sigh, relieved at the direction Wendy's statement had gone.

Chanting. Not "Enchanted." *You'll understand when we get there.*

"All right then. Let's—"

And that's when the creature leapt from the bush, grabbing Tinker Bell out of the air.

The Qqrimal

It was all predator. Sleek and slinky and black and lithe. Its paws had claws, long curled half-moons that easily ripped through the fairy's dress and closed around her waist.

Without thinking, Wendy threw herself at it, grasping at the beast with her own hands, naked, pink, and clawless.

One would suppose that after her experiences in Never Land she might stop and think twice about engaging a strange creature, an unknown entity who might have had any number of unpredictable and magical attacks. But the thing's closest approximation to any London beast was *cat*; an angry, starving alley cat. Fierce but not indomitable. Wendy had her share of experiences with those, ranging from pulling them off hapless songbirds to begging her parents to let her keep one.

And in fact, the twin mirrors on the front of its snub face could have been mistaken for cat's eyes with a light shining into them.

"Down!" Wendy cried imperiously.

Her hands closed tightly around its middle—but it didn't yowl as she expected. It dropped the fairy in shock . . . then sort of *thinned out* between Wendy's fingers. The creature slid through them like oil, dripped to the ground, and reformed into a weaselly, mink-like critter.

"Ugh!" Wendy looked at her hands. But they were clean and all she had actually felt was the soft fur one would expect.

With barely a pause the creature found Tinker Bell and again leapt on her.

The little fairy was a bit stunned and shaken up by its first attack; she was still on the ground and stumbling.

She emitted exactly half a jingle-wail before it had body-slammed her, smashing her straight down into the ground.

"I said, get *off*!" Wendy cried. She grabbed the first stick she saw and—though usually opposed to violence toward animals—whacked the qqrimal as hard as she could on its side.

It rolled out of the way but kept its claws around Tinker Bell, the fairy close to its belly.

Then it jumped upright on its four paws and—laughed?

"You—you—" Wendy stammered, indignant.

It really was. The horrible thing *was* laughing at her, chuckling and warbling. It bent its head and licked Tinker Bell with an ugly gray forked tongue. It smacked its mouth.

Wendy brought the stick down as hard as she could on its head.

It easily leapt out of her reach, landing on the side of a tree. From this new perch it chuffed one more time back at Wendy before scuttling up like a lizard into its branches.

"No!" Wendy dropped her stick and grabbed the trunk of the tree. "Come back! Come down here this *instant!*"

She shook the tree as hard as she could, expecting disappointment. But the tree was a slender tropical thing whose body was far more lithe and pliable than its London counterparts. It swayed easily under her efforts, and its long leafy fronds clattered and clashed satisfyingly.

The creature fell and hit the ground with an equally satisfying *whomp*.

"Tink!" Wendy grabbed the creature's tail to yank it off the fairy.

Only—its tail slid into nothing in her hands. Overpowered by the momentum she had created with nothing to balance it, Wendy fell back onto her bum.

The creature looked back at her and chuffed again.

Faint jingling sounds could be heard (pitifully) from under its stomach.

LIZ BRASWELL

The qqrimal waggled its tail at Wendy and took off into the forest. Tinker Bell dangled from its mouth; the poor fairy jingled desperately as it disappeared into the bushes.

"No!" Wendy got up and ran after it as fast as she could. Flying was out of the question—she wasn't an expert and the understory of the jungle was far too dense for her to even consider it.

And she already had a late start; the smaller, more lithe carnivore easily leapt over obstacles and slunk under them.

Wendy also jumped over fallen trees and ducked under canopies of vines, trying to keep the thing in her sights— but she was much, much slower. The qqrimal was black as shadow and made almost no noise as it flowed on the forest floor, just a pitter-patter and occasional chuff.

She burst out into a hot clearing, an empty hilltop whose dry pinnacle could support little life. The sun beat down like a physical force. It was no longer a happy lemon; it was a blazing ball of fire. Wendy spun around, looking for signs of the qqrimal. But the ground was dried and cracked mud that recorded no footprints. The edges around the outside of the clearing were staffed by half-dead, yellowed trees that all looked the same.

There was no hint of the creature.

"TINK?" Wendy cried. "Tink?

"No," she murmured, turning and turning.

"No!" she cried again, and her voice fell flat and quiet in the thick fetid air.

"TINKER BELL!" she screamed.

But the jungle was silent.

A Shadow (of a) Doubt

There was a very thin line between panic and giving up.

Wendy was filled with rage and terror—but also a split second away from collapsing onto the ground and weeping. And that would be the end of everything.

If she just started running—in the wrong direction—she would merely *continue* in the wrong direction and get farther and farther from the creature and the fairy.

If she retraced her steps looking for clues, she would be wasting time.

The image came to her mind ruthlessly unbidden: the black, formless creature biting down on the fairy's midriff; the resulting terrible *crunch*.

"TINKER BELL!" she screamed until her voice cracked.

Nothing.

Wendy choked back a sob and pulled at her hair. What to do? What would a hero do? What would Peter Pan do? What could *she* do? Where was the terribly clever deus ex machina or plot device that she would write for her own heroes?

What sort of nightmare creature *was* that thing—that qqrimal—anyway?

At least the crystalline guardian from before had made some sort of sense, pulled out of Michael's angry toddlerhood and a doll he had made out of clay. This animal was far too precise, too detailed for his young mind. And John would never have imagined something so horrible and vicious. Secretly he loved fairies as much as Wendy and delighted in designing the twig and acorn contraptions they used to simplify their forest tasks.

"What sort of child would come up with a carnivorous beast that *eats* fairies? That hunts and devours and tears them apart?" she wailed.

But of course there were other children besides the Darlings who believed in Never Land.

Children who . . . delighted in the destruction of fairies? Who hated beauty?

Or who didn't believe beauty was possible? That only ugliness and horror survived?

What kind of children were they—what were their lives like?

Wendy shivered.

"What do I do?" she whispered. What *could* she do, when there were monsters like these and worse roaming the fairy-tale world she had thought was safe?

That was when she noticed her shadow.

The black shape was doing the equivalent of jumping up and down—elongating and contracting, still connected to Wendy's feet. She waved her arms frantically, trying to get Wendy's attention.

"What? What is it?"

The shadow bent down and pulled at her feet. Then she stretched her arms, making a flying gesture, and pointed into the woods.

"What do you—oh, you want me to release you? So you can go look for Tinker Bell?"

The shadow nodded vigorously.

"You think you can find her?"

The shadow nodded again.

"But even if you find her—how can you help her until I get there?"

The shadow shook her head: *no time.* She pointed at their feet again.

"Oh. I suppose there isn't much of a choice, really, is there?"

The shadow nodded vigorously.

Wendy bent down, unsure what to do exactly. She placed her hands on her left foot and made as if to untie a boot.

Something . . . *gave.*

It felt like something untied from her belly and slid out through her feet. A wave of nausea washed over her, leaving her enervated. Everything, even standing, suddenly seemed exhausting.

It wasn't a simple thing to release one's shadow, Wendy realized. It wasn't all fun and games and a funny quest to reunite with it. The shadow—in Never Land, at least—contained something besides a lack of light and mimicry of movements. Some very visceral part of Wendy was in her shadow. And when she let go . . .

"You *will* come back to me, after you find her, right?" she asked before reaching for her other foot.

The shadow shrugged and shook her head.

No time.

No time to stop and think. No time to consider the ramifications.

"For Tinker Bell," Wendy told herself sternly and untied her right foot.

The shadow shot off out of the clearing, into the woods.

Wendy slumped to the ground.

Her energy and strength weren't *all* gone, she figured out after a few silent moments. She could still move and still stand up with a little effort. It was more like she didn't really care to.

"It's like I have the chills, or a cold, but of the soul," she said aloud to cheer herself up. "Nothing so *very* serious. Manageable. Peter has done without a shadow for four years. Certainly I can go an hour."

She did a few stretches and was satisfied with the way her body responded. Weakly, but up to the task if pressed.

She just hoped her shadow was going to do what she said—what Wendy *assumed* she was saying. That she would go find Tinker Bell before it was too late and somehow signal to Wendy. After all, despite whatever influence Never Land had, she was still Wendy's shadow. The shade of a good, well-meaning, honest girl must be a little good herself.

Unless all of Wendy's worst behaviors were contained in her shadow.

Like her betrayal of Peter Pan . . .

Wendy had a few long minutes of pondering these oppressive thoughts. But before she even thought it was possible there came a strange and ominous crashing in the woods. As if something was being flailed wildly back and forth. Thrown into the bushes, picked up, and thrown again.

And was that—was there the faintest jingle?

"Tinker Bell!"

Wendy made her feet move in the direction the sounds were coming from as quickly as she could manage.

She often had to stop, pause to listen, run the wrong way for a moment, trip over a plant, then turn the *right* way again (at least seven times), the way all heroes do when chasing through the woods on a rescue mission.

Like all good heroes she eventually found her quarry. But the scene made no sense at all when she first came upon it.

The qqrimal seemed to be throwing *itself* around violently. It growled, shook its head, leapt headfirst into a tree, then flowed down its trunk—and then began the whole thing over again. Like a dog with hydrophobia.

Tinker Bell was still clutched in its paws.

Wendy crept up quietly—but it didn't seem to see her at all.

When she accidentally stepped on a twig and snapped it, *then* the creature leapt up, alert.

Looking the wrong way.

Carefully, unsure what was going on, Wendy came up behind it as silently as she could, as close as she could.

She grabbed it by the nape of its neck.

Swinging it around quickly before it could flow out of her grasp, she seized its stomach with her other hand. She had to keep tossing it from hold to hold so it couldn't use its tricky thinning-out powers to escape.

The thing yowled and growled and hissed and batted out with his hind legs. It snapped is jaws wildly in all the wrong directions.

Something strange was going on with its mirror eyes. They looked dull and unseeing.

Wendy tore Tinker Bell out of its grasp and then slammed the qqrimal into the ground. Perhaps harder than was strictly necessary.

"Tink—are you all right?" She held the crumpled and bruised little fairy up for a better look.

Tinker Bell nodded woefully. She was bleeding, but not from the giant punctures Wendy had expected from the creature's claws. More like scratches from being shaken around while in its grasp.

It was taking me back to its lair. They don't like . . . fresh *fairy meat.*

"Oh!" Wendy said, swallowing.

The qqrimal stood up woozily, swaying and sick.

A black mist—no, *shadow!*—peeled itself off its face.

Wendy's shadow had covered its eyes, using herself as a mask!

The animal shook its head and blinked its eyes, back to their normal shiny silver. It gave Wendy a wounded, irritated look.

Wendy, pulling a Tinker Bell, stuck her tongue out at it.

The qqrimal leapt away into the underbrush and

disappeared as fast as it could—this time without a single snarky chuff.

Wendy's shadow triumphantly unfolded herself and stood tall, hands on hips. Her toes touched Wendy's and the human girl could feel energy and strength pour back into her.

"That was very clever!" Wendy crowed. "You blinded him! Oh, very clever indeed!"

The shadow bowed.

Then she saluted.

And then she took off.

Disappeared into the woods like the qqrimal, but high: into the branches of the canopy layer.

Wendy stumbled but didn't quite fall.

"I suppose I should have expected that," she muttered. "No one helps for free around here."

Tinker Bell, despite her wounds, looked up at the human girl with pity and concern.

That was brave and noble, giving up your shadow for me. Thank you.

"Well, what else was there to do, really?" Wendy asked, a little more tiredly than she wanted.

After the way I treated you—

"I mean, that's a fair point," Wendy said with a faint smile. "You're welcome."

I don't deserve it.

You can't go back to London now.

"What?" the human girl asked, startled.

(Well, that was interesting, at least: she could still feel panic, though muted, in her shadowless state.)

You can't return home without your shadow.

"But why? Peter left his own shadow in London. And he returned here!"

Peter is almost pixie. You are entirely human. Shadows are different here. They are less of a . . . requirement than they are in London. The rules of your world are very strict about that sort of thing.

I'm sorry.

"But I didn't *want* to go back to London," Wendy protested.

It was a little bit of a lie: she had always thought she would return, otherwise she wouldn't have insisted on a return ticket from the pirates.

And now that it looked like that option was taken away, she was suddenly a lot more concerned about it.

Never see Michael and John again?

Mother and Father?

Nana?

Even the evil old Shesbow twins, the smokestacks, the roofs, the clouds?

Tinker Bell seemed to read her mind. *You gave up a lot for me. More than you knew.*

"Well, I can't think about any of that now," Wendy told Tinker Bell—and herself—firmly. "Before anything else, we must rescue *Peter's* shadow and save Never Land. I can't go home until everyone here is safe. So let us continue to make our way to the En—no, the *Chanting* Peninsula. Are you well enough to travel?"

Tinker Bell looked at her with wonder. She nodded once.

"And is it very far away? Because—I'm afraid to admit it, but I'm a bit done in. All these adventures really wear a girl out. I'm dying to sleep." Wendy was very, *very* shaky in fact, but she ground her teeth and tried to sound as blasé as possible. The loss of her shadow made all of her aches and pains and tiredness worse—the exact opposite of the fairy dust.

Sleep on the way. That's what we do.

And although the idea of tiny winged creatures sleeping high in the sky with clouds for their cushions was positively delightful, Wendy couldn't see herself doing it without heading directly into a thunderhead, or a cliff, or the mouth of some sort of horrid Never Land creature.

"Oh, Tinker Bell, I don't think I could. I'd be terrified of falling, or smashing into something."

Tinker Bell smiled. *Go to sleep. I'll watch you.*

"Are you certain? I won't be afraid if you really will keep an eye on me. Sorry about being such a terrible burden. Big ugly human and all. Utterly useless."

Tinker Bell opened her mouth and out came great peals of strange, jingly laughter. Then she grabbed Wendy's hand and pulled her aloft, into the darkening sky.

The First

The next few hours were strange.

Or maybe it was a day, or a half day, or two. . . .

A glorious sunset performed its final bows across Never Land. Dark purple clouds rolled out along a horizon edged in fiery orange so bright it was like looking into the depths of a blacksmith's forge. The first stars were entering with some confusion into the not-quite-black sky. It was delightful to see them floating in a sea of turquoise ether.

"How often do they get to do that?" Wendy wondered aloud tiredly.

Tinker Bell kept rising up and up into the sky and then pausing, then dipping down, then going sideways—and then repeating the whole procedure. Wendy had just summoned enough energy to ask her what she was doing when, with a bright look of satisfaction, the fairy apparently found whatever she was looking for and dragged the human girl through the air to her.

Aha!

Wendy suddenly realized what the invisible object of her friend's search was: a calm thermal wind. It was so large and encompassing that when she slipped into its embrace the howling breezes of the upper airs immediately became silent, as if in the presence of a king. Here it was surprisingly warm and scented with things that didn't seem to come from the jungles of Never Land: exotic but somehow familiar, like Mrs. Darling's perfume when she kissed her daughter before going out.

Wendy had no trouble at all curling up on this invisible bed, and sleep came quick despite the confusing scenes she saw between languorous blinks. Instead of crisp sheets, comforting fire, and downy quilt, she saw nothing but empty space, sharp mountains, and trees a thousand feet below. But not even these could keep her from unconsciousness.

She drifted, literally and figuratively, the whole night, Tinker Bell always close by. One time the little creature took a sit-down *on* her, lying back on the big girl's shoulder and watching the stars. Wendy remained silent and as still as she could, reluctant to disturb her.

Eventually, the fairy woke Wendy with a tug on her ear—back to her usual naughty tricks. But as the human girl started, indignant, she saw that the sun was close to rising. More importantly, the fairy held a rather ridiculously sized rubyfruit to break her fast with. These were the fruits that heroes stranded on a desert island in Wendy's stories always hoped to find to quench their thirst and save themselves from starvation.

Wendy sat up as best she could on nothing.

"Thank you, that's most kind." She took the rubyfruit and popped off the stem like she had in dreams. It fell neatly into ten perfect, juicy sections. "Would you like one?"

Tinker Bell shrugged nonchalantly but took a section and immediately sank her face into its pale, creamy flesh, tearing out mouthfuls while somehow managing not to get any juice on her face. A delicate, civilized little beast.

It was rather funny when Wendy thought about it. Despite Tinker Bell giving Wendy the gift of understanding fairy tongue, they had just had an entire conversation without the fairy speaking a single word. In fact, most of Tink's communicating still seemed to be in gestures, facial expressions, and body movements. They weren't just affectations or simply to enhance understanding for those who couldn't decipher jingles; this was really just how Tinker Bell spoke. When she had to she could be as articulate and verbose as anyone else—including other fairies, who spoke clearly and wordily and whose hands didn't move at all during discourse (like well-trained boarding school ladies). Tinker Bell's meaning was wrapped up in movement; she *was* energy and gesture.

Wendy ate another piece of fruit and turned to watch the east. She wasn't normally fond of sunrises because she was barely awake when they occurred and because they signaled the end of the peaceful quiet of the house. Others rose at that time, and Wendy had to deal with the various personalities and problems of the day that were outside her own head. Sunrises were never spectacular in London, anyway: just a yellowish lightening of the fog, or, on a really clear day in autumn, a brightening of rare blue sky somewhere behind all the rooftops. Perhaps in some neighborhood east of the Darlings' house, east of their street, east of the park, east and east and east, maybe *someone* at the edge of London saw the sun come up properly, from behind something natural like the sea or a forest edge. But no one else did.

Now two days in a row Wendy got to witness the real thing, Never Land–style. First came the strange false dawn that presaged the sun's appearance, like the hopeful breath of an audience before a famous chanteuse steps out onto stage.

Taking its own time, the lemony Never Land sun finally

rose—and surprisingly hot for the morning, its first rays hitting Wendy's skin with an almost tangible pressure.

Through all this, the air and the sunlight, came a strange vibration.

At first Wendy's brain almost dismissed it, thoughtlessly categorizing the repeated drone as "waves crashing on a shore." But the girls weren't low enough to hear any waves—and they weren't over a beach at all. So her mind tried to resolve the sounds into words or hums: *ommm, nam-nam-nam-nam ommmmm* and strings of only slightly more complicated sounds.

Tinker Bell saw her frowning and smiled.

Chanting Peninsula, she jingled. *Get it?*

"Oh! Yes! Not 'Enchanted'! The whole peninsula . . . *chants.* That's amazing! But what is it that makes the sounds, specifically?"

Tinker Bell shrugged, no longer interested in the question or the subject. She pulled Wendy's sleeve and pointed down: directly beneath them was the recognizable forest of Never Land, and there, just beyond it, was . . . a blank wall.

Clouds, gray and white and eggshell and beige and every not-quite-color in between drifted over each other in unhealthy layers. Fingers of mist spun out almost purposefully, ensnaring a tree or a rock and then using that anchor to crawl along farther. Yet in other places the mist stretched thin and snapped away from wherever it was before, revealing seemingly untouched foliage and landscape beneath it. Wendy wasn't sure what she expected—dead land? Changed, unfamiliar objects?—but was nevertheless surprised the magical fog moved on without altering anything in its wake. It didn't *look* harmless.

Inside the mist itself, however, something seemed not quite right. There were hints of pale brown or orange, with ochre . . . some surface that reflected light not from the sun that was now twinkling over Never Land; a different star perhaps, dun-colored and morose. Wendy shivered. The pirates were frightening, the crystal guardian was murderous, and the mermaids were surprisingly hostile, but this . . . this was a hint of the completely unknowable. And far, far more terrifying.

Tinker Bell pointed down and began to descend, spiraling like a drill.

"But why?" Wendy asked, coming somewhat clumsily after her, skirts flying up into her face as she desperately tried to hold them against her thighs. "Can't we just skim low under the fog, and search for Peter that way?"

One does not simply fly into the Land of the First.

"I don't suppose it should have been that easy," Wendy said with a sigh. She landed fairly elegantly and slowly—she thought—touching her tippy-toes down to the ground first the way Tinker Bell did. The two girls reluctantly regarded the strange, unwholesome smog before them as it coiled around itself like the intertwined bodies of mythic serpents. Jörmungandr or perhaps Ouroboros.

Though Wendy could not have possibly known it, the fairy and the human had the exact same expression on their faces: wonder, distrust, false bravery.

Tinker Bell tentatively reached a tiny, bauble-decorated toe into the mist—and then quickly pulled it out.

"I don't want to suggest anything untoward," Wendy said after a full moment's hesitation, "but, since you said one shouldn't fly here, well, if you don't think it's beneath you, perhaps you wouldn't object to sitting—*riding* rather, on my shoulder? That way we will be on equal footing, together, with whatever comes at us. Also you wouldn't be lost, or stepped on, or . . ."

But the fairy was already zooming up to her neck. She perched daintily on the crook of Wendy's shoulder and held on to a lock of brown hair—but less like reins and more for balance and possible security. She did not tug.

"Very well then," Wendy said, lifting her chin and trying to muster bravado and dignity appropriate to the moment—and to disguise how tickled she was at the closeness of the fairy, despite their circumstances. She could just feel the tiniest weight on her skin and the occasional brief heat of a speck of fairy dust.

Together, they entered the mists.

The first thing that struck Wendy was how it felt nothing at all like she had expected. The clouds were neither damp, nor moist, nor cold. They were *hot*, and somehow drier than the land around them. Yet they didn't smell of smoke or smog or anything burning.

Strange noises streamed past her ear: whispers she couldn't quite make out, the distant echo of something very large pounding off in the distance. A rhythmic beat whose direction she couldn't put her finger on.

Then the flat yellow, white, and gray entirely surrounded her, masking the world. There was no distance or perspective. She closed her eyes and tried to put her feet in the same direction she had been heading. There was nothing else to do. And since nothing was *touching* her, there was no immediate threat to worry about.

After some period of time she couldn't quite keep track of, the whispers quieted. She opened her eyes. Like tears after a good cry, the mists quickly dried and disappeared— or perhaps they rose up, joining the uncolored sky to make a complete dome of gray and beige around everything.

They stood in what appeared to be very much a desert.

Wendy, of course, had never seen one in real life but had read enough adventure novels and explorer's narratives to recognize one when she saw it. Sadly, the ground was not quite as dramatic as the sands of Egypt were described; not an endless ocean of dunes and ripples, solid waves and particulate shores. There *was* sand, but it was gritty white here and streaked with yellow there, broken up with a band of gray beyond that, and red, red, red where the far-off ruby cliffs seemed to dissolve under their own weight into the floor of the planet.

There were also rocks strewn about everywhere untidily. Tiny rocks like pebbles, large rocks like you might build a wall out of, but in all the wrong shapes and colors. Perfectly black rounded rocks scattered randomly among the rest for no good reason. Countless flat, flaking red rocks that made more sense in the red-tinged landscape.

Keeping close to the ground were strange little plants. And though Wendy generally didn't like imposing subjective opinions on defenseless inanimate objects, they were quite ugly. Thorny, narrow-twigged, bunched up tight, and miserly with leaves of dull colors. Some of them looked dead but apparently weren't. There wasn't a single "normal" cactus among them. No barrels with spikes, no tall ones with rounded branches like letters from another language.

Disappointing.

And then there were tall strange boulders that stood by themselves, spires or pinnacles dotting the landscape like bowling pins set up by a giant toddler. They were higher than buildings but narrow, their bodies striped with layers of red and white and tan like half-sucked peppermint canes a hundred years old and yellowed with age.

A dead wind blew so dry it burned Wendy's nostrils. Sand got in her eyes and it wasn't even normal *sand*, the pretty round and faceted jewels of a good English beach. It was more like dust, tiny slippery flakes that soon found their way into every crease and crevice of her clothes and person.

As for the rest of the land, from her squinted eyes Wendy saw . . . *farther* than she ever had. Her brain hurt trying to make some sort of sense of the images it received. At home even outside the city there were always houses blocking the view, and trees, and hills; every couple of miles something like a hedge cut off one's view of the rest of the world. Here she could see for what appeared to be fifty miles in every direction, maybe a hundred, with no real end but for the ability of her eyes.

She felt dizzy, utterly exposed under such a huge, bright, dead sky and endless flat desert, with its weird chess-like rock figures, its unmeasurable walls of red rock and distant plateaus. There was nothing else; she herself was nothing.

She didn't even have her shadow.

Wendy collapsed to her knees, overcome by it all.

Careful! Tinker Bell exhorted, buzzing up off her shoulder for a moment before remembering not to fly. *You're going to get all sticky and mucky.*

"Mucky?" Wendy asked huskily. "Are you joking? Tinker Bell, are you feeling all right? Is the heat getting to you?"

Heat? It's cold and nasty and wet with all the mud bubbling up everywhere!

"Mud?" Wendy looked around. "All I see is desert, miles and miles of empty desert. What do you see?"

The fairy shifted uncomfortably on her shoulder. *I just told you. Mud. A whole world of it. A giant flat. Dead. World. Mud bubbling up. Nothing.*

"I wonder which one of us is right," Wendy murmured. "Do you think it's some sort of trap, some way of disguising themselves? Of keeping us from finding them and Peter? An illusion . . . like fairy glamour?"

They are the most powerful beings in Never Land. They are *Never Land,* Tinker Bell jingled darkly. *No need for illusion.*

"How does this place usually appear? Have you seen it before?"

Those who return never say. And no.

"Well." Wendy bit her lip. Even words spoken aloud here sounded thin and dead and useless. "If it's real at all, at least what I can see, from where I stand, there is no sign of Peter anywhere. Or anything living. You?"

Nothing. Mud.

"Hmm. Hold on then. We'll walk a bit, and see if we see anything or anyone. Let's just take a good look at where we started so we can remember. . . ."

She forced herself back up on her feet and looked behind them. To her relief, the air—or reality—seemed to ripple; shreds of white and gray blew aside and the desert petered out. Glimpses of the dark green jungle peeped from beyond.

"Well, good," she said, turning back the way they were headed. "We can always return. We shall mark our place with those three rocks there, and—oh!"

Not twenty feet from them, where there was nothing but scrub before, stood a giant monolith. A red-and-orange jagged-edged hoodoo reaching high into the sky. Its top was worn into three strange and slightly bulbous shapes. With just a little imagination Wendy could make out heads and maybe faces—blank, primordial ones.

"Tinker Bell," she whispered. *"What do you see?"*

Mud welling up. Bubbling up into three ugly mud statues. Sweating and bleeding and oozing mud.

Wendy was only a little relieved that she and her friend were both seeing different versions of what appeared to be the same thing. The stone effigy in front of her was terrifying in every way: in its size, silence, and sudden appearance.

Why are you here?

Nothing spoke. Nothing that looked like a head or a

face moved. No *sound* emerged, and yet the words reverberated across the dead landscape, echoing and unmistakable. There could be no doubt where it came from.

"If you please . . ." Wendy dropped into a small curtsy. "We're here in search of our friend, Peter Pan. Have you seen him?"

Silence.

Terrible, dreadful silence. It, too, echoed, blanketing the desert with a deadly finality.

Wendy waited and waited.

The dry wind blew past her ear. She felt Tinker Bell grow tense, tiny fingernails digging into her skin. Not urging her to do anything. Just nervous.

"I'm sorry," she began again after a while. "Peter Pan. Have you seen him? He's about my size, and wears green. . . ."

Peter Pan was here. Now he is gone.

"Ah. Do you know when he left? Or where he went to? Did you give him a new shadow?"

One question too many.

Despite the lack of change in the landscape, Wendy could feel its impatience.

The problems of the boy are not our concern. We sent him away. Why are you here. You are not from Never Land. You are—older.

"I beg your forgiveness if I am too old to be allowed here," Wendy said, immediately lowering her head. "I shall leave as soon as I help my friend here find *her* friend, and help him get his shadow back, and defeat the pirates with whatever they are planning."

There was a strange un-noise, as if the air were shaking.

Age is no rule of ours. It is a law created by you humans from the other side. We make no laws. We make no rules. We just *are*. It is humans who seek to name and regulate and shape this land to their ridiculous whims. Our world is crystallizing to the point of permanence, thanks to your ridiculous dreaming.

"I . . . don't understand. . . ."

Once we and the world were one. We *were* the world. Then humans came. Their dreams were simple at first. But soon came the rules and the laws and the ideas and the suppositions and the feelings and the wishes and the decisions and the hopes. With each one another mountain hardened and another sea narrowed into a river. Now you have your Never Land. And because children's dreams are the strongest, their dreams rule the world. Everywhere except for here, where we still rule. We, the First of this world.

"Oh, but isn't it all rather lovely?" Wendy asked. "Fair-ies and mermaids—despite their vicious tendencies—and dragons and flying and moonlit beaches? You have an amazing, beautiful world here. Never Land exists the way it does as a result of all that innocent childhood dreaming . . . all of their most magical and creative thoughts before they grow up and it slips away. . . ."

INSOLENT!

Wendy Darling you *know*

You know you and your brothers are not the only ones who dream

Wendy was forced to her knees by the strength of the words. She covered her ears despite not actually hearing anything.

When she managed to look up again, the rock formation had changed. There was something about it that *looked* different, and it appeared to be looming over her more.

Some children are so twisted by hate from others they can dream of nothing but hate.

Some children dream of going through a day without being whipped or beaten.

Some children dream of nothing more than a full meal. They smile in their sleep as their minds conjure something that would fill their bellies if it were only real.

Some dream that their parents are still alive, or at least that their ghosts come to visit.

Some dream of still being able to play with their friends and go to school although they no longer can.

This Never Land you see is the Never Land you and your brothers are used to. There are other parts of Never Land you never see, with no fairies or mermaids. Only dishes of food and clean water and kindness. Or beasts so horrible you would die upon viewing them.

Silence filled the space in Wendy's ears and mind when the First finished speaking. Her heart paused.

Other . . . children's dreams . . .

"The qqrimal," she murmured.

But that wasn't *her* fault. Was it? These other children weren't part of *her* Never Land, her world—were they? They weren't part of the London where she and John and Michael played in the nursery with Nana and cufflinks and perfume and Mr. and Mrs. Darling and tea and rain.

But . . . of course they were.

Wendy knew that.

She just didn't like to think about it.

They were out there somewhere, at the edges or hidden in plain sight. Orphans, beggars, children with bruises, girls whose parents really did force them into arranged marriages—without even the choice of going to Ireland instead.

Some of them may even have dreamed of a life where

all they had to worry about was growing lonely and old in a large house, where there was food and heat every day.

Why else would they have dreamed up a Peter Pan to rescue them?

"I . . . I just never even thought about that before."

The First didn't say anything.

"I'm sorry. I didn't—I still don't know how Never Land works. Or . . . my world, either, I suppose."

How much do you *care* about your world? Or this one? The mad pirate will destroy all of Never Land rather than simply quit it, once he has Peter Pan in his clutches to watch it all and weep.

"Yes, that's why I'm here. But I don't see what I or my world has to do with—"

Hook is the villain and star of so many of your tales. He was birthed from the tides of your world. And he will destroy ours.

"I didn't mean to . . . They were just stories. . . . But *you* can stop him, can't you?"

We cannot stop this, because of your world's hold over ours. He is of your making.

"What do you want me to *do?*" Wendy cried desperately. "I'll do it! Whatever you ask!"

Nothing. Silence.

Normally she was not a girl prone to perspiring—she

never moved much faster than a brisk walk, and remained inside on the hottest days. Now she felt sweat break out across her brow and uncomfortably under her arms.

But it wasn't from the desert heat.

"Should I leave now?" she asked.

Maybe she and the fairy should just go. Maybe the First were done with them. But it felt wrong to turn her back on these creatures, whatever they were, and walk away . . . rather like turning one's back on a king or queen. Were *they* done with her?

"Please. I'm sorry. I was so stupid. Never Land is a learning experience," she ventured, nervousness and sweat coalescing into words that just poured out of her mouth. "I came for adventure—perhaps wrongfully—and it's far more complicated than the place I dreamed of. Pirates who don't seem to want to be pirates, girls who have to hide their true selves to come here, monsters who only eat fairies, mermaids who will fight each other tooth and claw over an apple . . . And Hook. And *I* am responsible for his doomsday visions?"

Never Land is a reflection of your world.

Wendy jumped. She had no longer been expecting a response, much less one so calm.

Are things broken here? Save this world. Then go back to your own broken world and fix it. Perhaps we shall be mended as well.

"Me? Fix the *entire* world? I can't even fix my own situation at home! That's why I came here!"

Is escape to Never Land your only recourse for being made to grow up, for being sent away? For disagreeing with your parents? Is there nothing else you could do? For yourself? For others like you? For others *un*like you?

This was not how Wendy expected the conversation to go. After her outburst, she expected irritation from the strange beings and maybe a boulder or two hurled at her for perceived insolence. Being squashed would have made more sense than these strange questions.

"I'm just . . . I'm no one. I can't do anything. I can't even disobey my father."

Perhaps you should see if that really is true.

Go quickly. Time is running out for Never Land and for Peter.

There was a pause and a ripple in the atmosphere that Wendy realized meant a change in mood.

Goodbye, human not grown-up not child not hero not villain. Goodbye, pixie not pixie not human.

Wendy blinked and the monolith was gone. The others behind it in the landscape had also rearranged. There seemed to be fewer.

She let out a breath, not even realizing she had been holding it.

Tinker Bell decided that it was safe to flitter, and zoomed around like a nervous bee—keeping *very* close to her big friend.

"That was . . . very interesting. Educational."

She finally found the right word.

"Terrifying."

Tinker Bell nodded, swallowing.

"We really have to get out of here and find Peter and get Hook. Immediately. When even the gods of a world are worried about its destruction, well—it's serious indeed. And I know you think it's better to find Peter first and then deal with his shadow and the pirates, but perhaps we really should go after the pirates now? I think we'll find them more easily at this point. What do you think? Tink?"

But the little fairy wasn't paying attention. She tugged on Wendy's hair and pointed back the way they had come.

Wendy looked, very reluctantly. Afraid of what would be there—or rather, what wouldn't.

And she was right.

Never Land was entirely gone. The desert extended for a hundred miles in all directions, seamless and complete.

The Desert

"No," Wendy said softly.

Even though she had predicted it, even though now she could see the truth with her own eyes, she still fell down the long-familiar tunnel of childishness: wishing that what just happened hadn't. Denying with her full being that the vase had tipped and smashed, that the terrible thing just said had come out of her own mouth, that the soufflé had fallen moments before she served it to Mother and Father.

That she and Tinker Bell were stranded, cut off from the rest of Never Land, in what looked like an infinite desert.

Wendy carefully stepped back to the point she had mentally marked before, knowing full well it might be important later. Three red stones in increasing size were lined up like a fallen desert sandman. A scrubby little black and matte turquoise bush with two pom-pom-like appendages grew nearby. There were her footprints coming out of nowhere. Beginning the journey. She bent over, trying to feel a hint of moist air, of cool sea breeze, of pungent jungle funk.

But of course there was nothing.

Tinker Bell zipped around back and forth above Wendy, trying to see what she was seeing. Then she flew a little farther out, to the left and right and front and back with the neat, almost unnatural motions of a dragonfly hunting. Actually, she *was* hunting. For a way out.

"Anything?" Wendy asked, trying to keep the hope out of her voice.

Tinker Bell shrugged, shook her head, and jingled sadly.

"Maybe . . . Look, I know you don't want to disrespect this place, but the First seem to have abandoned us to our fates. For now. Maybe it would be all right if you just flew up—really high—into the air? And looked around?"

Tinker Bell nodded reluctantly.

She took a big, dramatic breath and rose into the pale sky. Wendy had to shade her eyes with her hand to see the fairy at all against the brightness. High, higher still, higher than a kite. Eventually she disappeared.

While Wendy knew her friend's invisibility was just a

trick of distance and the limitation of her own eyesight, she couldn't help fretting. She shuffled her feet and bit her lip until the fairy reappeared, falling down on the exact same path she had taken up with the inevitability and determination of an acorn freed from its twig. Wendy held out her hand, and the tiny girl landed on it with obvious gratitude.

"Anything?"

Tinker Bell shook her head, looking perplexed. She pointed: north, east, south, west, or whatever passed for them in this strange land. She put a hand to her head, much like Wendy had when watching for her, and mimed looking far out in each direction, frowning and squinting. Then she shrugged again.

"It just goes on and on, in every direction?"

Forever. Just that big muddy plateau in front of us—that is the only feature in any distance.

"But . . . we *saw* boundaries to it when we flew down," Wendy protested, not arguing with her friend so much as with reality. "It wasn't so big, this area. It only covered a tiny portion of the island."

Tinker Bell gave her a look.

"All right, all right, I know we're not dealing with normal forces here." Wendy sighed. "After telling us that we need to save Never Land, and soon, the First abandoned and trapped us here. One can only assume they think we can find our way out. It's some sort of test.

"So let's think about this logically. Their demesne seems to continue forever. It's all outside, beyond us. But where did the First go? I don't see any of those monoliths— er, I guess you would see mud piles—in any direction *far away* from us. They are only in the middle distance. So perhaps . . . perhaps there is someplace *inward* they go. Or *downward.* Yes, that seems rather backward and Never Land-y. What do you think, Tinker Bell?"

The fairy shrugged and nodded, pursing her lips. Like: *sure, sounds as good as anything at this point.*

"All right then, let's head over to those cliffs over there. Maybe there's a secret canyon that burrows deep into their lair. Race you!" Wendy raised her arms to fly.

Nothing happened.

"Up now! Happy thoughts!"

Her feet remained firmly planted on the ground.

Tinker Bell frowned.

"Oh dear," Wendy said.

The fairy spiraled up and down around the human girl, practically smothering her with fairy dust. Much of it was blown away on the harsh, hot breeze: thousands of sparkles spreading across the arid landscape in a cloud that grew taller and taller and more spread out as it dissipated into the air. "What a waste," Wendy sighed.

She thought of all good things. Candy floss, the first scent of lilacs in the spring, a really nice day in the shade of the backyard tree with her notebook, Nana under her hand.

Still nothing happened.

"Either I'm terrified to the core of my soul by this place," Wendy said thoughtfully, "or I can't borrow your fairy magic here."

Tinker Bell shook her head sorrowfully and patted her on the hand.

"Well then, onward anyway!"

Wendy straightened her back, gave Tinker Bell (and herself) a reassuring nod, and began marching toward the cliffs. That's what Englishmen did. They pushed up their sleeves, gritted their teeth, and did what needed to be done. Out in the midday sun, if need be. Like mad dogs.

And so went she.

It was hard going in the strange sand. There were occasional patches of slick white rock, flat as a tabletop and much easier to walk on. But these didn't always line up the way she was heading; often she had to walk along one until its end and then stumble in the sand until the next one. Any plant she accidentally dragged her legs against left scrapes of both kinds: harmless little white-lined reminders and truly defensive strikes, deep angry red welts.

Wendy was sweating profusely now although it evaporated immediately in the dry air. This caused her some confusion until she finally figured out where the potential rivulets of sweat were disappearing to. Which brought up another worry. In her stories dehydration was much less threatening: *"And they couldn't find water anywhere on the deserted island, not even a coconut palm to climb and crack the fruits thereof and drink the sweet nectar. And so the heroes wandered and thirsted and dreamed of lemonade. . . ."* And of course, Peter Pan and the Lost Boys eventually found something like a washed-up cask of cider or a hidden spring.

Here there were no trees at all, and it seemed very unlikely without Moses to find a spring in the middle of the desert. Lack of water was going to be a real problem, real soon.

Not to mention hunger . . .

She looked askance at her little friend, who was flying beside her with an equal look of determination. Her teensy brow was a bit dewy and smeared with dust, but it didn't seem like she was in any real discomfort.

It was hard to tell if time passed at all in that strange land. The cliffs and mesas did seem to grow closer—very slowly—but the light didn't change at all. Wendy noticed with fascination that the shadows of this land chose their angle and size with no particular logic. A stone might have a long shadow lying to the area she thought of as "east," as if the sun were setting somewhere to the west, while the bush next to it might have a barely-there black circle clinging to its twiggy skirts like it was high noon. Perhaps that was why Peter was drawn here; the First might have some sort of strange affinity to shadows and shadow magic.

Tinker Bell's shadow yawned and stretched and pointed here and there, but honestly, the little fairy moved too quickly herself for the difference between them to be that noticeable.

Unlike Wendy's lack of shadow, which was *very* noticeable. The ground looked bleak and empty beneath her. She found she missed even the shadow's not quite appropriate behavior, like when she grew distracted and did something Wendy wasn't doing. She wondered if the shadow was out looking for Peter. Did she also grow weak without contact with her mistress? Did she *need* Wendy? And once they found Peter and reunited him with his shadow—would her shadow follow suit?

Or would her shadow prefer to stay in Never Land, where she was free to do as she pleased, rather than return to London and a life of just copying Wendy's every movement? Would Wendy be able to convince her to go home with her?

She found herself missing deeply the cold and wet weather of that city. It was vastly preferable to the oven they were in now.

Minutes or hours passed. Wendy fretted and swore quietly to herself. Time was ticking away and they were no closer to stopping Hook, his nefarious plans now confirmed by the First.

"What sort of lunatic destroys *everything* when he can't win?" she growled. Perhaps it was her fault, as a storyteller. Perhaps recurring villains grew sick of their own recurrence.

Wendy tried not to brush back the hair that wound up in her eyes because then she would get red streaks from the ubiquitous dust in it and all over her face. Tinker Bell had plucked a tiny, thick leaf and tried to hold it as an umbrella above her head—perhaps to keep herself dry in whatever the landscape was doing in her vision. But no matter which way she tilted it she seemed unsatisfied with the results. Eventually she let it drop—but only after taking a tentative bite out of its flesh.

The look on her face was all that was needed to stop Wendy from launching into a lecture on the danger of unknown plants and their possible toxicity. The fairy wasted precious spit getting all of it—and the taste—out of her mouth.

Finally they arrived at the skirts of the red cliffs. Here giant slopes of rock that looked like they used to be part of the mountains finally succumbed to time and melted into piles of sand and rubble. Amongst their folds were multiple canyons twisting and leading deep into the plateau. Wendy picked a likely one and pointed. Tinker Bell nodded. They plunged ahead.

"So . . . Tinker Bell . . ." Wendy ventured after they had walked for a bit. "Your little—pardon me—your fairy friends back there . . . What were their names? Berryloon and . . . ?"

Thorn.

"Thorn. Yes, that suits the fellow quite well. *Thorn.* Like with his sword, stabbing."

Tinker Bell narrowed her eyes suspiciously.

Wendy slipped down a treacherous patch of slick rock covered in fine gravel. More of her skirt tore. Without even thinking this time, she simply ripped off the ragged piece and tied it around her middle like a belt.

"Cuts quite a figure, doesn't he? I mean, his apparel was most immodest—but he wore it well. Didn't he?"

Tinker Bell buzzed over to hang in Wendy's face.

Oh my phlox. You like *him.*

"Like?" Wendy said indignantly. "I hardly know the boy. I was just saying how handsome he was, and well-spoken, and his ears were *very* elegant."

You like Thorn.

Whatever the fairy was saying from then on grew incomprehensible as she lapsed into great peals of jingly laughter that echoed off the canyon walls. She actually held her belly and guffawed, wasting quantities of sparkling fairy dust on the sand below. This only irritated Wendy further. She had just grown used to flying and was now more than a little peeved that her power was gone.

"All right, all right, no need to be all gossipy and school-girlish about it."

It's just . . . Thorn. *He's so* dull. *And you're so* big.

"I was only making conversation," Wendy said grumpily.

Oh, I'm just teasing, the little fairy said, patting her hand, eyes wide with mock apology. *When we get out of here and rescue Peter's shadow, we can go find him in the fairy realms and you can tell him your true feelings.*

Or I will, if you can't.

"Don't you dare!" Wendy cried.

Tinker Bell wiped a tear of laughter out of her eye. *Kidding! I wouldn't unless you asked me to. It's just so weird.*

"I don't see why it's strange. But let me just make sure I am clear about this, so we don't get into trouble again: *you* don't . . . ah . . . *like* him?"

Tinker Bell made a sick face. Then she thought about it. Really thought about it. Then she shrugged: *nope.*

"You only have eyes for Peter Pan, don't you?" Wendy asked softly.

Tinker Bell nodded woefully.

"All right, well, we're not going to discuss him. But what about that other girl? Berryloon or whatever? She acted like she knew you very well. Are you friends?"

Tinker Bell frowned and made a sour face, like she would have spit if she had been less ladylike. Or perhaps had any spit to waste.

"Ah, so you know each other well, but aren't friends. There are girls like that in my neighborhood—the demonic Shesbow twins, as I call them. Mother and Father are always trying to make me spend time with them. Frankly, I'd rather be alone. Alone, hungry, thirsty, hot, and exhausted, really."

Tinker Bell nodded vigorously.

"Fairies . . . spend a lot of time . . . *together,* don't they?"

Tinker Bell rolled her eyes.

Fetes. Balls. Parties. Moon viewings. New moon festivals. Farmers markets. Pollen whispers. Nectar-ines.

"I should very much like to see a fairy Nectar-ine," Wendy said wistfully. "But I'm sure I probably wouldn't want to attend many, if I *were* a fairy. Like the parties and dances in London. I never know what to say that's appropriate, and everyone thinks I talk too much and I'm odd and . . . I don't know. Immature. Childish. Strange?"

Tinker Bell nodded meaninfully. But her eyes were focused elsewhere, on an incident, on the past.

"I guess neither you *nor* I have had many female friends—any, really?"

Tinker Bell slowly shook her head.

"What about that Lost Boy—er, girl? Skipper?"

Tinker Bell shrugged. *Lost Boys. You know. They're friends . . . but not friends.*

"I do understand," Wendy said with a sigh. "There are booksellers' nephews and vendors at the market . . . but no bosom companions."

Tinker Bell looked down at her chest, frowning.

"Ah, I mean, very close friends. You know, someone you can tell secrets to, who will always love you no matter what stupid thing you say or do."

Or will always be there to save you, no matter how mean you've been.

And for once, Wendy had the sense to just nod and smile and not say anything.

Ahead the canyon opened up wide and flat as it traveled into the heart of the mesa. *Inviting.* Strangely clear of even the hardiest scrubby plants, almost paved in alternating ribbons of soft silt and packed sand. Very easy to walk on. Tiny polished pebbles congregated in delta formations in the middle of the path and along the edges.

"Peculiar," Wendy said softly. "Almost like the bottom of a stream, without a stream on it. Yes, that's exactly what it's like. Like we're walking in a stream that isn't here. What do *you* see?"

Tinker Bell shrugged. *Mud . . . You're walking on flat rocks just above the mud. Your feet are getting filthy.*

"Well, whatever it is, sounds like a road to me. Let's take it."

Tinker Bell nodded. One very suspicious rock guarded the entrance of this new path, a boulder perched on a pedestal with a strangely intelligent look about it. Much, much smaller than the monoliths that had dotted the desert earlier, or the one that had spoken to them. Still . . .

The way gently twisted and turned, the high stony walls above them copying its movements in folds and wrinkles. But the rocks, the sands, the scattered plants, the strange shadows—they all looked more or less exactly the same no matter where they were. There was no discernible feeling of progress.

This was more walking than Wendy had ever done at once, and all without her shadow. At some point she realized she could barely feel her legs. Sometimes when she put her foot down she misjudged the distance and stepped bone-jarringly hard on the ground. Sometimes she felt the world tilt.

The inside of her mouth was rough and painful like sandpaper, but she feared spitting the dust out—afraid of losing any fluid at all, since they'd had nothing to eat or drink since eating that rubyfruit.

And while Wendy didn't like spending too much time dwelling on functions of the body, it had been a very long time since she had last needed to use the loo.

"Tinker Bell, I think I need a break," she finally admitted.

The fairy nodded glumly. Her hair was limp and her wings drooped, and she didn't jingle. They found a large shadow (cast from who knew what object) to collapse in.

"I think this might be a kind of an oubliette," Wendy admitted after they had both sat there silently for a moment. "A trick of the First. There's no end or escape. I put these things into stories now and then—paths which look useful but lead nowhere."

Tinker Bell nodded reluctantly. She had come to the same conclusion.

"This is *so frustrating!*" Wendy suddenly shrieked, using a last bit of energy to kick the canyon wall. "We can't be here—we have to be out there, saving Never Land!"

The fairy was silent.

"You haven't said anything at all about the danger your whole *world* is in," Wendy pointed out, somewhere between curious and peevish.

Without Peter—

"It's like you don't have a world anyway. Yes, I understand." Wendy sighed and put a very careful finger on the fairy's hand. "I'm terribly sorry. About him, and everything. But I'm not sorry we're together. Imagine if you had to face this alone!"

Tinker Bell shuddered. She looked up at Wendy with something approaching chagrin.

I'm very glad you're with me. And not just because you saved me.

"Those First, eh?" Wendy said wryly, trying to keep her humor. "Nice gods, those lot."

Tinker Bell was silent, neither agreeing nor disagreeing. Then she frowned.

"What? What is it?"

They said, "Is there nothing else you could do? For yourself? Perhaps you should see if that is really true."

"They were talking about whether I could change anything back in *London*. If I could fix our world, and therefore make changes here."

But . . . then they said goodbye and left us here. And you said this could be a test. What if they meant perhaps you should see if you can change anything or figure out anything here, first?

"Oh," Wendy said, and she thought about it.

Once she quieted her initial immediate objections the idea sort of tasted right. Like something that would happen in an adventure story. The villains who turn out not to be villains at all, really, just helpers on the hero's path to heroism. What seems like a serious setback is actually a test to see if the hero is worthy enough to proceed with the rest of her quest.

Basic storytelling, really.

"Maybe . . . maybe you're right. If I can get us out of here, I can find Peter and get his shadow back. And If I can do *that,* surely I can save Never Land!"

Tinker Bell nodded vigorously.

"Only . . ." Wendy's face fell. "Only I've never really done anything *real.* Solved any *real* problems or puzzles. What could I possibly do? There are no obvious riddles to solve here. This isn't a labyrinth. There isn't even an actual villain to test my strength against. All my skills are imaginary. And all my real talents are useless. . . . Mend a skirt? Run a house? Stare out the window, dreaming? Which do you think would help us here?"

Dreaming.

You can tell stories.

"Oh please—that's nothing. Anyone can tell stories."

No. Stop it. You told stories so wonderful that Peter Pan came to listen—to stories about himself! Your telling stories invited Never Land into your home.

Wendy blinked. "I . . . suppose that's true. I never considered it that way before. If I hadn't told the stories about Peter Pan, Peter Pan wouldn't have come . . . which is an odd thought in itself. But if he hadn't come, he wouldn't have lost his shadow and left it. And then *I* wouldn't have traded it to Hook to come here. What a strange series of events! It's all because I tell stories.

"But how does this help us now? I can't just make up a story about us escaping here and have it come true."

The fairy looked at her thoughtfully. *What happens in your world, the dreams of your world, affects our world. And we are in the Land of the First, the origin and heart of Never Land.*

"Oh, I see what you're saying. My stories change and shape Never Land—and other children's do, too. So perhaps *here* I could directly alter it, myself?"

Tinker Bell shrugged: *why not?*

"It's worth a try!" Wendy said, growing excited. "Let's see. What can I come up with . . . ? All right. Here goes.

"Once upon a time, there were two girls lost in a desert that went on and on forever, one fairy and one human. They seemed to have no means of escape, but then . . . a giant friendly bird, a Never Bird, flew down out of the sky and took them on her back, safely returning them to the Pernicious Forest and Never Land proper!"

Wendy waited expectantly.

Nothing happened.

Although she hadn't completely believed that something would happen in response to her words, she still felt an almost overwhelming sense of disappointment at the completeness of the *nothing* that happened. Not even a random sparrow appeared in the dusty canyon.

That's not a story, Tinker Bell said dryly. *That's a wish.*

Wendy started to argue and then actually thought about what the fairy had said. True: although it had a beginning, middle, and end, there was no character change—no character interaction at all, really. There was no setup, no grand description of the scenery, nothing. She should know better! She spent so much of her spare time writing. . . .

Wendy looked at the strange, washed-out path they were on and began to imagine.

"You know, once upon a time this was a thriving, fast-moving river," she said almost conversationally. "It was all sorts of different colors—clear white to the bottom, red from the sand of the cliffs, green with life and fish. Where it splashed out of its banks, lush grass and trees grew.

"But then one day, far north of here, a powerful warlord fell in love with a beautiful maiden who did not love him back. For she loved another, a young farmer who lived on the other side of the river—"

Farmer? Tinker Bell interrupted skeptically.

"Shush. This is *my* story. And I always thought farmers were rather dashing and romantic figures in their own way. Especially the Scottish ones. Anyway: The warlord grew angry and swore that the maiden would never see her lover again. He used his incredible strength—from years of rampaging and pillaging—and picked up the river and tied it in a knot. The waters stopped flowing to the south and dried up, turning the once lovely river valley, the very one in which we sit, into just another dead path through the desert.

"The knot was so clever and complex that the maiden and the farmer could not figure out how to untie it, even had they the strength. So they each got a little boat—well, hers was actually rather magnificent because she was a warrior princess, as it happens, with a golden prow and silken cushions. His was more fitting to his station, of course.

"But back to the story. Every day they rowed toward each other but could never find a way to meet, for no matter what path they chose the water kept them apart. The princess had her wisest witches and most wily wizards use their magic to try to help her cross. On the back of a clockwork crocodile, through a tunnel made from the breath of mermaids. . . . None of it worked, of course. And so the maiden and the farmer kept trying, and failing, and wept at their fate.

"All who saw them pitied the poor lovers and cried with them. Year after year the tears fell, adding to the volume—and the saltiness—of the river that divided the princess from the farmer.

"And then one day the tears were just too much for the river to hold. It overflowed its banks and burst the knot—*pop! pop! pop!*—straightening itself out like a snake waking up.

"Not completely, however," Wendy added as a quick aside. "The bumps in the knots became a series of tiny islands and beautiful, rich ponds and lakes known as the Maiden's Tears."

Why not the Farmer's Tears?

"Excellent point. They were known as the Farmer's Tears, and made for quite good irrigation. The two lovers, united at last, left their boats in the river and met in the middle of the water on one of the new islands, and that is where they built their house and lived happily for the rest of their lives."

Was it her imagination, or was a breeze picking up?

Was there a shimmer in the sky, a difference beginning in the otherwise flat white sheen?

All right, the fairy said, interrupting. *But . . .*

"Just wait. This happened *so far north* that it took *weeks* before the river joyfully managed to come all the way back down to the desert, greeting its old, lost friends and watering the sands around it. Careful, Tinker Bell. Come over here."

Wendy stood and took her friend by the hand, pulling her into the air and moving both of them farther up the side of the gully. She couldn't have said how she knew, but with a calm assuredness like nothing she had ever felt before, she was utterly unsurprised when a strange noise began somewhere up in the canyon.

A crashing, booming, terrifying sound.

Tinker Bell just had time to tightly grab Wendy's finger when a ten-foot wall of water came hurtling down the ravine. It foamed and roiled in all the colors Wendy had described, red and white and green. Rainbow-sparkling fish leapt along its crest, riding it with apparent joy.

Tinker Bell swooped up backward in surprise and delight. Wendy grinned.

The river crashed up against the bank nearest them, careened off it and continued, splashing the two girls. It was like when a hundred children run down the street, out of school for the day and well aware that the marionette performer was back in the square; all violence and speed and good nature and excitement and *force*, bouncing off the gates and fences and alleys of London, un-slowed and untroubled by any accidental crashes.

"The river eventually found its way back to the sea, and settled with great relief into its old banks and beds," Wendy continued, feeling that things should calm down a *little* bit. "Once again it divided Never Land, but never as permanently as when it was in knots."

It's great we have water now, Tinker Bell said, *but how does this help us? You can't swim—we've seen that.*

Wendy shook her head at her friend and made a *tch tch* sound.

"Don't you remember the story? The two lovers stayed on the island in the middle, and *left their boats in the river.*"

Tinker Bell opened her mouth, about to ask another question, when the boats in question came bumping slowly around the bend.

They looked a little out of place in the desert, drifting along the base of the high umber walls. The farmer's boat was a tiny wood-and-hide thing that could have been mistaken for a pile of driftwood. It was made for quick jaunts close to the land, for poking about ponds and lakes. Not for going down the rocky rapids of a canyon wash.

The warrior maiden's boat was far more intriguing. It was all dark wood, beautifully bent and fitted together with the complexity of a true seafaring vessel. Intricate gilded carvings covered the prow. The gunwale was painted a bright, cheery blue. A pole stood up in the back for steering. While there were no cushions left—they looked like they had been ripped out by the incredibly rough journey—the benches looked comfortable enough.

Tinker Bell clapped and jingled her approval.

The boat seemed to sense their need and nosed its way through the back current over to their bank.

"Shall we?" Wendy asked, trying not to sound too pleased with herself. "After you."

Tinker Bell gave a little bow in the air, and Wendy

returned it with a curtsy and a flourish. Then the fairy flew delicately to the fore bench and sat. On the bench next to her was a carelessly left, beautiful gem-encrusted dagger that hung on a useful necklace. Tinker Bell gave her friend a look.

"Oh yes. She also left her necklace behind, the one her mother gave her for protection," Wendy said, reaching in and putting it on. "All right, it's not really part of the story—but it seems like a weapon would be useful for me to have, don't you agree?"

She carefully held the side of the boat as it tipped a little with her weight, then settled herself in the back with the pole. She had done some punting on a visit to see her mother's cousin up in Oxford but wasn't entirely sure what use that skill would be in a river that was the topological opposite of a sleepy English canal.

A strange *tick tick tock* noise could be heard just above the sound of the rushing water, growing as it came closer.

Tinker Bell looked left and right, trying to find the source of it as Wendy experimentally maneuvered the pole. When the fairy finally figured out what the noise was, she squeaked, jingled desperately, and flew back to desperately squeeze her friend's arm.

But Wendy already knew what it was.

It was a *beautiful* gold-and-steel crocodile. Four yards

long from tip to tail. It skimmed the water, its black nose and glass eyes just sticking out of the surface, its sparkling, mechanical tail swishing back and forth rhythmically. It smiled at the girls with clear crystal teeth.

"Oh yes, that's the clockwork crocodile. Now free from its previous task, the toy beast sought its way downstream to find other people in need of help. And, I daresay, we might have use of a clockwork crocodile somewhere along the way—against pirates, maybe? One *particular* crocodile-fearing pirate?"

Tinker Bell stared at her friend in newly discovered admiration—and the teensiest bit of horror.

You've changed, girl.

Wendy smiled as she pushed the boat away from the bank.

There was more to her than just manners and wishing, as her little fairy friend had pointed out. A whole world of Never Land was inside Wendy . . . with beasts as well as fairies.

The Ride and the Rain

The beautiful little boat began its journey slowly, bumping along the bank until Wendy managed to push them away from shore. The steering pole had a well-hewn and polished handle that fit in her hands perfectly. She couldn't have imagined a better designed piece of equipment. Which was intellectually amusing since some part of her mind *must* have actually imagined or designed it. Of course, she hadn't really visualized every detail of the entire boat; she had just said *boat*, royal boat, and figured there would be gold and blue and fancy things on it and comfy seats. And regal-looking equipment, like this pole. But not specifically the pole she was holding. Which inevitably led to the question: Who or what *did* provide the details? When she invented the story, who filled in the missing bits? Was that just how the magic of Never Land worked?

But this was a deep thought for another time. She had to work the pole around and around with all her strength before finally getting out to the middle of the newly reinvigorated river. The little boat bobbed in place for a moment as if discussing matters with the waters around it, spinning a little as it found a good place to join, and then—it took off.

Wendy squealed with delight as they rushed along with the waves. Tinker Bell also squealed, but with terror, and held on to the seat for dear life. Then she looked over at Wendy and saw her laughing, and the fairy reassessed the dangers. Very slowly she began to smile.

"Yeehaw!" Wendy shouted as they rose up with a swell and then crashed down with a belly-flopping *smash*, spraying water into the sky with bright rainbows. The droplets were small and cool and very refreshing. Her parched skin soaked them up gratefully. She licked her lips: cold, clear, and lightly mineral.

Fish leapt in arcs before the bow of the boat, their scales glittering in the sunlight. The canyon walls raced by. Between her triumph at figuring out how to escape the First and the speed of the river and the water and the day, Wendy was almost overcome with joy.

"I had *no idea* boating could be such fun!" she cried to Tinker Bell. "It's almost like flying!"

Tinker Bell gave a definitive headshake to this. *No.* But Wendy just laughed.

She did worry a little whether the whole plan would really work, if they could really get out of the demesne of the First or if they would just ride the river forever.

But then the landscape around them began to change—slowly. Perhaps indicating that they were getting back to Never Land proper.

The thick red walls of stone that rose into the sky on the left and right of them fell away, too busy with the eternal task of crumbling into piles of dust to bother with the riverbanks any longer. And while there was still the occasional tor or small rocky hill, the buttes and hoodoos and columns and pedestals and other exotic formations grew far less frequent.

Just before these features disappeared entirely, two final ones appeared on opposite sides of the river. These were unbelievably massive, so tall that Wendy couldn't see their tops. Striped layers of red and white and black alternated with each other up and into forever.

She had the strange urge to salute as they passed between these two guardians. Both girls, fey and human, remained silent and still until the columns were far behind. Even the boat seemed to slow for a bit.

After that the land grew greener by stages. Tall, gracefully curving trees with branches like umbrellas marked the edge of the jungle. Canyon walls back in the desert were recalled in living format here as massive gray trunks of trees, barriers of thick foliage, and unbelievably substantial skeins of vines. The calls of monkeys or parrots or other Never Land creatures echoed hauntingly from the tops of emerald hillocks. Far in the distance they could once again just make out the toothy shapes of the Black Dragon Mountains.

Wendy never imagined she could be so relieved to see *jungle*. Or hills, for that matter, even if they were covered in exotic plants. The desert had been fascinating but she never wanted to be somewhere that flat again. It was so exposed—she had felt like a speck peered at by God through an infinite microscope. Now she could relax and breathe again with leaves between her and the sky.

Where does the river lead? Tinker Bell asked curiously.

"Why, to the sea, of course," Wendy said with bravado. Things had worked out well so far—why shouldn't it continue to do exactly what she predicted? "It feeds into the cove from the western side of the Pernicious Forest, skirting the Quiescent Jungle."

Tinker Bell looked around a little thoughtfully.

I wonder how all this new water will affect everything.

"Whatever do you mean?"

When you fly, you are aware of these things—air weight, rising, falling, moisture, winds. . . . Remember your tumbling back there, over the ocean?

"Oh yes," Wendy said with a blush. "But that was the ocean. *This* is just a river. I'm sure it will all work itself out."

Tinker Bell pointed.

Up ahead things grew cloudy.

Literally.

As the two girls watched the jungle began to disappear. Hills and vales faded—but not from supernatural causes. This time it wasn't the First playing tricks with geography; this was real mist and real fog. The world was blurred by something thicker than air but thinner than real rain. This swirled madly as stray breezes gathered considerable speed over the tops of the trees, rushing toward the river. Clouds of all sorts were pulled from across the heavens into the maelstrom: puffy white Never Land specials, thunderheads from the Black Dragon Mountains, mackerel-backs and mare's tails from someplace inland that must have been a bit like England.

"My goodness . . ."

Wendy had never seen anything like it. Whatever was happening was fascinating and hypnotic—and deeply unnerving on a very basic level. She felt the touch of terror that all animals experience when they instinctively know something is wrong with the world around them. When the weather goes south.

There was a giant *crack*. A moment later Wendy realized it wasn't the sound of thunder. It was the sound of thousands of gallons of water spilling out of the sky all at once. Giant, hot raindrops hurt as they hit her head and eyes; the percussion of them pounding the river was deafening.

"We need to get to land!" Wendy cried out, once again grabbing the pole and pushing. Tinker Bell nodded vigorously and started to fly up but quickly realized there was nothing she could do. Each drop was the size of her head; already her wings looked crushed at the tips.

She hid under the bench.

Wendy wrestled with the pole, dress and slip plastered against her body by the torrents of rain. Water streamed into her eyes whenever she tried to look up and see where they were going. Eventually she surrendered to the greater power of nature and just pushed as hard as she could, blind, hoping it was toward the eastern shoreline. The wind worked the surface of the river into a rippling frenzy; the boat spun on its hull like a compass, twisting every direction.

She finally felt the keel of the boat touch soft, sandy bottom. Wendy leapt out. The water was freezing, all thoughts of the desert washed away along with its red dust and sweat. She gritted her teeth and yanked on the boat, dragging it out of the river and as far up the bank as she could manage. It wouldn't do to leave such a pretty, well-made thing to drift out into the ocean or smash itself to bits on the rocks. And it might come in useful later. Things had a way of doing that in adventure stories.

Besides, it was the first boat Wendy had ever made.

"Tink! Come with me!" She held out her left hand. Without a single protest jingle, Tinker Bell zoomed like a well-trained bee out from under the bench and into her friend's palm. Closing her fingers gently over the fairy, Wendy put her head down and ran into the forest.

The noise of the rain was considerably louder here. Giant drops hit giant leaves with *splats* that reverberated like ancient drums. Just breathing was tricky in the constant deluge; Wendy came close to choking several times as she took in gasps of rain along with air.

Tinker Bell's glow peeped out of the cracks between Wendy's fingers.

Find a trufualuff tree, she jingled moistly. *Like at the Lost Boys' hideout. They're hollow to their roots.*

Wendy looked for one as best she could, since she didn't perfectly remember those trees and botany was not her strong suit.

There were no edges or shadows in the jungle, just a dark, twilighty gray that made shapes and distances difficult to judge. She stumbled to avoid nearly invisible, deep black pools that were home to playful but spiny seven-legged cara-paced things that leapt and splashed in high arcs between them. The whole exercise was exhausting.

Finally, Wendy saw a tree with a comfortingly wide trunk and giant knobby roots. Although she had a fair idea this was their goal, it was confirmed by an intense jingling and shaking of her fairy-holding hand. And there it was, at the base of the trunk: a triangular-shaped hole framed by several intersecting roots. Just wide enough for Wendy to slip through, if she held her breath and twisted herself round like a cork.

"Go take a look," she suggested, opening up her hand. Tinker Bell obligingly buzzed out and down into the hole. Fairy glow flickered and bobbled like a candle in a lantern as she zipped around inside the tree. She reappeared at the entrance and nodded vigorously.

"*Great,*" Wendy said, a little ironically. "A dry hole under a tree. Even more exciting than seeing a jungle again. What a day."

Glad there was no around to see, she awkwardly stuck one foot into the hole, dangling until it touched a hard-ish surface, then squeezed her other foot in place next to it. Spinning slowly with her hands above her head, she ducked down until she disappeared, a genie shrinking into a bottle.

The little cave wasn't half as bad as she expected: it was dry, didn't smell too musty, and didn't contain any fetid animal refuse. If she pulled her knees up there was even room to sit or curl around herself and sleep if she needed to. Rather than feeling claustrophobic because of the weight of the tree above them, Wendy felt safe under the roots that laced together to make their ceiling.

"On the whole, a very acceptable, ah, *hole*," Wendy said approvingly. "If I were a rabbit I should very much like to live in a place like this, permanently."

We're just here until the rain stops. Then we have to go find Peter, Tinker Bell jingled, a little anxiously.

"And save the world, don't forget. We have no idea where the pirates are, or exactly what they intend to do. And the First said that time was running out." Wendy sighed and put her hand out without thinking to comfort the little fairy.

Without thinking, the little fairy climbed up onto it.

"I can't even tell how much time has passed since we first entered the Land of the First. Do you have any idea?"

Tinker Bell looked thoughtful, then shrugged and shook her head, jingling meaninglessly.

"I wonder if time passes differently there. Like in fairy tales. No disrespect," she added quickly. "Was the time we spent there like centuries out here? As if we were asleep, or under a fairy spell having the time of our lives, while time passed out here? No . . . that doesn't feel right. I think it's the reverse. And that makes more Never Land sense, really: time passing slower for the dwellers in the infinite beginnings of the world. Oh, I do like the sound of that, don't you? I just came up with it. 'Dwellers in the infinite beginnings of the world.' I should write that down."

She went to take out her journal before remembering that her parents still had it. Worse than that: she realized that her bag was gone. When had she lost it? When the mermaids tried to drown her? When she slept in the air on the way to the First? Clambering around the rocks in the desert? The river journey? She couldn't even remember the last time she had seen it.

"Well, I suppose the pirates' gold buttons and thimbles will *not* become useful later in the story, as originally suggested," she said sadly. "Nothing in Never Land seems to stick around for very long. I must remember when packing up for my next adventure to choose a bigger, sturdier satchel. A solid waxed canvas one, maybe, that goes over my shoulders with tight straps, like a soldier's."

Tinker Bell pouted sympathetically but distractedly, still watching the rain.

"We'll fly as soon as it calms down a bit," Wendy promised. Glumly, she watched her friend's shadow squeeze droplets out of her wings—and the emptiness of the space on the wall where Wendy's own shadow should have been. She sighed and tried to think happier thoughts.

"This is a bit like a tiny version of the Lost Boys' hide-out, isn't it? I really liked their home, actually—it could just do with a bit of a woman's touch."

Tinker Bell turned away from the rain and nodded vigorously. Like it was a subject she had thought about often.

"I used to dream of being a sort of a den mother to the Lost Boys, you know. Keeping the house neat, maybe sewing a rug and curtains, mending their rather disreputable clothes . . . Being useful and loved and happy, and surrounded by a passel of adoring children. But children grow up . . . or at least, they're supposed to. In my world, like my brothers. And I think I've tried all that anyway and I'm a bit done."

It was funny . . . she had finally come to Never Land—but for entirely different reasons now. Not because she was a girl who wanted to take care of others and find a place for herself; because she was a human who wanted adventure and quests and a reason for getting up in the morning and a purpose in life. To escape the role and future others wanted for her.

Could her life in London have been different in such a way that she wouldn't *want* to flee to Never Land? She wasn't as brave and strong-willed as those women who went to deepest Africa and the outback of Australia, leaving their families and taunting their detractors.

(Also, she didn't have the money. The world opened up for everyone, girls especially, if there was money. Most of those adventurers were heiresses. Wendy basically ran the Darling household and knew firsthand the cost of clinging to respectable middle class. There was no money for jaunts to the Outer Hebrides, much less Africa.)

So what *would* make Wendy happy? That she could do—in London?

Tinker Bell was looking at her curiously. Time apparently passed outside Wendy's head even as ideas and feelings ran around for what seemed like forever inside it. Like time in the realm of the First and Never Land.

"Sorry, lost in my thoughts. Don't want to be a mother for the Lost Boys anymore, basically. But it *would* be fun to redecorate their hideout. Like your lovely little apartment. Oh, I just adored it!"

Tinker Bell smiled prettily, no modesty or self-deprecation at all.

"If I had a flat of my own, I'd set up a little house for you when you visited, a bit like your place now," Wendy said dreamily, wrapping her arms around her knees. "There's a fancy toy store downtown with the most cunning little furniture for dolls. . . . Tufted sofas and real Persian rugs the size of my hand. They even have tiny pewter dishes and the loveliest little porcelain claw-foot bathtub with a real miniature India-rubber stopper!"

Tinker Bell's eyes widened farther with each item listed.

"I've never much played with dolls, but I always loved looking in the window of that shop. I could make tiny beeswax candles with cotton thread wicks to put in the tiny silver candelabra they sell—they're almost like jewelry, they're so tiny and sparkling and delicate! Imagine if they really worked. Well, I don't suppose you need a candle at night when *you're* getting ready for bed—you carry yours around with you all the time."

Tinker Bell looked around at her glow and smiled smugly.

"Well, anyway, I'd have everything else all set up for you. You *will* come visit? When this is all over? And I return home?"

Despite the newfound (though mild) desire to return to London, the idea of the *end* of her adventure came down on Wendy hard, as solid as the dreaded end of a perfect summer day—or eventual end of life itself. She looked down at her ragged, dripping dress in wonder. She had been kidnapped, beaten around, almost drowned, nearly trapped in a desert for all eternity . . . and yet the thought of it all being over was terrifying.

The thought of never seeing Tinker Bell again . . . after they finally began to get to know each other . . .

The little fairy was frowning, but not angrily. It seemed like she was considering a thought that was so new and alien to her that she automatically distrusted it.

Me and Peter, you mean? Us come visit you? Come inside?

"You needn't bring Peter, if it makes you uncomfortable. It's funny, I came all the way to Never Land and haven't even actually met the boy yet. And I've still had lots of adventures. But it could just be . . . *you*, you know. I would miss you so terribly. You could take an afternoon. We could have tea, like my mother does with ladies she likes. I confess I've never liked the idea of tea out with anyone besides Mother before. Because I don't have any close friends—and because it's really a little silly. Flower plates and talk of the weather and only one lump of sugar. I'm supposedly a young woman and I still think tea tastes awful without at least two . . . but I have to put on a good show for the boys. Act like an adult, you know, set an example."

Tinker Bell was nodding, obviously a little perplexed as Wendy chattered on, too nervous about her heartfelt admission to do anything besides babble about inconsequential things afterwards. Belittling and dismissing her own deep feelings. As always.

The little fairy put a hand on her thumb and patted it.

I think I would like that. But we'll see.

"All right, plans for the future, better to concentrate on the now, eh?" Wendy said, shaking her head free of silly thoughts of fairies coming to a London bedsit to visit an aging spinster. "Let's keep an eye on the rain, and leave the moment it lets up."

And the drops fell, and time passed, the two girls from different worlds sat in companionable silence.

Meanwhile, on the High Seas...

The sun shone its absolute hardest. The sky it sailed in was a pure balmy blue, empty but for the occasional harmless puffy cloud and the impressive but subtextually unimportant albatross.

(This was Never Land. It was a giant white bird, distinguished from the smaller white birds—seagulls—only by size and call.)

The sea below stretched far and smooth in every direction, green as a precious gem. In London someone would point out how one can see the earth's curvature at sea after only twelve miles, but this was Never Land and nobody cared. The horizon *did* curve gently, and little wispy clouds would flock to it at sunrise and sunset for a perfect viewing.

That was what geometry and distances were for in Never Land.

A jolly pirate ship flew over the waves. Its sails puffed out like a giant wind child was blowing on them. Its skull-and-crossbones flag snapped merrily in the wind.

The whole scene practically screamed *adventure* and *shenanigans*, as in Never Land it should.

But something was wrong.

The crew on the deck was neither swabbing reluctantly nor singing lustily. There were no sea chanteys being belted out or harmonicas or pipes being played. No one was *avast*-ing, or *something*-ing the mainsail, or trying to figure out how to spell *fo'c'sle*. They sat or stood uncomfortably, rest-ing on their mops, unable to play mumbly-pegs, mindlessly hauling rope, end over end beyond its seeming use.

All eyes were directed to the front of the ship, where the reader's should be, too.

The prow of the *Jolly Roger*, a ship well-known to fans of Never Land awake or asleep, was decorated with a giant skull, as on its flag. But its famous figurehead was eclipsed now by a newer, more intricate, and far more terrifying dec-oration: a giant cage of golden wire and evil pointy bits that was suspended precariously over the water.

Captive inside was a squirming splotch of blackness that didn't quite resolve into focus. It deformed and swelled and shrank and stretched but somehow never managed to ooze out of the wickedly sharp pincers that held it in place. Four of them, sharper than Sleeping Beauty's spindle, were set around the thing at points of the compass. Each dug deeply into the material of Peter Pan's shadow. Four more were set in points indicating places only known to Captain Hook, Mr. Smee, and perhaps the shadow itself.

Its skin rippled around the barbs like a horse's flesh when a fly lands on a sore.

The shadow hunkered down, trying to become as small as it would be underfoot at noon on the equator; to virtually disappear, and thereby free itself of the points. But somehow it remained stuck. Long, thin, sickly strands of shadow ran from the barbs back to its center, refusing to snap free. The shade would vibrate for a few moments—like a hideous spider prevaricating in the middle of its web—before reforming itself and trying something new.

But for long periods in between it would give up and resolve itself into a version of Peter Pan, albeit a horribly distorted one. In terrible irony it put its arms out as if it were Peter: flying free, banking and turning on the wind.

Pulleys and wires under the cage attached to the pincers would then twist and squeak and groan, almost in ridicule of the normal creak of a ship's ropes and rigging. These wires ran through guides and eventually connected to the captain's wheel. When the shadow banked, so did the ship.

That the shadow was in unspeakable amounts of pain wasn't even a question. Sometimes its shrieks actually bordered on the audible. No pirate slept through the night comfortably even with bellies full of purloined grog and bits of cloth stuffed into ears and kerchiefs wrapped around weary heads. Even when the cries couldn't be heard, its torment could be *felt* thrumming throughout the ship.

The crew, already an unhealthy lot, looked even sicker than usual.

"Smooth sailing today," the Duke observed reluctantly, afraid—like all of them—to break the streak.

"Ain't right," Djareth mumbled.

"Go talk to 'im, go talk again," Screaming Byron told Zane.

The tall, skinny pirate spat in response to this, but without conviction.

"Go on then," Ziggy pushed. "You drew the short straw. You have to."

"Likely as kill me as reason with me," Zane sighed. "But better to be dead than caught in this misery forever."

He sauntered over to the captain's quarters and knocked. An irritated voice growled from within.

"Mr. Smee, could you get that?"

"SMEE! Where the deuce did you get to?"

"Dash it all, do I have to do everything meself. . . ."

"COME IN!" the captain finally roared.

Zane swallowed and took a last look back at the crew. They all gave him unconvincing grins and thumbs-up. He sighed and opened the door. He would rather have done many things, including face a fleet of sharks with just a bowie knife, rather than enter the dark, unwholesome hold of his captain.

Hook looked as resplendent as ever in the ridiculous red frock coat that Zane sorely coveted. But his face was an unhealthy pink, glowing and perspiring from something unnatural—certainly nothing wholesome and clean like working the masts, counting loot, or cutting a throat.

"Begging your pardon, Cap'n," Zane began, trying to remain polite—something he wasn't much used to.

"Ah! Alodon. *You* would appreciate this, out of the whole crew. I've come up with some tweaks to the Painopticon that not only enhance its effectiveness, but also add some very stylish flourishes."

Zane licked his dry lips and leaned over the table where Hook gestured. Apparently the captain had been scribbling away with a beautiful swan's feather pen on a sheet of parchment, his fury and passion betrayed by the untidy spots of ink all over his sketch. None of it made any sort of sense except for the flourishes Hook had described, which were drawn as neatly and intricately as an architect's diagram.

"Er, lovely, Cap'n."

Zane let his eyes roam over the rest of the desk, which was covered with black leather-bound books, scrolls written in what appeared to be Greek, and one particularly hideous tome labeled *The Necronomicon*.

"I knew you would like it." Hook grinned smugly and chomped down on the upper cigar of the twin cigarillo holder he sported.

"Yes, Cap'n. Amazing, Cap'n. So the boys were kind of wondering when . . . ah . . . all this would be over? It's a lovely spring day, sir, and we've got a cracking breeze. Perfect weather for despoiling a port or two."

"Yes, yes, I know, I feel it, too, Zane," Hook said with a sigh, looking nostalgic. "This sort of air reminds me of when I was a young man, skewering a few of the queen's finest. But you know, work first, play later."

The pirate was on the one hand relieved by this answer from the intemperate Hook. He had *expected* to be fired upon, or stabbed—or worse, to sit through one of the screaming, incoherent lectures the captain of the *Jolly Roger* so enjoyed.

On the other hand, the seemingly random tempers of Hook were actually quite predictable. This behavior was not, and therefore terrifying.

Knowing he was dangerously tweaking the crazy, Zane

nevertheless persisted. He had drawn the short straw, after all, and pirates did keep to their code.

"Ahh . . . and what work would that be, Cap'n?"

"Why, finding Peter Pan, of course!" Hook said, laughing at his crew member's idiocy. "Once we have him I can put my final plans into action. He must be there to watch the destruction of Never Land, of course. I mean, if we're short on time I could just . . . leave him to his and everyone else's fate. But that would be missing the point, wouldn't it? It would be revenge, but lacking finesse. Anyway, one way or another, after that we'll be free to do whatever we want. Maybe we'll upset the power structure in a small Caribbean island nation. That might be a nice change, eh? A little civil war and *revolución* for the masses? Roast some pigs, party like it's 1699?"

"That sounds lovely, Cap'n. It's just that the crew . . . well, this . . . *work* of capturing Pan seems to be dragging out a bit. . . ."

He continued quickly, seeing the look on Hook's face.

"*And* this whole involvement ye have here with shadows and black magic—it ain't right, sir. It ain't right or wholesome. That's the way of witches and sea sorcerers. We none of us signed up for a sea sorcerer as a captain, sir."

He swallowed but held steady. That was the truth, plain and simple.

"Ah, well, I suppose I could see your issue with that," Hook relented, tapping his chin thoughtfully with his hook. "But shadows—what can you do? There is no other way to deal with them other than black magic. They are . . . literally . . . black.

"But you're right about things dragging out a little long. Time's a ticking, Zane. You can practically hear it. That foul beast of a crocodile is nearly upon me. We don't have forever, you know. The sooner we get this done the sooner we can move on with our lives. I have to rid the world of Peter Pan and his silly Never Land friends before we can all be free."

Zane sighed.

The captain of the *Jolly Roger* was somehow both more reasonable and more insane than ever. There was nothing that could be done besides mutiny—and who was going to try a mutiny against a psychotic, hooked captain who now knew black magic and had captured the power of a shadow?

"What if," the pirate begged, "what if we went after some *other* annoying lad—one of the other Lost Boys, maybe? Or someone else entirely? Someone close and easy to grab? Then you can do whatever you want to Never Land and we'll all be on our way."

Hook laughed. "Well, what would be the point of that? This is *revenge,* Alodon. Peter Pan must see what happens to everything he loves and perhaps just die on his own—of a broken heart."

Zane ground his back teeth in frustration.

He tried a different course.

"You know . . . some would say your chasing after Pan isn't actually about revenge, sir."

"Oh? What else would it be, then?" the captain growled, holding up his hook. Despite his growing lunacy, he kept it regularly sharpened and polished; it glittered even in the low light of the lantern.

"Well, some would say—not me, necessarily, Cap'n—but *some* might say it's less about revenge and more about . . . well . . . chasing your own youth, sir."

Hook stared at him. In the dim hold, the two regarded each other silently for a long, awkward moment.

"What in blazes is that supposed to mean?" the captain finally demanded.

"Well, it's like this, Cap'n. Peter's young and adventurous and can fly, sir. And you can't never catch him, he's always receding from you, as it were, sir. Like youth. And also, he cut off your hand, which *might* could be looked at as representative of the end of your prowess with a sword, and—"

"OH, SHUT YOUR BLOODY NONSENSE UP!" Hook roared, standing up and throwing the desk over. As the books tumbled and he pulled out his flintlock, Zane felt

a strange sense of relief. This was the sort of ending he expected.

"I ought to shoot you in the head, you insane, Freudian dimwit," Hook growled. "We're only Jungians on this boat, you know. I can see all this focus on Peter Pan has made you a bit loony."

"*Me* . . . ? Loony? Focused on Peter Pan . . . ?"

But Hook wasn't even paying attention.

"Well, maybe we could all use a break," he said with an air of *giving up*. "A bit of R & R might do you and the crew some good. And, as it happens, although Peter's shadow is leading us almost directly south, I have a bit of an errand to get done first, at Skull Island."

Zane's face lit up. "Skull Island! The boys'll love that! We can dig up some casks we hid there, have a right party. That'll get you back to feeling yourself, sir."

"Yes, well, I suppose you and the crew can have an evening. *I* need to work. To prepare for my final showdown with Peter. . . ."

Hook's eyes flicked to a pile in the corner. It was almost indistinguishable from the other pirate bric-a-brac he chose to collect: pianofortes, urns, snuffboxes, an evil-looking and sinuous black dagger. But there were several tightly capped quarter-casks with what looked like three *X*s stamped on their sides, and a pile of rope or fuse.

There was also what looked like a broken-up clock.

Hook saw the surprise on Zane's face.

"Oh yes, I know. Usually I hate the dratted things. But it's just one last clock," the captain mused quietly. "*The* last clock. For Skull Island."

"All right, Cap'n. Whatever. I'll go tell the crew about landing at the island. They'll be happy to hear it."

But Hook was already picking up the desk and frowning at his drawings.

"If you see Mr. Smee, send him in here. That rascal's been missing all morning and I haven't had my tea yet."

Zane sighed again, shook his head, and prepared to deliver the tiny bit of good news to the crew.

The Thysolits

The sky above the jungle grew darker and lighter at the same time, shades exchanging depth and brightness. It took Wendy a moment of watching through the hole in the tree to realize what was happening: the storm was clearing up, the clouds were dissipating and leaving a streaky just-washed sky. A *night* sky, bright with stars and a moon that hadn't risen yet. Or moon*s*. Still inky; the world lay in shadow.

"Well, this is rather beautiful," Wendy said, pushing her way up and out of their den. The forest looked like it was covered in pixie dust—and transformed in other indescribably mysterious ways as well. A very *un*-tropical and refreshing breeze blew. The air smelled delightful and fresh;

there was no heavy undercurrent of the rot or foul sweetness that usually permeated the forest floor.

Winged things began to come out of their hiding places. Giant birds flapped heavily overhead like geese (if geese had four wings). Night singers, invisible in their slick black feathers, called out to each other tentatively. Insects began to chirp and *scrtch*.

One particularly wondrous Never Land creature hummed up right in front of Wendy. It looked like a very, very, *very* large carpenter bee . . . if that bee had a thorax the size and shape of a wine glass. Its wings, strangely geometric and crystalline, looked too small to be able to lift such a load. A pair of long legs hung out in front mirrored by a pair of tiny feelers above. Large faceted eyes stared dumbly ahead.

As Wendy watched, its bulb-thorax flickered and slowly lit up.

Not like a fire or an electric light, but more dimly, and sort of black-and-white, like a photograph.

Deep within this glow images began to appear.

A hazy blur resolved itself into a mermaid—perhaps even one of those Wendy had encountered—brushing her hair in the lagoon. Again and again and again. The little play looped around to the beginning again like a circle of yarn in cat's cradle. Sometimes it went in reverse and the mermaid's hair fell up in strokes.

Tinker Bell was rising in the night air along with the other creatures, stretching and looking a little grumpy. She was not, by any account, a nocturnal fairy.

"Tinker Bell! What *is* this creature?"

The insect flew very slowly and Wendy was able to move around it, regarding the thing from every angle. Also like a carpenter bee it seemed more interested in hovering than actually going anywhere with purpose or direction.

Tinker Bell made a bored, disgusted face.

It's a thysolit. They're stupid. Barely alive. Dangerous.

"Oh! Dangerous!" Wendy backed away from it immediately. The amount of poison in a stinger from a thorax that size would be enough to kill an army.

No, not like that, Tinker Bell said, yawning. *They . . . suck you in. Not you. Not everyone. Those who pay too much attention. Poison the mind, not the body. If you're that kind of person. And if you rouse a whole colony they get you.*

"But I won't get stung?"

No.

As if to illustrate, Tinker Bell approached another one of them that was just taking off from the ground and threw herself against it, hard. The insect fell to the side, confused, then shook itself and continued on its original path.

"Oh . . ." Wendy approached closely to see if it was all right—then peered at its images. These were of the same lagoon, but a different part of it. No mermaids, just lapping water and what might have been the fin of a fish about to surface, again and again and again.

More thysolits rose, buzzing drowsily and drifting into the sky like silky seedpods. Wendy walked among them, enchanted.

"But what is going on with their—derrieres? What are they showing?"

Anything. A moment of time from somewhere in Never Land. They collect them. Usually they're only a few hours old.

The next one Wendy saw had a monkey swinging from vine to vine across a high stream that fell down into the lagoon. The one after that showed Hangman's Tree.

"Oh, look, Tinker Bell! It's the hideout!"

And in fact, another one had a loop of the Lost Boys themselves (and Luna), sitting around the table and eating a plum pudding they had gotten from who knows where.

The next thysolit showed a placid beach, a scurrying crab. The next one showed an empty sea. . . .

"And the pirates!" Wendy cried as the *Jolly Roger* came riding quickly through the waves.

Tinker Bell jingled impatiently. *So? We should go! They are probably looking for Peter!!*

"No, wait," Wendy said, twirling around and searching all the other bees. "It seems like these creatures fly in clusters. Like they gather their *moments* together. There's always a number of the scenes that take place at the same spot. If we can find all the ones related to *this* moment, maybe we can see where the pirates are, or what they are up to!"

Tinker Bell thought about that for only a second before nodding. She began to zoom around the creatures, checking their sides with as much grace and care as an American cowboy searching the flanks of his herd for the right brand.

That is, not very delicately.

Wendy was still a little hesitant about just grabbing and handling the insects. She resorted to glimpsing and ducking and weaving and saying *excuse me* when the situation warranted a gentle pushing-out-of-the-way. Dozens of them were now aloft. Their lights blinked on slowly, one by one, like stars coming out in a hazy summer night.

Some of their scenes took a moment to figure out: one was the black eye of a large animal, blinking; in another, a set of children who *weren't* the Lost Boys danced and cavorted on a hilltop, ribbons round their heads and streamers flowing from their hands and toes.

Tinker Bell jingled loudly and excitedly. Wendy looked up and saw that the fairy was steering a bee from behind, flying it toward her friend.

This one showed a close-up of the prow of the *Jolly*

Roger. While the view wasn't far enough back to give them any geographical information, what it did show was interesting—and disturbing. It looked as though the pirates had hung a sort of cage off the front of the ship. The thing was extremely nasty-looking, covered on the insides with spikes and barbs and other horrid implements.

And inside this cage was a dark, oily figure that could only have been Peter's shadow.

Watching over it was Hook, unmistakable even at that distance in his bright red coat.

"What are they doing? It looks like they're torturing him!" Wendy took the bee into her hands without thinking, trying to get a better look. She had to resist shaking it to see if that would help.

What is the cage for? Why are they suspending it over the water?

"I don't know—is it to threaten the shadow with drowning, I wonder? Or are they . . . are they using him somehow to *power* the ship? Or maybe . . ." She spun around, letting that thysolit go and running back to where Tinker Bell had first found it. Now she batted the creatures carelessly in her zeal to find the right one. "Let's see . . . water, more water, no. Oh—I know that face," she said, seeing a surprised and angry-looking pirate in one, as if the bee had almost knocked him in the nose. "Ziggy. Interesting fellow. Sewed a patch on for him, sort of a lightning-shaped one. Look—a beach! With rocks! Tinker Bell, does this look familiar to you at all?"

Tinker Bell watched the rolling waves and strangely shaped boulders rewind and replay. She shrugged.

That could be anywhere on the eastern coast. If the thysolit is following the boat or the pirates, though, they are heading south.

Wendy frowned. "Why? Do they know where they are going? Did they somehow get the shadow to tell them where Peter is, do you think? Is that why they are torturing him?"

Tinker Bell shrugged again. But her brow was furrowed with worry. She made a little flying-off gesture with her fingers: *we should go.*

"Yes, of course. Peter's shadow is in more peril than ever—and Never Land as well. Let's be off." And Wendy turned to launch herself into the air.

But . . .

A thysolit drifted by with an unusually dreary image in its thorax. Almost entirely black-and-white and grainy, the interior of a dull house. Somehow the room seemed both vacant and cramped at the same time. There was an un-set table. Two ghostly figures sat at it. One looked like he was about to say something—but didn't.

"Michael! John!" Wendy cried.

She grabbed the next closest bee and peered desperately into its bulb. A misty view of the street the Darlings lived on, at dusk or dawn, empty of people.

"Tinker Bell! You said these thysolits only gathered moments in Never Land. How are they showing me London?"

She caught another one, her fear of the supposedly dangerous things now entirely gone as she tried to find another view of home.

Wendy . . . Tinker Bell jingled warningly. *We have to go. Stop. This is what they do.*

"But Michael and John! They looked so sad! Do you think they miss me? How much time has passed there since I left? Oh, do let me find just one more. . . ."

As she searched among the bees for more images of her brothers, she was vaguely aware of the insects' growing numbers. The air was filled with the pleasant hum of their ridiculous little wings. It was hard to see anything now, much less take a close look at their behinds.

Wendy! Tinker Bell jingled. *Your brothers are fine! They're distracting you! Poisoning your mind!*

"Don't be silly. I feel fine. Oh, look, it's the Shesbow household," Wendy said, turning another thysolit over in her hand. "What are they up to? Piano lessons? Funny, looking in on someone's house without them even knowing it. It's like being a peeping tom, one second at a time. I wonder if Mr. Crenshaw's house is here, too. . . . I would so love to see what he's up to."

Wendy!

Struggling, Tinker Bell wove her way through the tightening mass of bees. She grabbed the human girl's arm and yanked it. *This is exactly what happens. You get caught. You humans—too interested in what you can't see for yourself. You fill your heads with too much . . . noise.*

"Too much *news*, you mean," Wendy corrected. "Look! There's parliament. Oh my goodness, they're all arguing! Whatever do you think it is? Taxes or something to do with Europe? Wait, is that a view of Paris? I've always wanted to see Paris."

Wendy reached out for a bee with the Eiffel Tower flashing on and off in its thorax like a strange warning beacon.

It flew just out of her reach. She lunged too far—

But didn't fall.

Instead she found herself drifting softly several feet above the ground.

It wasn't the fairy dust; she wasn't concentrating on floating or flying or anything else but grabbing at the bee.

In some ways it was a far stranger phenomenon that held her aloft: her legs and body were now entirely supported by the soft, furry thysolits.

But she was only vaguely aware of this.

WENDY! COME! Tinker Bell jingled anxiously.

The dazed girl had finally managed to get hold of the bee she wanted. It was warm and plummy in her hands, comforting, not at all dangerous or disobedient.

(A bit like that stupid little dog her parents had given her—but quieter and far more pleasant.)

The smell of honey filled the air, sweet and soothing. The cityscape of Paris in miniature was enchanting. Everything was lovely.

Eventually done gazing at the Eiffel Tower, Wendy looked up. She was a little surprised to see that she was in a sort of nest or cocoon made out of the bodies of hundreds of thysolits. They ignored their unwary passenger as they droned and flew to whatever their eventual nighttime destination was, taking her with them.

The frustrated jingles of Tinker Bell were soft and fading as the little fairy tried to force her way in from the outside.

"Ah, excuse me?" Wendy addressed the bees, leaning forward. Those making up her "seat" underneath shifted themselves obligingly to better support her new position. "I don't mean to be rude, but my friend would like to come, too. . . ."

The thysolits in front of her turned themselves slightly so she could see all of their thoraxes—all of their moments—neatly lined up. Paris . . . the Shesbow twins . . . St. Petersburg . . . New York City! The bookseller's nephew . . . *Thorn* . . .

The smell of honey grew stronger.

"Oh, look," Wendy said. "Look at it all! It's like a thousand little plays . . . just for me. . . ."

Every once in a while, as if somehow sensing she had finished watching a scene, a thysolit would gracefully exit its place and another would come to fill in with a new image or scene.

"How thoughtful of them . . ." Wendy said dreamily. "I can just sit here and watch . . . don't have to lift a finger. . . .

"OUCH!"

Finally, having shoved her way through the wall of bees and apparently out of options, Tinker Bell had resorted to the last trick of fairies. She sank her sharp little teeth into Wendy's arm, forcefully enough to summon bright drops of blood.

"Tinker Bell, you . . . !"

But the pain cleared her head; the smell of blood was stronger than honey. Wendy took a fresh look at the scene around her through slightly more wakeful eyes.

Thysolits. Everywhere. Completely caging her.

"I'm surrounded by a bunch of bees with pictures in their bottoms. And they've kidnapped me," she said slowly.

Tinker Bell decided an extra little nip would drive the point home.

Wendy didn't even really react, thoughtlessly scratching at both wounds.

"Yes, you told me so. I really could have sat here forever, trying to satisfy my curiosity. And they would have kept finding something else to pique my interest, to make me continue. . . . And I would have been lost. A subtle kind of poison indeed. They promise to show you the world but just sort of hypnotize you instead while life goes on without you. What would they have done with me ultimately, do you think?"

Tinker Bell shrugged. *Something not good?*

"As succinct and correct as always. Shall we?"

Concentrating on flying the normal way—Ha, normal! As if flying had been a normal thing a week ago!—Wendy tried to part the bees like a curtain. Tinker Bell didn't bother with such niceties, kicking them in their rear ends and punching them in their eyes. Which actually seemed to be a better tactic, because the thysolits resisted Wendy's efforts utterly, pushing back with a force she didn't believe insects should have.

"Let me out!" she cried, finally also resorting to kicks.

The wall of bees opened—and then enveloped her leg, covering it with their combined weight. This threw her awkwardly off-balance; she flailed and swayed and swung her arms, trying to regain herself.

Concentrating and tipping only a little, she managed to draw her little dagger from its necklace sheath.

"Don't make me use this!"

No reaction. She might as well have been talking to a bunch of . . . well, bees.

Feeling a little guilty about the violence, Wendy swept her arm out with the knife held diagonally, her thumb on its top, like she was sawing off a strip of old cloth. The blade slipped harmlessly in between the first thysolits, who moved slowly out of its way . . . and then caught and sank into the bodies of those who couldn't or wouldn't escape.

The result was immediate: a black and amber ichor began to pour out of the torn bee bodies. The smell of honey became overwhelming. And sickening.

The humming changed; it was no longer drowsy but growling and angry.

The swarm turned and dove at her face.

Wendy screamed. She tried to knock them away, now using her dagger like a badminton racquet. But they didn't bounce away lightly like a shuttlecock. Every time she injured one, it *stuck* on the dagger—like thick honey—and she had to shake it loose before defending herself from another one.

"Tinker Bell! Are you all right? How are you doing?"

The jingles that came back to her were angry and loud but otherwise unintelligible.

The things were now bludgeoning Wendy's body hard enough to leave bruises.

"Let's just push our way through—maybe we can outpace them!"

Wendy covered her face with her arms, and, pointing her dagger before her, flew upward *into* the thick of the swarm. Hopefully where they least expected her to go.

She burst into the clear night air, shedding bees like ugly raindrops.

Tinker Bell zoomed through the path she had made and appeared by her side, disheveled and a little scratched. But red with anger and ready to go.

"Come on, this way!" Wendy pointed south, because that was the way the pirate ship had been heading. At least she thought it was south—she was turned around from the bees and there were no points of reference from which to take her bearings. Ursa Major didn't look quite right and there were no moons at all.

The two girls spread their arms and took off into the wind . . . and then Wendy looked behind her.

The swarm had caught on to their escape plans. Like a strange yellow-and-orange tornado, they crowded together and rushed at the two girls.

"Back this way!" Wendy cried, pointing. Tinker Bell nodded, understanding immediately.

They dove *under* the swarm.

Momentum—and insect stupidity—continued to carry the bees forward, now the wrong way, *away* from the two girls.

But it wasn't very long before they righted themselves and were in pursuit again.

"All right. Hide in the clouds?" Wendy suggested. But there were none now. The storm had finished and it was a perfectly clear night, not a wisp in sight.

I don't think we can outrun them, Tinker Bell jingled sadly. *This is why they're so dangerous—they're relentless. Once the colony is on the warpath, they will never let up.*

"Surely there must be some escape . . ." Wendy said, looking around desperately for a mountain or a cave or some other sort of answer to present itself.

This isn't London. You can't escape Never Land the way you could escape your life in the city.

"I feel like we should revisit this theme later, and less ironically," Wendy muttered. "Also: *Ouch.* All right. I suppose it's . . . fisticuffs, then?"

She tried to ready herself for the clash, putting her arms up the way she imagined a boxer might, but with her dagger out.

The bees came, their hum and bodies filling the sky to the horizon.

"They never actually *sting*," Wendy reminded herself bravely. They just had numbers and mass.

That didn't stop it from being utterly terrifying when they hit.

They slammed into her all over her body. She could barely get a breath in between their blows, which came like a massive, fuzzy hailstorm. Their droning drowned all her thoughts.

She tried her badminton strategy again, using the length of her arm and dagger together as one weapon, connecting with as many bees as she could with each blow.

This was moderately successful, at least for knocking them away—if not actually killing them.

Still they kept coming.

One clocked her in the head so badly she saw stars. She fell, spiraling to earth.

Only Tinker Bell's quick response and tiny hands on hers guided Wendy back into remembering which way was up.

A hundred, a *thousand* bees were waiting for her when she returned to battle.

Her arm throbbed. Her left eye swelled almost shut. Her stomach ached from the angry purple bruises that now covered it. Without her shadow, Wendy's reserves were depleted quickly.

And they just kept coming.

Every time she thought they had done enough, that she and Tinker Bell had killed *enough* of the creatures, they would try to fly away—only to be pursued twice as angrily by the remainders. They never gave up.

Hit, block, hit, drop.

Hit, block, hit, drop.

It was clear: there was no escaping, no flying away, no resting, no stopping for a breath, no doing *anything* else until the last bee was gone.

Wendy dispatched the thysolits one after another without thought, sending their waning lights and broken bodies down to earth. The whole thing was less like a heroic battle than scullery work: endlessly scrubbing and scrubbing a room of dirt and grime that would, given the chance, kill her.

She couldn't turn her attention away long enough for a glance at Tinker Bell. She heard encouraging jingles now and then and knew the fairy was doing the best she could, maybe one thysolit for every dozen or two of her own. Eventually exhaustion wore even the terror whisper-thin.

She lost her fear of falling and dying.

The stars wheeled overhead in a way that made little sense. The moon (moons) never rose. Nothing Wendy had ever done in her life, not the most menial, boring household task, had ever lasted this long. Or required such continual strength: acid burned in her muscles as she lifted her arm, hit, dropped her arm, lifted, hit, and dropped. . . .

She barely noticed when there were only a dozen thysolits left. She had begun to sink slowly groundward, losing whatever it was that kept her afloat with the fairy dust.

"I . . . can't . . . fly . . . Tinker Bell. . . ."

The little fairy grabbed her by the hand—while kicking a bee hard in its mandibles. Her touch helped but didn't stop the fall. So she guided Wendy's descent into the little boat, where the human girl crumpled into a ball. Tinker Bell defended her there, valiantly trying to drive off the last few bees.

One final thought occurred to Wendy before she passed out: *They don't talk about* this *in adventures.*

That being a hero is just work . . . and boring work . . . endless work . . . nothing more . . .

Meanwhile, in Another World...

But what of the family Wendy left behind? *Does* time pass in the real world as it does in Never Land? As it does in the Land of the First? How exactly are the two worlds (three worlds) connected? If it's teatime in Never Land, what hour is it on the east coast of the Americas? What does Wendy's father mean when he says, "It's gin-and-tonic time *somewhere* in this great, bloody world," and what exactly are cocktails? Does Wendy's family miss her?

We shall indulge the reader with the answer to exactly two of these questions, even as we indulge the author in a bit of fourth wall breakage.

In the empty, somewhat dark house of the Darlings, it was raining outside. John and Michael burst through the door with the endless energy and boundless enthusiasm of two young men, the elder of whom had just aced a botany exam and the younger of whom had toast and treacle for lunch as a special treat from the headmaster. Also there were puddles: Michael was soaking. John was trim and dry from the top of his ridiculous hat down to his spats, for he had a large umbrella given to him at Christmastime that he took with him everywhere and called Bella.

("Bella the *umbrella*, isn't that just perfect?" And maybe it was, the first twelve times. After that, even Wendy began to grow cross.)

"Wendy, we're home!" John called.

"Where's the tea? I can't smell tea," Michael said a little plaintively.

"You can't *smell* tea being made."

"I can smell the steam, it's all warm and moist and lovely," Michael snapped. "And I can hear the whistle. And if she or the cook has made buns, I can smell those, too."

"Neither hearing a whistle nor smelling buns has anything to do with smelling *tea*," John pointed out with the wise air of someone much older—and more often than not a pain in the thorax.

"I guess we shall have to make it ourselves," Michael said, completely ignoring his brother's freely given wisdom, as he often did. He poked cautiously at the stove and looked around for the box of matches. Lack of Wendy and how-to knowledge were only temporary impediments to teatime, not permanent ones.

"But where could she be?" John asked, now sounding plaintive himself.

Old Nana finally made it into the kitchen by this point. She had been slumbering in front of the fire in one of the upstairs rooms, happily dreaming of lying in front of a fire. She chuffed, demanding the sort of greeting an elder doyenne of the household deserved.

"Nana." Michael hugged her, and the dog didn't mind his wet and muddy paws—the same as Michael never minded hers back when she, too, was of puddle-jumping age. "Have you seen Wendy?"

Nana sighed. If the two boys had been a little more observant of her large, expressive brown eyes, they would have realized she was saying something to the extent of, *Oh, here we go again. You're not going to bother even trying to understand what I'm about to say, but I will try to tell you anyway, because that is what good dogs do.*

She walked over to the kitchen door, sat down pointedly, looked out the window, and barked once.

"She's gone out," Michael hazarded.

Nana sighed a moist pant of relief.

"Wendy? Gone out at teatime? Most suspicious. That's not like her at all."

"Maybe she has gone out to buy us special treats and got caught in the rain," Michael said hopefully.

"It's *London*, Michael. No one ever 'gets caught in the rain.' It rains all the bloody time here." John started off saying it amusingly, like his father would, but trailed off into something somewhere between wistful and bitter. For the slightest moment, a world had flashed in front of his eyes, a memory of bright sun and blue sea that wasn't a real memory at all, but a memory of imagination. There was a palm tree and the smell of coconuts.

Without being able to read his brother's mind and yet somehow sensing the mood behind it, Michael took the sort of cerebral right turn that babes sometimes manage when their too-learned betters cannot.

"We should get treats for Wendy sometime," he ventured, not coming to quite the right conclusion (but not the wrong one, either).

"Yes, we should," John said uncertainly. The two sat down at the un-set table, and the older boy's mind went the way the younger one's couldn't, wondering, perhaps, if it was too late for something like treats to rectify a situation they had been stupidly unaware of—despite how traces of it were pressed into every dark corner of the house, making itself widely known, and permanent, and sad.

———

When Mr. Darling returned home for a light supper before going to his study to get even more work done and Mrs. Darling finished her book club/charity drive/sherry session with the Tevvervilles and Miss Pontescue, the two entered to a half-lit house and an uninspired supper. Wendy rarely cooked unless it was a special occasion, but *every* occasion had her mark upon it. An extra garnish, a pretty bouquet, a little menu she had written out.

But this night the table was set minimally, napkins thrown down on chairs. The lamps weren't trimmed. The leftover roast, plopped in the middle of the table for anyone to steal or any mouse to nibble, was mostly cold. John and Michael sat glumly in their seats, politely waiting for their parents, not even bothering to sneak an early morsel. John had a book he wasn't reading.

"Boys." Mrs. Darling kissed them each on the head. "Where is Wendy?"

"No idea, Mother," Michael said. "She hasn't been here for hours."

"Oh." Mrs. Darling looked at Mr. Darling.

"Oh." Mr. Darling looked flummoxed. Wendy was never not where she was supposed to be when she was supposed to be there. "Has there . . . has there been a break-in?"

"Has someone stolen Wendy?" John asked, with a sneer and the touch of irony that often bloomed in an overbright boy with two mediocre parents. "Is that what you're asking?"

Mr. Darling frowned. His eldest son had reined in his tone at the last minute, couching it in what sounded like genuine surprise. Darling fruffled for a moment, feeling like he was being made fun of somehow, but couldn't quite put his finger on it. He wanted to be angry.

But Wendy . . .

Mrs. Darling, ever practical, was looking around the foyer. "Her umbrella is here, though her jacket is gone. She couldn't have gone out, or at least not far."

"I go outside without an umbrella all the time," Michael said.

"If there was fun to be had, you would go out without your own shadow," John said waspishly, rolling his eyes.

The two boys looked at each other, realizing the same thing at the same time.

"*The shadow,*" Michael whispered.

"*It's not real,*" John reminded him, also whispering.

"*We should check.*"

"We'll go look upstairs one more time, Mother," John said loudly as the two boys hurried away from the table. "I . . . pray she doesn't have a fever and lie collapsed, insensate, somewhere."

"That's a bit much," Michael muttered, realizing with a wisdom beyond his years that he would be saying very similar things to his older brother for the rest of their lives. Nevertheless, united in this mission they raced upstairs together into the old nursery, which was now John and Michael's room. It had been repainted, of course, and had a new chair and extra wardrobe, and a neat line drawn down the middle in chalk past which Michael's lead soldiers were not allowed to march.

The old bureau was still there and still had some of Wendy's old things in it: once-favorite toys, bits and bobs, sewing notions. The top drawer was stuck, as always happened in damp weather; John had to wrestle with it up and down until it finally flew open, sending him backward to land on his bum.

Michael ran forward to look in.

"It's not there!" he said in awe, rustling around the drawer, ignoring the pin and needle pricks from the untidy pincushion. John rose up behind him without the usual complaints that should have come from such a pratfall enacted on his serious, scholarly body. He, too, poked around, albeit more hesitantly. But there were no extra shadows to be found—nor even the silken bag and wrapper she sometimes kept it in.

"Was it ever really there?" Michael finally asked, in perfect innocence.

"I don't know," John admitted.

On the one hand, Mr. Darling didn't want a scandal that could jeopardize his position in society or at the firm. On the other hand, neither he nor Mrs. Darling was entirely immune to the stories of Spring-Heeled Jack and the dreary, mysterious gray fogs of a London spring. The police were quietly notified, though the Darlings were quietly notified back that young unwed girls had a tendency to show up again hale and hearty, if often wed, or at least with child. Since there were no signs of violence, no known enemies, and no bodies floating Ophelia-like down the Thames recently, the police weren't concerned.

Mrs. Darling didn't believe it was a boy, at least a boy they knew; whether or not she was the *best* mother (as John and Michael and Wendy believed), she was good enough to know her daughter. Wendy, being a strange kitten, was not interested in any boys that way, except for maybe the bookstore owner's nephew.

"She'll come back. It's all probably just to avoid being sent to Ire—" Mr. Darling began.

Too late he saw Mrs. Darling's panicked eyes and shaking head.

"Sent to—to *Ireland*?" John asked sharply. "You were going to send Wendy to *Ireland*?"

"Why? For how long?" Michael demanded.

"We just felt like your sister needed a little break," their mother said gently.

"Rid her head of fairy stories, the nonsense she continually writes down in that notebook of hers," Mr. Darling blustered, angry at being caught out, angry that he ever had to hide anything.

"You wanted to send her to Ireland to rid her head of fairy stories," John said. "Let me just get this straight: the land of the *daoine sídhe* and the *bean sídthe* and the *pookah*?"

"Now look here, John—"

"You're sending Wendy *away* because of her stories?" Michael shouted. "Did you take her notebook? Did you *read* it?"

"Michael, we're her parents. We have every right to read—"

"But then you know! You *know* she's ever so much better than Beatrix Potter and Robert Louis Stevenson!"

"But those are . . ." Mrs. Darling began. Maybe even she wasn't sure what *those* were.

Something went out of Mr. Darling.

He collapsed onto a chair, head in his hands.

And so the Darling house continued on in a state of uncertainty and gloom. No one would admit a mistake or a problem, but the problem presented itself readily whenever there was a button to be mended, or Nana sighed, or meal after meal was silent and somehow unsatisfying. Despite the cook and the scullery maid the house seemed darker and dirtier. Groceries weren't bought, objects were misplaced, clothing grew ugly. No one hugged Mr. Darling in that special way daughters did; no one fell speechless at Mrs. Darling's dress or asked to use her perfume.

And no one wrote stories anymore.

There, you see? Everyone was perfectly miserable, and for each day that passed in the real world, a day passed in Never Land, more or less. Though you probably have guessed that already because of the business of Peter's shadow going missing for so long. But tell me this, since you're such a clever reader: If Wendy ever *does* arrive back home, changed or unchanged from her adventures, will life go on as before? Do you really think that's possible?

The Darlings were beginning to think not.

Pan

Night slowly rolled into morning as the boat drifted down the last length of the new river. The sun was warm, the rain was gone, there were no maniacal mermaids, tyrannical pirates, unknowable gods, crystalline guards, or tricksy thysolits. . . . Despite their pressing quest, Wendy found herself relishing the quietude. If life back in London were as fraught and dangerous as in Never Land, she shouldn't have minded the quiet in-between days so much. A giant house with nothing to do seemed almost inviting after such travails.

Tinker Bell did not seem to be enjoying the lull in action. She had grabbed the prow of the boat and flew hard, trying to drag it through the water faster. Wendy laughed not unkindly at the look of fierce determination on the fairy's face and the tiny muscles popping out along her arms and base of her wings. A few sparkles of fairy dust sweated off.

The water grew shallow and spread into a silver delta, sculpting the soft sand into a thousand scales. The banks on either side became dunes. Once again Wendy was on a beach facing the sea.

Tinker Bell flew high up to get a better view, letting the boat go. It continued on, neither slower nor faster without her help.

"I wish you wouldn't get your hopes up about Peter," Wendy began carefully. "We still have no idea at all where he is, nor any way to find him. Hook should be our main concern now. We'll have to—"

But Tinker Bell dove down and grabbed her hand violently. She pointed across the sand. The fairy's eyes were the widest Wendy had ever seen, so wide they threatened to consume her face.

There, lying nonchalantly in the curve of a coconut tree, was Peter Pan.

"Oh," Wendy said, her mouth making the perfect shape of the letter she spoke.

He was unmistakable. Slender, clad in bright leafy green. Soft shoes with pointed tips. Soft hat with a red feather sticking jauntily out the back. Swooping nose.

Auburn hair and extremely distinctive eyebrows. Dagger dangling from a thin belt.

He let one hand trail languorously toward the ground and seemed to be conducting some sort of invisible orchestra with the other. His eyes were closed.

He was *so* Peter Pan it was ridiculous. He was realer than real. In brighter colors than Wendy ever imagined and far greater detail. Just like a dream but *more*.

"But how . . . ?"

They had been chasing his ghost all over Never Land and he wound up exactly where they were headed?

Tinker Bell was smiling devilishly.

Part of your magic. The stories. Part of his magic. Peter Pan.

Then she zoomed off to see him, abandoning Wendy and the boat.

Wendy struggled with a foot that was asleep and a boat that was tippy, only clumsily managing to disembark.

She started to haul the boat onto the beach—and then thought better of it. In Never Land one seemed to be stripped of everything: bags, modern possessions, decent clothing, ideas. Nothing material remained with anyone for long.

"Just look at what the Lost Boys wore and sat on, and what happened with Luna," she murmured.

Found and then lost again. Even her own shadow.

If they needed transport someplace else, they would improvise. Wasn't that what Peter always did in her stories?

Wendy pushed the boat back into the slow current and slapped it playfully on what would have been its flank.

"You go and help someone else now. You're free—of me, at least."

She watched it float away, so pretty and blue and gold like a toy, until it was safely far out in the sea. . . .

And pretended she wasn't trying to delay meeting her hero.

With a sigh she turned and began to head for him (and Tink). She watched the prints her feet made in the sand and the trailing threads and tatters of her dress dancing around her freckled legs. Not the way she had imagined she would be dressed when she met Peter. Not that she really ever had imagined clothing in the adventures. Only the accessories: a stylish cap, a sharp sword. Everything else was ignored or assumed to be the usual; Wendy in a light blue dress, probably.

A shadow—*her* shadow!—danced over the sand to her feet, daintily touching them with her own toes. Wendy felt a surge of completeness, of warmth and solidity. Some exhaustion faded away.

She kicked her feet, spraying sand and shadow sand at her shade.

Her shadow sputtered in surprise.

"Oh, you're back. Lovely to see you again," Wendy said dryly.

The shadow pointed at Peter excitedly.

"Yes, I know. We found him. Ourselves. No thanks to you. You didn't even come get us once *you* found him. Fat lot of good you are."

And with that, Wendy ignored her shadow, walking with great dignity toward the palms where her friends were.

(I'm afraid, dear reader, you can't see how the shadow reacted to this, for Wendy very steadfastly ignored her— literally refusing to see her. And since we are living this story in Wendy's point of view, you shall have to resort to your own imagination to decide what the shadow did.)

Peter Pan sat up and looked at Wendy.

The time had come to admit her wrongdoing and take her comeuppance. To begin the next part of her quest, where together the three of them would save Never Land.

She stuck her chin out and marched up to him.

Upon closer inspection she realized how small the boy was. Not tiny, but slender and no taller than she. Maybe even shorter. His face was *very* boyish—he hadn't lost all the baby fat from his cheekbones yet, and his teeth were suspiciously small . . . like his adult teeth hadn't come in yet.

Wendy swallowed, remembering the near-romantic thoughts she used to have of him. The eager young lad looking up at her now couldn't have been more than twelve or thirteen in London years. His eyes, though feral and dark, seemed somehow younger than John's.

"Hello, you must be Peter Pan." Wendy covered her mixed feelings and nervousness with accent and politeness. She did not curtsy.

"Tink here was just telling me you were going to help me find my shadow!" Peter said with a grin of undiluted happiness. His teeth sparkled and his eyes crinkled in joy.

All misgivings and reluctance disappeared. Wendy was immediately swept up by his energy. She would do *anything* with him—she could tell he was the most fun person in the whole world. His games would be the *best*.

"I can see you're having trouble with *your* shadow, too," he went on to say, smirking at Wendy's. She risked a look—the shadow was pouting, arms crossed.

"Well . . . wolves and shadows," Wendy said nonchalantly. "They have their own minds and motives. What can you do?"

"Ain't that the truth," Peter said with a sigh. Wendy felt her heart skip. He was *commiserating* with her! They were *bonding*! "'Cause say what you want about them, but it's hard not having a shadow, you know. It really tires you right out. I was just taking a lie down here, on account of my continual exhaustion and the pains."

"Pains?"

Tinker Bell and Wendy looked at each other, worried.

"Oh, stomachaches and heart aches, like I've eaten too much from the snacky tree," Peter said airily, dismissing it. "But ha, Wendy! I can't believe it! I used to come and hear your stories . . . and here you are, helping me! On this beach, no less!"

"Of course. But . . . what *are* you doing on this beach?" Wendy asked, curiosity getting the better of her—and her apology.

"Looking for my shadow, silly! Didn't I just say I was missing it?" he said with disgust.

It was approaching noon, and they were close enough to whatever passed for an equator that nothing had a shadow, except for the puffed heads of the palms directly over their roots.

And Wendy, of course, whose shadow sulked away from her on a sandy mound.

"But . . . there aren't any shadows here at all. . . ."

"Exactly! So mine would stand out, right? I'd see him immediately!" Peter crowed in triumph.

Wendy looked helplessly at Tinker Bell, unable to think of a response to this lunacy. The fairy, who had been looking up at Peter with wide eyes a moment before, a delicate hand on his, gave her a little shrug: *what can you do*?

"Peter, I *know* where your shadow is," Wendy said quickly, before something else stopped her from admitting the truth. "I had it. In London. I traded it for passage to Never Land."

And Peter Pan, for perhaps the first time in his existence, was silenced.

Tinker Bell gave Wendy a nod and a tiny smile, pleased at her friend's brave admission.

"You . . . had it?" he finally said, trying to work it out. "In . . . London?"

Wendy nodded. "You left it there. The last time you came, I suppose you surprised or upset Nana, our dog. She tried to bite you but grabbed your shadow instead, and I'm afraid she rather ripped it off of you. She didn't mean to, really. She's a good dog. She was just trying to protect us. I kept it all these years—folded carefully in a drawer, waiting for you to come back and fetch it."

"I remember now!" Peter leapt up, twirling, laughing and crowing. "That *was* the last place I saw him! Gosh,

I haven't been back to London at all since then! I haven't gone back at all, not even to look! That's strange, I searched everywhere else. I *should* have looked there. But Tink kept telling me . . . Tink kept telling me . . ."

He frowned.

Tinker Bell swallowed.

Wendy bit her lip.

"Tink," Peter said, eyes glowing with rage and suspicion. "Why did you keep telling me it wasn't there? That I shouldn't bother looking in London, or ever going back? Didn't you *want* me to find my shadow?"

Tinker Bell wrung her hands and swayed back and forth miserably.

I didn't want you seeing Wendy again.

"Wendy?" Peter demanded, confused out of his anger. "Why? What's wrong with Wendy? Is she—is she evil?"

No! She—I was jealous.

"What? *Jealous?* Of some silly girl?"

"I beg your pardon," Wendy said, her eyebrows rising.

Tinker Bell nodded woefully.

"And you were so jealous that you were all right with me going without a shadow for the rest of my life? What kind of friend *are* you, Tink?"

"She didn't *know* I had the shadow," Wendy interrupted quickly, seeing the flames in his eyes. "Not really. In fact, she came to London of her own accord to look for it, but I had already left for Never Land."

"Well, *thank you* for that," he spat, looking wrathfully at the fairy. "It's been like . . . hundreds of moons since I lost it! You're the worst, Tink."

The little fairy collapsed into a crumpled ball of wings and arms and legs and began to weep.

"Oh!" Wendy cried, scooping her up. "She made a mistake, Peter. She's trying to make up for it. She did it because she loves you. And didn't want to lose you."

"*Loves . . . ?*" Peter asked, sounding sick.

He stuck his head close to the teary-eyed fairy.

"Is this true, Tinker Bell? Do you . . . *love* me?"

The fairy nodded, sparkling tears still spilling out of her eyes.

"Well, that's all nuts," he swore, sitting back on his heels.

"Shh, don't cry, it's all right," Wendy murmured. The fairy tears stung and burned. For only a moment, but it was still a little unnerving. "Just give him a few minutes."

"And I don't mean nuts just about the love—*blech*—business," Peter continued, stomping up the beach, then spinning around and stomping back. "It's nuts and bananas that you say that you care about me and then wait *forever* to go get my shadow!

"Tinker Bell, you're *banished*! For *treason*!"

"Oh no, stop it! She did the wrong thing for the right reasons," Wendy snapped. Which was incredibly strange, because here was the hero of her dreams and she was talking to him like she would Michael or John when they were being silly. "Don't go about banishing her or whatever. Accept her apology and move on—we're wasting precious time. There are other things going on besides reuniting you with your shadow.

"Hook is planning to destroy Never Land as some sort of doomsday farewell gesture—he was just waiting to capture you before he carried it out."

"Oh? All of Never Land? Destroyed?" Peter asked, surprised. "That's huge. All right then. Tink, you're forgiven."

His switch from red-faced anger to forgiveness was so abrupt—and apparently free from reflection—that Wendy felt seasick.

I'm sorry, Tinker Bell jingled through a gap in Wendy's fingers. Golden light spilled out around her apologetic face. She looked like a tiny Renaissance saint.

"Apology accepted," Peter said, nodding officiously. "Don't do it again."

I never will. She said it with such warmth Wendy could feel it on her fingers.

"Now then, what's this about Hook wanting to destroy

Never Land?" Peter asked. "I mean, he's evil, but he's not *insane*. Well, all right. He's insane. But not *that* insane. If he destroys Never Land, where will he go?"

"Right out of my stories forever," Wendy said. "Along with the rest of you."

Tinker Bell shivered.

"Well, it all seems crazy to me. So how does he plan on doing it?"

"I don't know—I don't have any of the details beyond the fact that it has something to do with getting you first, maybe by using your shadow to lure you in. It's like he wants to punish you and erase his past at the same time. And," she added quickly, making herself say it again, clearly and aloud, "it's *my* fault he has the shadow. Because as I said, I traded it *to him* to come here."

"Hm." Peter looked her up and down as if seeing her for the first time. Reevaluating. "Yes, you are a bit old to come to Never Land the normal way. Plus, you're a girl."

"A silly one, I'm told," she said archly.

"Exactly. At least, you were when I first started visiting you. Now you're like . . . a silly young woman. Pretty clever, using my shadow as payment for passage. Even if it wasn't yours."

"Thank you?" Wendy said uncertainly.

"So wait—let me get this straight. You gave the shadow

I left behind to my enemy? Crazy old codfish whose hand I took, who's been after me ever since?"

"Ah . . . yes? Yes. I did. I did that." She cleared her throat. "I did the worst possible thing, and I'm so sorry, Peter, you don't know how—"

But she was interrupted by a loud crowing, a resounding *cock-a-doodle-do* from Peter's wide mouth.

He was grinning and spinning, hands on his hips, laughing, dancing.

"I get to fight the *pirates* for it!" he sang. "I get to battle old Codfish to get my shadow back! Oh, I've been meaning to give him another hook! This is a *perfect* opportunity! Well done, Wendy! You're brilliant!"

He grabbed her hands and spun her around, causing Tinker Bell to go flying head over heels through the air and then land with a hard *thump* on the sand.

Wendy should have been over the moon that the legendary Peter Pan was delighted by her antics and was now dancing with her. She should have felt a happiness and satisfaction in her heart that she had never known before. Rather than earning his scorn or hatred, she had *impressed* her hero. It was a glorious, greedy feeling. One that Peter Pan particularly inspired; she could see herself doing anything to recapture that feeling, to make him feel that way about her again and again—if he couldn't feel about her any other way.

But . . .

She looked over to where Tinker Bell had landed. The fairy was a little stunned and a little rumpled and glaring furiously.

At *Wendy*.

Not Peter.

If her eyes had been coals, they would have lit what was left of Wendy's dress on fire.

Wendy quickly dropped Peter's hand.

"Well, yes, but I'm still sorry. The shadow was never mine to trade. It was terribly selfish of me."

"Oh, it's all fine," Peter said, waving his hands at her. "C'mon! Let's go get the pirates!"

He turned and went to dive into the air, but paused on the ground in a ridiculous tiptoe pose.

"Little help here, Tink?" he asked.

The fairy shook her head forcefully, crossing her arms and pouting.

Wendy felt weariness descend upon her. *This* was the sticking point? *This* was where their quest ended? Despite the evolution of her and Tinker Bell's friendship, Tinker Bell remained very much a fairy: prone to sudden passions, savage angers, swift tears, and whatever one moment demanded but the next moment forgot.

Just like Peter Pan.

Just like characters in story after story who never change because you don't want them to. You want them to stay the same forever, like you wished your best friends or your relationship with your mother would.

Wendy watched the two of them bicker with a strange mixture of feelings. They were both like children. Wendy wasn't really, not anymore. Despite living in her parents' house and taking on tasks like Mother in a game of pretend and dreaming out the window and making up stories no one wanted to listen to. She had started to want other things, even if she couldn't name them yet, and had grown tired of her current life.

But was that change so terrible, really?

Would it be better to stay in Never Land forever and never change?

To be the same talky, nervous Wendy forever? To always have the same desire to make others like her by taking care of them? To always be the same lonely girl who never fit in any world? To always dream and never *do*?

Sometimes stories needed to be pushed along. Things needed to happen. People needed to accomplish things. And as long as Peter and Tink were somewhere in the world, never changing, and Wendy knew that, she would be happy with whatever happened to her. As someone who changed in the course of a story.

As someone who *changed* the course of a story.

"Actually, she's right," she said, her wonderful, story-telling mind coming up with a useful plan that would make everyone happy—and behave.

"I mean, you should still give him the fairy dust, but he should really *stay where he is*. The pirates have been running all over the seas looking for him—it would be much easier to work this out by just having them come to us, don't you think?"

Peter and Tinker Bell frowned almost identically in confusion.

"I've said this before: I really don't think the three of us can go up against the pirates all by ourselves. I'm not that handy with a sword—a real one. I'm sure Tinker Bell can be quite dangerous in her own way. But as someone who has been actually captive to those seafaring hoodlums, I don't know how much good fairy dust does against gunpowder and savage bloodlust."

"I don't need help!" Peter protested. "All I need is to be able to fly! I can take on old Hook by myself!"

"But can you, I wonder . . ." Wendy said thoughtfully. "I think I'm beginning to figure this all out. You've been tired and weak without your shadow, just like I was. And now Hook *has* your shadow, in a cage. A nasty one. And you were talking about strange pains and aches. . . . I think

Hook is getting to you through your own shadow. Maybe he can't kill you directly, but he can hurt *it* and affect *you*."

This gave Peter pause.

"A cage? He has my shadow in a cage?"

"I'm afraid so. With all sorts of nasty barbs and pincers inside."

Tinker Bell watched Peter closely for his decision. As he considered this information, he unthinkingly offered the fairy his hand up.

She grinned from ear to pointed ear.

"I don't like this. I don't like this at all," he swore. "Using my *shadow*. That's against the rules. That's bad form. So I guess what you're saying is that I need a crew. An army. All right then, to the Lost Boys! Yeah! Together we'll all save Never Land! Let's go get 'em!" He made to fly again.

"You should stay here," Wendy said, "remember? We decided that a moment ago? Even assuming you're back to yourself enough to fly, Tinker Bell would be fastest. She'll fly there, and you and I will . . ."

Tinker Bell narrowed her eyes at Wendy.

"I mean . . . *I'll go*. Yes, that's best," Wendy said, correcting herself quickly. "Tinker Bell can stay here and look after you. If that's all right? I'll just need very precise directions. And some more fairy dust, if you don't mind. For me *and* Peter."

Tinker Bell closed her eyes and bowed politely—*of course. For you.*

She flew up in a dainty spiral around Peter, gracefully whisking showers of golden sparks over him. Peter laughed in delight.

She threw the dust over her shoulder without looking at Wendy, getting her in the face. Not out of spite—it was just that the fairy's eyes were still on Peter.

"I'm not sure this relationship is very good for either one of you," Wendy muttered, wiping dust off her nose. No one paid her any attention.

"It's easy to get there," Peter said. He squatted down and pulled out his dagger to draw a map in the sand. "We're here, at Pegleg Point. Then hang right at Blind Man's Bluff. Then follow the river up—"

"Sorry, which river?" Wendy asked, trying to understand. All she saw were vague lines and gashes and one sinuous, perhaps watery, track.

"Whaddayamean, *which* river?" Peter said, laughing. He pushed his hat from the back so it dipped down over his face. "There's only *one* river in Never Land."

Tinker Bell jingled, shaking her head.

"There's two now," Wendy said. "I made one."

For perhaps the second time in his existence, Peter Pan was shocked into silence.

"When we were with the First," she continued primly, trying—sort of—not to be smug. Had Peter ever created anything from nothing in Never Land? Anything so grand?

"You went to the *First*?" Peter Pan gulped.

"The mermaids told us you went there to see about obtaining a new shadow."

"I did! Good-for-nothing jerks," he growled, kicking sand over his map. "They wouldn't even let me in. I had to walk the whole way and *they wouldn't let me in*! Told me to deal with 'my own piddling issues.' *Me!* Peter Pan! I'm practically the *king* of Never Land."

Wendy turned this declaration over in her mind. How often did Peter say things like this? How often did he act like that? How true was it? No wonder Slightly was chafing a bit.

"Well, consider yourself lucky, perhaps. They tried to trap us there—we very nearly could have spent eternity in a desert maze, trying to find our way out."

"I can't even believe you went there to begin with," he said, turning to Tinker Bell. "Tink? That was incredibly dangerous. You know, for someone who isn't me. You really did that? You went in there . . . for me?"

Tinker Bell nodded shyly.

"Huh. That's some powerful stuff there." He scratched his chin. "L—uh, whatever is you feel, I mean."

Wouldn't you do the same for me? Tinker Bell asked, the tips of her wings quivering.

Wendy felt her heart stop. She waited as anxiously as her friend for the answer.

"Yeah, of course," the boy said, shaking his head in disgust. "But that's not 'cause of love, that's 'cause we're buddies. You're my first mate. You're the most important member of my crew. I wouldn't let anything happen to you, ever."

Tinker Bell clasped her hands in delight and looked at him with shining eyes. He smiled and patted her on the head.

"Good enough," Wendy decided.

"Whatever river you choose, Hangman's Tree is here." He put an X on the ground.

Can you remember from when we went there before? Tinker Bell asked. *It's southeast of the Black Dragon Mountains, about halfway to the coast. In a round clearing, like a fire or a meteor cleared it out.*

"Thank you, Tinker Bell," Wendy said. "That was very precise and clear."

"Did you name it?" Peter asked suddenly.

"Name what?"

"The river! Did you name it yet?"

He was deadly serious.

"No—I don't suppose I have," Wendy said. "Hadn't we better—"

"We absolutely had better!"

Peter put a finger to his chin, thinking.

Tinker Bell furrowed her brow, trying to come up with something.

Wendy looked at both of them in exasperation. They didn't have time for this.

Peter's eyes lit up and he opened his mouth.

"How about—"

"We are *not* calling it the River Pan," Wendy interrupted.

"I wasn't," Peter said peevishly. "I was going to call it the River Peter."

Tinker Bell giggled, sparkles of dust falling around her.

"No. How about . . . the First River? *You* should like that. It makes sense, but it makes absolutely no sense at all. It's just Never Land's style."

"The First River! It's the River of the First . . . but it's *not really* the *first river*! I love it!" He clapped her on the back—rather a little too hard, and she fell forward.

But what if the pirates get here before you get back? What if Hook gets to Peter before we're ready? Tinker Bell asked.

"What about your fairy friends? Can you ask them to help? To at least—keep you company?" Wendy asked. "To keep an eye out?"

The little fairy gave her a nearly uncomprehending look.

"I know you aren't the closest with them, really, but this is an emergency. You're in serious need. All of Never Land is in trouble. Thorn might come—he seems a decent sort."

Tinker bell tossed her head and began to jingle something contemptuously.

"Don't," Wendy interrupted. "Don't let your ego get in the way of protecting yourself and Peter."

"I don't need protecting by fairies!" Peter squawked indignantly.

Wendy and Tinker Bell ignored him.

Finally, the fairy nodded. *All right. For Peter.*

"Good," Wendy said with a sigh. "Well look, I should head out. Stay *here*," she ordered, standing up and readying herself to go. "Tinker Bell, take care of him. Make sure he doesn't leave. But if the pirates appear, fly—if you can—into the jungle and hide."

Tinker Bell saluted her smartly.

But Peter just stood there gazing at her, mouth agape.

Wendy looked down at herself; she hadn't even realized how heroic a pose she struck. From her shadow—which took this opportunity to actually behave—she realized how she appeared: powerful, strong . . . with a scandalously short tunic cinched around her waist and improvised leggings that showed a prodigious amount of her newly tanned skin. Her hair was down around her shoulders. She bet she was the spitting image of an Amazon, short a bow.

"Gosh, Wendy, you sure look different from when I first saw you," Peter mumbled.

Tinker Bell put her hands on her hips and started to jingle.

"Well, I must be off," Wendy said quickly. "Bye!"

And she took off into the air, like Nike, triumphant.

And She Flew

Wendy fell backward into the sky a little more rapidly than she intended. It felt like a dream she'd had once or twice: suddenly being pulled up into the air, snatched out of a narrative, away from monsters or loved ones.

Her heart jumped at the unnatural movement but she didn't stop.

Barreling forward, she stuck her arms out and—*there*. Her fingertips brushed against the steady warm wind that Tinker Bell looked for when they had great distances to fly. It streamed almost directly due north, so she would have to get off it and take a right at some point, but it would ease the journey somewhat.

She banked into the thermal, feeling important. For the first time in her life she was on a quest where people needed her for real things—for *survival*, not for a popped button or an emergency trip to the market for some dinner veg. If she failed it would mean disaster for her friends and all of Never Land.

And what precisely would Hook do if she failed? If he succeeded in catching Peter? How would he end Never Land *rather permanently*? Would he use dark powers to call up a titanic storm and sink it like Atlantis? Could Peter's shadow have something to do with that? Would he somehow rain down fire and lava?

Well, Wendy didn't intend to find out. She stretched and frowned, flying a little faster.

Was that her shadow down there, also gliding? Rippling over the trees?

Feh! She wouldn't look. At least now she *could* return to London.

And speaking of . . .

What would *she* do, once Hook was defeated?

(As he must be.)

Wendy had wanted adventure; now she had gotten herself one. She could go back home and live the rest of her life on recollections from the past several days, spooning out carefully meted measures of memory to live on when existence grew dull. She could write an entire book on what had happened. She could actually try to get it published and watch with amusement as readers drank up her "fantasy." Or she could just keep it in her notebook, to be taken out and read to eventual children in her life.

She could stay in Never Land forever. . . .

No, that didn't feel right. She *had* grown up a little. And, like Slightly, she chafed at some of the unchanging and arbitrary aspects of Never Land.

Maybe Peter Pan *was* king of the island in his own way. They were similar, or maybe even dependent on each other, just in the same way Never Land was dependent on London—and the rest of the world.

So the real question was: What could Wendy *do* with her life? Back in the real world? What lay in between *household* and *mermaids*? What would give her adventure (of the London sort) and challenges, and a change for the better for both worlds?

John knew that he could choose between being a doctor, banker, academic, or barrister. Even shipping, if he had any ability that way (he didn't). These were known, potential futures.

But despite all her reading Wendy hadn't been exposed in any real way to the idea that there were any possibilities for her at all beyond *unhappy spinster* or *unhappy housewife*.

These were odd thoughts, and uncomfortable ones. She felt a little stirring of self-recrimination: Why hadn't she even *thought* things like this before? Why hadn't she even noticed the invisible prison she was in?

"Because," she told herself gently, "I've never been able to fly before."

Below her Never Land unrolled in shades of green except for the misty, unavailable area to the northwest. Wendy gave that place a salute.

The First had said there were people whose idea of Never Land meant a single warm meal for the day. There were girls who weren't held back by well-meaning parents or society, but by poverty or *genuinely* terrible parents who treated them like possessions to trade. There were girls who had no chance simply because of the color of their skin.

Sometimes stories needed to be pushed along. Things needed to happen. People *were needed to* do *things.*

Sometimes whole societies needed to be pushed along in the right direction.

The landscape below changed and the Black Dragon Mountains came into view, as blurry and smoggy as ever. It was time to turn east. Wendy felt her heart clench. She so wanted to see the mountains—and a real dragon. She wondered if maybe she would have time to dip by on her way back from talking with the Lost Boys. Just a peep.

She sighed and banked right. Probably not. It would be something for her to dream about later, to wonder about and imagine on dark days.

Meanwhile, on the High Seas...

Hook took long and precise military steps up and down the deck, his back straight as a knife blade while he inspected each cannon and musket, sword and dagger. Everything had to be *perfect*.

The pirates, more used to going into battle by the seat of their pants, were a little unprepared for such a military-style drill—and completely unfamiliar with the particulars.

Screaming Byron, for instance, had thought he had done a very nice job polishing the cannonballs at his station, and presented them to the captain with a bow and a proud smile.

Hook just stared at him.

"What good is a *shiny cannonball*?" he finally roared. "Is the barrel of the machine cleaned out? Are your powder cartridges stacked, dry, and ready to go? Is your friction primer up to snuff? In short, will your cannon actually *fire* your very pretty and shiny cannonball when it is loaded?"

"I think it looks very nice," Smee said sympathetically, upon seeing the poor pirate's downcast look.

"We're looking at the *final battle* here," Hook reminded Byron, leaning forward so he could look the other pirate dead in the eye. "Our very last run-in ever with Peter Pan and the Lost Boys. We want to look good, absolutely, but we also want to *finish* it for good. I want their bodies washing up on the shore, bloodied and broken. *All* of them. And I want Peter Pan to see it. Do you hear me?"

"Loud and clear," the pirate said, brightening a little at the mention of blood.

And maybe *final battle*.

Hook glowered: no one in his idiotic crew shared his passion for defeating their worst enemy once and for all. They only seemed to look forward to getting it over with and moving on to whatever fun activity was planned afterward. They were short on imagination and education; they had no taste for refined concepts like *nemeses* and *life conflicts* and *guiding principles*.

(They might also all have still been in recovery mode after their shenanigans at Skull Island. The entire crew but Hook and Smee dragged and stumbled a bit.)

No matter. Whatever it took to drive them to victory.

"Mr. Smee, take a note: I need you to go back and recheck cannon crews one, two, and six. They didn't pass muster. Also, have the Duke unlock the stockroom and distribute as many bullets and shells as needed. My personal stash of purloined weaponry will be available for general use, except of course these flintlocks on me belt. I want every man armed and ready."

"Oh, they'll like that, Cap'n. That'll get them in the spirit! Bullets and muskets! Right away, Cap'n!" Mr. Smee doffed his cap and ran off to deliver the news.

Hook twirled his mustache for a moment, enjoying himself utterly. *This* was what it meant to be a pirate captain! To be on top of everything, awash in the excitement before a battle!

Wait? What was that?

That sound . . .

He grabbed the nearest pirate—Djareth—by the earring. "Do you hear that?" he demanded.

The pirate, wide-eyed, tried to shake his head and shrug.

"*THE TICKING!* Can you not hear it, you villainous fool? The sound of the crocodile approaching!"

"N-no, Cap'n," Djareth stuttered. "Nothing, Cap'n!"

"Bah!"

Hook threw him aside. Of course, when he listened, it was silent now: wherever the beast was, it must have gone beneath the waves.

But it was close.

Hook stalked to the prow. A rope had been hung across the decking between the chart room and the railing along with a hastily painted sign that read NO ADMITTANCE. The words could, of course, just have been gibberish; few of the pirates could read. It was the angry red paint that got their attention.

Zane was on watch. He sat on a stool looking vaguely green, like a reluctant landlubber on a transatlantic voyage. This despite the fact that the wind was up and the ship cut through the waves as beautifully as a knife through a kidney. No, it was *what* he watched: the shadow in its golden prison of bars and sharp picks, the way its blackness recoiled in ripples away from those picks.

"Any change in the prisoner, Alodon?"

"No, Cap'n. He ain't moved an inch. Looks like he even gave up on the whole escaping-himself thing. He's just been man-shaped. Peter-shaped. The whole time. Pointing the same way."

"Hmm." Hook stroked his chin and frowned. The shadow had been pointing that way more or less directly for the last day. It only wavered a little, when the ship had to curve around a bit of coast or shoals, but always returned to face the same way.

The captain made his way back to the chart room. Zane apparently decided that was as good as a dismissal, or an order to follow, and hastily went after him, getting away from the unnatural scene as quickly as he could.

The cool darkness of the cabin caressed Hook's tortured brow. He bent over the table that held the map of Never Land with the help of two pressed-glass prisms, a bronze astrolabe, and a perfect skull. A little pewter model of the *Jolly Roger* stood in for the real one. He did some quick calculations for latitude and longitude. The breeze had remained steady; he pushed the little ship along, down and around the corner of Never Land. Then he took a ruler and tried to predict the route.

"No, it's the same, look at that," Hook said thoughtfully. "If this is all correct, Peter Pan has been in Pegleg Point for two days now—unmoving. I wonder why. That dratted boy can never stay still for more than a moment at a time."

"Maybe he can't fly, Cap'n?" Zane suggested. "That without his shadow, he lost some of his power, or the pixie dust don't work or somethin'?"

"True, true," Hook said, turning it over in his head. "But even if he couldn't *fly*, the boy could still *run*, if the notion took him. No, something else is going on."

"Maybe he's resting. Or sick. Or pining for the fjords. Or . . . captured!"

"But by whom? The First were last spotted on the exact opposite end of the island. The L'cki haven't been heard from in fortnights. The Fangriders of Upper Hillsdale swore they wouldn't bother with him again until they got their numbers back up. It's festival season for the Ragnarosti—they make peace with the deuced fairies and have those terrible musical concerts that go on forever. With the stupid flower crowns and ceremonial kombucha. No . . . it must be a trick. Something he's planning.

"I know, it's an *ambush*!"

He pounded his fists down on the table in realization. But he was smiling.

"Uh, Cap'n . . . ?" Zane asked, worried.

"Don't you see? *I've figured it out.* His ambush! I got it! Ha ha! Peter Pan can't get the best of *me*!"

"But what do we do then, Cap'n?" the other pirate asked carefully. "Surprise him? Go around the island the other way? Sneak in through the back side of the lagoon? Uh, *is* there a back side of the lagoon?"

"No, there isn't, Zane. No . . . I think I may try something else. Go present your flintlocks to Mr. Smee for inspection and see about making any requests from the artillery storeroom. And I need someone else keeping an eye on the prisoner. Someone a bit more . . . proactive, and less squeamish. You know who I mean, Zane. The one who was recently reunited with us."

"Uh, yes, Cap'n. Right away, Cap'n."

Zane shivered as he escaped the room, but Hook didn't notice or care. The moment the other pirate was gone he pulled out one of the black leather books obtained from Madam Moreia. Along with theories on how to capture and remove a person's shadow, there were passages in the book that discussed the connection that remained between them even after the two were separated. The bond between person and shadow was deep and possibly continued through the spirit plane. For if a person was hurt or weakened dramatically—say, an arm cut off—wasn't it true that the shadow was also affected?

So logically it followed the reverse was true, too. And now that Hook had the Painopticon . . .

A smile grew on his face, a genuine, devilish one complete with an evil gleam in his eye.

Finally Captain Hook was going to win. *Really* win against Peter Pan.

And after?

Skull Island.

Peter Pan and Tink

Tinker Bell performed the fairy call for aid as quickly as she could, just above the tree line at the edge of the forest. Then she zoomed back to where Peter lay talking to himself—and then to her, when he noticed she was back.

"I just can't wait until the pirates are here, Tink," he said in a tone only he could master authentically: dreamy and excited at the same time, wistful and full of resolve. "I'll show Hook. I'll show that stinky old codfish. This time, I'll finish him but good, and . . . ohhh!"

Suddenly he convulsed in pain. He fell, hard, to the sand.

Tinker Bell flew backward up into the air to take him in all at once: Was it a poisonous snake? A spiderphyl?

Something else she could beat back with fairy rage?

But . . . no. She could see nothing.

"Tink? Tink?" Peter cried, squirming and writhing in the dust. His eyes were screwed shut in torment.

She landed on his chest, put a hand on his face.

What? What is it? What hurts?!

He opened his eyes and tried to focus them on her, but they were glazed and unwilling to do his bidding.

"Tink, it burns! It's like . . . it's like something inside of me is being pulled—*outside* of me. Something is reaching up into me and is pulling my heart into knots . . . but it's not my heart . . . it's my . . . I don't know what it is. Oh, Tink, it feels terrible. I don't know what it is. I can't see it. I can't fight it. Tink! Help me!"

The fairy buzzed back and forth, helpless and angry. She thought about what she had seen on the thysolit thorax, the pirate ship and the cage. Wendy was right: whatever was happening to Peter must have something to do with the shadow. Something Hook was *doing* to the shadow.

She flew as high into the sky as she could and looked for the pirate ship at sea, Wendy in the jungle. There were no signs of either.

Hurry! she jingled loudly, knowing no one could hear her.

"Tink—where are you? Oh! Please! Tink! Come back!"

She returned to Peter, frustrated and powerless to do anything.

"Don't leave me, Tink. Wendy and the Lost Boys will be here soon. The Lost Boys will come. They'll help me out. They're the best. Even Slightly. He just wants . . . he just wants . . . Ohhhhhh!"

He spasmed, contracting over his stomach again.

"Tink! Where are you? Tink!"

Peter put his hand up to feel for her like a blind man. The little fairy took his thumb and squeezed as hard as she could. His face was pale and glittering with translucent beads of sweat. His breath came in thin-sounding rasps.

Tinker Bell hesitantly leaned over. She kissed him ever so gently on the lower lip.

A fairy kiss, invisible and seemingly ephemeral, whose effects and existence would last as long as pixie dust.

Perhaps his breathing eased. Perhaps he looked a trifle more peaceful, despite his eyes rolling beneath their lids.

She wondered what it meant, the touch of human lips on her own—if *it* left any trace on *her*.

Hurry, Wendy, she jingled.

The Lost Boys

Wendy found the trufualuffs and the clearing with Hangman's Tree in the middle of it fairly easily. Were men ever actually hanged from the nooses that dangled from its branches? She had never given it much thought when telling stories to the boys. . . .

Her landing was far more graceful than the first time there. Also more prepared for the slide down this time, she managed to use some pixie dust power at the bottom of the ramp to pop back up on her feet like a jack-in-the-box, immediately and somewhat unbelievably.

Luna, who had been lounging near the fire, leapt up joyfully and stuffed her nose into Wendy's hand.

"Good girl! Miss me? I've had the most extraordinary adventures. What's it been like here?"

The Lost Boys, figures of her tales of swashbuckling adventures under their leader, Peter Pan, seemed to be having a rare quiet moment. The older ones, Slightly, Skipper, and Cubby, were reclined in various supine positions on different furniture stand-ins: mushrooms, ledges, roots. The twins were playing some sort of game like jacks which involved swiping the *other* person's jacks. They looked almost demonic with their quick movements and shiny white teeth bared in grins that contrasted starkly with their black masks. Tootles had what looked like a bright pink dormouse that he was petting and whispering baby-nothings to.

"Wendy!" He put the dormouse in his pocket and smashed into her, wrapping his arms around her legs, squeezing in next to Luna.

"Did you find Peter or his shadow?" Slightly asked, hopping down from his root.

"I—we—found Peter, yes. Can I have this?" Wendy asked, suddenly distracted by the honeycomb on the table mushroom. She couldn't remember the last time she had eaten.

"I was saving it for—" Cubby began.

"Thank you," Wendy said, for the first time in her life being a little rude. And why not? Everyone else in Never Land was. She couldn't be expected to civilize an entire island of barbarians. "I'll just take a piece."

She broke it in two and immediately shoved half into her mouth, closing her eyes at the glorious golden deliciousness. It tasted like summer and flowers and something exotic. When she opened her eyes Slightly was regarding her with an amused expression.

"That's lovely," she added primly, not even bothering to look for a napkin. She wiped her mouth with the back of her hand. "Even without a bit of toast. Anyway, yes, we found Peter. He's at Pegleg Point with Tinker Bell. Seems a bit peaked. As for his shadow, Hook still has it and is doing something unspeakable to it, maybe using it to find Peter. Hook wants Peter in hand—excuse me, hook and hand—before he destroys Never Land so that Peter is forced to watch it. Or something. According to the First. Pretty over-the-top villainy there. Anyway, it's only a matter of time before the pirates reach him and Tinker Bell. Our job is to lure the pirates in, grab the shadow, and return it to Peter."

The boys—and girl—all stared at her.

"Maybe *she* should be the new leader," Skipper ventured.

Slightly raised a foxish eyebrow. "D'you mean to tell me you plan on using Peter as bait to catch old Codfish?"

"Yes. I'm just going to grab one of these apricots here. Before we go. Maybe three."

She wished she had a bag to tuck them into instead of

being forced to pop them all into her mouth at once. She was so hungry and they were so good there was a danger of the juice spilling from her lips and running down her cheeks. Which, again, would not have caused much of a scene in the den of the Lost Boys, but she wanted to keep up *some* appearances.

"Did you—did you talk to Peter?" Skipper asked in a low voice. "About me?"

"Or me?" Slightly added. "Is everything all right again between us?"

Wendy almost choked. "All of Never Land is in *danger*. Did you miss that part? I have left Peter tended by a tiny fairy while a pirate ship is coming after him. I've been nearly drowned by mermaids, fought off thysolits, escaped the realm of the First, and flown *all over* this bloody island. Somehow, during all of that, I may have neglected to launch into an invective against misogyny or a monograph about the necessary skills of a great leader. We don't have a lot of time here, is what I'm trying to say. Do you think you could get over your personal grievances and come to his and all of Never Land's aid? Are the Lost Boys really going to sit around while everything is destroyed around them?"

"Of course we'll help," Slightly said, pulling out his rapier and brandishing it. "That was never a question!"

"We'd never abandon Peter if he was in trouble,"

Skipper mumbled as she put one hand on her scimitar, the other on her bow. "Whatever our problems are."

"For Peter!" the twins said together, drawing the little knives that hung from their waists. "And Never Land!"

"LET ME AT THOSE PIRATES," Cubby roared, pushing up his sleeves and baring his meaty fists.

Tootles just narrowed his eyes and growled.

"Well, I'm glad to hear that," Wendy said. "I'm going to fly ahead and see how they're doing. How long do you think it will take you to get there?"

"Forced march?" one twin asked.

"Several hours," the other answered.

Wendy began to open her mouth, feeling her panic grow.

"We could use the tunnels through the Cenotaph Caves," Skipper suggested quickly, seeing her look.

"Just what I was thinking," Slightly said with a frown. "They lead right into the back of the cove. And maybe we could ask the Elephant Wheels for help. Let's say four hours, max. Depends on the cooperation of the various parties involved."

"All right, well, I suppose that sounds feasible," Wendy said uncertainly. Elephant Wheels seemed interesting. The other . . . perhaps a little dangerous. She worried about Tootles. "Pegleg Point, by the three clustered palms. If we're not there, it's because we're hiding in the jungle from the pirates, who have already arrived."

"Aye, aye, madam!" Slightly said with a bow, doffing his cap.

"Hmm. You're doing this all in a dress," Skipper observed.

"Not much of one, really," Wendy said with a smile.

"To arms, men—ah, mates!" Slightly cried, raising up his rapier.

"TO ARMS!" they all shouted.

The fox boy threw back his head and howled. The rest of the Lost Boys joined in, each in his or her own way, crowing, barking, screaming, roaring.

"Yes, well, all right," Wendy said. She gave Luna another good solid scratching on her head. "You make sure they find me. And remember where they are going."

Luna barked once.

Wendy wished the wolf could meet Nana; she felt somehow sure they would get along splendidly.

To Arms

The heroine appeared above the jungle like a tatter on the breeze.

Wendy had become just another one of the strange Never Land flying creatures, she realized; had anyone, even her own parents, looked up and seen her—well, they wouldn't have *seen* her. They would have seen a tanned, lanky fairy thing without wings, in strips and bandages of once-blue cotton, performing some unknown task within the realms of the magical island. And considering how many denizens she had interacted with—and almost grown comfortable with—she thought she was also well on her way to being accepted by the *natives* as just another weird flying creature.

Well, maybe not by the First. They were rather cranky about all the newcomers and dreamers who changed their world.

(Who could blame them, really?)

Although she *had* figured out their trap, so maybe that accorded her a smidgen of respect.

But unlike the endlessly cheerful and vicious full-time residents of Never Land, Wendy had hollows around her eyes from the constant flying, fighting, running, bleeding, strategizing, and worrying.

Peter's shape could easily be distinguished among three palm trees on the beach. A tiny golden glow shone against one of the harsh, tree-shaped shadows.

Wendy *tried* not thinking of herself as a ragged facsimile of a Greek god, but she did land as she imagined one might: delicately, cloth whipping around her, arms raised. Not for balance, but for *effect*.

Immediately, the golden glow zipped up and around her madly.

Peter is hurting somehow! They're doing something to him or his shadow, like you said they would!

Wendy now saw that what had at first looked like a lazy, reclining Peter was actually a taut-faced, wan Peter, collapsed into his own skin somehow. He shivered on the burning beach but had sweated through his shirt as if he were in the grip of a great fever. Sometimes he grimaced, eyes closed, and clenched his stomach.

"Oh my goodness," Wendy cried, rushing over and laying a hand on his brow. Tinker Bell didn't even object. He *wasn't* burning up—in fact, he was a little clammy.

Did you find them? Are they coming?

"Yes, though I'm afraid it will be a few hours before they get here. Are you managing to get any liquids into him?"

Tinker Bell nodded, pointing to a leaf she had been using for just that. A puddle of pink juice lay along its veins.

"Good. Well, that's something."

Wendy slowly collapsed on the sand next to them, exhausted and worried. The hard bark of the palm against her back felt like heaven, or at least something far softer than it actually was. She wiggled a bit to scare off any unicorn beetles—an opalescent one fell glittering to the sand, and without thinking, she scooped it up and placed it back on the tree next to her.

(Her shadow stood up against the palm trunk, watching Peter with worry.)

They're taking the Cenotaph Caves? Tinker Bell jingled.

"Um, yes. Do remind me to ask you about what those are sometime. Has Peter been like this the whole time I've been gone?"

"Wendy—you're back," the ailing boy murmured,

rousing a little upon hearing his name. Then his dreamy smile crumpled in a rictus of hurt.

Those terrible pirates! Tinker Bell wail-jingled.

"Well, we shall give them what for directly," Wendy promised, summoning brightness into her features.

The three settled in to wait for the pirates—or the Lost Boys, whoever came first.

The sun beat down hard until it hurt to have the tiniest bit of skin exposed beyond the shadow of the palm trees. Waves of heat danced like spirits between the sand and the sea, the latter of which lapped appealingly against the shore and seemed endlessly far away. Hurdy-gurdy gnats droned and riffed their unending calls.

Wendy reached out and squeezed Peter's hand whenever he went through a particularly bad bout of whatever was happening to him. Tinker Bell brought nectar, or sap, or—really, Wendy didn't want to think about the alternatives; beetle milk?—and carefully poured it into his mouth. But silence reigned over all of them; even the fairy's jingles were absent.

Wendy watched her shadow for a bit: she sat at the base of the tree, also apparently trying to keep cool.

"Really. Fat lot of good it did, you running off like that before," she murmured. "We've all wound up back at precisely the same place. *Again.*"

Her shadow shrugged. *Maybe* looking a little sheepish. Then she stood up, straight and proud—not sorry at all.

Tinker Bell raised an eyebrow at Wendy.

Are you actually yelling at your own shadow?

"But what good did she do?" Wendy demanded, feeling a little childish.

She rescued me.

"All right, yes, but then . . . after . . . She could have been a help, or . . . I was so tired. . . ."

And yet here we are. You won. You beat the thysolits and the First. We found Peter.

"But—"

You're different now. Maybe she is, too, in Never Land. Maybe drop it?

Of course Wendy was different. She was beat up and in tatters, although sometimes she had flashes of feeling heroic. That was something. She considered the black shape standing tall on the sand, her arms crossed. Maybe . . . her shadow wanted a chance to feel heroic, too?

"Maybe that's right," Wendy said slowly. "I've wanted an adventure my whole life—of course it follows that my shadow would, too. I suppose shadows have their own minds in Never Land. I'm not your master, merely your . . . I don't know, solid object. *Home*, maybe?"

The shadow nodded eagerly.

"Whatever you are, I need you and you need me. And we all will most certainly need your help to rescue Peter's shadow. So would you mind staying around at least until we get to the happily-ever-afters? I'll wager you have a better insight into how to aid a fellow shadow in distress than we do."

She reached out her hand and tried to place it on her shadow's. It didn't really work, but the shadow patted the air near where the flesh-and-blood hand was.

Tinker Bell sighed in relief.

And then, finally, something happened.

Tink was high in the sky on one of her lookout missions when she came diving back down like an angry bee (or thysolit).

I see them—the pirates! They're not far off, rounding Bloody Neck.

"We should move into the jungle," Wendy said, getting up. Tinker Bell looked skeptical. "Don't worry! I told the Lost Boys that's what we would do if Hook came first. We'll keep an eye on the beach in case they look for us there instead."

Mollified, Tinker Bell fluttered around Peter's face, trying to wake him up.

"Tinker Bell?" he asked softly. "I was just dreaming about you. . . ."

The fairy's face blushed in surprise—and pleasure—but that didn't stop her from planting herself on Peter's chest and gently slapping his chin.

Get up. The pirates are coming. We don't have reinforcements yet.

"I don't need no—"

Peter tried to stand up. Instead, he spun on his feet, falling back toward the sand. But Wendy was there to right him.

"No, there you go, easy now," she said, throwing one of his arms around her shoulders. "Let's just take it one step at a time."

Despite his slender build, it was still hard going for the two across the sand. Wendy tried not to imagine baby turtles making their ungainly way to the safety of the sea as predators swooped and salivated overhead. All three of them were terribly exposed—but to what, she wasn't sure. "If pirates can keep shadows as hostages and bees can steal bits of time," Wendy murmured to herself, "who knows what other horrible things in Never Land are on the side of evil?"

When the moist air of the jungle finally hit her nose and lungs Wendy nearly collapsed in relief.

"Here, sit down, and we can keep an eye on the beach," Wendy said, settling Peter on a soft tuffet of ferns which she hoped weren't carnivorous or itchy. Tinker Bell just hovered back and forth around her beloved Peter, not saying anything, so Wendy assumed they were fine.

There was a rubyfruit bush close by covered in the voluptuous red fruit. They were small and not quite the right color yet, but still fairly juicy. She cracked one open and tried giving a piece to Peter.

"Bleh! It's not ripe!" he cried, spitting it out.

"Stop being such a baby. It's all we have right now."

"Feh." He opened his mouth reluctantly to be fed more.

"You're welcome," Wendy said dryly.

Tinker Bell tugged on her sleeve, pointing into the jungle.

"Is it the Lost Boys?" Wendy asked with excitement.

But bouncing slowly through the bushes with great determination was a strange—and familiar— amber glow. It quickly resolved itself into Thorn, who landed and strode through the leaves like a fearless king and giant.

You came!

"You came!" Wendy cried at the same time. Then she blushed—she wasn't supposed to have known about the other fairy.

He gave her a knowing smile and the slightest wisp of a bow.

Someone gave the Call of Aid. Only someone with no honor at all would fail to respond.

Tinker Bell looked at the empty air around him and raised an eyebrow skeptically.

None of our kin will reveal themselves near humans, Tinker Bell. You know you are the exception. And you also know the Call is for the aid of fairies—not humans. You don't seem to be in trouble, so I can only assume it is your friend Peter again, and perhaps this mighty warrior human here?

Wendy didn't think she had it in her to react to a man's— no matter how tiny he might be—blandishments. But certainly *mighty warrior* wasn't the normal sort of pretty pap fed to girls? And it sounded genuine. *That* was why she felt a blush, she decided. And exhaustion accounted for her weakened knees.

The pirates are coming for him, Tinker Bell said. *In his state, they will surely get him this time.*

I believe Peter "got" Hook last time—and left him without a hand, Thorn countered. *Turnabout's fair play, wouldn't you say?*

"Yes, but this time they are coming for all of Never Land," Wendy interrupted as politely as she could. "No, they really are. It's not just another one of Peter and Hook's games. The First confirmed it. Once he has Peter, his plan is to destroy everything as a sort of payback, and then leave."

What? That's mad! Thorn jingled, horrified.

"I don't disagree."

Peter suddenly crumpled up, whimpering and breathing

too quickly to be able to cry out. Wendy grabbed his hand and squeezed. Tinker Bell looked bleakly at Thorn.

See? They have his shadow captured in a strange golden cage on their ship. I think they're torturing it somehow. Hurting Peter.

Black magic? The warrior fairy frowned. The tips of his long brown ears seemed to quiver in thought, or maybe it was a stray breeze. His hand brushed the hilt of his sword, almost thoughtlessly. *That's . . . new. And disturbing. Hook really is out of control. Peter may be a nuisance at times, but he's no blackguard. At times he has even done favors for us. All right, Tinker Bell, and Madam—*

"Miss," Wendy interrupted. "But you can call me Wendy."

Wendy, then, although it is a meaningless name, he said, bowing. *Better you were named Windy, Mistress of the Winds. And what in blazes happened to you? Since I last caught sight of you—yes, I saw you hiding in the bushes—it looks like you've been through hell.*

She helped me escape a trap of the First, Tinker Bell said proudly. *And fought off an entire colony of thysolits.*

Wendy was gratified to see his honey-brown eyes widen in surprise.

I knew you had the bearing of a warrior, but . . . the First captured you? And you escaped? Truly?

Wendy gave a slightly ironic curtsy.

"Aww, quit all your palavering and chitchat," Peter moaned. His complexion had brightened a little and his whole countenance had improved—whether it was the ruby-fruit, moving to the jungle, something finally *happening*, or all three, it was hard to say. "When do my boys come? Is there any sign of them yet?"

They should be here soon, Tinker Bell promised, fluttering over to soothe him. She even made little jingly cooing noises.

Thorn watched this, then sighed and looked over at Wendy: *what can you do?* Wendy couldn't help smiling. She didn't feel like she was betraying her friend; the boy fairy wasn't being snarky or obnoxious. More *resigned*, like a big brother. And she was relieved to see someone shared her feelings about Tinker Bell's obsessive relationship with Peter.

"Do you know, there's a rather popular—though scandalous—story called 'The Great God Pan,'" she ventured, desperate to keep their conversation going, "by a fellow named Arthur Machen. His Pan *is* an actual blackguard. . . ."

I'd rather hear the stories of your escape from the First and then the thysolits, Windy.

"Quiet!" the less godly Pan ordered.

Wendy turned, about to give him a piece of her

mind—then saw the expression on his face. He was serious for once. The the tips of his ears twitched, like a dog's in its sleep or a cat's when it isn't paying attention to you. Thorn frowned, also listening.

I hear it, too.

Wendy, the only one without pixie hearing, turned and cocked her head and strained.

After a few moments she finally caught the faintest sound of twigs cracking and something crashing through the underbrush. She grabbed her dagger.

"It's the Lost Boys!" Peter cried with delight. He leapt up, his cheeks growing rosy with excitement. "They've come!"

Luna came crashing through the underbrush first, leaping exultantly into Wendy.

"Good girl. How are you, girl?" Wendy hugged the wolf, wondering who was getting more dirt and mud on whom.

Now even *she* could hear the Lost Boys' approach: they were marching, singing some sort of military song—familiar in tune, the original lyrics replaced with something rude and unrepeatable. When they broke into the small clearing where Wendy, Thorn, Tink, and Peter waited, it was with glad eyes and weary triumph.

They were all streaked with blood and makeup. Skipper made for a particularly scary whatever rodent she was with dark blue woad streaks above her eyes and on each cheekbone. Slightly's jacket was stained with unsettlingly large dark brown splotches and his arm was bandaged with a strip of leather over gauze. But he also had a new necklace with the face of a hideous demon or god on it. The twins had new weapons to go with their slings: short, elaborately carved batons. Cubby and Tootles alone looked more or less the same, with just a few rips in their outfits and blue dots on their faces.

Wendy made a mental note to ask them about their adventures later. When she had tossed around *bloody* and *blood* and *terrible wound* in her stories (or, say, the idea of losing a hand in battle), she hadn't really thought about it. She had even basked in the praise when Michael and John said she could tell a good story "unlike most girls"—one full of violence and victory. But now that she was viewing the real thing and had experienced some fighting herself she found her zeal for the lurid somewhat tempered. She wondered about the strange wound on Slightly's arm.

"Well then, Slightly," Peter said, straightening himself up and regarding the other boy gravely.

"Well then, Peter," Slightly said back, trying not to sound wary.

The tension between the two of them was more palpable—and uncomfortable—than the humidity in the jungle.

"Looks like you've had a bit of an adventure," Peter said, nodding at Slightly's arm.

"The caves are still inhabited, don't you know."

"You showed 'em who's who, though, right?"

"Oh, we showed them all right!"

Slightly couldn't resist grinning, the whites of his teeth glistening like a real fox's.

The smile was infectious: Peter smiled back proudly.

"I'm awfully glad you made it, Slightly. I'm not in top form at all. Things would be pretty grim without you all here to help me against the pirates," Peter admitted.

"Well, things would be pretty grim without you around ever again," Slightly said softly.

Peter opened his mouth to say something else, but then Tootles broke in excitedly.

"We fought! And won!" he cried, pushing his way into the middle of the two older boys.

Peter grinned and swept him up into the air. "Of course you did! You're the best fighters a captain could ever want!"

But he looked at Slightly as he said it.

The fox boy smiled back.

Then all the tension was gone, and everyone was talking and shouting excitedly about what had happened and where Peter's shadow was and what the plan was next.

Peter looked grim. "Fact is, men, it could go down at

any time. Hook's got my shadow and he's been holding it prisoner, torturing it. And when he does that, it hurts *me*. They're rounding the Bloody Neck, or were a little while ago, and should be here any moment. They plan to get all of us, me first. Then all of Never Land. We need to be ready."

"We need to come up with a plan," Wendy added.

"All right then!" Peter said. "All together now—fairies, Lost Boys, Wendy, and me! Let's *do this*!"

Look, the pirates, Tinker Bell jingled nervously.

And there it was: riding a fair wind from the west, the *Jolly Roger* swept into view, its ghastly flag—and Peter's shadow—snapping in the breeze.

A Plan Comes Together

The Lost Boys and Wendy immediately crouched down behind the bushes. The two fairies hid their glow behind a tree and peeped out.

The ship came near enough to the beach that Hook could clearly be seen in his blazing red jacket marching up and down the deck, gesticulating and shouting orders. Pirates scurried everywhere frantically, dropping anchor and readying the skiffs.

"What is *that*?" Slightly whispered in horror. He pointed at the glinting golden cage and the black formless mass within.

"That's my shadow," Peter growled.

"That's why you haven't had any . . . attacks in the last few minutes," Wendy realized. "Hook has been too busy making preparations for landing to pay attention to your shadow."

That is an ugly desecration of nature, Thorn said in disgust. *I half thought you were wrong. That no one, not even pirates, would consider such a thing. My apologies. Anyone who would do this is capable of anything—including wiping out Never Land.*

Hook suddenly stopped and pulled out a spyglass, aiming it at the shore.

The little group immediately hunkered down behind the bushes again.

"Should we wait until they're all in the smaller boats?" Slightly asked. "They'll be easy pickings for Skipper with— uh, *his* bow, and the twins with their slings."

I cannot fly well over the water, Thorn said. *For us, it would be best to wait until they've landed.*

"I don't know how much good I could do," Wendy admitted. "Even on land. A bunch of bees without stingers is one thing—a bunch of pirates with swords . . . Well, I could try. . . ."

Me too! Tinker Bell put in. *I'm not a warrior like Thorn, but any good I do would have to be on land.*

The pirates had begun boarding the skiffs and lowering them down. There were at least a dozen of the men, all armed to the teeth.

Hook remained behind on the ship, one booted foot

up on the railing, a triumphant leer polluting his face as he watched his men row toward the beach.

Peter's face darkened.

"Here's what I think we should do," Wendy said. "When Caesar was invading Gaul, he—"

"*HOOOOOOOOOOOK!*" Peter cried, and flew out of the jungle, knife drawn.

"Oh," Wendy said, too stunned to do much else.

"You heard the captain!" Slightly shouted, shaking his sword. "HOOK! AND THE PIRATES!"

"HOOK AND THE PIRATES!"

The Lost Boys ran screaming out of the jungle, Thorn zipping reluctantly after them.

And the final battle between the pirates and the Lost Boys began.

A Battle on Land and Sea

The Lost Boys (and Luna) broke out of the jungle and ran screaming down the beach just as the first skiff touched shore. The pirates, undaunted, leapt out of their boats into the water, cutlasses and muskets drawn. They, too, screamed.

For one dizzying moment it was as strange and pretty as a picture: a small army of boys (and one girl) dressed like animals, wielding archaic weapons, their faces in masks or painted with ancient Celtic stripes, making for gaily dressed pirates in eye patches and bright bandannas and golden rings. Wendy knew that image would remain emblazoned on her mind for the rest of her days.

Peter had flown up and over everyone's heads, making

straight for the pirate ship and the few who remained aboard. Well, really, for *one* who remained aboard: Hook.

Peter seemed entirely recovered, but Wendy knew that as long as his shadow was still in captivity his current vigor was only temporary. And it was very suspicious that Hook stayed back when his men were going to fight his most hated enemy—he didn't even have his flintlocks out. He also wasn't overseeing the cannon fire. And he couldn't possibly shout orders from the deck loudly enough for anyone on shore to hear. So what was he doing?

Tinker Bell had, of course, zipped after Peter, knocking a pirate's hat off as she went. The enraged man (the Duke, Wendy was pretty sure) turned and shot wildly into the air after her, singeing the hair and possibly the ear of the pirate next to him. That pirate—Major Thomas—responded by laughing and then backhanding the Duke.

Thorn swooped right up to the first pirate he encountered and sank his blade deep into the flesh behind the man's right knee. Screaming Byron did exactly what one would expect him to do: he let out a high-pitched wail that hardly seemed possible from such a large, sturdy-looking fellow. Then he immediately collapsed onto the sand, unable to stand on that leg any longer.

The fairy immediately wiped his blade and moved to the next pirate without pause.

Wendy watched in disbelief and admiration. He, of course, *looked* like a little warrior. But in her rather prejudiced, giant human-sized head, she had assumed he could do no real damage.

"That will teach me to judge a book by its cover," she murmured.

And maybe that meant *she* could help, too.

Wendy took a deep breath, grasped her dagger, and marched out onto the beach.

But where to go? What to do? The scene was utter chaos. The twins had surrounded T. Jerome Newton and were taking turns smashing him in the stomach and back with their batons. Skipper had planted herself a little farther up the beach and was taking careful aim with her bow at the pirates on the periphery, the ones who hadn't quite made the beachhead yet. Wendy saw one go down with an arrow through his right shoulder. He fell *out* of the water and back into the boat. Slightly was in the middle of a rather amazing duel with Djareth, sword and scimitar flashing in the sun, Luna biting at the pirate's feet. Cubby was roaring and swinging his claymore at several pirates who were closing in on him.

"That's where I am needed! Cubby, I am coming!" Wendy cried and ran forward to help. She tried not to think about whether she would actually *cut* or *slice* one of the pirates; she figured instinct would take over at the last minute and she would do whatever was necessary for the sake of her friend.

"AAAAAAAAI!" she yelled—more for herself than with any real intention of putting terror into her enemy's heart—and aimed at a pirate whose name she couldn't remember, the one with the blue bandanna. She raised her dagger, thinking to get him in the neck maybe—

Wait, could she really do that? Could she *slice into the artery* of someone—even if it was someone who had held her captive—from the *back*, like a coward? What if he bled on her? What if . . .

Sheathing her dagger, she flipped into the air, and—with the help of fairy dust—spiraled down feetfirst, planting both as hard as she could into the small of his back.

"Take *that*, dread villain!"

With a distinct *oof*, the pirate fell facedown into the sand.

Because fairy dust was merely magical and didn't completely negate the laws of physics, Wendy *kept* falling, her beautiful attack almost ruined by a sprawling somersault over the pirate's head. She landed, straddle-legged and a little confused, sand now in every fold of her clothes.

"That was *brilliant*, Wendy!" Slightly called, saluting her from across the beach before spinning to riposte an attack by a new pirate he was fighting.

"You saved me," Cubby said, smiling dreamily as he used the flat of his giant claymore to knock his remaining attacker into the dust.

"But Wendy," one twin cried, makeup running down his face and pooling around his mask.

"Get *up!*" the other one, equally askew, urged.

Wendy staggered to her feet, feeling it was a bit much to ask of her right then. Hadn't she just taken out a pirate? Her body had been through a great deal over the past few days; she was broken like a doll. And where was Tinker Bell? Somehow this all would have seemed easier with her friend nearby.

Aha: she was still on the ship. Peter and Hook were crossing swords amongst the rigging. Peter balanced on the bowsprit, slashing down at the pirate captain. Hook held his hook behind his back and skillfully parried *up*. Neither one of them seemed in a haste to end the fight. Tinker Bell floated and buzzed around them, making the occasional jab at Hook.

Wendy couldn't see all the details, of course, but her mind filled in Peter's grand smile and sparkling eyes. Such a small boy, really, to be fighting so carelessly against such an evil, nasty, experienced, and *large* pirate (with guns and hooks). Yet that was not the impression the scene gave. He looked like the living embodiment of fearlessness, of seizing whatever the moment brought and assuming it would all work out somehow.

Wendy found that besides admiration she felt more than a touch of envy. He was everything that she, a girl so otherwise full of words and worries and doubts, wanted to *be*.

"But really!" she scolded herself. "Here I am, still thinking and observing and watching, when really I should be rejoining the fight!"

There. One of the twins was down on the ground, nursing his wrist. The other was backed up against a tree, trying to avoid being run through by Ziggy. Wendy began to push off into the air, but suddenly there were strong arms around her, holding her to the ground instead.

"*NO!* Unhand me, villain!"

She tried to bring her blade back down behind her, slashing wildly. "I'll cut you!"

"That was a short trip from Wendy words to prison patois," a voice spoke dryly in her ear. It was Zane, who despite his slender look had tautly muscled arms and rock-like, immovable shoulders.

"I'll not serve you again!" she cried. "I'd rather die!"

She wasn't sure if this was entirely true, but she was enraged at being unable to move, and anyway, she really did hate laundry.

"I'm not capturing ye, I'm saving ye, ye daft molly," the pirate said, exasperated. He dragged her to a tree, flinging her thoughtlessly upside down, face-first, into the sand in front of it. It was an extremely unbecoming, awkward, and most of all embarrassing position to be in—made worse when she realized he had done it so he could bind her wrists and legs.

"You brute! You villainous cur!"

He worked quickly and methodically, ignoring her words as well as her kicking legs while they were still free.

When he was done, he picked her up like a sack and sat her back down properly at the base of the tree.

"You don't belong in this fight," he said. "You have your reasons to hate Hook, but you're going to get yourself killed."

"No one ever dies in these battles," Wendy scoffed. "None of the good guys do."

Zane's look turned dark. "Hook is serious this time— he's completely mad. He means to do away with the Lost Boys for good. And Peter Pan, and everyone else."

"But . . . the Lost Boys . . . they're children!"

"They're children who chose to fight pirates," Zane pointed out. "They're children who cut the hand off a pirate and left him with one hand, one hook, no sanity, and a death wish for the entire world. Believe you me, I don't want to be wasting none of me time with this here folderol. I want to be out on the open sea, shooting down cargo vessels and looting them, then maybe take a month or two in some island port with coconut rum and time to think things over in the sun."

He took her dagger and threw it into the jungle. "The faster this is all over, the faster we can set sail and leave Never Land forever."

"Yes! *Forever!* Hook intends on destroying it after he's done with Peter!"

"Aye. Seems a bit much," he said with a shrug.

"But do you have any idea how he intends to kill everyone?"

"Not a whit. We're carrying some extra powder—or were. Maybe that has something to do with it. Who knows."

"Oh, you're useless. Why are you even saving me?" Wendy demanded. "*I'm* a child who chose to fight pirates."

"Oh, you're not a child anymore, lassie." Zane chuckled. "And you'd be no help to either side in a fight, eitherways."

He gave her a sparkling gold-doubloon grin and then went running back to the battle.

Wendy fumed. It would be so easy to sit there and watch the battle. No one would blame her: she was tied up. And Zane was right. She didn't really know how to fight—not humans, anyway.

"No help to either side," she muttered. "I'll—I'll show them!"

Struggling, she stood up. She twisted and turned wildly, trying to loosen the stiff old ropes he had tied her with. They wouldn't give an inch. Zane was, of course, an expert at knots. She had no idea where to start looking for her pretty dagger in the forest, and as far as she could tell, no one on the beach had conveniently dropped one for her to use. It seemed rather unreasonable to push herself into a fight and demand to be set free: *Mind loaning me your sword for a moment? And you, pirate, would you mind holding off attacking for that moment?*

She looked at her shadow, who was also tied up and struggling. Apparently sticking to her host had some distinct disadvantages—like sharing her fate while they were attached.

Wendy screamed in frustration. For once, she was *here*, in Never Land, not just narrating the story. And she still couldn't do anything! And Peter and Hook . . .

Wait. There *was* one thing she could do, she realized. She could still fly. Maybe there would be something on the ship she could use. It was full of pointy and jabby things. And then she could set about rescuing Peter's shadow, or snooping around the ship for a hint of Hook's plans.

Wendy grinned and took off into the air—

And immediately began rolling and flailing, her head grinding into the sand while her legs whirled around above her like a pinwheel. Somehow flying required more balance and use of her arms and legs than she had thought.

Stretching, curling up, and then keeping herself very still, Wendy finally managed to move forward. Very awkwardly. Like a caterpillar with all of its little legs bound together, inching along in an undignified fashion. Sometimes as little as a foot above the sand and in constant danger of plowing into it face-first. But she took it slowly and did her best to sneak around the fight, to not draw too much attention to herself.

(Though a twin saw her and nearly lost his ear as he stared, transfixed.)

When she made it to the edge of the water Wendy came in a bit too low. A wave crashed into her face, temporarily blinding her. It took her a bit to reorient herself and then swayingly cross the rest of the way to the ship. Finally, like a bobbing harbor seal, she popped up over the side of the *Jolly Roger* to surveil the scene.

There was the sword fight, of course. Blades flashing in the sun, the scrape of steel on steel.

"I'll get you yet, Peter Pan!" Hook cried, grinning.

"Just try it, you ridiculous codfish!" Peter taunted. He danced on top of the ship's wheel, causing it to spin.

Tinker Bell, hovering nearby, caught sight of Wendy.

"No—shh," Wendy mouthed. She jerked her head toward the prow of the ship, where the golden cage was. *"Meet me there!"*

Tinker Bell nodded and flew off.

Wendy followed, throwing herself over the railing and skidding to a painful halt on her knees, elbows, and chin.

The fairy immediately began to work on her ropes.

"They're very tight," Wendy whispered. "I don't think you have the strength. Maybe you can find a knife or a—"

But the bonds fell away.

Tinker Bell gave a smug little smile.

"Well! That's rather useful," Wendy said, bending over to release her shadow.

The shadow jumped and stretched in her newfound freedom and then slid into the cage, to Peter's shadow.

"Do what you can—see if you can release him," Wendy said. "Meanwhile, Tink and I will—"

But a pirate stepped out from behind the chart room and loomed menacingly over her.

"You didn't think Hook would have left this *unguarded*, did you?" he growled. His skin was pale and torn; his breath reeked of rot.

It was Valentine.

"But . . . you're dead!" Wendy breathed in horror.

"Oh, the dead don't always stay dead in Never Land," he sneered, his mouth full of rotting black and golden teeth. "Not when they're pirates. Not when Davy Jones's locker is full."

He aimed his musket at her belly.

"Not sure the same holds for the likes of *ye*, however."

He began to pull the trigger—

Wendy screamed.

"Wendy!" Peter cried, catching sight of her. "Blackguard! Don't you dare! Don't you dare lay a finger on her!"

"Valentine, lower your weapon," Hook ordered, joining the group with solid, sure smacks of his bootheels. "Miss Darling! Isn't this a nice surprise. Now you can witness my triumph—and Peter Pan's utter defeat. I was just enjoying one last bout with my old nemesis here before getting on with things."

"Defeat? Why, you old codfish, you . . ."

Hook ignored him.

"Valentine? Adjust the machine—to the limit, please."

The pirate grinned. Keeping the gun trained on Wendy with his right hand, he reached out his left to a greasy golden knob on the cage. Peter's shadow shivered and shrank and expanded in dismay, knowing what was to come.

The pirate spun the knob all the way to the left.

The shadow snapped into a thousand quivering tendrils

of pain. It vibrated and shook and trembled so fiercely that the air around it turned black. A strange not-noise—the opposite of noise?—filled the air as it screamed, almost breaking Wendy's eardrums.

Peter fell to the deck, unconscious.

Tinker Bell jingle-screamed.

"And that," Hook said with a smile, "is the end of Peter Pan."

A Plan Comes Together...
No, *Really* This Time

The few remaining pirates on the *Jolly Roger* surrounded Wendy, Tinker Bell, and the prone form of Peter lying on the ground.

"SURRENDER!" Hook bellowed toward the shore. *"Lost Boys, we have your Peter Pan!"*

The fighting paused as both pirate and Lost Boy alike stopped to figure out what the captain was shouting. It was hard to hear over the waves and wind.

"I have him!" Hook gestured dramatically at Peter—whom no one could see, hidden as he was on the deck behind the railing—and his shadow in the cage, which made no real sense if you didn't know what you were looking at beforehand.

"*I have Peter Pan!*" he tried again.

Nothing. Those on the beach shrugged and looked at each other in confusion.

Frustrated at the lack of response on shore, Hook reached down and grabbed Peter's shirt, holding him aloft and shaking him so all could see. The boy sagged like a badly made scarecrow, pale and limp.

It was a shocking display.

After all, Peter really was just a boy, and Hook was not a small man. The pirate had no trouble at all tossing his unconscious body about. The strangeness of it—of him manhandling the usually energetic and scrappy Pan—must have gotten even to Hook. His face slipped for just a moment in wonder, as if he was thinking, "*This is all of it? This is my prize?*" And maybe there was just a touch of disappointment, like that of a child who has finally and triumphantly caught a dragonfly, only to open his hands and realize he has killed it in the process.

On the beach there were collective wails and gasps. Even the pirates seemed a little surprised. Wendy was pretty sure she saw Zane blink and gawp before rousing himself and grabbing Cubby, thrusting the boy's hands behind his back. Then the rest of the pirates rounded up the dejected Lost Boys with exaggerated movements, ropes, and whips.

Hook seemed to get over whatever momentary lapse of

joy he had experienced and now leered and grinned and pranced about, dropping Peter's body into Valentine's waiting arms.

"That's right," the captain chortled. "Get them all—it's over now, over *forever*!"

The pirates tied the Lost Boys into a kind of chain and forced them onto the skiffs.

Thorn, aloft and uncaptured, jingled—but it was untranslatable, even for Wendy.

Wendy looked at her shadow. She was wrapped around Peter's, trying to comfort or free him—with little effect. Tinker Bell tried to wrap herself around Peter's flesh and blood body; Valentine kept waving her away.

Wendy Darling didn't normally consider herself someone who surveyed a situation, immediately understood what was going on, and then reacted in a timely and appropriate manner. She was a dreamy, thoughtful girl, slow to decide and act.

But a week was a long time in Never Land.

Without bothering to warn her, Wendy grabbed Tinker Bell and took off.

The little fairy fought and bit and scratched and made noises that were far more terrifying than jingles. Wendy kept her fist shut tight.

Did she feel like a coward, bombing away from the

pirate ship like a bee martin after its prey? Not really. Soon the ship would be full of pirates and weapons and guns, and Hook's attention would inevitably turn to her. It was only while he was gloating that she had a chance to escape—and from the belated *pop pop pop* sounds behind her, it was clear that though it had taken everyone a moment to notice her absence, the use of guns was not forbidden against potential Pan accomplices.

"We need to get away and regroup," she told Tinker Bell. "There's nothing we could have done back there."

The little fairy jingled furiously.

"No, I don't think I *could* have pulled Peter from either Hook or Valentine—I'm not that strong, Tink. I already tried to fight off Valentine when he was *alive* and I failed. And this is all assuming I could fly holding Peter and not drop him in the water, drowning him."

She's right, Tinker Bell, Thorn said, flying up beside them—as Wendy knew he would, even without a word or a signal. *I'm no coward. The odds were entirely against us. We need to strategize and come back again and hit them hard.*

Tinker Bell jingled something translatable—but unprintable.

Wendy skimmed along the water and the beach, keeping a wide swath between them and the pirates in the skiffs (and their captives).

"Wendy!" The twins cried together, spotting her. But it wasn't a cry of despair; it was a cheer. They were *glad* one of their number had escaped—and could maybe return to free them.

Slightly also caught her eye as she passed, but didn't say anything. Hope shone brightly on his face, and it spoke for his silence.

Wendy was also full of hope: she hoped she didn't disappoint him.

She flew above the jungle a little before finding a good place to break through the canopy. Curling herself into a ball, she plummeted to the ground through dense leaves and twigs, remembering to stick her feet out at the last minute.

The moment she opened her hand, Tinker Bell shot out and dove at her face.

"Please stop," Wendy said, as patiently as she could manage. But it came out the way she felt: weary, and maybe, like Hook, just a bit disappointed. Did her little friend *never* see the ramifications of actions? Never think a few moves ahead? Never grasp how ridiculous she was being? Wendy suddenly thought of Zane, and his perfunctory removal of her at the battle. He, too, was only trying to save a life.

Tinker Bell must have finally seen or understood what passed through Wendy's mind. She drooped.

Easy, little sister, Thorn jingled, coming close to the other fairy. *We will come up with something. It isn't over yet.*

Wendy felt a rush of affection for him that had nothing to do with his physiognomy or his manner. He understood why she did what she did, and he understood that Tinker Bell needed to be appeased. He was useful, kind, and like-minded. Good qualities to have in a friend.

"All right," Wendy said, sitting down at the base of a tree. "Let's see what our options are. Peter is out of the game—and possibly in real danger. While he's hostage I doubt the Lost Boys are going to try to escape. Even Slightly wouldn't risk it. And now that Hook has Peter, all of his little pieces are in place. We don't know how long before he sets into motion his plan to destroy Never Land.

"And we're the only ones who can save it. Of all the inhabitants of Never Land I've met, none of them—literally none of them—would ally with us. Or me, rather. Not the terrible mermaids or the unknowable First. Certainly not the mindless and devouring thysolits. I doubt the Cenotaph cave-dwellers would lend a hand and I have no idea what the Elephant Wheels are."

They keep to themselves, on the Lost Roads, Thorn said, which was both helpful and not at all. Wendy decided to file that with the now *very* long list of things to look into if she had more time in Never Land.

"Well, that leaves us and the fairies, then. And you have said they won't fight on our side?"

Unfortunately, we have no actual proof of Hook's plans. After seeing the blasphemous doings of Captain Hook, it might be possible to rally the Great Army to our side. But it would require a meeting at the Allthing, and just the scheduling of that is a bear.

"Oh, cripes, this is *impossible*!" Wendy tore off a piece of a plant and threw it at the ground. She had almost said *hopeless*. "We have *nothing*."

We have you, Tinker Bell jingled softly.

Wendy gave her a weak smile. "Thank you, but I don't see what I can bring to the table, other than a belated ability to fly and a dagger I seem to have lost."

You have your stories.

"But, Tink, those powers only worked in the realm of the First—where the stories and the land of Never Land haven't solidified or *set* yet. It doesn't work out here. Any stories I tell would just be stories."

Then we can be the powers for you. You tell the stories, and we will make *them come true.*

Tinker Bell's eyes were so wide and she sounded so sincere that Wendy felt like she was drowning in her friend's trust. She snuck a look at Thorn. He gave a slight nod. She wasn't sure if it meant *yes, we will,* or *yes, you can,* but either way it was an endorsement. For some reason he didn't think Tinker Bell was being ridiculous.

"Okay," Wendy said slowly. "But how—"

We need to take out Captain Hook, said the warrior fairy. *Without a leader, the pirates will collapse into chaos.*

"Agreed," Wendy said. "A queen for a queen, like in chess. I don't think they're loyal enough to mount a revenge or rescue. There seemed to be some difference of opinion about what pirates are supposed to do even when I was aboard—and getting Peter Pan wasn't high on the list for most of them."

Just then, a ragged black shape slithered through the underbrush toward them.

Tinker Bell leapt up, jingling in fright—but it was only Wendy's shadow.

"Ah! Good of you to join us," Wendy said, patting the ground next to herself. The shadow obligingly slid over and slipped into Wendy's shape. "Any luck with Peter's shadow?"

The shadow shook her head, then held her hand out and rocked it from side to side.

"You think you could help him escape? With more time?"

The shadow shrugged and nodded desperately. *Maybe* or *I have to* or *what else can we do?*

"All right. We were just talking about the pirates and their leader, and how they are not that devoted to their beloved captain. So there's somehow *killing* Hook, somehow *capturing* him, or somehow *disabling* him. And should it be the second two—as I rather hope—we will need the Lost Boys free and ready to battle the pirates if they do put up a resistance. Tinker Bell, when you released me from my ropes before—could you do that for all of them?"

Not from a distance. It isn't magic, it's . . . fairy knowing. Knots and traps are in our blood.

"I think that may still count as magic, to humans at least. But in any case, be clear: you have to actually touch the ropes."

Yes. Thorn cut in. *And we shine.*

"Well, of course you do. You're the best."

No, shine.

Thorn flew up in front of her and glowed so brilliantly she had to shade her eyes.

"Right, right," she said, feeling a little breathless that he was so close. "Not exactly a covert mission, I get it. But what if you could zip around and—I don't know—maybe *give* them something to cut their own bonds with? Drop something in their hands and fly away quickly? Maybe a knife, or a sharp shell?"

Yes, but someone may still see us. And how will that help, since as you said the Lost Boys won't rise up if their leader is in trouble?

"I think I'm getting there," Wendy said, trying not to let her heart quicken as it sensed her brain's ideas. Trying not to *hope* or *believe.* "I think you actually nailed it when you said *stories.* Hook certainly loves to talk—to hear himself talk, to hear himself tell stories. He has told stories in his head all his life about Peter and losing his hand. And crocodiles and clocks and time. It's what worked him up into this crazy obsession. I think stories—or plays—are the thing to 'catch the conscience of the king.'"

She sat back, feeling very clever.

The two fairies looked at her, uncomprehending.

"Shakespeare," Wendy said, disappointed no one got the reference. *"Hamlet."*

Oh! We know A Midsummer's Night Dream, Thorn said proudly. *I'm in it, sometimes.*

Tinker Bell shot him an annoyed look.

"All right, the point is that, like Peter, Hook loves hearing about himself. You know, they really are a lot alike, if you stop to think about it. . . . Anyway, the tale needs to be big and dramatic, just like Hook. Something that will distract him to pieces. I don't think it would take much to push him over the edge right now. Besides stories, *I* have a clockwork crocodile. Which, unlike my satchel, pirate treasure, or boat, really *will* turn out to be useful at the end of my adventure.

"And, finally, I have . . . myself."

Tinker Bell jingled curiously.

"Why, I'm giving myself up, Tink. I'm going to trade myself for Peter."

Wendy

While she walked out on the hot sand Wendy imagined herself strolling primly down the avenue with a parasol on her shoulder and a smug little Wendy smile on her face. As if she were going out to market or the bookstore when the demonic Shesbow twins were known to be about, thus requiring her to be extra prim and have an extra-smug smile as first lines of defense.

In reality, of course, it was not an ancient cobbled street she trod, and her pinafore had long since disappeared. Instead, she wore a tunic made of rags bleached white from the sun and salt water, her arms and legs and face darkened by the same powers.

And maybe—just maybe—her smile was less smug and a trifle more sardonic now.

Her shadow behaved like any well-behaved shadow would, copying her precisely. Although, of course, *her* smile was hidden.

The pirate ship lay on the water as pretty and perfect as a ship in a bottle. For a dizzying moment Wendy played with the idea that it *was* a ship in a bottle, that she was standing in her father's study, mouthing words to imaginary heroes and villains as the toll of too much time alone and lack of outside voices finally grew too great.

But her father didn't have a ship in a bottle.

And Wendy had scratches all over that itched terribly—boring, annoying little details that she would never normally imagine or narrate in a story.

External proof aside, internally she had changed as well. Permanently and deeply. She didn't need to see her scars to know that they were real.

She kept walking, right into the water, until it was up to her calves.

"Captain Hook," she called out, waving politely. "Captain Hook? May I have a word?"

Whatever was happening on the ship paused; all attention was directed to her by the antlike pirates and villains.

Hook, ever dramatic and unable to resist a cue, complied.

"WENDY DARLING!" he shouted, his voice a trifle

less unctuous than usual because he had to shout. "I WON-DERED WHERE YOU RAN OFF TO."

She curtsied.

"I'M AFRAID WE'RE RATHER BUSY AT THE MOMENT, BUT I WOULD LOVE TO CATCH UP FOR A CHAT JUST AFTER I'VE REVIVED YOUR GOOD FRIEND PAN HERE LONG ENOUGH FOR HIM TO WATCH THE NEXT PHASE OF THE PLAN. IF THERE'S TIME BEFORE YOU'RE ALL WIPED OUT, OF COURSE."

"I've come to give myself up," Wendy shouted.

"WHAT?"

"I've come to give myself up. To offer myself in trade for Peter Pan."

The red-coated, black-wigged effigy stood stock-still on the ship for a moment. Then Hook threw back his shoulders and bent double, guffawing heartily.

"AND WHAT DO I CARE ABOUT YOU, WENDY DARLING? I HAVE PETER PAN. I DON'T *WANT* YOU."

"But do you *want* Peter Pan? Really?"

"WANT? PETER PAN? MISS DARLING, HAVE YOU BEEN PAYING ATTENTION TO ANYTHING OUTSIDE YOUR OWN LOVELY HEAD WHILE YOU'VE BEEN HERE?"

"Of course I have, and I come with a warning. . . ." And here she lowered her voice, just a little, letting the wind take it where it would. She recounted the various stories of her time in Never Land, occasionally raising her voice just up to the level it was before, only letting key and cryptic phrases be carried across to the ship. "METAPHORICALLY SPEAKING, OF COURSE . . . NO LESS THAN AN ARMY . . . SURPRISED TO FIND . . ."

The red pirate-ant in the distance grew frustrated. She could imagine exactly what he was saying: *What the deuce? Can anyone hear? What is that dashed girl going on about?*

". . . INEVITABLE," she finished.

"YOU STAY RIGHT THERE, MISS DARLING," Hook ordered, face red with impatience. "I DON'T KNOW WHAT THE BLAZES YOU'RE UP TO, BUT YOU WILL COME ABOARD MY SHIP AND WE WILL RESOLVE THIS—*DISTRACTION*—IMMEDIATELY!"

Wendy curtsied again.

Tinker Bell hadn't understood this part of the plan— why Wendy couldn't just fly up to the ship and proceed from there. But Thorn did. It was all about playing a part, and gaining trust, and making Hook feel like *he* was the one making the decisions. The warrior fairy didn't put it quite that way, of course; he didn't think that way. He spoke in terms of *subverting the enemy's expectations* and *letting the trap draw itself closed.*

Wendy waited there as serenely as she could while the pirates lowered down one dinghy and two men—*only two!* She was insulted. Neither of them was Zane. They were nothing but tertiary characters, thugs whose names she hadn't bothered to learn when she was on board. They looked dangerous and unimaginative.

(Though one gave a kind of apology before tying her hands behind her back.

"No matter," she said. "It's improper, but understandable.")

She kept her spine straight and chin up, like a figurehead in the prow of the dinghy as they rowed back to the ship that had started all her adventures.

The deck was already quite crowded with prisoners and pirates. Members of the crew mumbled greetings to her with downcast eyes; the Lost Boys regarded her curiously. Hook stomped over, impatient and furious.

"Now hurry up with this foolishness, Miss Darling," he said, thrusting his face into hers. "You wanted to trade yourself for Peter Pan—which is ridiculous, ask anyone here. You're no Peter Pan, not half his worth to me. And anyway, I've captured you quite handily and made no sorts of promises to let you go, so you haven't even anything left to trade with. I've got you fair and square there, Miss Darling."

"Not half his *worth* . . . ?" Wendy started to object before getting control of herself.

The sun sparkled brightly on the sea, but something glinted in the rigging that didn't quite belong there. Possibly the head of a fairy peeping out to see how things were progressing.

"*WELL!*" she said dramatically, making sure everyone's eyes were on her. "Captain Hook, now that you *have* Peter Pan, what do you intend to do with him?"

She addressed him like a mother to a child with a song sparrow, or frog, or fox kit, or any other inappropriate pet. Patiently, like she wanted him to work out the ridiculousness of it all himself.

The pirates—and the Lost Boys—looked over at Hook with interest.

"What am I going to *do* with him?" Hook demanded. "Why, I'm going to exact revenge on him for what he did to me!" He shook his hook for emphasis.

"So . . . you're going to cut off his hand."

Hook's—and everyone else's—eyes drifted involuntarily to the unconscious Peter, pale and motionless. Defenseless. Wendy risked a quick look at his shadow: it lay limp in the cage, like the umbra of an unwound pile of string. She made the minutest nod toward it.

Her own shadow silently detached, rippling over the planks of the deck like a centipede. Again she felt the strange inside-out pain, the hollowness that pulsed along her limbs and torso.

A zip of light—Tinker Bell had also used the distraction when everyone was focused on Peter to get to the Lost Boys.

"I'm going to teach him a lesson he'll never forget!" Hook cried. "That all of Never Land will never forget! I'll make him watch as his beloved world is destroyed. And then I'll have him *walk the plank*—without any flying, or rescuing mermaids, or whatnot. Or maybe I'll execute him myself. One shot to the head."

He pulled out his pistol and aimed it menacingly at Wendy.

"You would really kill *Peter Pan*? Your archnemesis. Your greatest enemy. Your sole reason for living these days, it seems."

"Yes, well, maybe I'll find other reasons once he's gone," Hook said thoughtfully, looking at his pistol and frowning at a smudge on it. "Perhaps once again I'll be able to enjoy the simple pleasures in life: raiding a port town, attacking a merchant vessel and stealing its gold, a bit of plunder here, a bit of pillage there. . . ."

"Now you're talking!" Zane said encouragingly.

An amber glimmer swooped over the other side of the ship and disappeared among the prisoners. One pirate suddenly turned, having thought he saw something strange out the corner of his eye.

"But . . . you two have *fought each other forever*," Wendy said loudly, stepping forward—and drawing all attention to herself again.

Hook frowned and cocked the hammer on his flintlock with an ominous click.

Wendy shrugged as best she could with her hands tied to indicate no threat was intended. She continued to walk around Peter's body and Hook, appearing to think about both of them while blocking the pirates' view of the Lost Boys and any fairy goings-on.

"Hook and Peter, Peter and Hook, always battling it out on the seas or in secret hideaways. . . . You're so archetypal, so famous, so *ever-present* in Never Land that everyone knows your legendary exploits. Both here and in the nurseries of London, where stories of you are told to frighten little children."

Hook gave a modest dip of his head.

"And that's the beauty of the two of you. Peter Pan, always young and full of life. Captain Hook, scurrilous sea dog and villain of the tale. *Blast you, Peter Pan! I'll get you next time!* You're equal, you're opposite. You *can't* get rid of one or the other. Not forever. It's balance. Nothing ever changes here in Never Land.

"Or . . . does it?"

She frowned, as if puzzled.

"Everyone knows the story of the time he cut your hand off. So there must have been a time *before* you had your hook."

The captain looked at his hook with something like surprise.

"It was a long time ago . . ." he said, almost as if he was having trouble remembering.

"But it's still a change."

The pirates looked at each other, confused. Even the Lost Boys looked uncertain of where she was going with this. Slightly alone seemed to be concentrating on something else—but the minute wiggles of his shoulders hinted it was probably because he was trying to cut himself free.

"There have been other changes, too," she added, trying to think of something else to say. She had lost her train of thought—what else could she mention that would keep Hook interested? Where was she going with this all?

She began to panic. Maybe she *couldn't* pull this off. Maybe she was actually terrible at weaving stories on the spot that captured everyone's attention.

"I grow tired of your very obvious delaying tactics, Miss Darling," Hook growled. "What *changes*? How do they relate to *me*?"

Slightly's arm spasmed; he had probably just cut his way through the last of his bonds.

Valentine noticed this movement and frowned, pushing his way forward to look.

"There are so many . . . unexpected things . . ." Wendy babbled, trying to find something that worked. "Not just from children's imaginations . . . Never Land itself is making changes. . . ."

"*I* have!" Skipper suddenly stood up—awkwardly, arms behind her back. "I mean, I *am* a change!"

Everyone turned to stare at the Lost Boy. She stood terrified and defiant.

Wendy's heart nearly broke with gratitude.

"Skipper, tell them who you are," she said gently.

"Explain yourself," Hook ordered, aiming the pistol at her.

"I'm a girl."

Her giant animal ears were already off, thrown back over her shoulders, making her look more human. There was nothing more she could do—no taking down of her hair, no revealing a corset, no obvious sign to indicate what she said was true.

"I'm a girl," she said more loudly, when she saw everyone's confusion. "I just cut my hair. And stuff."

"A Lost Boy who's a . . . girl?" Captain Hook said incredulously.

Zane's eyes were wide with interest; his face acquired a light that Wendy hadn't seen in it before.

"Aye, a girl," Skipper said a little more defensively, and stuck her chin out.

"A girl . . . *what*?" Ziggy asked.

Everyone looked at the pirate.

"What?" he demanded. He pointed at the rest of the Lost Boys. "That one's a fox, that's a bear, easy enough to see. What in the bloody deuce are *you* supposed to be? A girl *what*?"

"Ah . . . a bilby?" Skipper cleared her throat and spoke more forcefully: "A bilby."

The pirates looked at her blankly, in silence.

The Lost Boy grew red and shifted on her feet, now uncomfortable with all the attention.

"A marsupial. Kind of like a hare, but with a long nose and tail," Slightly explained helpfully.

"Oh! You mean like a bandicoot?" Djareth said, recognition dawning on his face.

"Exactly."

"They're highly endangered, you know," Screaming Byron told Zane.

"All right, all right," Hook said impatiently. "This is certainly a bizarre turn of events, but what has any of this to do with whatever *warning* you said you were giving me? What has this to do with changes?"

"The warning is about precisely this; it's about *change*, Hook," Wendy said. "It comes slow to Never Land, but still it comes. A girl Lost Boy, for instance. And surely you've heard about the squabbles between Slightly and Peter?"

"Of course," Hook said with a sniff, looking exactly like a schoolboy who has been left out of a good gossip but desperately doesn't want anyone to know. "Who hasn't?"

"Well, then it must have confounded you as much as everyone else! The inseparable Lost Boys! Peter's endlessly brave and loyal crew! With leadership issues! Power struggles! *And* one of them is a girl!"

"I still don't see what this has to do with—"

"Things are changing, Captain Hook. Never Land is changing. Slowly. It is settling in, *aging*.

"And, it is obvious—*you are as well*."

Silence blanketed the ship. The pirates looked aghast.

"Now see here, Miss Darling," Hook said with a lilt in his voice as if it were all a joke—but his voice was shaky, and he raised the pistol to her.

"Everyone knows why you *started* chasing Pan, the youthful, adventurous, dashing young fellow—"

"It's because he took my hand! He's our greatest enemy! Isn't that right, men?" Hook demanded.

The pirates muttered and shook their heads.

"All right," Hook allowed. "Perhaps he's *my* greatest enemy. He's my nemesis. He's my final opponent. He's my—"

"*He's your youth*, Cap'n! Everybody knows it!" the Duke finally exploded.

"What?" Hook roared. "Not this nonsense again!"

"He *is*. Your youth," Zane said tiredly. "Get it through yer thick skull. You've been chasing him all over Never Land and the seas between the worlds because you think you can recapture it. And him."

"Stuff and nonsense!" Hook said, shaking himself all over and resettling himself. "He's an irritation, a thorn in my side, a veritable pain in my—"

"And when you had your famous confrontation with him, finally," Wendy interrupted, "*he took your hand and fed it to the crocodile*. The tick-tock croc, Hook. The one whose very sound puts a thrill of fear up your spine, reminding you of time passing."

Hook again glanced involuntarily at his hook.

"What will Peter take next time?" Wendy asked, stepping closer, speaking more softly. "If you don't finish him off?"

The pirates were silent, all eyes fixed on her and their captain.

(A bouncing glow shot over to another Lost Boy.)

Peter let out the slightest puff of a groan and twitched.

Wendy's shadow must have roused his shadow, but Wendy didn't dare risk a look over to see.

"There are people like me, all over the world, telling the story of the deadly Captain Hook and how he is . . . *changing*. Bits of him slowly hacked off, going gray, unable to take a single ship or port anymore . . . Not even wanting to! All he can think about is this one small boy and his island home. This *boy*. This slip of a thing you wouldn't have thought twice about making walk the plank and being done with years ago. He's gotten into your mind and skull, subverting your every thought and happy moment."

"It's true," Hook moaned. "I haven't had a moment's peace since the appearance of Peter Pan."

"What has it done to you, Captain?" Wendy whispered.

"But I *have* Peter Pan now!" He backed up toward the mast, waving his pistol wildly. "It's all over. I'll finish him and get rid of Never Land—then I'll get it all back. My peace of mind, my life . . . I can go back to being a real pirate!"

"But is it too late, I wonder?" Wendy said thoughtfully. "Peter has already used up every moment of your time. Time passes, even in Never Land. You can practically *hear* the ticktock of the hours as they pass. . . . Listen. . . ."

Tick.

Tick.

Everyone on the *Jolly Roger* grew perfectly silent and strained their ears.

Tick.

Tock.

Hook's eyes practically rolled up into his head, the whites showing all around.

Tick

Tock.

Tick

Tock.

"Yes, that is the sound of time, Hook," Wendy said. "Ages passing, even here, and taking you with them. . . ."

"*No.* NO!" Hook shrieked. "That's the crocodile! No! He has my hand! He's coming for the rest of me!"

"Crocodile, clocks, life, time, it doesn't matter, Hook. It's coming for you. Whether or not you kill Peter Pan."

The clockwork crocodile surfaced, spines gleaming in the dying scarlet light of the day. It circled the ship, snapping its jaws and slapping its tail.

Several pirates looked over the side at it and blanched.

"I really thought it were dead," T. Jerome Newton whispered.

"*SMEE! IT'S COME FOR ME!*" Hook cried, sliding down against the mast until he was crumpled at the base. "SMEE! HELP ME! HELP!"

Wendy waited, unsure how to deal with a potential rescue.

None came.

"Smee . . . Please . . . can't you *do* something?" Hook moaned, beginning to cry. "Get it away. I *have* Pan. I won! Get the crocodile away. He can't get me anymore, really, can he, Smee?"

Slightly leapt up, throwing his bonds dramatically aside and striking a heroic pose.

"To arms, men—and Skipper! We must overpower our captors!"

The Lost Boys leapt up right behind him.

The pirates . . .

Did nothing.

"Don't bother," Zane said, sighing. "I think, as they say, we're done here."

Endings

"What?" Slightly asked, taken aback—and not a little disappointed.

"It's over, Lost Boys. You won. All right? Is that what you want to hear?" Zane looked at his captain and shook his head sadly.

The clockwork crocodile had taken a turn closer to the boat and its ticking grew louder. Hook buried his head, whimpering into his knees, continued calling for Mr. Smee. Wendy reached over and gently took the pistol out of his grip. He didn't even try to resist.

"Who *is* this Smee I keep hearing about?" she asked curiously.

"There *is* no Smee," Djareth spat. "Didn't you get that, love?"

"I beg your pardon?"

"Aye, no Smee at all," Zane said, patting Hook on the shoulder. "Never has been. There've been others—that giant rabbit, Barney . . . Remember that one, mates?"

"Aye, that was right cuckoo, that one." Ziggy nodded sagely.

"Oh . . . my. I thought Mr. Smee was like . . . a first mate, or yeoman, or cabin boy, or something," Wendy said in wonder. "I did think it was odd I was never properly introduced."

"Our old captain here hasn't been right for years . . . maybe he never was." Zane shrugged. "Thanks to Peter Pan, or not. Anyway, you've won. We were on the point of mutiny anyway, if you want to know."

They made a strange pair: the crumpled, pale Peter, whose eyelids were just beginning to flutter, hat tipped back—and next to him his nemesis, hunched over, shivering, black wig askew.

"This raises a lot *more* questions about Never Land," Wendy murmured.

Slightly had directed the Lost Boys over to the golden cage. The moment the knobs were all reset and the gate swung open, the two shadows shot out together like captive birds set free.

Wendy watched the shadows, now elongated by the low, failing red light, enjoying their last moments that day together hand in hand, swooping and soaring over the water before merging into the dusk.

She smiled, lost in thoughts of other possibilities, other stories: where she was younger, Tinker Bell didn't mind, and she and Peter wound up together.

In reality, Tinker Bell nervously hovered over Peter. He rubbed a hand over his brow and tried to sit up.

"Wha-what happened?" he asked, somehow sounding both imperious and demanding despite the weakness of his voice.

"We won!" Slightly said, kneeling down to pat his hand. "All thanks to Wendy here, and Tink, and this brave fellow, Thorn."

Thorn bobbed demurely next to Wendy.

"But where's my shadow?" Peter asked, looking around. "I still don't have it!"

"He will be back, I promise," Wendy said. "He's just taking a little jaunt. But he has a good keeper this time. Shadows have their own minds in Never Land, and deserve some freedom, I think."

"Well, then, it doesn't seem like a victory to me," Peter Pan said peevishly. "The whole point was to get my shadow back."

Tinker Bell's eyes widened. She flew in close and *pinched his cheek.*

And save Never Land, you acorn!

"Aw, I'm just kidding, Tink," Peter said, waving her away and laughing. "I couldn't have asked for a better rescue. You all did amazing without me. I guess I taught you really well."

Wendy rolled her eyes. Tinker Bell gave Peter a kiss on the nose. Slightly laughed and bumped knuckles with him.

"You think *you've won,"* Hook whispered. "All of you standing around congratulating yourselves on a job well done. Well, you haven't won. Peter was supposed to watch all of you die. Everyone and everything he loves. But if I can't have Pan, no one can. Time comes for everyone, eh, Wendy? Tick . . . tock . . . *Boom!*"

He lapsed into a fit of psychotic giggles.

"What do you mean, exactly?" Wendy asked softly, addressing the captain the way she used to her great uncle.

"Goodbye, dear," Hook hissed. "You'd be safer if you had stayed in London. Safe as *houses*. Here you'll be quite exploded."

It sounds like an incendiary, Thorn jingled.

"It's a bomb!" Peter Pan exclaimed, standing up. Color was coming back into his face. "That's how he's going to destroy Never Land! He tried to blow up the hideout once— remember? It was attached to a clock!"

"Oh, that was a good adventure, that one," one of the pirates said with nostalgia. "*That* one almost worked."

"There was a clock in the chart room," Zane said. "And powder. Makes sense."

"A bomb to blow up all of Never Land?" Wendy demanded. "It would have to be huge! Where is this bomb, Hook?"

"I'll never tell—*never*," Hook said, holding a finger up to his lips. "We'll all go together!"

"We've got to find it. All of us," Slightly said. "Right now. Who knows when he set it to go off?"

"We'll set sail right now and search the coastlines," Zane said grimly. "With the right wind, we can make quick work of all the perimeters."

"I'll check the most explody places," Peter Pan said. "The volcanoes and the geysers. Those would be *great* places to hide a bomb."

I'll rally the fairies, Thorn said.

Yes, yes! Tinker Bell jingled. *We can cover all of the jungles if we spread out.*

"We'll take the caves around the mountains," Slightly offered. "And the tunnels, all the places underground where it's possible to hide a giant bomb."

Wendy watched the unlikely group before her—Lost Boys and pirates, fairies and shadows—work together to excitedly plan how they were going to save the world.

She cleared her throat.

"*Gentlemen!*" she shouted.

Everyone stopped talking.

"And ladies," she added. "And those who haven't made a decision one way or the other, or have chosen not to choose. This is *Captain Hook* we're talking about here. A pirate. He is not exactly over-imbued with imagination, or unpredictable. No disrespect intended."

Slightly, Peter Pan, Tinker Bell, Thorn, and Zane looked at each other, a little chagrined.

"Skull Island," they all said or jingled at the same time.

"We just stopped there afore coming here," Zane added, scratching his head. "For something or other secretive."

"*Really,*" Wendy said, crossing her arms and shaking her head. "The *deuce* you say."

"That's where the bomb is!" Peter Pan cried. "I'll go at once!"

I'm going with you! Tinker Bell jingled.

"And me as well," Wendy said. She turned to Thorn. "You should come, too, since you know about these kinds of things."

I don't think I'm needed right now, he said with a wise smile. *Or wanted. I'll still rally the fairies—just in case. Go save Never Land, Wendy.*

"All right . . ." She *wanted* to lean over and kiss him—on the cheek, of course. She had a feeling they might not see each other after this. But however overwhelming the urge, she was afraid it would terrify him. So she kissed her hand and blew it at him gently instead.

At first he looked surprised at the gesture—and then he grinned.

I will see you again someday, Windy Wendy. If not in Never Land or London, then somewhere else heroes go.

Wendy sighed and looked away. Tinker Bell was giving her the side-eye.

"What? Mind your business."

The little fairy grinned wickedly, and the three leapt up into the sky.

Skull Island

"There it is!" Peter cried.

As clear as a print in a child's book, there was the tiny island: a gray stone skull rising out of the sea as if the rest of a giant gray skeleton lurked in the depths below it. While the formation couldn't possibly have been natural—nothing in Never Land *was* strictly natural—perhaps it arose organically, having felt a need in stories for a spooky landmark. Or maybe it was built and carved by ancient peoples who never truly existed, only appearing in convenient side notes to explain how the island came about. Whatever the case, pirates needed it, and here it was. . . .

Although it was a bit different from when Wendy had told her own stories of Never Land to Michael and John.

The eye sockets, nose, and mouth, previously open and accessible to boats, mermaids, and pirates (and seagulls and ravens picking the bones of those murdered there) were all sealed up. Quickly and sloppily, in true pirate fashion. Boards crisscrossed the sockets with no plan or finesse. Half-hammered nails stuck out. Bricks and stones were piled up in awkward slants to fill in gaps. Cement or spackle had been slapped on the edges like a poor plumber's job.

"He's closed off all the entryways!" Peter said in dismay, pulling up to a stop in midair.

Tinker Bell flitted back and forth worriedly.

Wendy wasn't *quite* skilled enough to do either of those things, so she had to content herself with drifting to and fro over as narrow an area as she could manage.

Peter flew up to an eye socket to investigate more closely. Despite the slapdash appearance, the job was pretty solid. He couldn't pull out any of the stones or boards, or break up the cement.

"No good." He swore, kicking at the island. "That's a pickle."

I can slip in, Tinker Bell said, pointing. *There.*

The childish, potty-humored pirates had left a chink in the nose hole toward the bottom left. Some extra cement had been guided to pool around the base to give the appearance of snot.

"Tinker Bell, do you even know how to disarm a bomb?" Wendy asked.

Pirates are unencumbered with imagination, as a wise lady once said, Tinker Bell jingled with a wan smile. *Hook tried this before. . . . Easy-peasy!*

"Aw, Tink can do anything," Peter said, waving his hand. "She's a *tinker.* This ain't nothing to her."

"Be careful," Wendy pleaded. "Even defused it's dangerous."

Tinker Bell gave her a quick kiss on the cheek, then snapped to attention in front of Peter, touching her hand to her brow. Then she dove into the nose hole.

"Huh, that's funny," Peter said. "She gave *you* a kiss and *me* a salute."

But that was all he said, and he seemed merely to be puzzled by it, neither offended nor amused.

Wendy fretted while they waited: What if Tink couldn't defuse the bomb? What if, failing, she brought the bomb outside so the three could figure it out together? Wendy didn't know how to defuse a bomb—did Peter? What if they couldn't? What would they do with it?

Meanwhile, Peter whistled, checked his nails, made little churches and people with his fingers, stretched out in the air on his back.

At one point he sat up and noticed his shadow on the

rocks below, reinvigorated by the bright light of the two moons. Wendy's shadow was playing cat's cradle with her friend, using a shadow piece of string from somewhere.

"*Hey,*" Peter said, a little vexed.

Shadow Peter turned to look at him, which of course was no more than a shifting of flat black shapes. But even Wendy could feel the look he gave the solid Peter. *Really? You want to start this again?*

"As you were," Peter said quickly. "You could ask us if *we* wanted to play, though."

This was such a ridiculous and impossible idea that everyone just ignored it.

And then the bomb went off.

It was a noise like nothing Wendy had ever heard before, an earsplitting sound preceded by a blast of air so strong it knocked her back like a carriage pulled by eight panicking horses. Somehow Peter flung himself around her and wrapped her body with his.

The two were thrown, the world went black.

Flotsam and Jetsam

She must have only been out for a moment or two, but when Wendy came to she found the world a topsy-turvy place that made no sense. It was almost perfectly silent, for one thing; noises like rocks falling and gulls screaming sounded almost hollow, as if very, very far away. Dust and grit poured from her lashes as she tried to make sense of gravity, light, and pain, all of which were coming at her from strange angles.

Peter Pan was lying next to her, one arm still thrown protectively over her waist.

"Peter," she whispered. Even that sounded wrong; she felt the vibrations in her throat but couldn't hear the words.

Wincing at the extreme, *wrong* pain in her back, she managed with great difficulty to push herself onto her elbows and knees.

"Peter, wake up."

She gasped at how bloody he was; a thousand lacerations covered him from forehead to feet. After a panicked moment of wiping it off—with his own soft hat—she was relieved to see they were just tiny divots and scrapes from the grit and scree shot out by the explosion. No wound seemed especially deep.

"Where's Tink?" he murmured. At least, that's what it looked like his lips said.

"I don't know!"

"I can't hear you," he said accusingly.

"The explosion." She touched her ears, then waved to the black and windy sky.

"I can't hear you!" Peter shouted.

This Wendy could hear a little, which was a relief. She forced herself to stand up. Her back was a throbbing mass of pain—but it obeyed her will, albeit reluctantly. No permanent damage except for maybe a cracked rib. No tingling in her feet. She was all right, though the crimson streak in the corner of her right eye was a little worrisome.

"TINK!" she shouted as loudly as she could, unsure how loud it really was.

The landscape was much changed in the last five minutes. Skull Island was almost entirely gone. What Wendy stood on were its remains: a whole new atoll of big, ugly chunks of gray rock, some of which were still rolling and shifting into place like knucklebones. Dust had risen up and nearly blocked out the moons and stars, diffusing their light strangely and, turning the sky the same sort of monochrome white she associated with the First. A wind had sprung up and the water was an ugly shade of lead.

"TINK!" she screamed.

"Tinker Bell!" Peter yelled, and this time Wendy thought she heard him. He shot into the air, darting back and forth over the sea in the same random, unorganized way Tinker Bell would have. Wendy struggled to fly, buffeted about by the winds and very, very unsteady. She coughed and spat up sand and blood.

"Tinker Bell!"

In snippets and wisps sound was coming back, but it was confusing and snarled. Somehow the noises made her want to vomit. She gagged and ordered her stomach to settle.

"Tink! TINKER BELL!" Peter Pan called again.

A faint shadow appeared over Wendy's vision. *This is it*, she thought; she was going to pass out again.

Then it blinked away and everything was light . . . and then it was dark again. On and off, like a signal.

Confused, Wendy put her hands up between her face and the sky.

Her shadow appeared on her palm, shrinking quickly to fit. She had been trying to get Wendy's attention! She pointed and waved her arms toward what might have been north. Wendy dropped her hands and the shadow fell to the sea, just visible in the dim light. The shadow skittered across the water, still pointing. Peter's was close behind.

"Peter!" Wendy shouted.

Whether he was less injured or his pixie ears healed faster, Peter Pan heard her immediately. He looked to where she pointed and flew after the shadows.

The four skimmed together over the surface of the sea.

And there she was: a glittering lump of golden hair and wings, floating lackluster on the foam.

Peter scooped up the tiny fairy and landed on the closest pile of rocks. He gently lowered her down and cleared the water and silt off her face.

But Tinker Bell wasn't breathing. And she wasn't glowing.

"Don't die, Tinker Bell!" Peter begged. "Don't go out! Tink! You mean more to me than anything!"

"Come on, Tink," Wendy begged. "You can make it. I know you can. I believe in you. I believe in you and fairies and Never Land. I know you wouldn't leave me or Peter Pan or this world. Please, Tinker Bell. I believe in you."

Silence.

And then . . . the faintest of jingles.

No, Wendy.

I believe in you.

Endings Again

The pirates sailed away to resume wholesome—well, normal—pirate activities. Zane promised to find a nice tropical port where they would deposit Hook, along with enough gold for a comfortable house and a caretaker. Which was, perhaps, more than the violent, insane captain deserved—but then again, the bomb hadn't really worked all that well after all, and it did nicely set him up for recovering and returning for revenge when he was needed again.

Captain Zane saluted Peter Pan and declared their enmity at an end, but said that he and the crew would cheerfully resume aggressions any time Peter wanted to interfere with their operations. The boy politely offered the same.

The pirate then shook Wendy's hand. "It was a pleasure knowing you, Miss Darling. You . . . brought change. And as you said, change comes to all things. Even Never Land. It was high time."

He turned to Skipper.

"Should you be looking for . . . other employment, my ship is an open and welcoming place to *anyone* who wants to loot and plunder, no matter what they look like, who they snog, or how they dress. As long as you're into murder and burnin', these days we keep an open mind on the *Jolly Roger*."

Skipper cracked one of her small sideways smiles.

"Thanks, Captain. Maybe someday I'll take you up on it."

And so the pirates sailed away, the *Jolly Roger* growing smaller and smaller until it disappeared into the horizon.

On the white sands of the tropical beach now remained only the Lost Boys (and Luna), Peter Pan, Wendy, Tinker Bell, and everyone's shadows.

It was how Wendy had once imagined a perfect end of an adventurous day . . . and yet entirely different. Peter Pan was covered in ugly wounds. Tink sat slumped on his shoulder, not quite recovered enough to fly. The Lost Boys looked less lost and more real under this Never Land sun, pores and hair and dirt and scratches and eyes and smiles and all.

"Now then, what's this about you being a *girl*, Skipper?" Peter Pan demanded.

Skipper shrugged.

"She is what she is," said Slightly.

"You wouldn't have taken me if I wasn't a boy," she pointed out.

"But it's the Lost *Boys*," Peter said, exasperated.

"Maybe it shouldn't be," Slightly said. "Maybe it shouldn't be *Boys*. Or *Girls*. Maybe it should be *Lost People*."

"Lost *People* . . . ?" Peter repeated, a little distastefully.

"Maybe it shouldn't be *Lost*." Cubby spoke up unexpectedly. "You *found* us, Peter. We're *found*."

"Found People," Slightly said, nodding, "I like that."

"I like it, too," Skipper agreed.

Slightly and Peter stared at each other for a long, silent moment.

Finally, Peter rolled his eyes.

"Lost Boys, Found People, Tiny Bunnies—I don't care what you call yourselves. I just don't ever want to be fighting with you again. I *missed* you guys. I don't know if it was arguing with you or losing my shadow that made me more sick. And I know it was at least half my fault.

"You've, ah, you've grown into quite the position of leader—under my wise tutelage," Peter added, putting his arm around Slightly. "I definitely think it's high time we gave you more responsibility over this little ragtag group of heroes."

Now it was Slightly's turn to roll his eyes, but he did it with a smile.

"Bring it in, Peter," he ordered.

And the two boys hugged and made up.

Tinker Bell disentangled herself from Peter and slipped down his arm. Wendy put out hers and Tink landed on it as gracefully as a ballerina.

What will you *do now?*

"I think . . . I've been thinking about this a lot, Tinker Bell. And I think because you are wiser than you let on—when you're not distracted by boys—you can probably guess what it is."

The fairy pulled a face.

You're returning to stinky London.

"Yes, I'm afraid I am," Wendy sighed. "Just like in all those terrible stories I said I would never, ever tell or write. The ones English authors love so much, about experiencing magic and wonder as a child and then giving it all up and putting it away to become an adult and take on responsibilities and children and a job—and all that somehow making it all right.

"But I cannot forget what the First said, about how Never Land is a reflection of London, my world. My world has a lot of problems. And not only is it unfair to foist them upon this unfinished, innocent world, it's unfair to ignore them by staying here and pretending they don't exist.

"Somewhere right now a toothless old grandfather is shivering in a poorhouse, starving and without visitors.

Somewhere an orphan—who *wasn't* rescued by Peter—is being beaten by a harsh nurse or sold as a slave to a factory owner. And everywhere in the world, girls have little ability to make their voices heard, or the power to change things. I think about the way *I* changed things in the Land of the First . . . and here, with your and Thorn's help . . . and I wonder if I can use a little of that magic at home.

"I've had the best adventure a girl could ever want—and that is more than I ever dreamed was possible."

But . . . I'll miss you.

"I can't even think about it, Tinker Bell. It hurts dreadfully. You're the best friend I ever had. I feel like I'm cutting off a part of me. Forever."

The little fairy drooped, and she was a sad sight indeed: tattered wings, trembling lips, limp hair out of its messy bun and draping her like an old cloak.

Then she looked up.

Maybe just one last adventure? For goodbye?

"I'd dearly love to see a dragon," Wendy said eagerly. "I didn't get to do that."

The two girls smiled, and gently touched scratched-up, bruised hands.

Epilogue

In one of the less pleasant—but eminently affordable—
neighborhoods of London was the in/famous flat of Ms.
Wendy Darling.

Her apartment was modest but large enough for Wendy,
her books, and gatherings of like-minded people. There was
hot running water, electric lamps, and a private entrance.
Every room had windows. There was a dining area large
enough to serve as the nexus for organizing protests, staging
letter-writing campaigns, publishing pamphlets, planning
speeches, strategizing actions, and occasionally even feeding unannounced hordes of supporters who dropped by.

And none of them said Wendy talked too much. Some
came from a hundred miles away just to hear her speak.

(Even Mr. and Mrs. Darling came over to attend her

speeches. They were mostly embarrassed and *very* slightly proud, but more than anything else *surprised* by this enterprise of their eldest, dreamiest child.)

(Michael and John were absolutely on their sister's side about changing the world and voting rights for women, even to the point of marching with her—but that might have been partially due to the number of passionate ladies attracted to the cause.)

Wendy looked mostly the same as an adult; her only nod to the passage of time was the decision to keep her hair up in a messy bun modeled after a dear friend's style. She also found that her years of dreaming had either left her myopic or caused her to let it go unnoticed for a long time. She now sported a pair of glasses very similar to John's.

(These were removed when fisticuffs were expected, as when she joined a number of ladies of Caribbean descent at Saxelbrees Café and Salon for a peaceful sit-in. Tea was an English right, regardless of race, color, or creed.)

This particular evening, all was quiet; constituents and suffragettes and equal-rights advocates and rabble-rousers had all been ordered out. Wendy was indulging herself in a pastime with which even her closest confidants were unacquainted.

First she set the kitchen table with a pretty cloth and her best un-chipped tea service.

Next to this she carefully placed another tea set—but this one was *tiny*: so dainty and perfect that an outside observer would have blinked in astonishment. For Wendy Darling was gifted, passionate, forgiving, and talkative, but not cracked in the head or prone to strange hobbies. And she did *not* have any cats.

(Or dogs. Nana had passed on peacefully. Snowball was happily adopted by Phoebe Shesbow.)

"Oh, I've forgotten a spoon, and a fork for the cake," Wendy realized. She ran up the cramped flight of stairs that led to a dormer. Her neatly made bed was nestled under a brilliantly large pair of windows that looked out on the sky. Next to it was a rickety nightstand that supported a tall stack of pamphlets, chapbooks, and monographs. And next to *that* was a chest, on top of which was a very large dollhouse decorated with every conceivable realistic detail.

("You never played with dolls as a child, Wendy," Michael had pointed out upon seeing it. Perhaps with a touch of envy.

"Maybe this is just a physical manifestation of your reframing the desire for a child, the natural impulse of which has been subverted by mannish occupations?"

John was very fond of modern psychology.

This sort of thing was usually answered with a disappointed look from Wendy—and sometimes a slap.)

It was a work in progress. If Wendy had a little extra money for herself it went to things like having an exactly 1:12-scale Chesterfield sofa made to her specifications and upholstered in real leather with tiny covered buttons decorating the tufts.

If she had a little extra *time* for herself—even rarer—she tatted miniature antimacassars out of single-strand silk, or rolled tiny real beeswax tapers. Teensy gas and oil lamps she hadn't quite worked out yet without teensy explosions.

She carefully opened the miniature china cabinet in the pantry and used the tip of her pinky to pull out a dainty silver spoon and matching fork. It was part of a brilliant charm set she had seen in a jeweler's shop.

(She had received *very* funny looks from the jeweler when she had asked him to pull open the jump ring and separate the eating implements off it.)

She hurried back downstairs, laid the spoon and fork next to the cup, and put the kettle on the hob.

Then she proceeded to wait.

It looked like madness: a famous suffragette sitting at an empty table with two very different-sized saucers laid in front of her.

And if one managed to peep into the mind of Wendy Darling—well, that too might look like a bit of madness.

It had been ten years since she had reappeared in the garden of the Darling household, practically naked and covered with injuries, all of which the Darlings managed to keep a secret.

She was not sent to Ireland.

Those ten years had been full of hard decisions, harder work, and fights with her family and friends and even strangers on the street as her notoriety grew. There were small victories, large setbacks, and of course the endless, tiring, and unglamorous work that no one tells you about when you decide to change the world. Boring stuff like writing letters, keeping accounts, assigning funds, constantly reminding people to show up, and politely pursuing them to hold them to whatever promises they made. Usually about funds.

By the end of most days, her writing arm would ache like she had been battling thysolits the whole time.

But she kept herself going with hopes and dreams, with memories of severe deserts and voices that couldn't be heard. Nothing she did, she reminded herself, was more dangerous than battling pirates—or more terrible than doing their laundry.

And on certain nights, when it *felt* right, when the moon was friendly and she didn't recognize all the stars, she set out two cups of tea and waited.

And waited.

Of course, things happened at a different pace in Never Land, even if the years matched up. Peter Pan was a hard boy to keep in line. Promises over there could be put off for years when the promiser thought only an afternoon had slipped by.

"I have so much to tell her," Wendy said to herself. "The protest outside of parliament where they hit me with that rotten tomato . . . and then that funny tree I saw growing at the botanical gardens that reminded me so much of rubyfruit!"

The mantel clock in the other room (humorously decorated with a TIME TO CHANGE sign penned by one of her friends) continued to ticktock.

As midnight approached, Wendy sighed and stood up to clear the dishes. Again.

At midnight oh one, a golden glow appeared in her kitchen window.

Upon seeing it, Wendy's face also glowed.

"Tinker Bell!" she sighed, and opened the door.